10/21

National Library of Canada Cataloguing in Publication Data

Hayter, Sparkle, 1958-
Naked brunch

ISBN 0-7710-3795-3

I. Title.

PS8565.A938N34 2002   C813´.54   C2001-904304-X
PR9199.3.H39N34 2002

We acknowledge the financial support of the Government of Canada
through the Book Publishing Industry Development Program for
our publishing activities. We further acknowledge the support of the
Canada Council for the Arts and the Ontario Arts Council for our
publishing program.

Typeset in Bembo by M&S, Toronto
Printed and bound in Canada

McClelland & Stewart Ltd.
The Canadian Publishers
481 University Avenue
Toronto, Ontario
M5G 2E9
www.mcclelland.com

1 2 3 4 5   06 05 04 03 02

Naked Brunch

SPARKLE HAYTER

Naked Brunch

Even a man who is pure in heart
And says his prayers by night
May become a wolf when the wolfbane blooms
And the autumn moon is bright

– from the 1941 film *The Wolf Man*

Dear Tweets,

Well, it's another deceptively candy-coloured day here in the Grimm's fairy tale that is our city. Don't you love those two Teuton brothers? In their bloody fairy tales, the woods teem with trolls, tricksters, giants, ogres, dark princes, and vengeful old women who devour innocent children. A plotting courtier darts out of the shadows of an apothecary shop with a dram of poison to further his ambitions. An old witch or an evil giant comes to an unhappy end, thus freeing the beautiful young princess and handsome prince to ride off into the gleaming white future.

And they live happily ever after, or so they claim.

This is where the Fratres Grimm let me down. Shame on them. They give a perceptive and unflinching view of the world, then cop out at the end with the Official Palace Version of things. Name one princess who lived happily ever after. There are no happy endings, only unhappy endings and happy beginnings.

This where I come in. With the help of my happy minions, I promise to cut through the sweetly scented fog of the Official Palace Version to give you the real stories about the Kings, Queens,

Princes, Princesses, Bluebloods, Bluebeards, Scheming Ministers, and Callow Knaves of our Grimm City, every day except Sunday, right here in the Downtown Eye.

– from the first "Dear Tweets" gossip column, June 8

I

The Strawberry Moon

June

I

The wolf crouched atop the low-slung iron awning of a whole-saler in the Meatpacking District. The smell of meat was every-where, raw, rotten, and cooking – the humid summer air threaded with smoke from the neighbourhood's latest steakhouse, this one defiant enough to call itself Carnivore. It had been described by *Time Out* as "nouvelle caveman cuisine, slabs of meats marinated in lightly spiced nut oils, accompanied by imaginative side dishes and postmodern presentation (don't miss the Flintstone-size rack of ribs basted with jalapeno honey and beer and served with smoked apple-bacon salsa)."

The wolf was more interested in another smell, approaching from Carnivore on two legs, an odour so strong it could be tasted. It wasn't a pleasant smell. Every soul has a unique scent, and this one smelled of enthusiastic compromises with dictators, devious ambition, greed, lost children. This smell was not detectable by normal humans but if they could have sensed it, they would have been overcome by the stench of wormy meat that had been kept in a dirty sock in the hot sun for a week or so, then set afloat in petroleum.

On the empty cobblestone street below, Robert Bingham searched for a taxi to take him back to his hotel. It had been good to be in the city for a while. His meeting at headquarters had gone well and he was rewarded with more stock options and a hearty handshake from the head of the entire organization, Lord Harry, who said, "Good job, Bob," so many times in their last meeting that it was now his nickname, Good Job Bob. When Lord Harry, who had a naming whimsy, bestowed this particular blessing on someone, that person was golden. And though Lord Harry had had to back out of their dinner at the last moment, he promised to make it up to Bob. Lord Harry always made good on his promises to the people who counted, and he was particularly pleased with the way Bob had handled overseas operations and put down the threat to the company's operations.

"I have big plans for you, Good Job Bob," he said.

Bob was speculating about what those plans were, and hoping they'd take him far from sub-Saharan Africa, when what looked like a bear leapt from the awning above him. He only had time to think, "No, it's a dog!" before his throat was in its jaws. The wolf broke his neck with one snap, ripping out his throat in the process, leaving Bob on the cobblestones in his own pooling blood.

The wolf sniffed the body as all life left it, then headed home.

2

Sam Deverell had been lucky most of his career.

Some people are just like that. They are blessed from birth with everything they need to win friends and influence people. They may be good looking, but not too good looking, and smart, but not too smart.

If they are too smart or too good looking, they learn to play it down.

Sam didn't have to. He wasn't too smart, not in the way the kids in the newsroom were, and he knew it. It wasn't that he didn't try to improve himself. He had always tried to keep up on the big news stories of the day, and back when he was an anchorman he made sure he knew how to pronounce every strange foreign name perfectly. Before he did an on-set interview, he humbly consulted with his producer to find out what questions to ask, and if the producer barked a new question in his ear during the interview, he asked it without skipping a beat. Afterwards, if anyone said, "Hey, great interview," or "Good show," he always said, "Yeah, tell the producer and the crew that. They did it all."

He'd watched too many too-smart guys who insisted on showing it go down to defeat, just like that guy Ichabod who made the wings of wax and feathers, flew too close to the sun, and fell into the sea. The too-smart guys, some of whom were unlucky enough to be too good looking as well, had their way while things were going well and ratings were good. Then they got arrogant, they made demands, they pissed people off, and the whispering campaigns began. The first major fuck-up brought the glint of hidden knives. Just the glint, just enough to make the smart guy paranoid.

Performance soon suffered as viewers picked up on the arrogance and the paranoia. Ratings dropped. The guys who were too smart ended up dropping in weight class to smaller media markets, where they bitched and moaned over their copies of *Atlantic Monthly* and *Foreign Policy Review* about the injustice of a culture that rewarded mediocrity and punished brilliance.

Before he came to the city and Citywide Cable News, Sam had been the top anchor in four markets because he was likable and he read news well. He'd worked his way up the TV news ladder from Lincoln, Nebraska, to Albuquerque to Phoenix and to Atlanta, where he'd been pretty happy, co-anchoring the six P.M. newscast with his wife, Candace Quall. They were both southerners and felt at home. They had a two-million-dollar house in Buckhead, they were Atlanta A-list, and whenever they went to the mall or to a Braves baseball game people would get excited and ask for their autographs.

Sam had been lucky. He hadn't gone to college, and until he got a job at seventeen sweeping up and fetching food at the local radio station, "The Voice of Eastern Arkansas," he'd had no career aspirations. When the too-smart guy who was DJing the afternoon easy-listening show quit in a principled dispute over the mandatory playlist, Sam got his chance to test his pipes, and he was on his way.

After that, it all just fell into place. Soon he took over the late-night show with an eye on that morning drive-time hour. On a clear night, a station owner from Nebraska, in Nashville for a convention, happened to pick up Sam's show from Arkansas. He found Sam to be a refreshing note in a time of antiwar protests and crazy hippies, a young man with a friendly, soothing voice who played Perry Como without any sarcasm and cheerfully took requests from the middle-aged women who tuned in, always calling them "Ma'am." The Nebraska station owner called in his own request and Sam took off for Lincoln and his own drive-time show. Soon he was anchoring on television.

Because Sam was so careful and deferred to others he rarely made a mistake on the air. He was no Ted Baxter. That's why he had always been loved, almost universally.

He was lucky in his career – and he'd be the first person to say so – until his station in Atlanta was sold to a big conglomerate and he was laid off and replaced with a younger man. His young wife, Candace, fared better. Synergy TV had courted and won her, so he followed her to the city and hit up an old friend for a job at CCN. He had hoped to be an anchor, but he didn't fit in with the network's anchor strategy, so he grudgingly accepted a job as a low-level features reporter.

When the kids at CCN looked at him, they didn't see a nice older guy who had had a bad break, they saw a guy who didn't know

Icarus from Ichabod, who had his job because the owner owed him a favour – and there was a lot of speculation around the newsroom about just what that favour was for. They saw the two production assistants they could have hired for Sam's salary, or the five all-in-one audio-video cameras called Gizmos they could have bought. Or one production assistant, two cameras, and ten thousand Krispy Kreme doughnuts . . . a group of them had spent a slow news day translating Sam's value into various other commodities, like doughnuts, condoms, and Budweisers.

It wasn't just that he was so much older than almost everyone else, though they were trying to "brand" themselves as the edgy news network with a young, eclectic and "post-ethnic" look. Sam was incompetent as a reporter, everyone knew it, even the owner. It's a temporary thing, the owner told them, Sam will be here just long enough to get on his feet here. Six months tops. Give him the easy stuff.

Six months went by, Sam had no other job offers, and he was still at CCN. Complaints about Sam escalated to the point where even the owner knew he had to go, though he didn't have the heart to fire the guy. Instead, he put Sam on the overnight shift and instructed the desk to only use him if they had to. He dropped hints about openings at easy-listening radio stations just outside the city. Eventually, he figured, Sam would take the short sword, quit on his own, and maybe go back to radio.

The overnight shift at CCN was considered a transit point for reporters on the way up or the way out. At fifty-two, almost twice as old as the other two overnight reporters, Sam's direction seemed clear. He'd been shoved onto the newsroom equivalent of an ice floe.

Sam knew this, but he didn't let on. He knew the kids in the newsroom made fun of him and wanted him gone. That made friendly old Sam turn kind of bitter, like those too-smart guys he'd outrun in the past. His wife was busy with her own career and had little time for him. Lonely, isolated, and frustrated, Sam fell into a stupid affair with a nutty young woman, which blew up in his face. His wife left him and the young woman, Micki, wouldn't even take his calls.

His luck had almost run out the night of that full moon. Then he got lucky again.

6

The newsroom was so quiet he could hear the hum of the fluorescent lights above, along with the soft *ticka-ticka* of an old-fashioned teletype news wire, kept around in case the computer system crashed. The overnight newscast was playing on a monitor near the assignment desk, where the night editor occasionally laughed at something or swore. Flies, which had invaded the news-room with a promotional basket of gourmet fruits and meats left too long by a sunny window, buzzed around. The police scanner crackled with police talk. It was Sam's job to listen to the scanner, and he was half-listening to it while shooting flies out of the air with his can of industrial strength hairspray, when he heard the words ". . . Caucasian male, dead of neck injuries consistent with dog attack."

What a way to go, killed by man's best friend, Sam thought as another fly paralyzed by lacquer plunged out of the air mid-flight.

It took him a moment to realize that this was a real story, not a photo op of the Mayor's wife or a spot piece about a downtown club being closed down for violating the city's noise ordinances or any of that other idiot-proof crap he was sent to cover by the smirking assignment editor.

I found a story, he thought. Ha! He looked up at the assign-ment desk. The producer was leaning on it, talking to the assignment editor. When he got up and walked towards them, Sam had every intention of telling them what he'd just heard. But as he approached, the looks on both their faces changed. They looked superior and mocking. If he told them about this, they might just pull one of the other reporters from the field and put him on it.

About halfway to the desk, he smiled and said, "Just heading out to grab a bite. Haven't had my lunch yet."

On the way to the elevator, he circled back to the crew room to grab a Gizmo.

Forbidden to use a news car because of an excessive number of parking tickets, he had to take a taxi to the Meatpacking District, where the body had been found just around the corner from a trendy new steakhouse called Carnivore.

It was the first real story Sam had had in the six months since he moved here from Atlanta. Before CCN, he hadn't really done much . . . well, any . . . reporting. He was an anchorman and he found the reporting part hard, but he'd eat his own foot before he'd ask one of the young reporters for help again, not after the alligators-in-the-sewers fiasco. Those kids didn't appreciate that he'd been in the news biz a lot longer than they had. Where had they been when Reagan defeated Carter, when the Iran hostages were released, when the U.S. was bombing Iraq? Where were they while Sam was covering the local angle to the world's big stories in Lincoln, Albuquerque, Phoenix and Atlanta? Well, he hadn't actually reported on those stories, but he had anchored the newscasts and read them to the viewing audience. He was there, on camera, speaking with authority about places like Baghdad and guys like the Ayatollah Khomeini.

The city's overnight news crews were covering two big stories that night, a five-alarm fire in the warehouse district and a late-night post-premiere party that a horde of celebrities was attending. That alignment of stars was another lucky break for Sam. There were no other media at the scene yet, just cops and emergency medical guys, and a handful of stray trendoids coming home from a club who had stopped to see what all the cops were doing. The body was still there, lying in a brightly lit circle and surrounded by uniformed cops. To the side, a plainclothes detective – a short blonde woman – was going through a wallet and talking into a cell phone while a tall black man, Detective Macy, took notes. A police photographer took pictures while a second video-taped the scene.

Sam turned the Gizmo on and casually approached the circle, in the centre of which was a middle-aged white man, his head snapped to the side like the head of a broken doll. He lay in a pool of congealed blood that formed a shiny red halo in the bright police lights. The victim's mouth was wide open as if he had died in the middle of a scream. His eyes were also open wide.

Sam moved around the circle to the plainclothes detectives. A uniformed cop held his arm up.

"Crime scene, stay back," he said.

Sam flashed his press pass.

"Citywide Cable News."

"You should talk to the media people at headquarters. We're busy with an investigation here," Detective Macy said. He was chewing gum.

"I just have a few questions. Who's the victim?" Sam asked.

"Can't talk right now," Macy said.

"His neck was ripped out in an attack consistent with a dog attack. Right? Because that's what I heard on the police scanner."

"It would be irresponsible to put anything speculative on the air before we have a chance to do our jobs and develop our leads," Macy said.

"I was just . . ."

"Uh huh," Macy said, cutting him off. He walked away without saying goodbye. To his partner, Foster, he said, "Fuckin' asshole."

To the side, two young women were standing in the doorway of the Carnivore restaurant. They'd come out to see what the commotion was, and Sam managed to find out that they'd seen nothing of the crime, but that the victim had ordered the Buffalo prime rib with baby baked potatoes, asparagus in piquant lime sauce, and Winesap-apple dumplings in a light brandy cream sauce for dessert. He'd come in on a reservation for two people, one of whom hadn't shown up. He'd paid with a credit card but the waitress didn't remember the name and her manager wouldn't let her look at the charge slip.

As the body was taken away, Sam got a good clear shot of it and by the time photogs and news crews from other stations and papers got there, the body was gone. Sam got the only video of the dead man.

⑥

When he got back to the newsroom, he told the surprised assignment editor about the story and sat down to write. The writing part was really hard. Most of his stories for CCN came with press releases, and he just rewrote what the PR flacks sent. But this was different. For a moment he was frozen.

Think, Sam, he thought, think hard. You've read copy about crimes before. Try to remember what it sounded like. He wracked his brain for some similar story from the past, and remembered a story he read on the air about a murder in Atlanta. He shut his eyes and focussed, trying to see the teleprompter rolling in front of him. "A man was found dead last night in what appears to be a brutal skinhead attack . . ." he saw, and he opened his eyes, turned to the computer and typed it, changing "skinhead" to "dog." Then he closed his eyes tight and focussed on the imaginary teleprompter again.

Across the newsroom, the assignment editor turned to the producer and said, "What's he doing?"

"I don't know. Thinking?"

"Looks painful. Better hold his hand in edit so he doesn't mess it up."

After massive editing and the combined wizardry of the producer and editor, Sam's piece aired first at five A.M. He had the only video of the "Mad Dog Murder," as he dubbed it. Pretty clever, he thought. Sam was feeling proud of himself. Yeah, he was getting the hang of this reporting stuff. Those kids in the newsroom who thought he was just a washed-up talking head, a "haircut" they could lampoon on the in-house joke reel, dubbing his words over pictures of a toupee on a tall stick at various scenes all over town, well, they had another think coming.

3

It may have been an attack dog, Dr. Marco Potenza thought, but he couldn't quell a sudden feeling of dread, which coincided with a shadow falling over the room as a cloud passed in front of the sun outside. Because the killing had happened during the full moon, he had to proceed as if it were, well, a werewolf, in street slang, a word Marco hated to use because of superstitious fear and the erroneous belief that a werewolf was something supernatural.

If this was a werewolf, and not some random killer with an attack dog, as the media seemed to believe, it had to be found as quickly as possible before further killings led to discovery, which would threaten his program.

For years, every now and then, Marco had turned over in his mind the idea of "coming out," which would allow him to publish the many papers he had written on Lycanthropic Metamorphic Disorder and bring the Potenza family the recognition it deserved for its groundbreaking work with werewolves, or, as most preferred to be called, "people living with LMD." It was frustrating to be a great scientist and have to keep it secret. But his father and brother had vetoed the idea, and after long thought Marco had to agree: people were not yet ready to accept werewolves among them. By the time a werewolf was found, he was a killer, and people had little tolerance for random, solitary killers, no matter the root cause. It wasn't the kind of thing that could be paraded on *Oprah* or *The Beth Tindall Show* to foster acceptance and understanding. My God, there was still racism against blacks and Asians. The general population hadn't quite come to grips with the idea of feminism or same-sex marriage. They'd hardly be open-minded enough to accept werewolves.

While he was formulating a plan to make contact with the new wolf, his wife Carol came in with a pot of herbal tea, then sat down in a nearby armchair and began sorting through cheques.

"Darn," she said. "Ernie didn't sign his cheque. Don't let him leave the Centre tomorrow without signing, Marco."

Marco ignored her.

"Hee. Look at Fritz's cheque design," Carol held up a cheque. "Clowns and balloons."

"Carol?"

"Yeah?"

"I'm thinking here."

"Sorry, sweetie. I forgot. The new werewolf. Why don't you call Rudolfo?" she asked.

"I don't need a tracker. I can do it myself."

"Of course you can. Marco?"

"Carol, what did I just say? I'm thinking here."

Sometimes it was like talking to a child, he thought. Carol was not the brightest bulb in the marquee, and she was a little loose in her socket. She was not the kind of woman he was attracted to, but a man with LMD, even one who had learned to control it, couldn't be too fussy. She was a plain woman but with a heart so big and expectations so small that she hadn't even blinked when Marco had told her about his condition, just after they were married, thirty years earlier. She asked him to show her and prove it, and he did. That, to her, was an amazing talent, something he could make a fortune from, and the fact that he'd devoted his life instead to saving other, more primitive werewolves and giving them as normal a life as possible was nothing less than noble. "You're like Mother Teresa for werewolves," she said. "And I'm like Mrs. Mother Teresa." She worshipped him.

"Marco."

"What?!"

"Sorry dear, I just found a sticky." She held up a yellow square. "Mike Burke told me to tell you we're out of ketamine. Marco, how will we handle confinement next month if we don't get more ketamine?"

"We'll do the best we can."

"But Marco —"

"There's nothing I can do. It's this new Mayor. I didn't even vote for him. We'll use lots of Thorazine and we'll carefully step up the dosage of the other drugs."

As a psychiatrist, Marco could get his hands on all the Thorazine he needed, though it wasn't nearly as effective as the ketamine in combination with midazolam. But only a veterinarian, animal trainer, certified anaesthetist, or drug dealer could get ketamine in the quantities he required without arousing suspicion. It was a powerful animal tranquilizer and anaesthetic abused by club kids under its street name, Special K. The new mayor had cracked down hard on Special K, and the centre's sources had now all disappeared.

He wasn't ready to tell Carol that if they didn't find this new werewolf soon, she and Mike Burke would have to handle confinement not just without ketamine, but without him while he went out to track the new wolf during the next full moon. Handling the patients without ketamine was painful. They'd had to do it once during another ketamine drought under the previous mayor and it had been hell.

He'd wait to tell her. With luck, he'd be able to find the new werewolf while it was in human form, and it wouldn't be necessary to leave Carol alone with the patients. To start, he'd put an ad in the papers and have Mike and the others put up some posters downtown. Chances were, this new wolf was shocked to learn of his condition and anxious to get help. Nobody wants to be a freak – everyone wants to fit in – and wolves seek their pack. But if ads and posters didn't work, he'd have to go after the wolf during the next full moon.

"Marco?"

"*What?*"

"It's almost nine. You have to relieve Mike Burke and check the patients at nine."

"I'll go down in a few minutes," he said.

He looked back at his notes.

What triggered the metamorphosis? he wrote in his notebook. *Can he be managed?*

He underlined managed three times.

4

In the Pink Pony Coffee Shop, the thin, dark-haired waitress chastised Jim.

"You haven't been in for three days," she said. She was pouting slightly, her head tilted, her hand on one hip, the other hand holding a tray with his grande cappuccino. She looked like she'd escaped from a *Rowan and Martin's Laugh-in* sketch, in a pink-and-green-check mini dress, eyeliner, and frosted-pink lipstick.

"I had a deadline," Jim said.

"You always have deadlines. Don't you ever play?"

He just smiled at her, a not-too-friendly a smile. He didn't want to encourage her.

"You can't work all the time," she said. "Some of us are going to see Aerostar tonight. Want to come? My roommate dates the drummer so we can get you on the list."

"I can't, thanks," he said. He hadn't even heard of Aerostar, but he dared not ask about it and risk having another long conversation with her, which would be mainly about herself and her acting career, except for a few probing questions she'd pose to find out about his private life. All she knew about him, all he allowed her to know, was that he lived down the street, alone, that he was a ghostwriter named Jim who liked coffee. That's it.

Without trying to know anything about her, he knew that she was twenty, an acting student in a program that didn't allow its students to audition for outside work for the first two years, but she'd snuck in "a few auditions anyway because after all one can't just practice one's craft in a cloister one has to go out and test it in the world and also it's really good to get your name and head shots out there to the directors even if you don't have a shot at playing a thirty-year-old married woman!"

Not only that, but she was putting together a one-woman show about Edie Sedgwick she hoped to do at a "performance space" on the west side. It was taking a little longer than she had hoped because she had to work part-time. Her wealthy father thought it would be good for her to work for her spending money to build character, "as if being the tallest girl in school, the child of divorce, the only artist in a family of business people, and the daughter of a woman whose closet is organized alphabetically by designer and then by colour didn't build character!"

Jim knew she lived across the street in a tiny one-bedroom with a roommate, Chrissie, who was an artist and with whom she was often annoyed because Chrissie was a slob and always late with the rent and thought her waitress roomie was a spoiled trust puppy just playing at the "bohemian thing."

About all Jim didn't know was her name, which was Meredith. She had told him once but he'd forgotten and didn't want to ask again because she might take that for interest. When he was younger he might have been interested in something sexual with her, maybe even something a little more, but not as much as her eyes told him she wanted and needed. He could smell her soul, but just barely. It was so lightweight it was hardly there, a whiff of rotten egg in a mist of baby powder.

"Oh come on. You'll have fun," she said.

"I can't," he said.

"Why?"

"Busy."

"Doing what?"

"Working," he said. "My coffee?"

"Oh. Heh. Yeah, here you go."

Ignoring people at other tables who were trying to get her attention, she stood for a minute to watch him drink.

"It's okay?"

"Fine."

"Okay." she said.

The coffee had cooled down while he'd waited, but he didn't mind. It went down faster. It took a lot of coffee after the full moon to cut the lethargy of the ketamine hangover. This moon he'd been low on the stuff and had thrashed about all night, alone in his apartment, then spent a couple of days just sleeping.

It was after ten and Jim's connection still hadn't shown up. It didn't look good and Jim was worried, though he'd been meaning to go off the ketamine anyway. It was a weird, dissociative drug that made him feel separated from his body. If the dosage was just right, it produced an all-over numbness, followed by deep sedation and merciful sleep. Dosing had to be continuous, which meant he had to prepare an IV drip to keep the drug flowing into his body as he didn't have anyone to administer regular shots throughout the high-risk period – the day before the full moon, the day after, and the day of the full moon itself, when the risk was exponentially greater than at any other time.

Even when it went perfectly, the ketamine left him sluggish for a week and occasionally caused memory loss. It was highly addictive psychologically, the only addictive psychedelic drug, and there was always the risk of overdose. This could lead either to actual death or a living hell known as a K-hole, where users were trapped in a hallucinatory state, unable to escape the monsters and other terrors of their nightmares. When he'd first come back to the city, after being off ketamine for years, he'd gone to the very rim of a

K-hole, and the things he'd seen made him take extreme caution after that.

His . . . guru, for lack of a better word . . . in India had advised him to do ketamine just for a month or two while he adjusted to being back. That had stretched into six months. Adjusting wasn't so easy after living in the Indian wilderness for five years. The city had changed a lot in that time.

Still lethargic, and his throat still dry from the endotracheal tube he had inserted to ensure he could breathe properly while he was sedated, he ordered another grande. There really was a deadline looming and he had a meeting with a possible client, a former politician, about an autobiographic article. He'd been out of it for three days and had to sharpen up fast.

The guy at the next table had left behind a newspaper. Jim grabbed it to see if anything earth-shattering had happened in his absence; it might come up in his meeting. He read the article on the "killer dog" attack during the last full moon, twice. Everyone else who read that story likely shivered to their bones, but Jim was thrilled. There was another free werewolf in the city. He wondered how long it would take for Marco to find him, and if he, Jim, could find him first.

"Isn't that awful?" the waitress asked, reading over his shoulder. "They think it's a Canary Island fighting dog, maybe crossed with a mastiff. One of the girls in my program at school belongs to a group that liberates animals and they liberated some fighting dogs in March. She thinks they were pit bulls and Dobermans but she can't be sure because the dogs, like, turned on them after they freed them and she says she was so scared and running so fast she didn't get a good look at all of them. The city only rounded up ten. That means there is still at least one, maybe two, on the loose. Scary! Another grande?"

5

Annie Engel had had the wolf dream again. As clearly as Annie could remember, the wolf dreams had begun when she was around five or six, but they hadn't become regular until she was thirteen. In them, she usually ran across vast fields of snow, bayed at the moon, drank from streams. Sometimes she slept in them, curled up with another wolf in a nest of leaves and grass in a cave sheltered from the wind. This always struck her as funny, sleeping in a dream.

The last dream was different. For one thing, it took place in the city, and in summer. It was always a vivid dream, but this one felt more real than any she'd had before. This time she could see and feel the stinging blur of street lights and neon signs. The screech of horns and howl of traffic on busy streets still echoed in her ears. As she bounded on all fours, she could feel the wind blowing over her and the sandpaper texture of the sidewalk as her paws hit the ground, running. Sharpest of all was the taste of blood. It was metallic and bitter on her tongue, but its thickness and viscosity was soothing.

When Annie awoke from this nightmare, she felt sick to her stomach, a heavy, sour feeling, like she'd eaten something rotten, something that would make her increasingly miserable as it worked its way through her system and out of her body. Her arms and legs felt stiff and cramped.

Stranger still, she had blood on her chest. She put her hand to her forehead to check for fever. It was slightly hot. A wave of sourness rose inside her, slowly at first, but by the time it got to mid-chest it was rolling like a tsunami. She jumped up and ran to the bathroom, getting to the sink just in time. A spurt of watery rust-coloured vomit shot out of her mouth, followed by a second, more solid, spurt.

After hoisting herself off the floor, she glanced in the mirror and saw the blood on her face. She scrubbed it off and rinsed her

mouth with mouthwash, then crawled back into bed and called in
sick to work. Her boss, Bo, was in London, so it was a good time
to be sick. With a cold washcloth on her forehead, she lay back and
listened to the messages on her answering machine, hoping they
would shed some light on the night before.

Mrs. Mackie had called, her late grandmother's best friend and
next-door neighbour, calling her by her grandmother's name.

"Kay, you've got to get me out of here," Mrs. Mackie said, with
a child's sing-songy rhythm and the voice of a woman who had
smoked a lot of cigarettes and emptied a lot of Bushmill bottles.
In a loud whisper, she said, "They expect me to eat with Negroes
in this place."

"This place" was the nursing home where Mrs. Mackie and
Annie's grandmother had worked and then lived when they got
too sick to take care of themselves. Her grandmother had been
dead for a few years, but Annie still went by sometimes to visit
Mrs. Mackie and help the staff. Not that Mrs. Mackie noticed.
Alzheimer's had sent her spinning backwards to her girlhood in
the 1930s, not a very sunny or pleasant place to be. As it turned
out, Mrs. Mackie had been a horrid little girl, bigoted and cruel.

After Mrs. Mackie, a woman had called to say she'd found
Annie's purse in front of her apartment. Annie's ID and credit cards
were still in it, along with about fifty dollars in cash, her keys, and
two bills that gave the Samaritan Annie's phone number.

Annie returned her call. The nice lady had found the purse on
the sidewalk, on its side as if it had been flung there and not just
dropped. Other than that, she had no insight on how it had ended
up there. After Annie answered some identifying questions about
the contents of her purse, including her lipstick shade, the nice lady
agreed to have Annie send a messenger for it the next day.

How she'd got into her apartment without her keys was a
mystery, until she noticed the open window by the fire escape and
the glass on the floor. The window had shattered, leaving nothing
but a jagged fringe around the edges. Something had hit it with a

tremendous force. Must have been me, Annie thought. That would explain the blood.

There was a piece of something stuck between her teeth, but her arms still felt too heavy to lift. She tried first to dislodge it with her tongue. Five minutes of probing didn't dislodge it, so she willed her hand to her mouth to work it free. It looked and smelled like raw meat, gone grey from being in her mouth for so long.

She was a vegetarian. What did I eat last night and what did I do, she wondered, trying to bring the evening before into better focus.

After work, she'd gone to a birthday party for her friend Henry at Liz's place, a one-bedroom apartment in the Meatpacking District. Annie had been feeling funny all day, nervous, itchy and very sensitive to people's perfume and body odours and by the time the party came she was feeling very weird. If she could have, she would have cancelled and just gone home after work, but Liz needed her there to help. A celebrity was coming, a participant from the reality show *Marooned*, and Liz wanted everything to be perfect for Buddy, the happy-go-lucky bartender who had come to the city to start a modelling career after being voted off the island and back to civilization.

Before the party, Annie had had three black-bean tortillas. At the party, while she put out the food, she snacked on pumpkin chips, some pea pods stuffed with lime-chili dip and a half-dozen falafel balls with garlic tahini, but nothing with meat in it.

As the guests arrived and the party got going, the smells of sweat, cigarette smoke, perfume and alcohol had made her queasy. She'd ducked out to get some fresh air. On the street, she'd leaned against the building wall and taken some deep breaths.

That's all she remembered.

She hadn't been robbed. She was sure she hadn't been raped, because whenever she had sex she always felt it the next day, especially if she hadn't had sex in a long time. She thought she should call the police, but to report what? What crime had been committed, if any, and what could the police do, considering she remembered so little? The combination of flu and vodka must have blacked her out, she thought. But she had made it home safely, so all was well.

No more drinking, she vowed. Not that she'd ever been a big drinker, but she'd never been a very good one. She'd had only one vodka-cranberry and that only because Liz was so nervous she'd poured Annie a drink, even though Annie had said she'd wait and have one later. Drinking it was preferable to saying anything that might set Liz off. For a year Liz had been trying to set up a party-planner business while working full-time on a TV talk show. She often met celebrities at work, as it was part of her job to make sure the green room was supplied with refreshments and the guests had everything they needed. But this was the first time she'd convinced one to come to a party, and she was edgy and snappish. If she had to bark at five people, including the birthday boy, in order to make one celebrity happy, it was a small price to pay.

Considering he was supposed to be the centre of attention, Henry was cheerful about Liz's outbursts. Once Liz explained that the celebrity was needed to get an item in the columns, and that the item would likely mention the celebrity was at Henry's birthday party, Henry played along. Twice in six months Henry had been mentioned in the press, once in a man-on-the-street interview and once in a *City Magazine* article on gay male personal assistants who worked for women, "The Gay Valet (or the answer to the plaintive cries of professional women everywhere – 'I Need a Wife!')"

All of this was part of Liz and Henry's plan to be famous in a year. As long as Annie had known them, as far back as secretarial college, the two of them had wanted to be famous. The time frame of a year had been added because Henry had decided a deadline was needed as incentive. The year was almost up and they were getting a tad desperate. It had been three months since the *City Magazine* piece and Henry was hungering for another press mention. Liz was hungering to break out of doing discount bar mitzvahs and promotional parties for self-published books.

Annie was just hungering. Lately, she couldn't seem to get enough food to fill her. Even now, as sick as she felt, she was ravenous, only she was too tired to get out of bed again and make herself something to eat. Her skin felt itchy, she had heart palpitations. Exhaustion won out over hunger and she fell asleep and into a dream. This time, she was back on the snowy expanse.

6

After two days away with what felt like mild flu, Annie went back to work.

On the subway, she wondered if she should have stayed home sick again, even at the risk of angering Bo, who was due back from London that day. She was still very sensitive to sounds and smells. The metal-on-metal sound of the subway train screeching through the tunnel pounded in her head long after she left the station. When she entered the immense lobby of the Synergy Enterprises Group building, the usual murmur of shuffling shoes and morning mumbling blended into a low-pitched howl that rose up to the high black ceiling. Yet through this she found that she could tune her hearing to pick up the voices of specific people speaking all the way across the great hall of a lobby. She wondered what Judi Cybulski from Syn-PHARM was saying to Jill Brickman from Syn-MACH, and a split second later she heard Judi's quiet voice cutting through the white noise, saying, "I keep waiting for my real life to begin."

Smells were strong. In the elevator, she was able to tell who had showered and who hadn't, and pick her way through the cacophony of perfume and aftershave to discern separate scents – cedar, orange, rose, musk, human sweat. The man to the left of her had a rotting tooth. To her right was a woman who used Ivory soap. Beneath that was another smell that Annie couldn't quite identify, but for some reason it made her instantly dislike the woman.

It took a great deal of Annie's concentration to tune all this sensory stimulation out so she could focus on work. When Bo got back he would have a lot more work for her, on top of the stuff he'd left that she hadn't been able to get to yet. Before Bo took off for London, he had dropped a dictatape on her desk, full of memos to be typed, and the legal department of Syn-EG rarely sent a short memo. The first one ended up being five pages about possible loopholes in the pension plan of a company Syn-EG was taking over, loopholes that would allow Syn-EG to withhold or, at the very least, reduce its employer contributions. The second was a three-page response to another Syn-EG lawyer's memo on strategy in a class-action lawsuit against the automotive division. Bo was the head of the Syn-EG legal department, and that meant he was ultimately responsible for the legal details of everything from lawsuits over exploding tires to the case of a woman in Ohio who was suing both Syn-EG's Silicones and Adhesives and its Pharmaceutical divisions because she'd mistaken a tube of superglue for a tube of anti-itch ointment and glued her hand to her butt, causing "scarring, great embarrassment, and emotional distress."

(True, both the anti-itch cream and the superglue were made by Syn-EG divisions, and the tubes were the same size and used the same colours in their packaging. But the woman had weak eyesight and hadn't upgraded her eyeglass prescription in five years. There were witnesses who claimed she once mistook a dog for a fluffy slipper. Syn-EG was fighting back in the courts, and by leaking the story to the media. If the woman thought she'd suffered great embarrassment before, wait until the late-night comedians got hold of this.)

This story was Annie's contribution at lunch, which she ate with Liz in the green room after the late-morning taping of *The Beth Tindall Show*, the talk show Liz worked on at Syn-TV. Part of Liz's job was to keep the green room stocked – with fresh vegetables and dip, little sandwiches, mini-bagels with flavoured cream cheese, cakes and cookies and soft drinks. There was usually left-over food that would just get thrown out if Liz and Annie didn't eat it. That day Beth Tindall had taped a show on "the Next Super-models," Elizabeth Agg, Barbara Hibbard, and Melissa Cooper, who, Liz assured Annie, were on the verge of stardom. Except for a few crudités and the mini-bagels their handlers had eaten, the food was largely untouched.

Henry wasn't with them, but he was there on the speakerphone. He was at "home," the home of his employer, Rosemary Frost, the cosmetics queen. He lived in, attending and deferring to Mrs. Frost, a woman once-widowed, twice-divorced, who had made her fortune in husbands. "Pulled herself up by her bra-straps," Henry put it, privately.

Henry saw possibilities in the superglue.

"Maybe that will work with the Czarina," he said, using his nickname for Mrs. Frost.

"Switch her hemorrhoid cream with superglue," Liz suggested. She was looking through the *Downtown Eye* for mention of her party, while Annie looked through the *News* and Henry looked through the *Post* on his end. "But if you do that, the bee up her ass will never escape."

"She only uses that cream for the bags under her eyes. Her hand would get stuck to her under-eye," Henry said. "Liz, nothing about your party. Lots about the man who was killed near your apartment."

"Nothing in here either," Liz said. "Two days, no mentions."

"Someone was killed near your apartment?" Annie asked.

"Yeah, the night of the party, a man was attacked by a dog and killed," Liz said. "Don't forget, Annie, party tonight at Dan Denton's. It's B-list, not like those crappy things we went to last week."

Liz's boss, Beth Tindall, went to the best things and excess invitations were put in a box from which her staff drew blind. Lately, Liz was drawing the short straw a lot and getting the dud

invites – a CD release party for a band "nobody" had heard of at
a club "nobody" had gone to since 1999, a reception for a right-
wing member of the Israeli Knesset, a party for a new book on
trade policy.

"Dan's party is to promote celebrity wrestling. . . . Something
like that," Liz said. "The Party Line did the party – they're getting
a lot of good jobs lately. I want to check out what they're doing."

"I'm still feeling weak," Annie said.

"You have to come," Liz said. "Henry's going to be late and I
can't go alone. It's important. You have to."

"I'll go for a little while –"

"Great. I'll meet you outside Denton's loft at nine," Liz said,
and, having obtained what she wanted, she turned her attention
back to the *Downtown Eye* and to Henry on the speakerphone.

When Annie went back to her desk, she took the other newspapers with her. "Dog Bites Man," the *Post* blared, above the
picture of the dead man, Robert Bingham, adding in only slightly
smaller type, "Oil man's throat ripped out in killer dog attack."

She got a strange chill when she read that. Maybe she had seen
the attack or been menaced herself, she thought, and then blacked
out due to some post-traumatic stress disorder. That could have
triggered the wolf dream and caused it to be set it in the city.
Maybe she should call the police. But since she didn't remember
anything, what would she tell them? That, and something else she
couldn't put her finger on, held her back.

She wished she could call her therapist to get some guidance,
but she had quit therapy and she was not on good terms with the
doctor. They'd fallen out over the question of Annie's "repressed
hostility." Annie didn't feel hostile, and said so, nicely. After
probing Annie's vulnerabilities for six sessions, unable to elicit any
hostility at all from Annie, the doctor finally lost her temper and
yelled, "You are *not* working with me. You are hostile! *Why can't
you admit it?*"

Annie replied, "Because I just don't feel it. Sorry!"

"Do you know what hostility is? Have you seen hostility?"

Too polite to point to the angry psychiatrist, whose face seemed to be drawing blood from every other part of her body, Annie cited several examples she saw on a regular basis: Liz, who was hostile in a snappish way; Bo, who was hostile in a bellowing way that rattled the venetian blinds in his office and blew her hair back; and the guy at the newsstand in the lobby of the Syn-EG building, who never said anything hostile but always had a seething tone to his voice. "Here's your change," he'd say, as if it were a threat.

"I don't feel angry like they do," Annie said.

"Because it's repressed!" the therapist said.

"Good!" Annie said. "There are entirely too many angry people in the world."

Finally, rather than continue to upset her therapist, she'd just stopped going to therapy.

⑥

Bo came back to work at around three in a terrible mood. London had been rainy and everything had been expensive. He hadn't gotten cabs when he needed them and everything had closed too early so that when he got back to the hotel after late-night meetings he was forced to make do with an overpriced club sandwich from the bare-bones after-midnight room service menu. He hated London almost as much as Paris, which he found "frou-frouey" and full of snobs who took long lunches. Bo liked cities full of hard-working people who didn't seem to be having more fun than he was having. This city fit his bill, despite its many parties, clubs and entertainments, and the fact that it wasn't hard to have more fun than Bo, since he was one of the most unhappy people Annie had ever met.

The London trip had been fruitful, if not enjoyable, and, as she'd expected, Bo dropped a bunch of work on her desk when he returned. He was in a bearishly bad mood, and smelled strangely of bitter herbs, but she was able to shrug it off, as usual. It was always in the back of her mind that she was much better off than most people in the world, for instance elderly people with arthritis and bad livers, beggar women in poor countries, children forced to weave carpets for fifty cents a day, and people who had lost their legs; people who would have counted themselves lucky to be able to be called into their boss's office, yelled at for having four errors on one page, and then walk out with a fully-functioning liver, on two healthy legs, to collect an annual salary of forty-one thousand dollars.

Somehow, Annie got everything done and faxed, and Bo let her go at seven. On the subway ride home she finished reading the papers, paying special attention to the killer-dog story. There was a brief obituary of the dead man, an American who had been working in the oil business in sub-Saharan Africa and had come to the city for some meetings. He was fifty-nine, divorced, a graduate of Southern Methodist University. He worked for Synergy Petroleum, and had run Syn-PET's sub-Saharan oil operations for the last five years. No other information was given out about him.

Caught up in reading, she almost ran into an old con artist named Razz when she came up from the metro. He was singing for money in the station, with his dark glasses on and his white cane propped on the wall beside him. He'd been gone for a few months and she was surprised, unhappily, to see him back. She was tempted to call the police and tell them about how Razz had mauled her and stalked her last winter, but she couldn't prove anything against him. Maybe he did accidentally fall, his open hands landing exactly on her breasts, his mouth exactly on her mouth.

Though she was sure he didn't know she was there, she plunged into the departing crowd to lose herself and took an alternate route home, just to be on the safe side. When she got to her building, her super, Mr. Hamernich, was out sweeping the steps. He told her he had replaced her window.

"You say you fell against it, from the inside," he said.

"Yes. I'm clumsy."

"That's strange, because there was glass on the inside sill but not the outside."

"That is strange," Annie said. "I guess it bounced back in."

"Yeah, I guess it did," he said, but he didn't sound convinced.

Lying had seemed better than telling the truth, that she'd broken in after losing her keys. Then she would have to explain why she didn't just buzz Mr. Hamernich to let her in, and she'd have to tell him she'd been drinking and had blacked out. He was a reformed alcoholic who'd found religion and often commented on what a nice, sensible girl she was, a rarity in this city of tarts, feminists, and drunkards, and she didn't want to disappoint the old guy without a very good reason. After her parents died, she'd been raised by disappointed old people. If Mr. Hamernich thought her mortal soul was being corrupted, he'd tell her the story again about being rescued from the "bowels of the earth," and maybe even drag her to another service at the Jesus Saves Tabernacle, which had been built with the first sober earnings of its converts.

In theory, she thought it was wonderful that Jesus Saves went into the shelters and flophouses to drag out drunks and make them sober up and accept Jesus Christ as saviour. The Tabernacle got them back to work and tithing regularly. But the service she went to was too depressing. The church was in a little storefront, just a large room with fluorescent lighting and bare walls except for a cross, a picture of Jesus, and inspirational posters about staying off demon drink. The congregation sat on folding chairs. Every person there looked angry and ashamed at the same time, what a friend of hers called "dry drunks, people who are just gritting their teeth to keep from drinking." Every movement seemed measured and methodical, lest some part of them lose control. They were a joyless bunch, but at least they weren't drunk on the sidewalk or in some shabby flophouse.

The urge to drink had been replaced by an urge to give testimony and convert and Annie heard more of this than she really needed to while she was waiting for the post-service coffee and

cookie, which cost her two dollars for the coffee fund. To avoid
going back, Annie told Mr. Hamernich the outing had inspired
her to return to the Catholic Church she'd been raised in, an easy
ruse to keep up since on many Sundays she went to visit Mrs.
Mackie at the nursing home. Other Sundays, she dressed as if she
were going to church anyway and went to the movies, rather than
be caught in a lie by Mr. Hamernich.

"There was hair in the broken glass, stuck in blood," Mr.
Hamernich said.

"My hair?"

"It was coarser and a darker colour. You don't have a dog, do
you?"

"No. I cut myself when I fell into the window. Maybe the blood
made the hair look darker."

"No pets allowed."

"Yes, I know. I don't have a pet. Honest."

"Okay."

"Thanks for fixing my window," Annie said.

"That's my job," Mr. Hamernich said, probing her eyes, a look
her ex-boyfriend Hayden called his Sin Searchlight, before grimly
turning back to his methodical sweeping.

Maybe it was time to move out of this neighbourhood, she
thought, into a new apartment. This was something she'd been
meaning to do since she and Hayden had split up. It had been hard,
being in the apartment she and Hayden had shared, coming home
at night not to him but to the ghost of their life together, sleeping
in the bed they had shared. Even something as simple as sitting in
front of the television could strike a deep blue note in her, the television they bought one Saturday and then lugged home in a taxi,
after making the driver rearrange everything in his trunk and close
it with a rope so the television would fit. On the ride back, Hayden
had sat with a big plastic jug of anti-freeze on his lap, which left a
smear on his pants. He had been furious.

Hoping he'd return to her, Annie had stayed in their apartment longer than she should have. When it became clear he wasn't going to come back, she'd tried to change the apartment around, moving things in the medicine chest to fill in his vacated section, rearranging the furniture, buying new curtains and even a new toothbrush so her old one didn't look so lonely by itself.

But it didn't help, and since she was having neighbour trouble anyway, she had decided to look for a new place, not an easy task on a legal secretary's salary. But, as both Liz and Henry pointed out, if you're not in this city, you're nowhere. Look at all the people they'd known from the old neighbourhood who either stayed there, or went back there after a short run in the city. "Nobody" went to see them out there.

⑥

Tarts and drunkards, if not feminists, were out in force at Dan Denton's loft party later that night. Dan Denton was a dot-com millionaire who had gotten out before the crash and now produced "events." His loft was cavernous and dim, except for the bright lights in the far corner illuminating a wrestling ring and the pale glow of the bar, which was a twenty-five-foot S-shaped aquarium teeming with brightly coloured fish and topped with an S-shaped slab of pink marble. There were several people with video cameras roaming through the crowd. Every now and then the scene on the giant screen on the back wall would switch to the massage room, or a crowd shot, or the people steaming in the steam room.

"This is a B-plus-list party," Liz said. "I'm moderately impressed. Hip too, there's a guy from Andy's Factory talking to Renee and Lenore Gothmann, from last month's *Playboy*. Talk about party cred. An Andy guy talking to identical twin Playmates. I have got to schmooze them onto my mailing list, as soon as Henry gets here."

At every party, Liz liked to start by casing the joint to get a handle on the celebrity quotient and the quality of the entertainment, refreshments, and promotional treat bags given out to guests.

Annie, with her sturdy stenographer's memory, was very useful during this part of the evening, cataloguing the snacks and keeping track of which things were popular with guests and which were not. But charming and chatting people up, that was Henry's job.

Henry arrived schmoozing, entering the party with a man he'd met on the elevator up, who took Henry's card before he turned away into a clutch of male models.

"Who was that?" Liz asked.

"The guy who writes 'Dear Tweets,'" Henry said.

"What's 'Dear Tweets'?" Annie asked.

"Annie, catch up. It's the new gossip column in the *Downtown Eye*," Liz said. "You gave him your card?"

"Of course."

"Did he give you his?"

"No. He doesn't have cards yet. He's still trying to decide on the design."

"So he says. He may have been blowing you off."

"I don't think so. We had a vibe. Who's he talking to now?" Henry asked. "I don't want to look over."

"That horrible British journalist."

"Which one?"

"You know, the old, gay one."

"Which old gay one, Liz?"

"I can't remember his name. Nigel . . . Nigel . . ."

"Nigel Findyke. He's not gay."

"He's not?"

"No, he's a beardsplitter. Asian girls. He just acts gay. Let's walk around and judge people."

They manoeuvred through the room, trailing Annie, who had to lean in behind them to hear their commentary through the party music.

"Look, there's the model who does those Calvin Klein ads. Her skin looks like hell from the heroin."

As they passed the model who did the Calvin Klein ads, Annie heard her say, "It was court-ordered rehab so it was like jail. I felt like those Russian sailors who were trapped in that submarine, or Anne Frank or someone."

"She's looking very butch these days," Liz said out of the side of her mouth to Henry.

"Overalls? Just came from a barn-raising perhaps," Henry said out of the side of his mouth as they glided past the model and turned their high beams on to a TV news anchorwoman and anchorman from Syn-TV, where Liz worked.

The music was too loud to make out what was said next. Annie was getting a headache. She amused herself for a while counting the designer shoes in the crowd. Her statistical sample indicated there was well over a hundred thousand dollars of footwear holding up the 150 or so guests.

"Liz, look over and see who Dear Tweets is talking to now."

"Joey Something, the musician —"

Henry looked quickly. "Oh no. He's an idiot. Speed-limit IQ."

"Freeway?"

"School zone," Henry said. "Is there a vibe between them? Sex vibe?"

"I can't tell. Is Joey Something gay?"

"Yes."

"No way. He seems very hetero —"

"You can't always tell, Liz. You know that," Henry said. "Trust my gaydar."

"I'm not feeling well. I'm going home," Annie said. Her radar was going off too. It wasn't gaydar, it was smell-dar, or something. Both Henry and Liz were giving off a very sour smell.

"Stay for the fights," Liz said.

"I'm tired and I have to work on a birthday present for Mrs. Mackie."

"Annie, you are too nice. You're going to leave a party to do something for an old lady who doesn't even remember you?" Henry said.

"I'm not too nice."

"Please. The old con artist who stalked you?"

"I thought he really was blind."

"Until he stalked you."

"Yeah, but –"

"For three blocks."

"Okay –"

"The last one running."

"I suspected he could see the night he took me bowling."

"You should have suspected when he tried to sell you that hot fur coat," Henry said. "You are just a lamb among the wolves, Annie."

"You can't get anywhere that way. You have to be sharp, on the ball," Liz said, snapping her fingers to punctuate "sharp" and "ball."

Liz and Henry went off to talk to the twin Playmates and Annie slipped away. As she got on the elevator a bunch of "wannabes and almosts" (as Henry had dubbed their breed) got off, young hipsters looking for an angle. The elevator was designed for freight, grey and black with a chain-mail door, a leftover from when the building was a meat warehouse. As it went down, it ground and rattled in its cage. She could smell the meat in it still. It seemed to her the kind of elevator that would take you down to hell.

Outside, looking for a taxi, she passed a poster taped to an aluminum light pole.

"A. Wolf. I need to talk to you. I can help," it said, with a box number underneath.

She didn't see it. She was thinking how sad those parties made her feel, and how that one had seemed particularly sad and made her think of the Edgar Allan Poe story, "The Masque of the Red Death," in which the rich and powerful isolate themselves inside a sumptuous palace in an endless party while plague rages in the countryside. The Red Death breaches the quarantine though, in the guise of a guest.

A voice in her head said, "There comes a time when a girl gets tired of spectacle and cheap sensation, and yearns for a deeper feeling." Whatever that deeper feeling was, she was hungering for it.

7

The week after Sam's scoop, he basked in the glow of a sudden success, a success just as surprising to Sam as it was to his many detractors in the newsroom. They had done everything they could to get that guy off the air and off the premises only to have him pull one motherfucking rabbit out of the hat at the last minute.

It was a fluke, right? The old anchorman's last gasp of the rarefied air of TV news before he got out of the way of the future? Over the next couple of weeks he dug up nothing to refute this theory. Granted, he worked hard, even if he didn't seem to know what he was doing and his follow-up stories sounded like they'd been written by a generic newsbot.

If only he'd accept his fate and go, instead of trying to milk the story. The rest of the media may have abandoned the killer-dog story for other things, but Sam Deverell was more tenacious than a pit bull. Still, as his coverage dribbled off into increasingly lame sidebar stories, it became clear to everyone but Sam that the Mad Dog story was the last flash for him.

Sam got the news when the owner of CCN called Sam in to congratulate him on the story.

"But Sam," he said, "I don't think we can keep you much longer. You'd be happier somewhere else. A radio station upstate is looking for a DJ from midnight to five. I could give them a call."

"You can't let me go yet. That killer dog is still out there —"

"And it may never be found."

"This is a bad time. Candace has moved out. She says she needs some space . . ."

"That's bad. I'm really sorry. But Sam, it's tough all over, pal. I gave you a chance to get on your feet here, but we've been changing to a certain . . . look and energy and you don't –"

"When we were back in Albuquerque," Sam started, his voice trailing off. That was all he had to say to remind his boss of the heroic deed Sam had performed for the then-owner of Mesa Broadcasting, who now sighed between gritted teeth and looked down.

"One more month, Sam. Look for another job in that time, because when that month is over you're going to have to . . . move on. Let go of this story and work on getting yourself situated elsewhere."

There was no way Sam was going to let go of the story. This was the only scoop he'd had in his entire career, and it was the only thing that could, at this point, save him from the big chill of midnight-to-five radio. It was getting harder and harder to milk it though. There had been only one killer-dog death. Then nothing. Sam had been making do with stories on coyote sightings, breeds of attack dogs, pepper spray sales, and by eavesdropping on other reporters for rumours to report – but that wasn't easy and it wasn't reliable.

Somehow, he was going to have to find a real source. He needed someone in the police department, he was pretty sure of that. Since the police kept transferring his calls to public affairs, which gave him the official story ("We are continuing to investigate the death of Robert Hunt Bingham"), the only way he could think of to meet someone from the police department was just to go down there and turn on the charm.

This probably would have worked in Albuquerque, or even Atlanta, where people were more friendly and polite and Sam was a celebrity. But in this city it earned him smirks and sneers. When the cop at reception at Police Division South wouldn't help him, he tried randomly stopping people who looked like they could be cops. It was a desperate move, and his desperation was so strong even the cleaning people leaving for lunch could smell it on him.

He finally gave up – roughly at the same time he was asked to leave the building and quit bothering people.

Outside, a swarthy man sidled up to him and without turning his head said, "Don't look at me. I can help you. Wait five minutes, then come to Griffin's, two blocks east. Ask for Vincent."

Then he walked ahead of Sam and kept on walking.

A few blocks later, Sam came to Griffin's, a dark-windowed bar and grill with a Police Benevolent Association sticker in the window, which led Sam to believe he had found a real cop hangout. When he got inside, he couldn't see the man who had spoken to him. He walked the length of the place and did not see him.

At the bar, a short, dark-haired woman watched him walking back and forth. Her eyes moved but the rest of her was still.

"Are you looking for Vincent?" she asked.

"Yeah!"

"Come with me," she said.

Sam followed her through a faux Oriental rug nailed over a doorway into a small back room, the air warm and steamy with meat, tomatoes and onions from the nearby kitchen. The swarthy man was there, sitting at a butcher-block table under an exposed light bulb. Across from him was a lean, fair-haired man with a prominent nose. They were eating plates of brown-grey stew. The swarthy man asked the woman to bring them all some beers. His name was Vincent, and he and his friend Ivan were not cops, it turned out, but part of the cleaning staff at Police Division South.

"I've seen you on television," Vincent said. "Talking about the Mad Dog Murder."

"I'm a reporter and I'm looking for a source."

"I know. I heard you," Vincent said. "Ivan here, he cleans Homicide. He hears everything."

Ivan nodded.

"Will you be my source?" Sam asked.

"A hundred dollars for Ivan, and a hundred dollars for me," Vincent said. "You can't use our names."

Vaguely, Sam remembered someone saying something about it being unethical for journalists to pay money to sources for information, but since he couldn't remember exactly what that was, and suspected it might just be one of the news kids' pranks, he ran out to an ATM, withdrew the cash, and paid them when he got back to Griffin's.

"The police are worried because the oil man was killed on the full moon, and there's a full moon in a few days," Ivan said, after he'd counted the twenty-dollar bills.

"They think there's a connection?"

Ivan nodded. "It happened before, men killed by dogs during full moons. Four years ago a man was killed, five years ago a man was killed, and seven years ago two men were killed, all in the city, the same way. Always during full moons. That's all I know. You give me your numbers, and I will call you when I know more."

"Okay. And let me get your numbers."

"No. I'll call you. And if you tell anyone where you got this information –" He slid his finger across his neck.

"You can count on me," Sam said. "But I want this . . . exclusively. You talk to me only."

"Okay," Vincent said. Sam had paid so quickly that the price was already going up in Vincent's mind. The next tip would cost more.

Life was funny. Just the night before, Vincent, Ivan, and Vincent's wife, Marguerite, had been worrying about where they were going to find the money to pay the rent. They'd invested all their savings into the bar in hopes of leaving janitorial work for good, but the bar was costing them more than it made. Vincent had had to go back to driving a cab at night, and Marguerite was running the place on her own most of the time, while Ivan moonlighted in the kitchen.

"The Lord works in mysterious ways," Marguerite said after Sam had left.

"Six tips a month and we have rent," Vincent said.

Back at CCN, Sam bounded through the newsroom like a man half his age. Cooper, the young managing editor, was in his office talking on the phone.

"Hold on, Jon," Cooper said. He hit the hold button. "What is it, Sam?"

"Can you put me on the set? I've got new information." He felt like those two guys who brought down Nixon, Woodward and Bernknopf, who met Deep Throat in *All the President's Men*, which he'd rented and watched to pick up some reporting tips. He'd learned a lot from it.

"What is it?"

"Put me on set . . ."

"Not until I hear what you've got." Cooper gave Sam a steady, intimidating gaze, no doubt something he learned from one of those books behind his desk, Sam thought, like Sun Tzu's *Art of War* or Strunk and White.

"Bingham wasn't the first victim. This has happened before, and always during full moons."

"Really? Sounds like it could be a serial killer," Cooper said, perking up.

"Does it?"

"Yes, Sam, like the Zodiac Killer. Someone timing their murders to astrological events. Do you have details on the previous killings?"

"I have last names, and roughly when they happened."

"Where did you get this information?"

"From my sources. Two different sources," he added.

"Who are they?"

"I can't tell you," Sam said. "It would violate . . . that journalism rule."

"Okay. What do the cops say?"

"No comment."

"You're sure about these other killings?"

"Absolutely."

"I'll have Jennifer Ray get the details on the names of these victims. If it checks out, I'll have her write something for you to do on-set."

"Which Jennifer is Jennifer Ray?"

"The brunette with the heart tattoo on her collarbone. She's a writer and a producer. You go to makeup. She'll meet you there."

Cooper picked up the phone. "Jennifer Ray, can you go meet Sam Deverell in makeup? I want you to check out some information he has."

Sam gave Cooper a thumbs-up and took off. Cooper watched him leave, wondering what had happened here. The newsroom deadwood still had some sap in him. He was oddly glad to see it, though he'd been one of the loudest critics of Sam's hiring, and had pointed out to the owner, "I don't care how nice he is. Look at him. If you want to buy a used car or life insurance, this is the guy you go to. If you want edgy, provocative news, no."

Still, Cooper had to respect the guy for finding a story and working it, for making an effort. He could have easily hung around at CCN collecting a paycheque until the owner had finally repaid that legendary favour and showed him the door. Then he could have just lived off his wife, Candace Quall, a rising star anchor-woman at Syn-TV, and golfed or whatever it was he did when he wasn't at CCN.

So it was with a certain pleasure that Cooper watched Sam do his piece on-set. It was a good story, snappy, full of previously unre-ported facts, thanks in large part to Jennifer Ray's writing, but also thanks to Sam's apparently sharp investigative skills. Who knew he had it in him?

After Sam finished his shift, Cooper gave him some books on basic journalism, and Sam promised to read them. There remained the problem of trying to make Sam fit in with CCN's look and agenda. Cooper had been thinking about this a lot, if there wasn't some way to "hip" Sam up without making him too much like the hopelessly out-of-touch high school teacher who dresses young and drops lyrics from last year's pop songs into his lessons so as to appear relevant. There was a big risk of this with Sam, because he was just so square, and not in a hip-square way. It would be too easy to make him look ridiculous.

At the end of the day, Cooper called Jennifer Ray in and told her, "I'm putting you on the story full time."

"Lucky me. I must have made a deal with the devil I don't remember because I was drunk at the time," Jennifer Ray said. "That would also explain the new toaster-oven."

Cooper smiled. "Good story, bad reporter. He needs help."

"I know."

"What does he look like to you?"

"Like a televangelist."

"Yeah, a faith healer a month before the inevitable sex scandal, circa 1987," Cooper said. "We need to 'brand' him somehow, some way that will make him appeal to our viewers."

"It's going to have to be a subtle transformation. The helmet hair has got to go. No more hairspray. And the suit. Burn it."

"And we'll replace them with what?"

"I don't know. Maybe some serious glasses would help, some black-rimmed Clark Kent thing," she said. "Or something really retro."

"Example."

"Make him look like one of those old-timey reporters."

"A trench coat?" Cooper asked.

"Too obvious," she said. "Maybe a slate-grey London Fog raincoat with a matching hat. Subtler, more Bogie, less *Front Page* cliché."

"You're a genius, Jennifer Ray."

8

The whole week leading up to the full moon, Annie was in a bad mood. It started with a trip to the nursing home to deliver a painting she had done for Mrs. Mackie's birthday, a portrait of a guy called Dusty Rhoades, whom Mrs. Mackie wanted to marry "when I grow up." Annie had gone to a great deal of trouble to paint this for Mrs. Mackie. She'd looked up Rhoades on the Internet to find a picture of him. He was a star of movie serials for a while in the 1930s, playing a singing gunslinger in *High Noon Hill* and a space-ship pilot in *Zip Parker, Astroman*. Then he had some bit parts in B-movies until he was pushed from a balcony in Hollywood in 1951.

That story got her down, and seeing Mrs. Mackie got her down, and not only because she missed the old Mrs. Mackie, the one in wire curlers under a floral scarf who chatted with her grandmother over the fence as they hung their wet laundry on the line behind their semi-detached houses in the old neighbourhood. Back then, Mrs. Mackie always had a cigarette hanging out of her mouth, a Lucky Strike. She knew how to smoke and talk without the cigarette falling out of her mouth, as she and Grandma Kay passed judgment on the rest of their neighbours or lamented all their lost chances, the men they could have married, the land they could have bought when it was cheap, or that time Mrs. Mackie was one number off in the lottery, and it was the last number, so she didn't even get a consolation prize. If the ash didn't fall off by itself, Mrs. Mackie would just press the cigarette between her lips and jerk her head till it fell. For years after she quit, she still spoke and laughed out of one side of her mouth, like Popeye.

This was how Annie wanted to remember her, not as the hateful child she'd become.

When Annie arrived at the nursing home, Mrs. Mackie didn't recognize her at all, not even as her Grandma Kay.

"Who are you?" she asked through slitted eyes.

"Annie, Kay Katch's granddaughter."

"You have to get me out of here. I need to go home. My daddy will miss me," she said, abruptly changing subject to taunt Annie about her freckles. "You're spotty!"

"They're freckles."

"Spots! You've got spots. Ugly spots."

Of the painting of Dusty Rhoades Annie had worked so hard on, she said, "It doesn't even look like him!" And everything was "Mine!" including Annie's purse, which Annie then had to wrestle away from the poor old bird. When the Jamaican nurse came to take Mrs. Mackie for her dialysis treatment, Mrs. Mackie had hissed at her and appealed to Annie, "Don't let the Negro take me. Take me home!"

"The good Lord will take you home soon enough," the nurse said, unperturbed.

Mrs. Mackie smelled strange too, swampy and rotten. Privately, Annie asked the nurse if Mrs. Mackie were more sick than usual. The nurse said her condition was about the same, which was bad enough. Mrs. Mackie only had a short time left, months at the outside, and that made Annie sad too, less for Mrs. Mackie than for herself, though she didn't like to give in to self-pity for too long. At this point, trapped as she was in the 1930s, death seemed a mercy for Mrs. Mackie, who was the last link Annie had to her family.

As if she wasn't feeling blue enough, when Annie got home Liz and Henry called to alert her to a wedding announcement in the *Times* Style section for her ex-boyfriend, Hayden Lipp, and his girlfriend, Elizabeth Clark Barrow.

"Mrs. Lipp, who goes by the name Clark, is a graduate of law school . . ." Liz read, as Annie searched through the paper to find it.

"Too bad, Annie," Henry said. "If it's any consolation, a friend of mine does weight training with Clark Barrow and says she has tiny tits and cellulite."

"And big shoulders. Those horsey-looking trust puppies piss me off," Liz said.

"Thanks. I have to go," Annie said, hanging up in tears.

Annie thought she had handled the break-up relatively well, but this went to her heart like a shot of poison. Her old dream was shattered. Annie thought she was going to be Mrs. Lipp. In her mind, their whole life had been planned. Hay would make a lot of money as an attorney-slash-writer-of-legal-thrillers, and she'd give up her job to paint and do volunteer work. Eventually, after his first bestseller, he'd quit the law firm and they would both be artists in an apartment with bookshelves everywhere, cats, even kids one day. They'd work on their masterpieces in their separate blue rooms in the apartment (apart, yet connected by a powerful soul-cord), driven by their own creative forces and desire for each other, until they couldn't stand it any longer, and they'd rush from their masterpieces to make love wherever their bodies met in the apartment.

It was a very detailed fantasy – and one Hay said he shared, until Clark came along. The fantasy included the inevitable difficulties most marriages face, but which they would overcome and be stronger for, and it went right up to her mourning his death at age eighty-five in the entire townhouse they would then own, being comforted by their children, grandchildren, and the city's brilliant, beautiful people who loved them both, despite their envy of Annie and Hay's deep and lasting love.

It was devastating, as break-ups are, but Annie quickly came to understand it. These things happen. As Hay advanced in school and began to be courted by tony law firms, his self-esteem rose. Meanwhile, Annie was advancing from file clerk to typist to administrative assistant to help support them both, and her self-esteem remained pretty static. She'd tried to keep up with him in every other area, reading voraciously, keeping fit, snagging one college course per semester to help complete her own degree – she even took up rock climbing because he enjoyed it and she wanted to share that with him. But on the self-esteem front, her progress was glacial, and his broke the sound barrier. He needed someone who loved herself just as much as he loved himself.

Still, even though she had known they were engaged, seeing their union there in black and white, with a picture of them looking so happy, made her not just unhappy, but angry. All week after that, she was short-tempered. When the hostile guy at the newsstand in the Syn-EG lobby handed over her change with his usual sneer and implied threat, she said, "Do you have to be so rude? Would it kill you to be polite?"

Afterwards, she had walked away, stunned by her own outburst.

Even Bo got some of his own bluster back at him. It started out with a few simple, firm statements. When he asked Annie to complete a huge task in a short time, she said, "No, I can't do that," and walked away. When he complained she wasn't fast enough in making some changes he'd scribbled on a draft of a memo about a lawsuit filed by people who claimed they'd hallucinated and had psychotic episodes after taking Zonex, she snapped, "I'm going as fast as I can, Bo. Take a pill. Take a Zonex."

It was weird, like she was channelling Liz, who also felt the unfamiliar sharp edge of Annie's tongue when she called to ask Annie to swipe some card stock from supply. Annie snapped at her, "I can't think about things like that right now, Liz. Jesus Christ. Buy one less pair of Christian Louboutin shoes this month and buy your own card stock."

"Man, are you touchy," Liz said.

Annie's eyes had become very sensitive to light and her sense of smell was heightened to the point where she could tell that a kid across the aisle and down two seats on the subway had vomited earlier after a great deal of liquor. She could feel – or imagined she could feel – her blood rushing through her veins. She could hear her blood too, like water in pipes. And the hunger . . . the hunger was profound and insatiable. For breakfast, the lightest meal of her day, she was now eating two bowls of granola, four fruit muffins and, to quell an inexplicable desire for meat, a whole package of fried tofu sausages. Every day she had to shave not only her legs and underarms, but her arms and her face, as she had started to develop a soft, blond fur all over her body.

Above all, she felt a growing agitation and energy. She felt like she was about to break out of her skin, like it might just split, and everything inside her would go flying.

II

The Buck Moon

July

9

When Dr. Marco Potenza, following in his father's footsteps, first set up his practice, he looked for a place where he wouldn't arouse suspicions, something spacious with good soundproofing, where he could have both a confinement centre, an office practice, and a home. The places that were suitable for confinement were not conducive to a soothing therapeutic atmosphere and even less suitable for gentle, cultured living. He looked at warehouses in various parts of the city and was about to settle, unhappily, for a former corrugated-paper warehouse, when he stumbled upon a paragraph in a book about speakeasies in the Prohibition era:

There was said to be one in a secret underground room in the West 20s. Known as Marie's, after the proprietor P. Marie Liddick, it attracted the city's most famous and most fascinating, from movie stars to the notorious spiritualist Madame Victoria Ball, who described Marie's in a letter as a "large, low-ceilinged room originally built as an opium den and retaining much of its original decor. It reminded me of the harem room of a Turkish pasha who once consulted me in my girlhood. There one might find oneself drinking a 'pink' on a cushioned banquette next to Bette Davis, the Prince of Wales, Ernest Hemingway or a dapper gangster named Joey 'No Questions' Gagliardi with carious breath while a Victrola played low music. I first went with Edith Piaf, who was visiting her friend, a poet, in a building called the Chelsea. It was very popular with the artists, who convinced me I should stay in the Chelsea when I was next in town. I have never stayed anywhere else since."

The poet, named Virgil, and a contemporary named Alice were still alive and living in the Chelsea, and Marco was able to win an invitation to meet with them to discuss "speakeasies and Marie Liddick" for a journal paper he said he was writing on the psychological effects of prohibition on the different social classes. The secret basement, he learned, was located right there beneath the Chelsea. Alice said it had been closed and filled in for years, but Virgil later told him it was still there, it had just been sealed off so the only access was through a small crawl space leading from the basement.

The room had low ceilings but it was long and wide. It measured one hundred by two hundred feet and extended out beyond the Chelsea below the street. There were still remnants of the speakeasy decor, patches of red and gold brocade wallpaper and the remains of light fixtures. Marco took one look and knew this was the place. He rented an apartment on the eighth floor of the Chelsea while he renovated the secret room, and later moved into a three-storey penthouse with roof garden on the top floor. He found the old door and a secret staircase that opened into the basement of the Chelsea in a furniture storage area just off the boiler room. Marco arranged to store a large cabinet there, which concealed the entrance. With the help of a patient, he added better ventilation and a plumbing and drainage system, a group shower room, heat and air conditioning. They installed cubicles where his patients would be contained.

There were a lot of werewolves around at that time. Nobody noticed because it was the seventies, the disco/punk rock era, swingers clubs, anything goes. With the help of his father's tracker, Rudolfo, Marco found them and brought them into the program. The Centre had been in its heyday then, everything was experimental, and there was a strong sense of mission. From that original group, Marco had picked a protegé, trained him almost to his own calibre, and dispatched him to London, just as his father had dispatched him here and his brother Enzio to Hollywood, just as his grandfather had sent his father to America from Switzerland in 1946. None of the original patients was still with Marco now.

Marco always confined the patients a day before the full moon until a day after, longer if behaviour warranted. It was rare for someone to transform before the moon was full, but the signs could be seen as much as a week before and a week after, depending on health or emotional factors. The patients' body hair grew faster and more profusely, they were hypersensitive to all sensations, and this was often accompanied by aggressive feelings and sexual arousal of increasing intensity as the moon neared full. Their growing wolfish nature showed itself as rudeness, loss of temper, or something as simple as forgetting table manners.

When a patient first entered the program Marco liked to keep him at the Centre, observing him for a week before the full moon and a few days after, depending how long it took for the sickness to recede. But as a rule, a three-day confinement was sufficient in conjunction with talk, drug and self-hypnosis therapy during the off-peak weeks.

The day before the July full moon, the Buck Moon, the patients arrived at the Centre in the morning with a change of clothes, their toiletry kit, a few personal things, and a cheque for the month's treatment. Marco and his protegé, Mike, escorted them downstairs, where they stripped, showered, and changed into disposable paper pyjamas. After Marco checked their vital signs, they were strapped into a bed, their arms and legs manacled with padded iron restraints embedded in concrete. They were then connected to monitors to record their heart and respiratory rates, along with brain activity.

At that point, endotracheal tubes were inserted, and the patients were catheterized and hooked up to two IVs, one supplying fluids and glucose, the other supplying a drug mixture tailored to the patient's body weight, health, hormonal and adrenal levels. Marco liked to use a combination of benzodiazepine, a "Benzo" called midazolam, with the animal tranquilizer ketamine. The Benzo caused amnesia so the patients couldn't recall either their transformation or the ketamine-induced hallucinations.

Drugs alone didn't suppress the transformation during the full moon, but they weakened it and allowed the patients to sleep, saving not only the lives of their would-be victims but the lives of werewolves everywhere.

Once the patients were all in place and asleep, Mike kept an eye on them and Marco went back upstairs. Every morning during treatment, Marco would go back down with Carol to rouse them, hose them down, exercise them, put them in clean paper pyjamas and strap them down again. After two days in manacles, they were taken off the drugs and given a day to sleep off the effects of treatment before they ate a big communal meal upstairs in the Centre.

Marco hadn't told them that he'd be gone for this full moon, nor that they were low on ketamine. That would just worry them, and anxiety increased adrenal and hormonal reactions, which meant greater sedation was needed. Without the ketamine, the job of restraining them was tougher. It was important the patients be kept calm and made to feel secure and looked after.

The morning before the full moon, Marco checked the patients. They were fine. After lunch, he put on his favourite silk robe, a gift from Carol, and then sat in front of a big round mirror and lit a candle, which he placed on the table below the mirror. The room was dark except for the candlelight and a sliver of streetlight. The door was open to bring in the scents of the outdoors. The air smelled like rain.

Nine times out of ten, all he had to do to lure a werewolf back to the Chelsea was to show up and send a non-threatening signal, telling the other to follow him. Werewolves, like common wolves, need their pack and would follow Marco to his with little resistance. When there was resistance, he tried to lure them in with ads and posters while they were in human form. If that didn't work, he was supposed to call his father in Washington, and ask for Rudolfo. Rudolfo was ruthless. If a werewolf continued to resist, Rudolfo killed him and disposed of the body. It was necessary.

After an hour of concentrating, Marco had to take a break. All he'd mustered up so far was some hair. He sat back down and tried again. It had been six months since he had last transformed. He hadn't had to transform in three years, but as a rule he would force himself to every few months, just to stay in practice. It was a painful process, mentally as well as physically, requiring tremendous concentration and mind control to summon the wolf up from his DNA. It was easy enough to transform once one turned on the natural adrenal and hormonal triggers – and the moon was full. But he needed to adopt the form and the powerful instincts while maintaining his total human intelligence and complete control – no cheap trick when one was rusty.

But he had to track this new werewolf and bring him in tonight, before there were any more killings. Already, a reporter at CCN had discovered the previous killings – several by werewolves in Marco's program, and two by a former patient and protegé. The rest of the media followed like a pack of jackals. The pressure was on the police and the new mayor.

That meant the pressure was on Marco. He'd never responded well to pressure, as his father and brother liked to point out. They could trace this back to his brief career as a child prodigy pianist, when he got stage fright in the middle of a recital in Washington and abruptly left the stage to throw up. Even now, something as simple as a game of charades with the family at Thanksgiving made him nauseated, especially if he had to play with his wife Carol, who took off-the-wall guesses like "Man walking a pickle" for the movie title *Wag the Dog*.

These thoughts were impeding his progress.

You are not a man, he told himself. You are a wolf. A powerful wolf. He repeated this mantra until he could do it without words, until he could see nothing but his own eyes in the mirror. Soon, he began to feel the wolf in him come alive.

10

Jim got up in his underwear, drank some orange juice, took a Valium and looked out at the world through windows blurred with rain, which always made him think of the monsoon and India.

This would be his first full moon off ketamine since he'd left India, and he was feeling it. He had heavy beard growth, he was hyper-energized, every nerve in his body alive and reaching for something. It was useless to write when he was like this. Several days before the full moon, his ability to use words declined. Images, sensations, visions came to him, and he couldn't express them properly. It was frustrating. There was always a moment, the last moment before the moon was completely full and his consciousness changed over completely from human to wolf, when he was sure he saw the secret of life, only to find he couldn't quite grasp it and describe it later, after he'd recovered from the moon and become wholly human again.

He hoped the rain would stop. It would be harder to find the other werewolf in the rain. He knew it was his job to find him before Marco did, that this mission was the reason he'd felt the strong urge to return here, despite the risks. He had missed this city, but that wasn't the reason he'd come back. The place he missed had changed so much it was barely here any more.

In India, he'd been at peace, living among other free werewolves, patrolling the Sunderbans National Park wildlife refuge for poachers, and writing under a pseudonym. It was a strange, beautiful place where the animals drank saltwater and fish climbed trees. They did good work there, the werewolves, keeping out the poachers and the geologists surreptitiously exploring for oil, with the occasional road trip to pick off a brutal village warlord. To come back to America seemed folly on the surface, but even the man who ran their commune, the ironically named Wolfgang, had said it was time for Jim Valiente to return. So he'd come back on a false passport, drawing on his Swiss bank account and picking up writing assignments where he safely could. His agent knew him only as an American who had lived and worked in India until recently. He found Jim enough ghostwriting work to keep him busy and keep him from getting depressed. Depression was his biggest foe. Aside from the loneliness and his uncertainty about why he had felt compelled to come back, there was always a crash a few days after the full moon, which took over a week to recover from.

By the new moon, the depression had lifted, and by the full moon, he was feeling almost euphoric with anticipation of the hunt ahead of him.

I I

By Friday, the day of the full moon, Annie was so foul-tempered, relatively speaking, that even Bo was avoiding her. Every once in a while, he'd spread the slats of the venetian blinds in his office to peek out at her at her desk, but he waited until lunch before he dropped more work on her desk. He wasn't sure what to make of this Annie, who had never spoken back in all her years with him and who had always taken criticism with a deep blush, a bowed head, and a promise to do better. She had never before, to cite a recent example, rolled her eyes and said, "Oh for God's sake, Bo. What do you expect when you give me half an hour to process five pages of changes in your illegible handwriting?"

When she opened his office door on Friday before lunch and said, "I'm feeling strange. I'm leaving," he was relieved. He was glad to have an explanation for her appalling sass lately. She was sick, and that was affecting her behaviour. Some bed rest over the weekend and she'd be back to the efficient and unassuming assistant he had come to rely on more than he'd ever admit to her.

Even though Annie felt strange, she didn't feel bad. She was energetic and decided to walk home, all the way from midtown, ignoring the intermittent bursts of rain, which turned into a downpour just a block from her apartment.

When she got home and had towelled off, she ate like a horse – three Gardenburgers sautéed in walnut oil and a side of saffron and green-raisin rice – and she was still hungry. A pint of Cappuccino Almond Fudge Rice Dream Supreme left her wanting. She had another Gardenburger and a package of tofu breakfast sausages, and went to bed, feeling her joints tighten and her limbs cramp.

As she stared at the ceiling, watching the shadow of dusk spread over it like a water stain, her mind went absolutely blank. The rain had stopped. It was the blue hour, twilight, and the room took on a dim, silver-blue cast. A dreamy feeling came over her. As the room first darkened, and then brightened with the moon, she fell into a semi-conscious state, and was soon completely asleep.

Annie couldn't be sure how long she'd slept, but when she awoke, she felt a surge of pure energy. The cramps were gone. One of her hind legs jerked involuntarily before she adjusted and got control of her new body. Annie raised herself up to all fours, and didn't think there was anything strange about that. A low growl came from her throat. She didn't think there was anything strange about that, either. She turned to the window and saw the ghostly reflection of a wolf, but larger than a timber wolf. It stared back at her with big amber eyes.

She sprang off the bed. At the window, she inserted her nose in the crack between the frame and the sill, pushing the window open with her snout, then widening the gap with her head. It opened onto the fire escape. She stepped out.

A scent on the wind made her head north, but instead of going down the fire escape, she climbed up to the roof, and then began bounding her way across buildings, keeping to the shadows, leaping across a landscape of black tar-paper roofing, dimly glowing skylights, wooden water towers, and darkened roof gardens, everything still wet from the storm. Every now and then, she stopped to let out a howl, a low-pitched howl below the range of human hearing.

When she reached a street too wide to leap across, she jumped off the roof to the top of a truck, landing with a soft thud. Her body flattened against the truck roof. She lay low until she leapt into the back of another truck heading uptown.

12

Gunther Hamernich was walking home from his nightly twelve-step meeting when he saw a large black thing jump up the steps of the fire escape to the roof of the building, then disappear. His heart stopped for a moment, and he put his hand to his chest to thump it back into beating. Had he just seen that, or was he having a flashback to his days as a drunk living among the Mole People in the city's abandoned underground tunnels, before the police cleared them out and he was rescued by the pastor of the Jesus Saves Tabernacle? During those wretched days among the other drunks, druggies, and crazies, he had hallucinated many things, ghosts of people he'd wronged who came back at him accusingly, the disembodied voices of people he'd loved and lost, the contorted, mocking face of the devil himself. But he was always sure he had not imagined that beast he saw down there, five years ago. He had looked into its eyes and seen life there. He'd known in his heart it was real.

He looked up at the sky, where smoky grey puffs of cloud, the tail end of the day's storm, blew past a fully full moon, and he knew this one was real too.

13

When Armin Sunga was first contacted about buying the technology for the Porcupine missile, he was sure it was a sting operation. The only question in his mind was, who set it up? A hostile government, the FBI, the CIA, a rival dealer? When he met with the contact Albert Moud in a Russian steam bath to discuss it, Sunga said straight off, "If you are setting me up, Moody, be sure I will have you hunted down like a dog, tortured until you see the face of God, and then I will have your penis cut off and delivered to your wife in a red velvet box."

"My wife will thank you," Moud said, shaking the sweat off his face. "She's been trying to do the same thing for twenty years. I understand your concern. It's a rare opportunity, but it is completely legitimate. I've always delivered before, haven't I?"

Moud worked for the defence company that made the Porcupine and the two of them had done business before – a few thousand Tumbleweed rolling land mines here and there and some small arms, but nothing of this size and consequence.

"Even allies like Israel and the NATO countries can't buy Porcupines. It's a U.S. exclusive. Nobody has the Porcupine except –"

"Except the company that made it. My company," Moud said.

Sunga's first thought was that Moud had been caught in a crime and had turned state's evidence, promising to reel in some big fish. In the arms market, Sunga was currently the biggest fish of all, and also the slipperiest. Nobody in the world knew Armin Sunga as an arms dealer, not under that name. Armin Sunga was an importer of manufacturing equipment, a Malaysian national who lived with two wives, six sons, and several daughters in Lahore, Pakistan, and Geneva, Switzerland. In fact, he rarely saw his family. Most of the time, he was travelling the world, dealing arms under a series of aliases. To his customers he was known simply as Mr. Singer.

"You have the plans for the Porcupine," Sunga said.

"No, but I know who does. He wants to keep his name out of this for obvious reasons."

"What is he asking?"

"Fifty million for the blueprints and specs."

"Does that include the Ghost technology?"

"It does."

"Why is he selling?"

"He needs the money. Fast."

"I need to meet him," Sunga said.

"He doesn't need to sell to you. He can go to Ghazli Fez –"

"Ghazli Fez is nearly bankrupt. Haven't you heard? He sank most of his money into Afghan heroin just before the Taliban cleared out the poppies, then he sold his stake before the market recovered," Sunga said. "You want fifty million fast, I'm the only game in town. And for me to play, I need to meet the supplier."

"I'll do what I can do," Moud said.

The Porcupine was a beautiful missile, a reusable homing missile, studded with smaller missiles that were programmed to shoot off in all directions when the missile reached its target. Among its many beauties: it came in three sizes, its "quills" could be filled with anything from nerve gas to nuclear warheads, and, best of all, it was the first weapon to employ new Ghost technology to elude radar. After it had discharged its quills, raining missiles over a selected radius from one to fifty miles, it soared abruptly upward and then flew home again, landing gently in its specially padded berth in the Porcupine Homing Unit. It would be checked, any damage repaired, and rearmed with more quills. If it was shot down, it self-destructed so the technology could not fall into enemy hands, but not once in the years of testing had a Porcupine failed to make it home.

Everyone wanted the Porcupine, but Porkies were harder to obtain than bomb-grade uranium. A lot harder. Beijing wanted the Porkie, North Korea wanted it, and a central Asian dictator wanted it so badly he was willing to pay fifty million dollars for the blueprints and specs.

Two days after his initial meeting with Moud, Sunga was told to go to the Humming Tombstone in the Bramble, a heavily wooded section of the city's biggest park, to meet the supplier, who lived nearby. A man, dressed as a bird watcher, would approach him there. Sunga would recognize him when he said, "I'm a friend of Moody's."

When, at their first meeting, Sunga saw who the contact was, he very nearly swallowed his own tongue. It was Peter Gorgon, the president of the company who made the missile. Money was missing from his company's accounts, Gorgon explained, and he had to replace it before its absence was discovered. Gorgon was genuinely and desperately frightened and Sunga believed him. Though it was classified information, Sunga knew for a fact that Syn-DEF had lost about fifty million dollars on its armoured-hovercraft prototype because of a design flaw that made the engine seize up in rough seas, causing the craft to sink with all aboard. Gorgon needed the money, and it made sense he'd do this deal himself to limit the number of possible witnesses.

All the same, Sunga was careful to set up the deal so he had almost complete deniability and was reassured to see Gorgon had done the same. Neither man wanted to be caught, and their mutual suspicion bred a perverse kind of trust between them.

After Sunga transferred the first instalment from his secret offshore account to Gorgon's secret offshore account, he got word to meet Gorgon again in the Bramble to get instructions on where to find the plans. Once Sunga had the plans and his customer had determined they were authentic, the remaining millions would be transferred to Gorgon.

Annie kept to the wooded areas as she ran through the park, skirting the footpaths and clearings. She could see without being seen as she ran past a jogger, who caught her eye for a moment. But he did not smell of the moral rot she was seeking, and she passed him by, as she did two illicit lovers meeting under a rose bower, who smelled of deceit and dishonesty, of the most common kind. The thread of a more terrible scent was pulling her forward.

It was sulfurous and festering, this smell. When she found the source, she ran past it to find a good perch.

(6)

It had been a very good day even before Sunga got the call. He had made a big deal that afternoon with a representative of a fundamentalist rebel group fighting the government of a Central Asian country. A religious fanatic in one of the OPEC countries was funding them, and they had a lot of money to spend. The rebels wanted Tumbleweed rolling land mines, small arms, and surface-to-air Mistral missiles. With a little creative selling, Sunga unloaded some Gimlets, Gophers, and Russian Grumbles on them as well. It seemed only fair to sell to them, since he had already sold the government they were fighting some Russian anti-tank Songsters and Kazoos, and had promised them some new tank-killer Brimstones too, as soon as he got his hands on them.

But that was nothing compared to this deal. As Sunga walked into the Bramble, he stopped a moment to breathe in the green woodsy air, freshened by the day's storms. Life was good. He was king. There was nothing he could not buy or sell. There was not a man on this planet who scared him.

Perched on a dark brown rock, Annie watched the man get closer. Her legs tightened into spring posture. Her mouth opened, baring her large teeth.

Coming around a tumbling stream, Sunga heard a noise and stopped, putting his hand on the Luger in his pocket.

Annie leapt from the rock. Sunga's instincts were sharp enough for him to duck slightly, so her jaws got the corner of his face, gouging out his eyeball. But he never got a chance to pull the gun from his pocket. All he managed was a gurgled "oh" before Annie's jaws were on his throat, snapping his neck in two. After twisting the body back and forth several times, she flung it over a rock.

She stuck her snout into the humid air and picked up the thread of another compelling scent, sending her bounding towards the Humming Tombstone, an electrical control box covered in granite. She zeroed in on the source: a man on the ground. She approached cautiously and circled the body until she saw its dead black eyes, its throat ripped open.

Someone had already killed him.

14

Jim Valiente had taken Peter Gorgon out with one bite, and was heading away when he smelled the female.

Because Annie was upwind of the male she did not sense his presence quite as quickly. It wasn't until she saw him standing on a large black rock that his scent hit her. She came to a thudding (and not completely graceful, she'd later note) halt in a patch of mud. For a moment they stared into each other's amber eyes.

She was confused at first. She could smell his body, but not his soul. She was wary, but attracted.

He leapt off the rock and she backed away slightly. She paced in front of him in a half-circle, and he followed suit. She growled softly, and he growled back, more softly. Her eyes flashed, not in a threatened or threatening way, but in an invitation – come closer if you dare. Emboldened, he circled closer to her, slowly. Her pace slowed too. The attraction between them was powerful. She was ready for him. He mounted her.

⑥

Dr. Marco Potenza tracked Annie at first by following her periodic howls as she travelled to the park. Inside the park, the smell of blood helped him approximate her location. By the time he got to the tumbling stream and saw the dead Armin Sunga, Annie was gone. It took him a few minutes to pick up her scent again, along with the sharp scent of fresh blood elsewhere. When he found her, she was with another werewolf, rutting like the rough beasts they were and howling in that low-pitched way humans couldn't hear.

(At the south end of the park, carriage horses heard this howl, pulled their heads out of their feed pails and began to snort and rear up. One carriage horse, transporting an adulterous couple around the park, stood up on his hind legs and let out a bellow, tipping the couple and the driver into the road. Dogs within a three-mile radius began to bark and howl; the fur on cats' backs stood straight up and they hissed at unseen things; rats turned on each other in their crowded nests; sleeping birds suddenly woke and took flight.)

Marco crouched nearby, but not so close they would see him. There was something familiar about the male werewolf. He felt uncomfortable watching them pump and grind and howl, but he dared not look away and risk losing them, should they complete coitus and bolt. Quietly and cautiously, he drew closer to them. When he was within fifteen feet of them, the male pulled away from the female and began to growl. He turned and looked into Marco's eyes, then jumped towards him, pacing quickly in a semi-circle to confront Marco, the interloper.

Marco adopted a non-threatening posture, sitting on his haunches. Using his body language, pheromonal signals, and what the maverick British biologist Sir Rupert Sheldrake called

"morphic resonance" – wordless telepathy between members of .
the same species – he communicated this, loosely translated: "You
both must come with me. I can save you."

Jim thought back: "No."

Marco got back up to his feet and signalled to Annie. "She's
coming with me."

"Don't go with him," Jim thought towards Annie, and he
growled louder at Marco and bared his teeth.

Marco pounced. He and Jim rolled around, snarling and biting.
This close, Marco clearly recognized the male werewolf. Though
he tried hard to control his emotions, anger roared up inside him
and he fought harder.

"Run," Jim thought to Annie.

She ran. Jim held Marco back as long as he could to give Annie
some lead time, then broke away and ran in the opposite direction,
forcing Marco to hesitate and choose which wolf to follow.

Jim could have called it. Marco went after the female.

Just north of the park, Jim found the entrance to an abandoned
metro tunnel, the lock broken off and the wooden door splintered
by vandals. After descending, he followed the tracks east for a while,
then turned and crossed three sets of tracks to a second abandoned
tunnel, and made his way downtown. He came to the surface a
few blocks from home. The streets were empty so he travelled in
the shadows for a half-block before climbing up a fire escape to the
roof of a religious souvenir warehouse. From there, he went by
rooftop to his building.

Meanwhile, Annie galloped out of the woods without a
thought in her head, going on pure instinct and adrenaline. Once
outside the park, she took shelter on the roof of a deli until an
open-backed truck came along. The truck, full of dirt, took her
south to within blocks of where she lived. From there, she climbed
fire escapes and crossed roofs to get home, at one point startling a
pair of freshman film students who were out on the roof under the
full moon after smoking hash and eating some mushrooms, nursing

a couple of beers, talking about whatever came into their swim-
ming brains. They'd already discussed the movies they wanted to
make, meandered into girls they wanted to slam, which somehow
led into a discussion of space-based weapons and the tragic futility
of war.

"Why isn't it crazy to build nuclear bombs, but it is to make a
laughing-gas bomb? Why – did you see that?"

"What?"

"That big . . . I dunno . . . I think it was a bear."

"Where?"

"It ran right behind us and then jumped to that building." He
stood up to look for it. "It's gone now. It was, like, a bear crossed
with a dog."

"Dude, you are *fucked up*!"

On a neighbouring roof, Annie crouched behind a glowing
skylight and waited until the two boys went back inside. Then she
bounded to the roof of her building, trotted down the fire escape
and slipped through her open window. After shaking the dirt off
her pelt and stretching her legs, she curled up on her bed and slept.

(6)

By the time Marco got to the edge of the park, Annie was gone.
Her scent had grown faint, and since she had killed and mated, her
howl was now muted. He had to get home before sun-up. He had
to face facts: he'd lost her.

He was bleeding from the shoulder when he got back to the
roof of the Chelsea, where Carol was waiting. When she tried to
get close enough to tend his injury he snarled and licked his own
wound. It took him almost an hour to will himself back to human
form, which left him feeling cramped, with knots in his leg and
arm muscles. He was exhausted. Now that it was safe, Carol rushed
to him and began to massage his arms and legs.

"They got away," he managed to say in a weak, coarse whisper.

"They?"

"A male . . . a female."

"A female!" Carol said.

"The male is . . . Jim Valiente."

"*Jim Valiente?*"

"He's alive . . ."

"Oh my God," she said.

"The others . . ."

"Mike is still with them downstairs. They had a very rough night, lots of bruises, sprains and cuts from fighting the manacles. But they're all asleep now. Marco, we have to get more ketamine −"

"That's the least of our worries at the moment, Carol," he said. "I'm going to have to rest, but I'll need you to pull everything we have in the files on Jim Valiente − his patterns, his strengths, his vulnerabilities."

He was still panting. He stopped to catch his breath before he continued, "Leave it on my desk. I want you to wake me no later than noon, and give me a shot of Benzedrine if I need it. I can't waste any time."

"Jim Valiente, alive," she said. "That bastard! He let us all think he was dead, cry for him and everything."

"Tell Mike I'll need to speak to him tomorrow while the others are sleeping."

"Marco, I don't understand. Why would Jim come back here? Why wouldn't he go somewhere nobody knows him?"

"There's only one explanation. To destroy me," Marco said, and he said it so sadly, she stopped massaging his legs, took his face in her hands, and kissed him.

"I fucked up −"

"You did everything you could tonight," she said.

"No, I should have gone after Jim instead of the female. He's more dangerous. My judgment was bad. I was vain, overconfident −"

"You mustn't talk like that! You were alone. You didn't know there were two werewolves loose," Carol said. "Come on, let me help you up and into bed. A nice vitamin drip and some power sleep, and you'll be able to figure this out."

He was very weak, and she had to half drag him into bed. She put his favourite blue flannel pyjamas on him, fluffed his pillow, and then hooked him up to a vitamin-enriched IV solution before she went to pull the files on Jim Valiente. There wasn't much time. It was almost dawn and that meant the patients were transitional, morphing back into human form. Soon she'd have to go downstairs to help Mike hose them down and change the sheets. She'd make them all drink a glass of water with a dash of glycerin in it to soothe their throats after the tubes were taken out, and then she and Mike would hook them up to their breakfast IVs and let them sleep the day away.

She put everything she could find on Valiente on Marco's desk, stopping to take down the portrait of Marco's father and put it behind the file cabinet. When he got up, he wouldn't need the old man looking over his shoulder. When he'd been beating himself up over letting the two werewolves get away, it was the old man's voice Carol heard coming out of Marco's mouth. Luigi. The Count. He was bound to be upset when he heard about this.

Even when Luigi wasn't upset, Carol had to hold the phone away from her ear whenever he called, otherwise his booming voice made her fillings vibrate and gave her a splitting headache. Luigi didn't like her and hadn't approved of Marco marrying a woman who was not only normal, and half-Polish, and uneducated beyond high school, but unable to have children. She just wasn't the cloth for a future countess. He saw Marco's choice of Carol as yet another sign of weakness in his first-born son.

Carol didn't like Luigi and called him "Lwee-Gee" in a cartoon voice behind his back, but she always tried to be courteous to his face so as not to make more trouble for Marco. She didn't care if Luigi liked her. It was the way he treated Marco that made her mad. All the academic honours Marco had achieved, all the werewolves he had rescued and restored to normal life, and all Luigi could talk about were the failures, the ones who got away. Luigi had never let any get away, or so he claimed, all too often. Nor had his other son, Enzio, in Los Angeles, or so Enzio claimed.

Carol thought that Enzio was an ass too, and his wife Audrey was one of those slithery bitches who could systematically cut her down in a sweet voice with false compliments that were really insults. Audrey did it with a tone, a look, a carefully chosen word that pushed a button, a way of phrasing things. Carol didn't know how to respond, other than spitting in Audrey's coffee in the kitchen. Audrey clearly resented that Marco was in line to be the next count and Carol the next countess, when she and Enzio were better suited. The titles were meaningless in America, as far as Carol was concerned. Enzio and Audrey were so arrogant, yet it was them that Luigi favoured, not Marco and his frugal, hard-working wife.

God spare her from another Thanksgiving in Washington with that gang, the Great Potenzas.

As an afterthought, she unplugged the phone so Luigi couldn't call. Then she went downstairs with bandages, antiseptic, and glycerin water.

15

As inveterate bird watchers, Ila Dalcourt and her friend Ellen Moushey found the sightings were richest at dawn, when the birds were starting to sing. Since their first sighting, a magnolia warbler, as children in 1946, they had spotted over a hundred of the 230 species of birds that had been recorded in the park.

For safety reasons, they always went to the park together. Ila carried the mace and the binoculars, Ellen the cell phone and the camera. Aside from a harrowing mugging in 1985, they'd been very lucky, and very conscientious about preserving that luck by taking

all possible precautions. The most frightening thing they'd encoun-
tered since had been the occasional pair of lovers' bare bottoms.

Spring and fall migrations were best for bird spotting. Summer
was less hectic yet full of surprises, like green herons, Acadian
flycatchers, and once an albino red-tailed hawk. Someone in their
Usenet newsgroup had claimed to have seen several ruby-crowned
kinglets the previous week, and Ila and Ellen had come out every
morning hoping to catch a glimpse themselves. As is so often the
case, while looking for one thing, they often stumbled upon other
things, most of them happy surprises, such as a nest of mute swans
and a roof-nesting oystercatcher.

As they were tramping towards the place of the alleged kinglet
sighting, they noticed two large birds circling above, just ahead of
them. Ila put the binoculars up to her eyes.

"American black vultures," she said. "Odd."

"What are they circling?" Ellen asked just as the birds flew
down to the ground. By the time Ila and Ellen caught up with
them, they were already making a meal of Peter Gorgon, who
looked to the women like one of their own, a bird watcher. His
binoculars were hung around his neck and he had a small book
tucked into a jacket pocket, *Guide to Night Birds of the Northeast*.
Ila called the police. An hour later, a park worker stumbled upon
the body of Armin Sunga.

⑥

Both Sam's phones started ringing at the same time. On the night-
stand, the home phone was ringing. In the pocket of his jacket,
hung on the door, his cell phone was tweetering. Sam opened his
eyes and looked at the clock radio. 6:14 A.M.

After turning down the radio, he answered the phone on the
bed stand. "Hold on," he said, then lifted himself slowly out of bed
and went for the phone in the jacket.

"Hold on," he said, keeping the cell phone to one ear and
putting his home phone receiver to the other.

"This is Sam. Who's this?"

"It's Ivan," Sam heard in both ears. "Hang up one of your phones."

"Okay. What's up?"

"Two more mad dog murders last night in the park, in the Bramble, one near the Tumbling Stream and one near the Humming Tombstone. Come by Griffin's tonight to pay us."

"Where's the Humming Tombstone?" Sam asked. But Ivan just hung up.

Sam called Cooper, who conferenced him with Jennifer Ray.

"You two head over there. I'll send a live truck to meet you," Cooper said.

"Over where?" Sam said. "Where is the park?"

"Sam, grab a cab, stop by J.R.'s to pick her up. She'll know how to get there," Cooper said.

After Sam hung up, Cooper kept Jennifer on the line.

"Got the *Eye* there? Read the 'Dear Tweets' column, second item in," he said.

Which two local TV news "aces" were seen canoodling at Cornichon the other night? It's not the first time for this carelessly public duo, Tweets. Things could get sticky for the pretty pair. He and she work at the same station and three is not a lucky number for love. Kids, your secret's safe with us . . . and our hairdresser . . . and our manicurist . . . and the boys at our gym . . . and the folks in our car on the metro this morning. . . ."

"Aces: Cand*ace* Quall and Wall*ace* Waring. Three: Syn-TV is channel three, or it could mean three as in odd man out – Sam. You going to tell him?" J.R. asked.

"Hell no. It's just gossip. Let the guy enjoy his scoops before his heart is ripped out through his eyes."

"You're getting soft, Coop," J.R. said.

In the cab, Sam applied his on-air makeup while the cabbie

watched in the rear-view mirror. Sam felt compelled to explain he wore makeup because he was on television, but it wasn't necessary to explain. The cabbie wasn't looking at him funny because he was a big, burly man applying foundation and mascara, but because he recognized him.

"I seen you on TV, talking about the Mad Dog Murder."

"Yeah, that's me."

"Hey, a famous guy, in my cab."

"Yeah."

"Can I get your autograph for my wife?"

"Yeah, sure," Sam said. It was the first time he'd been asked for an autograph since he'd left Atlanta.

"You're married to Candace Quall, at Syn-TV, aren't you?"

"Yeah," Sam said.

"That's channel three, isn't it?"

"Yeah."

"You read the *Downtown Eye*?"

"I haven't had time to read any of the papers yet today," Sam said.

The driver gave him a pitying look, which puzzled Sam, who was more accustomed to men looking at him with envy when they found out he was married to Candace, a tall cool blonde who looked a bit like Grace Kelly or Gwyneth Paltrow.

He wondered how Candace was doing now. Since she'd walked out, she wouldn't take his calls, so he just left messages for her. She "needed some space to think," she'd said after she found out about his affair. That stupid, stupid affair. But even though Candace had stomped out, he knew in his heart she'd be back. She needed him.

"Mr. Deverell," the cabbie said.

"Yes?"

"What was the building number?"

"Thirty-seven."

Jennifer Ray was outside waiting. She jumped in the cab and told the driver where to take them. Without first saying hello, she informed Sam what they were going to do for the live shot.

When they got out of the cab, she walked ahead of him, quickly, and he followed.

"Over here," Jennifer Ray said, waving Sam into the woods. The bodies were gone now, but the cops were there, combing the area for evidence. Quite a large area was cordoned off with yellow crime-scene tape strung between trees. The CCN live tech was already there.

"Those women over there found one of the bodies," he said. "No ID on the victims but one of them was a bird watcher, like the women who found him."

"Great," Jennifer Ray said. "I'll go get SOTs while you set up. Sam, you just standby."

Sam stood by. When Jennifer Ray came back she handed the tech the tape to feed to HQ for cutting while she wrote something for Sam to intro and outro the tape. Ten minutes later, Sam was all wired up, and Jennifer Ray was giving him the countdown.

He said exactly what she told him to say, tossing to taped sound bites from the bird watchers, who were so agitated by their discovery they seemed like fluttery birds themselves. When he gave his sign off, "Sam Deverell, CCN, reporting to you live from the crime scene." and got the all-clear on his earpiece, Jennifer Ray smiled at him. It was the first time she'd ever smiled at him.

For the next two hours they did live shots, with Jennifer Ray adding a bit more information every update. After that, they went back to the newsroom to package a report to run for the next few hours, something that could be updated if necessary from the anchor desk if new information became available.

"Good job, kids," Cooper said to them afterwards. "But Sam, you've got to get to know this city better. Everyone knows the park."

"Yeah, I heard of it. I just didn't know where it was," Sam said.

"Get yourself a detailed map of the city and study it hard. There *will* be a quiz."

Cooper had a sarcastic tone in his voice – understandably. It appalled him that a reporter could be so woefully ignorant of the city.

But Sam didn't react to the sarcasm. Earnestly, he said, "Detailed map, study, quiz. Got it, boss."

The newsroom theory was that Sam's brain hadn't yet evolved to the stage where it was capable of recognizing sarcasm, but Cooper saw this lack of defensiveness as an endearing quality that had more to do with a genuine humility than utter stupidity. Sam wasn't stupid. He wasn't overly smart, but he wasn't the idiot that majority opinion held him to be, and he didn't pretend to be smarter than he was rather than suffer the horror of admitting he didn't know everything. Too many of his staff and his friends did that. Sam was actually a pretty nice guy, and he took orders like a trouper. It was refreshing in a newsroom where Cooper was surrounded by witty, neurotic, defensive *McSweeney's*-reading kid geniuses who presented a constant challenge to his own insecurities.

On the way out, Jennifer Ray took Sam by the arm and said, "Come on. We're going shopping. We need to get you a hat, and a coat, and a haircut."

She had been skeptical about Sam too, but she was warming to him. When she saw that piece in the "Dear Tweets" column about his wife, Candace, her heart just bled for him. Fortunately, he didn't seem to know about the item. Unfortunately, everyone else seemed to. Even the clerk in the clothing store brought it up, obliquely, with sympathetic but vague comments about "lots of fish in the sea," and didn't Sam look handsome in the slate-grey Burberry – too bad the outfit didn't come with a big stick, for fighting off the women!

"Looking good is the best revenge," the clerk assured Sam. Sam had no idea what the clerk was on about and gave Jennifer Ray a puzzled glance. She just shrugged.

Poor Sam. That was the price of fame in the big city. The more known you were, the more people were poking into your affairs and blabbing about them. The higher up you got, the more there were grasping little hands tugging at your trouser legs to bring you down. Often, those grasping little hands belonged to people who were kissing your ass at the same time. The shitty thing was, this piece of scandal would probably make him more famous than his Mad Dog story.

Jennifer Ray's cell phone rang and she went into a fitting room to take the call, leaving Sam with the obsequious clerk. When she came out, she said, "The heat's on at City Hall. The Mayor cancelled his daily briefing and has just issued a written statement which says nothing much but gives a tip-line phone number. Cooper wants you to do a live update from City Hall. Come on."

16

When Gunther Hamernich saw the news he knew for certain he had seen what he had seen the night before on the fire escape. He picked up the phone and called the police tip line.

"I know who killed those people, the ones with their throats ripped out," he said.

"Who?" asked the cop on the other end.

"A werewolf."

"A werewolf?"

"Yes. I saw it last night, leaping, almost flying, up the fire escape –"

"Flying? Was it alone?"

"Yes."

"Are you sure it wasn't a dog?"

"It was too big to be a dog. Twice as big as a big dog maybe. It was too big to be an ordinary wolf. And you know, there was a full moon last night?"

"Right. Call this number, 777-3456. That's our Special Werewolf Squad," the cop said.

When he hung up, the cop next to him said, "777-3456?"

"Moviephone," said the first cop.

17

This time, Annie's wolf dream was not only very vivid, it took place all over the city. She could remember every bit of it, seeing her reflection as a wolf in the glass of her window, running over rooftops and leaping onto the backs of trucks and buses, pressing her body tight to the warm metal. She had killed a man, had sex with another wolf, was chased by yet another one, came home, became human again and then dreamed herself sleeping.

That was just the beginning of strange. When she woke up, she felt like she really *had* had sex. She felt that good old post-sex throb between her legs. Her arms and legs – in fact, every part of her – was stiff and sore. She was naked, disoriented, and had blood on her chest. The window was open, though she was sure she had only opened it a crack the evening before. There was dirt on the bed, and coarse brown-blond hair.

I'm still dreaming, she thought. It's one of those dreams where you dream you wake up, but you're really still asleep. She had those dreams a lot too, dreams where she was in great danger – or great embarrassment – from which there seemed no escape, until she thought in her dream, "A-ha, if I wake up, I can escape the man with the gun, the woman with the needle full of poison, Liz, Henry, and the famous people who are laughing at me because I forgot to put clothes on before I came to the party." Then she'd "wake up," only to find herself in a different dream, or a worse nightmare.

That's what happened here. I've awakened into a worse nightmare, she thought.

She shook her head to try to wake herself up.

Before she could tell if this worked, the nausea started. She ran to the bathroom, where she puked up the same rusty, red-coloured water she'd barfed the month before. The second wave felt more solid. As she looked into the sink, she saw a round white thing with a gelatinous sheen, finely veined with blue-red lines, as it swirled round and then vanished down the drain. It looked like a big marble on a string.

She calmed herself down. It was delirium associated with the flu, or whatever it was she had. She'd had it the month before too, and she'd survived it fine. It was probably some kind of menstrual thing. If she wasn't better by Monday, she'd call in sick to work, and she'd make an appointment for a checkup when her doctor came back from her vacation. Some television and some sleep, and she'd be fine.

Whatever it was she had, it exhausted her, and she slid rapidly into sleep when she got back into bed. When she woke next, she flipped the TV on. It was near the end of the five o'clock news.

"Two more people have been killed in killer dog attacks, bringing the number of victims to three in the last month. The bodies were found early this morning by bird watchers and park workers," said the anchorwoman, Candace Quall. "We'll have a full report at six, coming up on Action News, right after this break."

When Action News said that one victim, whose body was found by the Tumbling Stream in the Bramble, had had his eye gouged out before he was killed, Annie shivered. The Tumbling Stream, where the first body was found, looked like it came straight from her dream, and when the video shifted to the Humming Tombstone, it looked like the spot where she'd had sex with the other werewolf.

I'm cracking up, she thought, just like a former boss of hers, a computer programmer at WOW, the World on the Web network, who flipped one day and suddenly started speaking in binary code. Annie hadn't understood him, but apparently he'd been saying, "Help me."

At the age of twenty-nine, after a lifetime of prudent behaviour, Christmas club accounts, good citizen certificates, and trying like hell to be a ray of sunshine in the world, she had suddenly gone completely stark-raving crazy. Oh God, Annie thought. It's what her former shrink had predicted. "If you don't work out this hostility, Annie," she had said, "you're going to act it out."

That was an understatement. It was one thing to inexplicably start wise-assing her boss and barking at the guy at the newsstand, but it was another for a grown woman to think she was a wolf and tear peoples' throats out. Had she killed men, made their wives widows and ripped fathers from their children forever? My God, what had those poor men thought when they saw a crazy young woman coming at them, lunging for their throats, Annie wondered. They must have been so surprised they didn't fight back, at least not in time to save their jugular veins. That poor man, the bird watcher, probably went out to look for some owls or something, only to be attacked by a psycho woman with a wolf delusion.

If she had to go mad, why this? Why couldn't she fall in love with a dead cowboy singer like Mrs. Mackie, or believe she was a great actress like a woman in her neighbourhood who thought Annie was trying to steal her "ideas," which was annoying but harmless? She would have rather had a vision of the Virgin Mary, or Elvis, something inspirational.

She had heard of things like this, people who believed they were animals, imagining themselves to be werewolves, vampires and more mundane creatures like monkeys, dogs and chickens – nice, quiet people who snapped one day, like her former boss at WOW (now Syn-WOW), who had been shipped off to a pastoral care facility, treated, then resettled into a lower-pressure job designing children's educational software. The authorities wouldn't be so indulgent with her. She would be shipped off for a long time. Her face and name would be in the papers. If she was ever free again, who would hire her, a man-killer? Children would run from her. Forget about ever having a boyfriend again.

No, no, there has to be another explanation, she thought. But no, no, there wasn't. The coarse hair on the bed and the throb between her legs, the blood on her face and chest said so. And either she'd been eating marbles, which was crazy enough, or she had barfed up an eyeball.

There was only one thing to do. Suicide. Luckily for her, she had no family to miss her. Mrs. Mackie didn't even know who she was. Liz and Henry would get over it, after they'd talked to the local news media about the tragic young woman who had thrown herself off a bridge. Or had taken poison, perhaps. That might be easier, something that killed almost instantly and painlessly, so she only had to take it and lie down in her bed.

Mixed with the dread, shame, guilt, and terror was that terrible feeling that comes when one wakes up one day and doesn't recognize oneself any more. Something dark and dangerous had pushed itself to the surface, in some form or other. All these years, she had thought of herself as a Good Person, doing good deeds for people, turning the other cheek, understanding and tolerating the nasty habits and quirks of others, putting others first most of the time, volunteering for bingo night and special Sundays at Mrs. Mackie's nursing home.

But no, she was evil, a killer, a widow-maker.

The only reassuring thing she could think of was that, provided she had not dreamt the events of the night before, there might be more like her – the one she'd made love with, and the third one who had attacked them. Until she found the others, she wouldn't kill herself. That would give her time to select the proper method and just the right wording for the suicide note.

For tonight, she would lock herself in as securely as she could, in case it happened again. If she was resourceful, she could manage this temporarily and protect the outside world from her, Annie Engel, former altar girl, meritorious Girl Scout, winner of her high school typing competition two years in a row, small investor.

In her cupboards she found two thick rolls of duct tape, bought on sale when a nearby hardware store was going out of business. First, she covered the bed thoroughly with Saran Wrap, then she filled a bowl with water and placed it near her pillow. She pushed a chest of drawers in front of the window next to the fire escape. She left the television on to keep her company and put on her most comfortable flannel pyjamas, the white ones with tiny pink and green flowers.

After she'd taped her feet securely to the bedposts, she fastened her left hand, leaving the other free to untie herself later, when she was out of danger. Secure in her homemade restraints, she fell back to sleep.

Early in the evening, Annie was awakened by the phone. She listened as her answering machine picked up. It was Liz, conferenced with Henry, calling to make sure Annie showed up for the book party Liz was handling for the author of an aphrodisiac cookbook.

"Sunday, seven P.M. Don't forget, Annie. I need you to help me out with the food and bus service. No celebs, just writers you've never heard of," Liz said to Annie's machine.

"You wouldn't believe the day I had," Liz went on. "Beth caught me trying to call Susan Sarandon about the fundraiser I want to do. She called me into her office, accused me of Rolodex abuse."

"Is there a newsgroup for that?" Henry asked. "Alt dot sex dot rolodex-abuse?"

"It doesn't stop there. Apparently, I mixed up the food for the morning and afternoon tapings, so the Orthodox Jews with drug problems got ham and cheese and shrimp salad and the gay cops got the kosher platter. I sent a car to Garden Plaza instead of the Plaza. She told me I have to cut back my party business or I'll be fired. I'm on warning."

"Honey, you had a bad day," Henry said. "But at least you didn't have to loofah the Czarina's feet and then massage mink oil into them."

Oh, you've got problems, Annie thought. She only now realized how whiny and selfish Liz and Henry were. She tried to reach over her body with her free hand to turn off the machine, but her arm didn't extend that far.

"Mink oil, my God, how decadent," Liz said.

"It's supposed to be good for softening old cow hide but this old cow is beyond such feeble measures. She's on a beauty tear right now because she's husband-hunting again. Shit, what time is it?"

"Almost seven."

"I have to prepare the Czarina's table for dinner at eight. Oh, Annie, hope you feel better."

"'Bye, Annie."

They both hung up.

Water was running somewhere, loudly. Annie wished it would stop. It made her want to pee, and even though she'd covered the bed with Saran Wrap she didn't want to let her bladder loose if she could help it. Her legs were spread-eagled and cuffed to the bedposts, so she wasn't able to squeeze her thighs together.

The water was gushing now. It sounded like it was the apartment below.

Think about something dry, she told herself.

Clean sheets, old toast, sand . . .

When the urge had almost passed, a sudden pounding at her door almost made her pee her pants.

"Annie! Annie! Are you in there?" A man's voice called. It was Mr. Hamernich.

He pounded again, and called her name. A key turned in the lock.

"You check the kitchen, I'll check the bathroom," he said to someone.

It was possible to get to the bathroom without going through the bedroom, and Annie prayed Mr. Hamernich would pass her by. On the upside, her muscles were tensed so tight now that she couldn't pee if she wanted to.

"Looks like something blocked the line," Mr. Hamernich called to his unidentified assistant. "The pressure of backed-up water musta caused a pipe to burst."

"I'll be right there," the assistant said. His boots went thumping down the hallway past the bedroom door.

"The water's leaking over his bedroom," the assistant said. "Where is that in relation to this place?"

"Same layout as this apartment," Mr. Hamernich said. "I'll check the bedroom."

His footsteps came to the door and it opened.

"Omigod, what happened to you?" Mr. Hamernich asked.

The other guy came to the bedroom door. It was a plumber.

"Who did this to you, you poor lamb?" Hamernich said. To the plumber, he said, "Call the police."

"No!" Annie said.

"Why not?"

"It's not what you think, it's . . . a game."

"A game?" He looked puzzled, then realization dawned. A sex game.

Almost the last thing Annie wanted this guy to think was that she was having a kinky sex relationship, but what else was she going to tell him?

"My boyfriend is going to be back soon. He just went out to get . . . some videos," Annie said.

Hamernich looked very disturbed.

The plumber said, "We have to remove a board by the bed and put a clamp on the leak. It won't take long."

While they worked, Annie closed her eyes and tried not to die of embarrassment. What was Mr. Hamernich thinking? That nice girl in 3-C who is never late with her rent, always holds the door for people with packages and sends a card to everyone in the building at Easter or Passover or – in the case of Dr. Mohammed Siddique in 5-J – Eid. That nice girl, she's into sexual bondage.

"Annie, listen to me," Mr. Hamernich said. "This boyfriend, he's no good. He's leading you astray."

"Mr. Hamernich –"

"Do not do this. Your soul is at stake. I have seen where immorality leads, the depths of misery. Lust, self-pride, alcohol, it took me to the bowels of the earth –"

"Yes, yes, you're right," Annie said, sure she was blushing all over now. She'd say anything to shut him up at this point. She wished she was merely a pervert into bondage. That was so much better than the truth. Nothing poor old Mr. Hamernich could say now would save her mortal soul.

"Whatever was blocking it is gone," the plumber said. "To clog this pipe, it must have been about the size of a quarter, or a big marble."

"It's okay now?" Hamernich said.

"Yeah, that clamp'll hold it." He replaced the board and packed up his tools, leaving without looking at Annie.

Hamernich didn't look at her either.

Night was just falling, and she was grateful for one thing, that he hadn't been here to see her turn into a man-killer. She did experience some rapid hair growth, itching, and cramping of muscles that night, but that was it. She didn't break out of her bonds and go out to cause even more mayhem.

The window was still closed the next morning and she was still duct-taped. According to the news, no men had had their throats ripped out the night before. Physically, she felt better, still very sensitive, but not as sensitive as she had been before the full moon, and the queasiness had passed. She felt well enough to get out of bed and do some research on the Internet, where she learned there was a condition called Lycanthropic Disorder, which causes its afflicted to believe they are werewolves. It is sometimes accompanied by excessive hair growth caused by extra testosterone. It didn't change her suicide plan, but it made her feel . . . not quite normal, but not as abnormal as she had originally thought. It was something along the lines of those men with two Y chromosomes who reportedly went extra crazy during full moons.

She took the next few days off work and spent them instead in a fog of organic wine, self-loathing, and soap operas. When she ran out of wine, she lay there in pure terror. The fat nun on one shoulder kept intoning about widows, orphans, and eternal damnation, while the wolf on the other side howled in a way that made her want to tear off her clothes and bolt out of the room. The further she got from the full moon the louder the fat nun got and the more distant the wolf sounded.

After three days, she pulled herself together enough to shower, shave, and go out to look after a few grown-up human things, like getting more wine. Before she left, she hesitated, her hand hovering above the doorknob for several heart-stopping minutes. Even if Mr. Hamernich hadn't seen her in that embarrassing position, she didn't want him or anyone else to see her now.

Finally, she turned the knob, promising herself it would be a quick trip. She only had to go to two places, the ATM and the health food store.

6

Coming out of Mother Earth's Bounty with a half-dozen bottles of Bergerac and a bag of groceries, she saw Razz, the blind guy who had stalked her a few months earlier. He had befriended her just after she'd been dumped by her ex, telling her on a street corner she smelled nice. She'd been such a soft touch – giving him money, running to his aid at all hours when he called and said he'd fallen, smelled gas, or heard an intruder. He always seemed okay when she got there, but she'd stay a while to make sure, maybe make him a bite to eat and listen to his hard-luck stories. He always had something he wanted her to buy, a toaster, a fur coat, a gold chain, ten pairs of white tube socks for men. Got a deal on it, he said, and hoped to resell it to get money for food. Sometimes, she bought something just to be nice.

One day he told her what he really needed was a girlfriend. When she told him she was flattered but not interested, having just broken up with the man she thought she was going to marry, he "fell" against her, grabbing her breasts, his mouth landing right on hers. She had to hit him with his own cane to get away. She would have called the police about him then, but she couldn't prove anything. And after all, he couldn't see, what threat was he to anyone? She would feel terrible if she put some blind guy in jail because of a misunderstanding.

After that, she wouldn't take his calls, so he stalked her, lurking outside her building at odd hours and eventually chasing her down the street.

He was on the top ten list of the last people she wanted to see right now. While she desperately tried to flag down a cab, he approached, his cane striking a menacing metre. By the time a cab came and she got her stuff into the car, he was beside her. She could smell him, the combined smell of sour cabbage and fermented sink clog. That was all she needed now, that psycho coming back into her life.

My God, she thought, look who I'm calling psycho. This man, for all his faults, was a better human being than she was. She climbed into the cab, and he just kept tapping his way along the sidewalk.

Before she got back to drinking herself into a stupor, she took time to tidy her apartment, which was a mess. If she was going to hell in a handbasket, she planned to go well-groomed and with a neat apartment. She made herself a decent meal, setting the table for one, with a placemat, silverware, and her good china because it made her feel normal. She poured a glass of wine, guzzled it, and poured another.

She glanced through the newspapers while she ate, reading up on her crimes. The police were withholding identification of the two new victims and other information, in order to "protect the investigation." According to the papers, though, the "crazy dog" and "wild coyote" theories had been discredited. There was a serial killer at work here, one who had killed before, years earlier, employing a killer dog as his weapon.

His weapon.

Right there she felt a small glimmer of . . . something. Misguided pride, perhaps. It occurred to Annie that nobody would ever suspect her. This made her feel good, then the fat nun on her shoulder roared back to life and she felt guilty about feeling good about killing people, and turned to the *Downtown Eye*, the back page personals, looking for the St. Jude novena.

She and Liz and Henry used to read the personals at lunch every day. Henry liked the ads for human guinea pigs, placed by hospitals doing studies in everything from eczema to heroin addiction to PMS. Liz liked the ads placed by disconnected people trying to contact real or imaginary lovers in economical shorthand – "O train 5/11 6pm. U: gr dress, rd hr. Me: Free Mumia T, jns, smile. U smiled back. I should've spoken. 2nd chance? shyguyonatrain@wow.com."

Annie liked the messages to St. Jude, the patron saint of hopeless cases, the novenas printed with a promise that if you recited them nine times a day for nine days, your prayers would be answered. When they were, you were expected to thank St. Jude with an ad. Every week, two or three people did. It always made her feel better to know some lost causes had been won somewhere, by someone.

Whose cause was more lost than hers? Running her finger down the page, she searched for the novena. Halfway down, she was stopped by this:

"Miss Wolf. I was moonstruck in the park. Must see you again. You're not alone. I can help."

A cell phone number was listed.

18

When Jim saw the ad, he was sitting in the Pink Pony. Meredith, the waitress whose name he could never remember, was holding his double cap hostage on a tray carefully balanced above her right shoulder while she chattered about her one-woman show on Edie Sedgwick and all the great sixties clothes she'd collected to wear in it.

He hoped the female werewolf hadn't seen the ad, and if she had, that she realized he hadn't placed it. He could place one too, but he couldn't give any contact info because Marco would use it to track him down. Still, it might be worth a shot to do it, just to warn the female.

"Gotta have my coffee and run," he said to the waitress, interrupting her in the middle of a description of a white micro-mini with clear vinyl across the midriff.

The *Downtown Eye* was just a few blocks away. He filled out a form for the back page personals, and paid cash. His ad said, "Miss Wolf, do not go with Moonstruck. He is not who you think he is. Wait. We'll find each other again."

From there he headed uptown to the Chelsea. He didn't know what else to do. If she saw Marco's ad before his ran the next day, Marco would lure her here, to the Chelsea. Maybe Jim would recognize her in human form and be able to get to her before Marco.

He took up a spot leaning on a building across the street from the hotel, his sunglasses on. Like a spy in a James Bond movie, he hid his face behind a copy of the *Downtown Eye* and watched the canopied doorway of the hotel. Lots of young women came and went in the next few hours, but none of them were her. He still had enough of the wolf in him to smell their souls. Werewolves couldn't smell the souls of other werewolves.

He figured he'd know the female werewolf just by sight, that he'd feel that same mule kick to the solar plexus he'd felt when he'd looked into her eyes in the park. He knew nothing about her, and his shallow male side worried about whether he'd like her as a human. What if she was a bitchy twenty-something publicist who wore designer minidresses and walked around all day in Jimmy

Choo shoes, a cell phone glued to her ear? What if she was a married grandmother of six?

And what if she was absolutely lovely, and too good for him?

But in the grand scheme of things, none of that mattered. The priority was getting her away from Marco.

He watched until his legs got tired from standing, then he gave up. The girl hadn't seen Marco's ad. He stepped out into the street to get a taxi and before he raised his arm to hail a cab, one stopped right by him. He held the door for the departing passenger, a petite brunette.

"Thank you so much," she said, before rushing across the street. On the other side she abruptly stopped, and looked back at him, then turned and went into the Chelsea.

Even across two lanes of traffic, he knew it was her. She was a werewolf all right. He could not smell her soul, as he could a human soul. By the time he got across the street and into the lobby, she was gone. Marco would keep her there all night, going by his previous M.O. Nevertheless, Jim waited until it was dark, then he went home.

19

It had taken Annie five tries to complete the call, because she kept hanging up to rethink what she was going to say. Finally, she got her courage up enough to say, "Are you him? The one from the park the night of the full moon," in a timid whisper.

"Are you A. Wolf, from the park?" he asked.

"Yes, I guess I am," she said.

Marco had already had a number of calls from men and women surnamed Wolf, who had seen the ad and imagined it was for them from some remote beautiful person they were in love with.

"Are you A. —" he paused. "— Wolf, from the Humming Tombstone in the Bramble?"

"Yes," she said.

"Then I'm waiting for you," the man on the other end said. "Come to the Chelsea. I'll meet you by the phone booths off the lobby."

Then he hung up.

His voice hadn't been what she expected. She wasn't sure what to expect. For all she knew, he was gas-guzzling right-winger, or one of those grown men who stripped to the waist, painted his body in team colours, went to football games and waved a giant foam-rubber finger that said, "We're Number One." He could be married.

Immediately, she hopped into a cab and went to the Chelsea, straight to the alcove off the lobby where the telephone booths and mailbox were. A tall, elegant-looking man was standing there, looking up at a papier mâché sculpture.

"Hello," he said. He smiled. "Are you Miss Wolf?"

"Are you Mr. Wolf?" she asked.

"In a manner of speaking. You can call me Dr. Marco Potenza. I put the ad in the *Eye* because I can help you. I help many like you."

It dawned on her now that this wasn't the wolfman she'd had sex with.

"You were in the park that night?" she asked.

"Yes."

"You were the one watching?"

"Yes. I tracked you that night because I want to help you."

"What about the other wolf? The one I . . ."

"We're hoping to bring him in too. Why don't we go upstairs? My wife is waiting. She'll make you some tea. And then, I'll show you the Centre."

"The Centre?"

"Where we help people like you. You'll see," he said, leading her to the elevator.

His soothing manner, the promise of help and the mention of the kindly wife made her trust him and she followed. They got off on the tenth floor and went up some stairs to the roof. At this point, she worried. What if he was a rapist or something? Or a mad scientist who wanted to clone her? But his smiling wife was waiting at the top of the stairs, and Annie relaxed.

Carol threw her arms around Annie. "Welcome," she said. "You're our first girl in, gosh, over five years. What's your name, hon?"

"Annie."

"Annie, I'm Carol Dickinson Potenza." She threw her arms around Annie and hugged her tight again. "Can I get you some tea? We have decaf Darjeeling, Moroccan mint, Japanese twig . . ."

"Mint, thanks," Annie said.

"Come on in. Don't stand out there attracting flies," Carol said. She waved Annie into the penthouse, and Marco followed, guiding Annie with one hand under her right elbow, very gently.

"Let's go into my office," Marco said to Annie, steering her away from Carol, who continued into the kitchen.

The office was lined with floor-to-ceiling bookshelves. There was a desk, an armchair, and a chaise longue. On the door were diplomas in German and Latin from Harvard Medical School and universities in Vienna and Berlin.

"Have a seat," Marco said, gesturing to the chaise longue. "Relax." Tentatively, she sat on the chaise longue.

"Take your shoes off and stretch out," he said. "You have a lot of questions, I know. Let me make it simple for you. I'll give you all the answers. If I miss something, you can ask me questions when I finish."

Annie started to say okay, but he didn't wait.

"This is a Metamorphic Disorder Centre, which I run. You'll see by my diplomas on the wall, I am a board-certified psychiatrist as well as a general practitioner. This is obviously quite a shock for you. Let me reassure you first of all that what you are experiencing is a completely natural thing. It's not the 'supernatural,' it's not insanity. You suffer from a rare genetic aberration we call Lycanthropic Metamorphic Disorder, LMD, and you are not alone. Just here in this city, there are nearly thirty LMD patients. You are the

only female at the moment, as full female metamorphosis is increasingly rare. As a result, the breed is dying out. There is no cure, but
some of our patients learn to suppress their transformation."

"Excuse me. Full metamorphosis?"

"At the full moon, when you transform into a wolf –"

"So it isn't just that I get extra hairy and think I'm a wolf –"

"No. That would be Lycanthropic Disorder. You have Lycanthropic Metamorphic Disorder. You actually do become a wolf.
The good news is, there is treatment. That's what we're here for."

There was a knock. The door opened and Carol came in with
two pots of tea, Japanese twig for Dr. Marco and Moroccan mint
for Annie.

"Thank you," Annie said.

"Oh, my pleasure! I'm so happy to have another girl around –"

"Okay, Carol."

"I can't help myself. This is such a nice surprise," Carol said.
"Okay, okay, don't give me the look. I'm leaving. We'll catch up
later, Annie and I. 'Bye now."

Marco waited for her to shut the door behind her then he said,
"Let me try to explain this as simply as I can. Most scientists believe
all people are descended from a single male ancestor. That's not
quite true. People with LMD are descended from a different ancestor who bred with normal humans as well as with his own, thus
sending that gene spinning through human history."

"It's like a missing link?"

"No, a link on a different chain. A different branch of the tree.
Have you ever seen a human embryo develop to full fetus?"

"No."

"In the early stages, the human fetus goes through a number
of other animal forms, a segmented worm, a reptilian creature
with gills and a tail . . . at one point it resembles a small pig. This
is part of its natural metamorphosis; those evolutionary stages are
encoded into the DNA. Our development is slightly different.
People who suffer from LMD are wolflike at the small-pig stage,

and have other chromosomal and hormonal variations that can lead to full-blown LMD. The full moon triggers a rapid release of thyroid hormone and adrenaline, which in turn can trigger the lycanthropic metamorphosis."

"How does the moon do that?"

"It's a primeval trigger for a lot of things in nature, far beyond just the pull of the tides. Some species get a signal when the moon is full to crawl out of the sea and mate on the beach, some to hide, some to change genders. Our bodies tell us to become wolves."

"You have it too, LMD?"

"Yes. But in my case, it's completely under my control. Some of our patients have also achieved self-control, which we call Transcendent LMD. That's the ultimate goal here, but I'll tell you right now, it isn't easy, and most of our patients never achieve that level of self-power."

"Meaning what? They no longer become werewolves?"

"They could, if they chose to and the moon was full, but they choose not to. They choose to control the wolf inside."

"How do they do this?"

"It takes years of treatment and training in self-hypnosis. Our treatment uses a combination of group and drug therapy in the initial phase. You will then advance to self-control exercises and self-hypnosis training. Until you can control your transformation, you are required to do confinement every month. I like to confine patients the day before the full moon until the day after, longer if there are problems outside that confinement window."

"I have a job. I'm a legal secretary –"

"I'll write you a doctor's note that excuses you from work for those three days every month. In your case, it should be simple. I'll just call it a menstrual abnormality, hemorrhagic ovaries."

"Is that a real thing?" Annie asked.

"Oh yes. It causes the ovaries to swell with fluid. They can become as large as oranges, causing great pain, backaches, and discomfort when you eat. Your company will buy that. From now on, you see no other doctor than me. It's too risky for you to go to an outside GP."

"You're saying I can go back to work?"

"Yes you can, but what I'd like you to do is apply for a leave of absence. During the initial adjustment, we find it is better to –"

"I'll never get a leave. Secretaries never get things like that where I work. Besides, I have to go to work. They need me there and I have to work for a living."

"We'll get you back to work then," he said. He preferred to isolate new patients from their families, friends, and jobs while they went through the fragile first stage of treatment, then reintegrate them into the normal world. But he didn't want to say anything to scare any werewolf away from treatment, particularly a female.

"You can live a nearly normal life in our program," he said. "I should warn you, the program isn't cheap. But if you have financial trouble, we can work out some arrangement."

"This may seem like a silly question, but do you take insurance?"

"Yes. What insurance do you have?"

"Synergy Medical."

"We take Syn-MED," he said. "We like you to pay us directly and then bill your insurance company, for bookkeeping reasons. Any more questions?"

"No, but I'm sure I'll think of more later."

"Good. I have a few for you then. When did this transformation first occur?"

Annie told him about her dreams, which started when she was a child, not long after her parents were killed in a car crash. But they were just dreams, and they always took place in a snow-covered landscape – until the month before, when she had the vivid dream about killing a man in the Meatpacking District.

"When I read that a man had been killed there, by a crazy dog or something, I thought maybe I'd witnessed something. I had no idea I'd killed the guy."

"Before that, you didn't go out and kill."

"No. I'm sure of it. I don't even eat meat. And I wouldn't hurt a fly. Seriously, I open the window and let the fly escape."

"Don't feel bad. You couldn't help killing. But you can now, with my help," he said.

"That's so reassuring," she said, and her whole body relaxed.

"What triggered the transformation from dream to reality?"

"I don't know."

"Have you been sick lately, or suffered a head injury? Did you go off any medication . . ."

"I went off the pill," she said. "About three months ago."

"Oh!"

"And Xanax, two months ago."

"How long were you on the pill?"

"Since I was fourteen," Annie said, quickly adding, "Not for contraception. I took it because it was the only thing that kept my skin clear and –"

"Controlled the hair growth."

"Yes!" Annie said, surprised she hadn't put this piece into the puzzle before. From puberty on, she'd always had a problem with excessive hair growth and severe acne. The pill suppressed both those things. "If I go back on the pill and the Xanax, will this wolf thing stop?"

"No, now that the genie is out of the bottle, that won't be enough to stop it. Occasionally the disease goes into remission as LMD patients age and, as I said, some learn to suppress it, but usually once the disease is active, it is with you for the rest of your life," he said. "We find even massive amounts of tranquilizers aren't enough to suppress it in its full-blown phase, just manage it. And that's what you now have. Full-blown LMD."

"LMD," she said. "That sounds like something almost normal."

He smiled. "Tell me about your parents. Did they suffer from LMD?"

"They died in a car accident when I was five, but I'm sure I would have noticed if they did."

"Not necessarily. They may have had ways to manage or hide it. Did you spend a lot time with relatives, away from your parents during full moons?"

"Not before my parents died," she said. "I'm pretty sure they weren't werewolves."

"Perhaps not. It's a rare and recessive gene. Two are required to make a werewolf. You only inherit it if both parents carry the gene, and neither parent may show outward signs because each may have only one of the genes. If you now have children with a normal man, your children will appear completely normal."

"How can I possibly have children with a normal man? How could I explain this to a normal man?"

"For the time being, you should not have any intimate relationships with men. You're too fragile. But we'll work on the relationship problem. Nothing is impossible and no obstacle is insurmountable. Okay?"

"Okay," she said. "It's just . . . the other werewolf, from the park. I felt something for him."

The door opened. Carol stuck her head in and said, "I made some dinner. It will be ready in about ten minutes."

"Let's discuss this over dinner. We've made a good start, Annie. We'll go a little deeper next time."

"So what do I do now?"

"I'd like you to stay here for a few days, so I can do a few tests. Carol has fixed up the guest room for you. After dinner she'll get you settled. You feel better now?"

"Oh, much," she said.

They ate in the roof garden, the three of them clustered at one end of a long dining table shaded by trees and lit by coloured lamps that hung from the branches, giving off a pale, diffuse light which made the night air seem grainy.

"We're vegetarians," Carol said, walking around the table with a huge bowl of cold pasta salad to serve Annie. "I hope you don't mind if we don't have meat for you."

"I'm a vegetarian too," Annie said. "This looks delicious, thank you."

"My secret is to mix the noodles, rigatoni with corkscrew pasta with macaroni, and use a lemon-juice-and-garlic-scented sunflower oil as the dressing, it goes nicely with the cured black olives and the minced peppers."

"Do you have a drinking problem, Annie?" Marco asked. He was uncorking a bottle of wine.

"I . . . I don't drink much as a rule but I get drunk far too easily. And the last few days . . . I was very depressed . . ."

"I guess we can risk one glass of wine for you." He poured. "We'll be putting you on a special diet. No caffeine or other stimulants, no refined sugar, or drugs other than what I prescribe, and no drinking except for special occasions. If you have trouble giving up drugs or alcohol, we have our own AA group to help."

"We had a rule, no smoking, but that one turned out to be too hard for the patients to give up," Carol said. "So Annie, where are you from?"

"I was born in Canada. My dad went there with my mom to dodge the draft, so he wouldn't die in Vietnam, but then he died in a car accident in a blizzard, along with my mom. So I came to live with my Grandma Kay."

"How old were you?"

"Five."

"It was just you and your grandma?"

"And her husbands, whenever she was married, and her best friend Mrs. Mackie who lived next door."

Marco sat back while Carol asked questions. It put the patients at ease if Carol chatted with them casually over dinner in this dreamy garden. Information flowed more easily and was less censored. Annie seemed surprised, and grateful, that Carol was interested in her. Marco took note of this. Bit by bit, a picture of Annie's life emerged. She was an orphan, raised by old people in a neighbourhood full of old people, and as a consequence, she liked

to play it safe. She took care of her health and had started a retirement fund before she was twenty-one. Her religious training was
Catholic, and though she hadn't gone to church since her grandmother's funeral, she still seemed like a good parochial schoolgirl.

"You have a boyfriend?" Carol asked.

"No. I had one. He . . . we split up. But the other night, in the
park, during the full moon –"

"Carol, Annie was asking about the other werewolf from the
park," Marco said. "I told her we were going to try to bring him
in too –"

"You have to try!" Carol said. "It's important to get him off the
street. But it will be really hard to have Jim with us again after what
he did."

"You know him?" Annie said.

"Excuse me," Marco said. "I'm going to go get some more dried
chilies for the pasta."

After he left, Carol said, "He likes spicy foods. You're not allowed
to have much spicy food on the LMD diet, by the way. Anyway, Jim,
Jim Valiente, yes, I know him. He was Marco's protegé and best
friend, and Marco doesn't make friends easily. It's hard in his position, and having LMD. And he's just so brilliant. That intimidates
some people."

"What did he, Jim, do?"

"Gosh, I hate to even think about it. It was a terrible time for
the Centre. A young girl came into the program, Sarah Weinman.
Darling young woman, so funny, full of life. She and I would get
going and laugh so hard we'd pee our pants. It was hard for me
to have close friends too because there are things I can't open up to
them about, things like LMD. You know.

"Anyway, Sarah just lit this place up, everyone loved her, and Jim
fell hard in love with her. They were involved for a while, secretly.
Well, it wasn't completely secret. I knew about it. It was obvious,
but I didn't say anything to Marco. He has this 'no fraternization'

rule for female patients so the guys won't compete for her and turn the joint into one giant cockfight, and I think he had it in his mind that Sarah should marry a Potenza. There aren't that many female werewolves around who aren't Potenzas, and the family's getting a little inbred, just between you and me.

"Once Sarah got mixed up with Jim, she kind of drifted away from us, which is natural, I guess, when people start relationships. I liked them both and hoped for the best for them, but it caused problems with the other patients. It's hard for them to find girl-friends and they all suspected and were jealous I think. It put a strain on the whole program, and that put a strain on Jim and Sarah. Long story short, they broke up."

"Was it a bad break-up?"

"Oh honey. The worst. They broke up just before confinement. As Marco said, this girl really had the pick of the litter, ha ha, of werewolves and she was new to the 'werewolf thing.'" Carol made quotation marks in the air. "She wasn't ready to be pinned down to any one guy. I could see that in her. God, the stories she told about her exploits. I was a young woman in the sixties and I had my share of adventures. In Berkeley, I dropped acid and had sex with two folk-singing brothers. But Sarah had done things, with other women and leather, in public places like restrooms. You know, she'd joke about the restraints when she went into confine-ment. She called them foreplay."

Carol laughed a little, and took a drink of wine.

"The Potenzas don't talk about things like that, so it was refresh-ing. She was a wild and free young woman and Jim wanted more from her than she could give, I guess. He didn't take the break-up well. Marco said he even accused him, Marco, of forcing the break-up. They had a big screaming dust-up. Marco figured he'd calm down but... You have to understand, Jim was lonely, and here comes this free spirit, they're both writers and he's a very sensitive guy –"

"What happened?"

"Jim killed her in a mad fit of jealousy. It was five years ago, but the pain still feels −" She put both her hands over her heart and closed her eyes. Tears pooled in her wrinkles and then spilled down the sides of both cheeks.

"Oh my God."

"Drug overdose the night of the full moon. Marco thinks Jim didn't kill her, consciously. It wasn't premeditated, where he sat down and said, okay, if I can't have you nobody can. But subconsciously, he wanted to punish her, and he mixed up a lethal drug combination for her IV. When he realized what he had done he was so racked by guilt − or so we thought − he killed himself.

"About a month later, the police contacted Marco − Marco was listed as Jim's next of kin − to say they'd found Jim's clothes and wallet on a pier at the shore, nailed to the wood with a knife. A few days later, a rowboat washed ashore, and they found Jim's blood in it. But they never found his body."

"He faked his own death?"

"It seems so −" The words were choked off by sobs. She grabbed Annie's hand and held it so tightly it hurt.

"I was away visiting my sister in California during all this. When I left, they were a cute couple in love. When I came back, they were both gone, Sarah and Jim. We had this beautiful memorial service for him and for Sarah. It was so tragic, like Romeo and Juliet, except homicidal. I forgave him for killing Sarah because he was crazy with love for her, so crazy he went and killed himself. He just couldn't control the wolf in him, that's what Marco said. He had enough self-control not to transform, most of the time, but the wolf was still there, and the wolf told him to kill the woman who spurned him. That's what I said at the memorial. We had to forgive him because he couldn't help himself, and love can make anyone crazy, you know?"

She reached for a cloth napkin to wipe her nose. Then she poured herself another glass of wine. Her eyes were red and swollen from the tears. Her mascara was running now, mixing with her tears to form little muddy trails down her face. She turned the napkin over and daubed her face with it.

"Jim made a fool of Marco, and me too. He broke our hearts. I should be glad he's alive but he hurt us all so much, and so cold-bloodedly. I don't think I could have made it without Marco and the others, my werewolf family. I didn't smile for a year."

"You're happy now?"

"I . . . Yeah, but in a different way. I know more now. Annie, Marco was so worried Jim would get you before we did. Jim's very charming and very dangerous. He has incredible charisma, the quiet, lurking kind, you know what I mean?"

"But in the park, I felt something for him, in my heart."

"Werewolves, around the full moon, can sense people's souls, normal people's, that is. It's a great gift. But when it comes to other werewolves, you're as blind as any girl in love, because werewolves can't smell another werewolf's soul."

"I smelled him, and I liked his smell —"

"You smelled his body, but not his soul," Carol said.

"You're sure that was Jim Valiente with me in the park?"

"Marco is sure. And Marco knows."

"Wow. I'm so glad you told me. I — I had sex with him," Annie said.

"Thank God you're here now," Carol said, reaching over to squeeze Annie's hand again. She sighed. "Here with us."

"Thank God," Annie said.

"Marco wants to find Jim and bring him back. That's going to be hard on all of us. Especially me. But I am going to make the best of it, and try to be loving."

"Are you a werewolf too?" Annie asked.

"No. I'm normal, much to my father-in-law's chagrin." She smiled.

"How long have you and Marco been married?"

"Over thirty years. Hard to believe."

"How did you meet?"

"She chased me and chased me until I caught her," Marco said. He sat back down and sprinkled a handful of dried red chilies into his pasta.

"We met in a bar," Carol said. "Nineteen sixty-nine, right Marco?"

"Yes, dear."

"I had come from California with a band, the Neon Nightingale, to go to Woodstock. Afterwards, I stayed on in the city. I was waitressing at this bar, under age, then crashing wherever at night, dropping acid, going to parties, grooving. Heh. I was a wild little hippie chick."

"But she was already burned out on it when I found her," Marco said.

"So I'm at this bar, waiting on the usual losers, stoned kids, and old, hard drinkers, serious drinkers, you know the kind? They come into the bar as soon as they get off work and they sit at the bar, silent, staring, pounding back shots until closing. You'd think they were made of stone if you didn't see their elbows bend to raise the glass to their lips. You don't even realize how hammered they are until they get up and stumble."

"You're digressing, Carol."

"Sorry. So. I'm leaning on the bar, talking to the bartender, and this man walks in. He's very elegant, he's wearing a topcoat and a hat." She poured herself more wine. "He comes to the bar, and he asks me if I know Sandie Herron. Sandie was my roommate. I said yeah, and he asks if I know where he can find her. I said I wasn't sure where she was, she'd run off with a roadie for Moby Grape —"

"Digressing."

"So I couldn't help him find Sandie, who he wanted to hook up with because he was trying to find one of her ex-boyfriends, a patient of his. I knew the patient! He came in almost every night, so I told Marco to wait. We got to talking and I really liked him. Marco was so handsome then."

"Then?" Marco said.

"Then and now, honey," Carol said, patting his hand. "He was boyishly handsome, and smart, and suave. You know, European, spoke a bunch of languages and had gone to all these prestigious universities. Here I was, a half-Polish high school dropout from Coosa County, Alabama. Coosa County is a funny name, isn't it? Coosa. It sounds like something I'd show the boys for a quarter while I was waiting for my mom to get off work at the bait shop. Anyway. I was impressed. I went home with him and we had sex that night. On our first date."

"*Carol.*"

"She's a grown woman, she knows about sex, Marco. Besides, it was the sixties. Marco doesn't like it when I tell that story. But I love to tell it. I especially love to tell it to my father-in-law, Lwee-Gee. It drives him nuts to know the future countess picked up his son in a bar."

"Future countess?" Annie said.

"That's enough, Carol," Marco said. "And I think you've had enough wine as well, dear heart."

"You're right, Marco. Just enough," she said. "I'm just so happy to have Annie here with us. It's so nice."

"Yes, it is, dear," Marco said. "Let's have dessert now."

"Oh, let's," Carol said, getting up. Annie started to get up too.

"You relax, Annie," Marco said.

When Carol had gone into the penthouse, he said, "Carol told you about Jim and Sarah."

"Yeah."

"Carol really loved both of them, and she took their deaths hard. What Jim did to Sarah, it broke Carol's heart. But then Jim's suicide, it just shattered her. It was a long time before Carol stopped crying. To learn now that he faked it —"

"How will you bring him in? And how can you trust him if you do?"

"He still has a human side, Annie. I know that side. We'll work on that. And you can help."

"How?"

"He likes you. You can be a good influence on him. You can help bring him in."

"How?"

"We'll work that out later. In the meantime we'll have some dessert, and then I'll do some tests before we get you settled for the night. I'd like to keep you off work one more day. I'll give you a doctor's note for your boss."

"Thank you."

"No thanks necessary," he said. "I've been thinking about this and I think you should stay here at least a week before you go home. You can go back to work, but if there are any problems we should try to get you a medical leave until you're ready to reintegrate. For now, we'll take it a day at a time, but I think this is what will work best for you."

"Okay."

After dessert, Marco checked Annie's pulse and temperature, peered into her eyes, listened to her heart, wrote things down and said he'd check her again the next morning.

"Come see the room I fixed up for you," Carol said, leading Annie by the hand upstairs to the second floor of the penthouse. Marco followed them into a small guest room with one sloping wall. It was painted pale yellow and dusty rose. The opposite wall, the sloping side, had two windows. In the middle of the room was a double bed with a rose-coloured duvet and two big fluffy pillows.

"It's a cozy little room. And the bed is heaven," Carol said.

"It's already equipped for you to use during confinement next month, so you don't have to suffer the indignities of transformation among a bunch of crazed male werewolves," Marco said. "And it will keep your female pheromones out of their airspace during transformation."

"You have a nice window so you can look at the stars," Carol said. "I've left cold water for you, under here, see the pitcher? And here are some pyjamas. There's rosewater-and-glycerin face wash in the guest bathroom, Tampax, whatever you need."

"Thanks," Annie said, and she started to cry now. She couldn't believe how kind these people were. She had awakened that morning wondering how she should kill herself, and in the course of a day she had found hope, a community, a family. Even the way Marco and Carol stood in the doorway, Marco's arm around Carol's waist, smiling down on Annie, made her think of family, or rather, the families she saw in TV shows. It was how she imagined her own parents might have looked at her after putting her to bed, before they turned out the light and closed the door.

"You're tired, Annie. You get some sleep," Carol said. "Everything's okay now."

She turned out the light and closed the door.

Annie changed into the pyjamas, sank into the bed and looked up through the sloping window above her at the deep blue night sky and the one star that was visible. She thought about making a wish, but before the right wish had crystallized, she was asleep.

20

Marco saw Jim's ad in the *Downtown Eye* the next day and sent Carol with Annie to pick up some things at her apartment. Jim could not know who Annie was, or where she worked or lived, Marco thought, and so her anonymity would protect her, but he didn't want Annie out there unsupervised, not until she was more settled, able to make logical and mature decisions. She wanted to go back to work the next day. Initially, he was against it, but then decided it was a good way to test her and flush out issues that needed to be dealt with in therapy.

When Carol and Annie got down to the street, Carol looked both ways to see if Jim was lurking about. She didn't see him. They got a cab and headed to Annie's place.

In a parked cab down the block, with the meter fare at thirty-five dollars, Jim said, "That's them. Can you follow that cab, try not to lose it?"

"That your wife?" the cabbie asked, pulling away from the curb. In the back seat, Jim pulled his baseball cap down to shade his face so Carol wouldn't be able to see him. He was heavier, with a different hair colour than before, but he couldn't take any chances now that Marco knew he was still alive.

"Yeah," Jim said. Better to be a suspicious husband than a random stalker.

"Left you?"

"Yeah."

"Bitch."

"No, she's not," Jim said, then thought, well, yeah, she is a bitch in a sense, in the she-wolf sense, and maybe in every sense. He didn't know her. He'd felt something profound and intensely moving when he saw her and then had sex with her, something he wanted to believe in, but how many times had that happened before? If he stopped to count, he could recall, just off the top of his head, a dozen times – before his LMD had manifested – when he'd looked across a room and had eye contact with some intriguing woman. Their eyes met, there was that magic *click*. Always, one or the other, or both, was soon disillusioned. Sometimes it took a few weeks for the illusion to shatter, but often it started as soon as they spoke. A girl with an angelic face and searching eyes might just be using them to find a man of sufficient status and power to raise her to her rightful place in the world. Hope might blind him to this, on a conscious level at least, but any doubts would be filed away until there was more information and the weight of it broke the bubble.

And no, he wasn't really in a position to judge, he acknowledged, because he'd once been a hotshot magazine writer who used his status and power to obtain pretty young women for sex, ego-gratification, and the prestige that comes from having a beautiful woman on your arm. After the LMD manifested and he could sense the souls of normal women, he did this even more. Convinced he'd never have a real relationship, he cynically exploited women who were cynically trying to exploit him. But after about a year of cross-exploitation, he'd begun to want more. He wanted what he couldn't have because of the LMD, a normal, intimate relationship with a woman. That bred a certain desperation and hopelessness for which he overcompensated with more casual exploitation – until Sarah came along, Sarah with her free ways, joie de vivre, and secret soul he could only guess at by the way she made him feel.

That was the thing about the female in the park. She made him feel like Sarah had. But, because of what happened with Sarah, he needed to be very careful now. That kind of mad instinctive passion addled a person's brain. He didn't want to ever feel that grief and madness again. This time, things had to be different.

While Jim was thinking about all this, the cab driver had been talking nonstop.

". . . Jesus. Like women need any help getting ideas. What do women expect of us?" the cabbie asked, turning around to look at Jim in the back seat. "They want us to be sensitive, and cry, except when they don't want us to. Then we're wimps. They want the right to have careers, except when they want the right to quit work and stay home. They expect –"

"It's tough all over," Jim said.

"My wife, she's from the old country. I had an American wife before her and she was a lot of trouble, so I went overseas to get the next wife. She's been here a year, she's turning into an American woman already. I come home from work, I'm tired, all I want is some dinner, a little TV, some affection. But she wants to talk about something she saw on *The Beth Tindall Show*. Some guy, Dr. Dennis, tells women how their husbands should behave and then she tells me everything I'm doing wrong as a husband!"

When Annie's cab stopped and she and Carol got out, Jim asked his cabbie to park down the street while he watched Annie's building with binoculars.

"I figure she's lonely without her mother and her four unmarried sisters in Siberia but why does she have to talk so much?" the cabbie continued. "It's as if she stores it up all day and lets loose as soon as I walk in the door. She can't be quiet for five minutes. I thought I could slow her down by making a rule that she can only speak English with me, but that hasn't helped. She talks just as much, but half the time I can't even understand her. She heard the word 'smirk' on television and couldn't find her English dictionary. She calls her sister in Siberia to ask her. Her sister tells her it's a sex thing a man does to a woman. I come home, she asks me why I never smirk her. We have a big argument before I figure out what she's talking –"

"Ssssh," Jim said.

Carol and the girl were leaving, each carrying a suitcase. When they drove off, Jim said, "Okay, follow them. Please."

The two women returned to the Chelsea. Marco was planning to keep the new werewolf there, Jim realized. Sneaky fuck. Even if she could resist Marco, it would be hard for her to resist Carol. He still got a twinge when he saw Carol. She'd been like a sister to him.

"Take me downtown," he said to the cabbie, interrupting the driver's rant about how he'd had to put a lock on the telephone because his wife was calling her mother and her unmarried sisters too much. On top of that, she sent them money, and he was pulling a lot of double shifts to put food and vodka on the table of "that Siberian henhouse."

If Jim, as a man instead of a wolf, met this female patient, he wondered, would she choose him over Marco and Carol? What could he offer the girl except a life underground as a freak of nature and a killer? What a catch he was. Marco and Carol would promise her a chance to have something resembling a normal life again, he thought, and a sense of belonging in their family of werewolves. A net of intimacy and habit would be woven around her. The longer she was in their hands, the harder it would be for her to escape.

⑥

"What time is it?" Carol asked as she helped Annie unpack a suitcase.

"Eleven-thirteen," Annie said.

"I have to get the tea ready for the group this morning. Marco wants you to sit in with the group."

"The group? All the werewolves?"

"No, just the gay ones. Marco thinks best way to integrate you into group therapy is with the gay males instead of the heterosexual groups. Want to help me with the tea?"

"Of course."

"Listen, don't mention Jim or Sarah to the other werewolves. Marco hasn't told them Jim's alive. He's waiting for the right time. It was hard on everyone. You know?"

"I understand."

The members of the group, three patients and Marco, were already sitting casually around the living room when Carol and Annie came in with tea. Carol poured for everyone from three different pots and Annie passed the cups.

"This is Annie, the girl I told you about. She's going to join us today," Marco said. "Tell her a little about yourselves. Briefly. There'll be lots of time to tell your full life stories later. Fritz, why don't you start?"

A lean, blond man with horn-rimmed glasses stood up.

"My name is Fritz. I'm thirty-five and I've been in the program, living with LMD, kill-free, for ten years. I'm a dentist, so if your teeth need work, I'm your man. I'm gay, and I'll tell you, one good thing about being a werewolf is it makes it comparatively easy to come out as a gay man. I called up my friends and family who didn't know and said, I'm gay. Live with it."

"Fritz is our unofficial social director this month," Marco said, smiling. "What's up next?"

"Potluck dinner and showing of *Stalag 17* in the roof garden," Fritz said.

"Annie, if you have to go anywhere socially in the next two weeks and neither Carol nor I can go with you, Fritz will go with you. That way, if anyone asks any difficult questions, one of us will be there to finesse you through it. Ernie?"

Ernie wore a grey suit with a dark wine-red tie. He was a stock exchange hotshot before the LMD manifested, three years earlier. He'd killed two people.

Annie asked, "And while you were actually killing, how did it feel?"

"We don't go into any details, Annie," Marco said. The other three were shifting uncomfortably. Specifics about kills had the same tempting effect on the patients that talking about a heroin high had on junkies.

"Oh, sorry," Annie said. "Can we talk about how it feels afterwards? I mean, the guilt —"

"But we can't help it," Fritz said. "And we chose to stop."

"That was then. This is now," Ernie added. "I had to quit my job after the LMD. I manage portfolios for small investors' clubs now. It gives me more flexibility, working for myself. A full-time office job is tough with LMD."

"That's one of the things that makes you feel alienated and disconnected, in general," Fritz said. "It's hard to keep a job or a relationship when you have to be in confinement three days a month and you can't confide your condition to anyone outside the Centre."

Max, the youngest looking of the three guys, was a fashion designer who supported himself with freelance illustration work and the occasional dressmaking job or consignment sale. He seemed the most comfortable with his LMD status. He wasn't looking for a relationship; he was into being a boy about town, dating here and there, having a few casual lovers. What bothered him about "living with LMD" was the crimp it put in his career.

After that, Annie sat quietly and listened to them discuss each other's problems. They had parents and half-siblings who didn't understand them – couldn't understand them, really. For those without a regular paycheque, the cost of treatment at the Centre made money tight. There was a general feeling of being a freak, or cursed, which Marco quickly discouraged with soothing comments such as, "It's a disease, not a curse. It's organic, not spiritual."

At the end of the hour, Carol called them for lunch, which they ate at the big table in the roof garden. Marco had some work to do, but Carol ate with them. Annie learned that Ernie and Max roomed together to save money and were trying to redecorate, on the cheap. Carol had seen a lamp that was perfect for them. Fritz lived all the way out in the suburbs in a small one-bedroom he paid $750 dollars a month for, and was looking to move downtown, maybe with a roommate so it would be more affordable.

Carol's cell phone rang and she went inside to talk in private.

As soon as she left, Max said, "Why don't we go to Hamburger Howie's after we leave here, have some meat."

"He's kidding," Fritz said to Annie, but he looked at Max nervously. "Meat isn't allowed on our diet except for special occasions."

"I'm a vegetarian anyway," Annie said. "Can I ask you a question?"

"Sure."

"You're a dentist and you can't afford more than seven-fifty a month?" Annie asked Fritz. "Sorry, that sounded rude. I didn't mean –"

"It's okay. You haven't been here long. Treatment is expensive. Even though most of the cost is covered by insurance, we all have to chip in to help pay the other expenses of running the Centre. But it cuts into the disposable income. So if I move downtown, I'll need a roommate."

"There's not much privacy with a roommate," Ernie said. "You sure you want to do that, Fritz? Max and I get along okay, but if one of us wants to bring a guy home, it gets tricky."

"Fritz doesn't go out much. He hasn't been laid in two years. He's dating a homemade German porn website," Max said to Annie.

"Max, chill. We're not just-us-boys sitting around. There's a lady here," Fritz said.

"Did I offend you, Annie?" Max asked.

"No."

"I didn't think so."

"I was a real party boy once, you know," Fritz said, "when I was in college. But those days were over for me before LMD, and not just because of the AIDS epidemic. It just gets old and sad after a while. You'll see."

"He makes me sound like such a slut," Max said. "I date several nice guys. I don't sleep around recklessly."

"One of them will get jealous, or you will. Then all hell will break loose," Fritz said. "I don't mean to be a noodge about it, but we have to protect the Centre. The last thing we need is some lovesick model stalking you here."

"Relax. I'm not going to do anything to endanger the program."

"Just be careful. We've had problems before," Fritz said, and his face tightened.

He was probably thinking about Sarah, Annie thought. She was now intensely curious about this girl everyone had loved, the last female werewolf in the program. But she couldn't say anything. Not only did it make people cry, but mention of Sarah might bring up the subject of Jim Valiente. She would have liked to have talked about Jim, she would have liked to talk about what it was like having sex with him as a werewolf, and about what it was like to kill. But rules were rules, and Marco had instructed her not to discuss these things with other patients. That's what he was there for.

21

Dear Tweets,

I once knew a man named Steve who had his gallstones faceted and set in a tiara for the daughter of a tribal lord in Afghanistan, or so he claimed. A crown of gallstones! Every girl should have one in this tricky world.

Our glittering hamlet has been overrun with royalty and the celebocracy lately, not to mention gall. You remember the engaged blue blood who looked all set to ride off into the sunset with her blue-collar megastar? She's here auditioning caterers and ordering orange blossoms (not just orange blossoms, we hear, but 10,000 Balinese tangerine blossoms which will be flown in a private, climate-controlled jet after they are freshly picked by hordes of happy little Balinese children who would gladly work their fingers to the nub collecting fragile flowers for the great beauty even if they weren't being paid 14 cents an hour and a big, steamin' bowl of rice).

Where is her low-born prince? He's in Europe doing a movie – and half the people on the movie, as well as every comely maiden who manages to elude security and make it to his hotel room. He's done both his co-stars, one of the producers, the makeup woman, his personal assistant, the continuity girl, even the writer! Why would he be so reckless?

For the answer to that question, we consulted the Council of Queens, a.k.a. my mother's bridge group. The Queen of Cold Creek, a.k.a. Mrs. Pat Tracy, says, "He doesn't want to marry her but for some reason he can't get out of it. He wants her to dump him." The Queen of Black Hill, a.k.a. my mother, says, "This explains why, if you look closely at pictures of them together, he looks like a hostage."

We don't want to say the words "self-sabotage," but if we know the delicious and dirty details, the future missus must know what he's been doing with whom. Why does she put up with it, or has she just been blinded by love?

Speaking of blind . . . Everyone in town, it seems, knows about a certain TV lady and her paramour – and her husband, who is also a reporter. But one scoop he hasn't got is the one everyone in the local newsbiz is talking about. The wife and the bachelor knave have been out and about almost every night looking very intimate. I've seen them myself, picnicking happily at Opera in the Park. The two lovelies are even more stunningly beautiful up close.

The bachelor knave still insists the lady is "just a friend seeking comfort during some personal difficulties and is separated from her husband while she works them out." He has threatened legal action against us if we print her name. Even we skeptical types are touched by the wording of the threat. "Don't do anything to besmirch the lady's honour," the Ace said to one of my happy minions. Besmirch? Did he say besmirch? It's nice to see chivalry lives alongside adultery, just like the good old days of yore. As for the husband, our sources tell us he is completely clueless. Nobody has the heart to tell him, and he doesn't take hints very well. Can a city of millions continue to keep this secret? We dare you to try.

Finally, we went to a sublime party the other night at Reverie. Most of our favourite monsters and magical creatures were there. We cocktailed with a stunning giantess just signed to a major cosmetics contract who confided she is the current quarry of that latest Aussie troubadour. The man from Down Under has sent flowers, fruit baskets, a pair of Australian songbirds, a poem, but her heart is unmoved. Doesn't he know she prefers men of a more, shall we say, kingly age?

Later we supped with an enchantingly evil queen who was trying to cast her spell on the mighty, mighty king she arranged to have seated at her table. This grande dame is not nearly as cool as her name suggests, but the hirsute-sounding king was charm-proof.

But all love's labours were not lost, as yours truly got her crown jewels polished by a scrumptious lad in the back of a limousine at the end of the evening, making her one very happy princess. So there you go, a happy ending. For today.

22

Cooper called a staff meeting before Sam got in.

"I don't want anyone to mention this to Sam," he said, holding up the *Downtown Eye*. "No jokes, no oblique references, no questions about his wife, no anonymous e-mails."

"The guy deserves to know," said an assignment editor. "Everybody knows."

"If we tell him about the rumours now he'll not only find out about his wife, he'll find out everyone knows about his wife, and that's going to shatter him. Let it die down, then I'll tell him if he still hasn't figured it out. Some other story will come along to amuse the gossips."

"He reads the *Eye*, doesn't he?" someone else asked.

"Yes, but he doesn't understand it," Cooper said.

"Someone's going to tell him sooner or later."

"Probably, but I don't want it coming from anyone at CCN."

"We're a news organization. Should we be holding back on the truth?"

"Um, it's not truth, Patricia, it's gossip. Have you seen his wife with Wallace Waring?"

"I did," said Jody Epstein, an entertainment reporter. "At a première."

"Were they having sex in front of you?" Cooper asked.

"No."

"Necking, fondling each other?"

"No, but they looked very . . . cozy."

"So what Wallace says could be true, they could just be good friends and colleagues."

"Oh please," someone said.

"Until you have incontrovertible proof that Sam's wife is having a sexual relationship with Wallace, keep your big trap shut."

"He's a laughingstock," the assignment editor said.

"No," Cooper said. "He isn't. He's getting enormous sympathy. He looks good and noble in this. And we're getting higher and higher ratings. People really like him."

When Cooper said that, there were only a few sarcastic and offended snorts, a fraction of what there would have been six weeks earlier, and those few who snorted drew dirty looks from everyone else. Even the hipsters of CCN were starting to warm to Sam. The guy was just so likable, and not just because he was bringing serious ratings to the beleaguered network with his story. Even with strangers now asking for his autograph, maître d's giving him the best tables, love letters from fans, he didn't have a big head. "I'm just lucky to have a job in this great business," he said, and he said it like he meant it. And he was always quick to credit "Jennifer Ray, my producer, and the staff backing me up at CCN. They do the real work."

But the real surprise was Sam's ability to dig up information. While Wallace Waring had the girl – even Cooper, for all his talk about gossip vs. news, had to admit it looked bad – Sam Deverell owned the story. He was the first to break the story, the first to learn of similar killings years before, and the first to identify the last two victims as Armin Sunga, "a foreign businessman," and Peter Gorgon, the head of Syn-DEF. Every day he had some juicy new tidbit about the investigation.

As soon as Cooper got back into his office, Sam was on the phone with more.

"The police may have a suspect," he said. "Can you send J.R. and a live truck to 347 West Broome Street? I'll meet them there."

23

"347 West Broome. Okay." Detective Macy put the phone down and turned to Foster. "Come on. The two-four may have the dog guy."

They didn't even see him, Ivan, the guy in the drab grey jumpsuit who emptied their wastepaper baskets and mopped their floors. When the cops spoke to him, they did so in very slow, simple English, as if speaking to a child, and it was always an order to do something – "Someone – was – sick – in – the – interview – room. You – mop – up." Often, this would be accompanied by pantomime, to make sure he understood. Possibly, this was because he'd gone out of his way to make them think he didn't speak English. It seemed safer that way. His knowledge of police had been gained in the former Soviet Union, where he had also learned how to be invisible.

As soon as Macy and Foster grabbed their jackets, Ivan swept his way out into a quiet corridor, where he took his cell phone out of his overalls and called Sam.

"This one's free," he said to Sam.

"Great," Sam said. This had been costing him a bundle. He could afford it, but still. "Why?"

"Just because." Poor guy, Ivan thought, being cuckolded by a younger reporter so publicly. He deserved a break.

⑥

The super at 347 West Broome didn't read the warrant all the way through. He grunted and waved the police to follow him up the stairs to the fourth floor.

"He's not there," the super said, unlocking three padlocks and a dead bolt. "He took off the night before the last of those murders, owing four months rent. We locked him out so he couldn't get his stuff until he paid up."

When he flung the door open, they were all hit by a gust of warm, sharp air smelling of old dogs, old men, and something dead.

Foster went in first, followed by Macy, and then George Bastable, a detective from the 24th Precinct. It was a small studio apartment, cluttered with the detritus of twenty years. The walls were covered with stories about attack dogs. Books about attack dogs lined the baseboards, along with a few non–dog-related books, books on UFOs, a few detective novels, and a copy of John Gray's *Men Are from Mars, Women Are from Venus*, which Detective Foster found strangely touching. On top of a chest of drawers, next to a hot plate, was a framed photograph of a woman that looked like it had been taken in the 1970s.

It didn't seem like there had been a woman in this apartment, ever. There was no kitchen. A plate, a fork, and a knife – the only dishes in evidence – were soaking in the bathroom sink in a thick, stagnant pool of water spotted with islands of green mould. Scraps of old food were rotting in the garbage – a piece of maggoty meat, a dry husk of bread, a fruit pit which, when lifted by rubber-gloved-hands into an evidence bag, disturbed a flock of fruit flies.

In the other room, Foster slowly opened the pint-size refrigerator, the kind you usually find in college dorm rooms, afraid of what she might find. The only things in there were a half bottle of vodka, a wrinkled apple and a huge, open can of dog food, its crust the colour of dried blood.

"He left a couple nights before the full moon," the super told Foster. "Took the dogs."

"What kind of dogs?" she asked.

"Crossbreeds, shepherd and some kind of fighting dog I think. Mean bastards, bit the ear off one of Mrs. Keech's terriers. She woulda pressed charges but she wasn't wearing her glasses so they couldn't prove it was his dogs."

"How did she know it was him?"

"Bruno cussed her out and laughed when his dogs bit off the other's ear. He told her she was next."

"Any other neighbours have complaints?"

"All of them," said Detective Bastable from the two-four.

"All of them?" Foster asked.

"Everyone in this building called the tip line and reported him."

"Hey, look at this," Macy said. He had pulled a brown cardboard file box out from under the bed and was reading through a file. "Letters to CEOs, politicians, celebrities."

"Complaints? Threats?"

"Complaints, threats, advice. There are four more boxes under the bed."

He pulled another one out for Foster and she opened it up. After she'd riffled through it she said, "This one is devoted just to copies of letters to Madonna."

"Listen to this, from the Syn-EG file. It's to Synergy Pharmaceutical. '. . . Your Gentle Laxatives gave me terrible stomach cramps and intestinal bleeding. I suppose you think because you're rich and powerful you can put any crap on the market without regard to how it affects your customers who are all brainwashed by advertising.'"

"This could be our man," Foster said.

Macy stayed behind in the apartment with the forensic cop while Foster and the precinct detective interviewed the neighbours, slowly putting together a picture of Bruno Barotti, a sixty-three-year-old divorcee, alone for thirty years, estranged from his only daughter, who lived with her husband and kids in Florida.

6

Sam was putting together a picture of Barotti too. First, of course, he had to get into the building with his Gizmo while he waited for Jennifer and the live tech to arrive. There were cops outside but the door was open. He figured he couldn't just breeze past them, so he shoved the Gizmo into his pocket, stepped past the cops, casually, and pressed one of the buzzers.

When a woman answered, he said, "Mom? It's me." Then he went through the open door and up the stairs.

Most of the neighbours were on the fourth floor or clustered on the stairwell leading up to it. Sam was easily able to mix in with them, pushing through towards the open door where the cops were. He adjusted the Gizmo in his coat pocket till its lens was just poking out slightly and turned it on as he got to the doorway and looked in. A cop in the hallway stopped him from going farther.

"You catch the guy?" Sam asked, moving back and forth to give the Gizmo the full scope of the room.

The cop didn't answer. He gestured for Sam to step back, and gave him a puzzling smile. Sam wandered back towards the stairs. As he went down, he stopped a young woman heading in the same direction and asked her, "They catch the guy?"

"No. He took a flyer just before the full moon."

"Did you know him at all?"

"Just a little."

"Can I talk to you about him?" He showed her his press pass.

She didn't even glance at it before she said, "Yeah, sure, Sam." She nodded for him to follow her to an apartment on the first floor.

"Get you a drink, Sam?" she asked.

"No, I'm fine," Sam said, taken aback because she knew his name. This was happening more and more. He hitched the Gizmo up to his shoulder. "What's your name?"

"Fran Read."

"Age?"

"You're asking my age?"

"Yes, please."

"I'm twenty-nine."

"Profession?"

"Actress. I'm appearing in a comic retelling of August Strindberg's *Miss Julie* at the 447 Theatre."

"How long have you known the suspect . . . what's his name?"

"Bruno Barotti. I've known him as long as I've lived here, which is three years." She cleared her throat and continued. "I met him the first day I moved in. He was on his way out to walk his dogs; they growled and one of them snapped at me."

"What did you do?"

"I jumped back, and he pulled the dogs away from me and gave me a dirty look, as if I had somehow provoked them. But the next time I saw him, without the dogs, he was really friendly. He started talking to me at the mailbox."

"Go on."

"After about five minutes I just wanted to get away from him. He told me he'd been in show business once. He was a folksinger in the 1960s, until Lyndon Johnson and the CIA destroyed his music career, and that led to the end of his marriage. I think he told Jeanne Rawluk in 2-B that he filed an alienation of affections suit against Johnson and the CIA."

"What happened?"

"It was thrown out, of course."

"Oh. Of course," Sam said.

"He filed quite a few lawsuits. He never sued me but he sued some of my neighbours and he sued the company that manages the building a few times. Otherwise, they would have evicted him long before this."

"Did he go out much with other people?"

"Oh no, he was a real loner. He went out late at night a lot, with the dogs. This whole thing doesn't surprise me in the least. You should talk to Jeanne Rawluk. She knows everything. He once accused her of breaking into his apartment, putting a stain on his favourite trousers, and then sneaking out again. Oh, and he believes Madonna can read his mind."

"He was nuts?" Sam asked, as if there was any doubt.

"Um, yeah," she said. "I have a picture of him. You want to see?"

"Sure."

"I took this for my cousin who apartment-sat for me last winter, so she'd know who to avoid."

Sam shot the photograph with the Gizmo. Bruno Barotti was a bald white man with a white whiskery face.

Jennifer Ray called as soon as she and the tech got there. They were parked across the street, ready to go live any time.

"Will you come outside with me and talk to me on camera? Live?" Sam asked.

"You bet," Fran said.

After he did his live shot with Fran, he spoke to Jeanne Rawluk, a registered nurse, and Lesley Keech, who carried in her arms the one-eared victim of Bruno Barotti's dogs. Fran Read came down after the noon live shot with bottled water for everyone. After the last live shot, Fran handed Sam her card.

"In case you need any more information. Or anything at all," she said, smiling. "Anything."

"I don't know why people say folks in this city are so tough and unfriendly," Sam said to Jennifer.

On the drive back to CCN, the live tech turned on the radio. The DJ was reading the newspapers and making jokes with his sidekick. When he said, "Let's see what's in 'Dear Tweets'..." the live tech turned to another station.

Jennifer Ray was of two minds about this. On one hand, she agreed with Cooper that Sam's ignorance was bliss. But how long could they keep him uninformed? And didn't he have a right to know, so he could go to his wife, confront her, and deal with it? Yes, he'd be hurt. It seemed inevitable that he was going to be hurt anyway. And yes, it might affect Sam's ability to do his job. She worried that Cooper's motives in this had more to do with the story and the ratings Sam was getting than it did with his concern for Sam's emotional well-being. She worried that her motives did too.

24

The Mayor was meeting with his media guy, Seth Kirk, and the Police Commissioner when Lord Harry Teufel, the chairman and majority stockholder of the Synergy Enterprises Group, called.

The Mayor turned to the media guy. "What am I going to tell this jackass? I've been dodging his calls for days."

"We're doing everything we can. You've been busy with this; apologize for not getting back to him. The police have identified a suspect. Blah blah," Seth said. "But you may have to take a meeting with him. He donated a shitload of money to your campaign."

"He did? Hell. I hate that guy. Damn. Do I have to take this call?"

"Yes. Put him on the speakerphone. I'll get you through it," Seth said.

The Mayor told his executive assistant to put the call through.

"Mr. Mayor," said Lord Harry. He had a South African accent. "Lord Harry Teufel here. I've been trying to get through for days. What's the problem over there?"

"Lord Harry, we're doing everything we can. I've been so busy dealing with this Mad Dog Killer I haven't had a chance to get back to you. My apologies. I wanted to have all the information in hand before I called you."

"Don't blow smoke up my arse. Two of my people have been killed, Bingham and Gorgon. I want this stopped now."

"The police have identified a suspect –"

"Have they arrested him?"

"They are in pursuit –"

"So they haven't got him?" Lord Harry said. "Look. I want to meet with you and the Police Commissioner here at Syn-EG. I have an opening tonight at –"

Seth was shaking his head. He whispered in the Mayor's ear.

"I'll get back to you about a good time and place to meet," the Mayor repeated after Seth. "So we can make the proper security precautions for you and for me."

"Get back to me soon. I've been going easy on you on Syn-TV and in my newspapers, but if my people keep getting killed —"

"I'll get back to you as soon as I can, Lord Harry," the Mayor said. Lord Harry hung up without saying goodbye.

"Good. You don't want to be seen as being at Lord Harry's beck and call," Seth said. "That's all you need, a piece in his newspaper or on Syn-TV about him calling you into his office."

"The guy is the world's biggest asshole. Have you met him?" the Mayor asked.

"Didn't he sue his own children?" asked the Police Commissioner.

"His mother," Seth said.

"There was a court case with his children too, as I recall, about ten years ago."

"Yes, he asked for a paternity test to make sure his children really were his children. They were twelve and thirteen at the time I believe, and had lived with him that entire time."

"And?" asked the Mayor.

"They were his children, much to his disappointment, apparently," Seth said. "We can all agree, the man's a grade-A prick. But we have to appease him because he's too damned powerful."

"We could appoint him to the task force on these murders," the Mayor said. "And get a gag order so that task force members can't speak to the news media, so they don't disrupt the investigation."

That's what a previous mayor had done when the current mayor was just a prominent businessman complaining about a garbage strike.

"Good idea," Seth said. "That way you have Lord Harry on your side, but gagged." He was impressed. The Mayor was getting the hang of the spin game. It hadn't been easy convincing the plainspoken grocer to play the game.

"We've got to plug up those police department leaks too," Seth added. "Find out how this guy Sam Deverell is getting his information. If we have to, have the police talk to him, and if he doesn't reveal his source, have him arrested for obstructing justice."

"Is that necessary?" the Mayor asked.

"It may be."

"I'd hate to have to put that guy in jail. His wife is cheating on him, he's so clueless, and he seems like such a nice guy," the Mayor said.

"It's hard to get a judge to throw a reporter in jail in this state," the Commissioner said.

"I know how," Seth said. "On grounds of public safety. If his reportage is compromising the investigation and jeopardizing public safety, he can be cited for contempt for not revealing his sources."

Seth looked at his watch. "Shit. I've got to go meet with that gossip columnist at the *Downtown Eye*. You have lunch with your wife. I'll be back at one for the sanitation meeting."

"Right."

"Marva's still okay with the whole thing?" Kirk asked.

"Okay, no. But she's hanging in there. Thanks for keeping it out of the press."

"That's my job, your Honour," Kirk said.

"You and Marva still living . . . apart?" the Commissioner asked, after groping for the right word, because the Mayor and his wife, while living completely separate lives, were still under the same roof at the mayoral mansion. The few people who knew referred to this darkly as the Curse of the Mansion, since this was the second mayor in a row to have to suffer that peculiar hell.

Granted, they were keeping up appearances for the sake of the city and the Mayor's career, but Marva had made it clear that as soon as things settled down for him, she was going her own way. She'd had to give up her seat on the boards of her various organizations when he became mayor, to avoid any appearance of conflict of interest. Then she'd been asked to minimize the socializing she did with her bohemian artist friends. It was fine to see some of them at an opera gala or a reception at the mayoral mansion, but it just wouldn't do for her to be seen at some wild gallery opening where an art dealer might be found dead of an overdose in the john, as had happened at one event she was supposed to attend. Luckily, their daughter had gone into labour and he and Marva were at the hospital that night. Close call.

"Is there another man?" he'd asked Marva.

"Oh no," she said.

But he wondered. She was close to her sculpture teacher Serge, an artist whose work was next to pornography, in the Mayor's opinion, and she got very upset when he suggested she discontinue her lessons for a while. At lunch today, he planned to make that argument again. So far, nobody had noticed Serge's visits to the mansion three times a week, but one couldn't be too careful. Look at how people were talking about this guy at CCN, Sam Deverell, and his wife's carryings-on.

25

Annie had intended to go back to work at Syn-EG more or less full time, until she watched the CCN report on the identities of the latest victims. Sam Deverell reported that the man dressed like a bird watcher found near the Humming Tombstone was the head of Syn-DEF. That meant two victims, Peter Gorgon and Robert Hunt Bingham, were executives at subsidiaries of Synergy Enterprises Group. The third victim, Armin Sunga, was a foreign businessman who, so far as anyone could see, was unconnected to the other two. Sources said Sunga may have seen the killer and died because of being in the wrong place at the wrong time. It was not known why he was in the Bramble after dark.

Knowing her victims' names was bad enough, but knowing that two of the victims were her "co-workers" in the Syn-EG family was almost too much.

"That was then, this is now," Marco reminded her. "You smelled the souls of your victims during the full moon, when the scent of the soul is powerful, and that sent a signal to your brain. You couldn't help yourself then."

"Now you can. That's why you're here!" Carol said. "You've done the right thing. You should feel good about that."

"Perhaps you should just quit your job at Syn-EG. Fritz's receptionist is going on maternity leave in a few weeks and he doesn't think she'll be coming back. You could work for him," Marco said. "Until then, you could work for me and I'll cover the cost of your treatment. Carol's got so much to do here. You would be a great help to her."

Their reassurances, and a good dose of Valium, calmed her down. She had been resisting the idea of leaving her job, but decided after that to give her notice. She still had two weeks of vacation coming, so she could give three weeks and only have to work one. Marco thought she should quit immediately, but Annie would lose three weeks of pay and benefits that way. Not only that, her anniversary was in two weeks, and at that point her company pension plan would be seventy-five per cent vested.

Absurdly practical, Marco wrote in his notes that night, alone in his office with his books, diplomas, and portraits of illustrious Potenza ancestors.

Annie found it strange to go back into Syn-EG after her whole world had changed. Carol rode the subway with her, saying goodbye in the immense black and pink marble lobby, which she described to Marco later as resembling "the mouth of a big machine with clocks showing various time zones in a row near the ceiling, like big teeth."

"Call if you have any problems," she said to Annie, and hugged her.

It was hard. At work, one of the first memos she read was for another condolence website, this one for Peter "Go Go" Gorgon, the head of Syn-DEF. On the home page was a photo, the corporate photo, of him shaking Lord Harry's hand. He had been born and raised in Connecticut until high school, when his family moved to Utah, where his father had taken a job for an aerospace firm. He was a star punter for the school football team as well as president of the junior businessman club. He attended Yale and went to work in his father's business. While serving in the Utah National Guard, he met and married Patricia Pedersen, a "honey-haired beauty," and Miss Flaming Gorge Utah 1970, who served him pink lemonade and cookies at a USO rally to raise money to send shaving soap to the fighting boys in Vietnam. In 1981, Lord Harry hired Gorgon to head the defence company he had just purchased and the Gorgon family moved east. Peter and Patricia had two children, Dwight, who worked for Syn-DEF, and George, who worked for Syn-EG's private prison arm, Syn-JUST. Peter had enjoyed hunting, fishing, and spending time with his wife and children.

At the bottom of the page was a link to sign the online condolence book. Annie clicked it and a response form popped up beneath another picture, this one of Gorgon with his wife and two sons, picking apples in the sunshine.

They were so blond, so beautiful, and they looked so happy, it tore Annie's heart out to think that she may have ended this sunny idyll. She wasn't sure who she had killed, Gorgon or Sunga, but either way, she was a killer.

Guiltily, she signed the condolence book. "I am so deeply, deeply sorry for your terrible loss. Mr. Gorgon sounds like he was a great man, and he will be missed terribly."

Everyone was buzzing about it. Bo was out most of the morning, in company security meetings. When he came back before lunch, he asked Annie to put together a file of threatening letters he'd received from disgruntled litigants.

She handed him her letter of resignation.

"You can't leave, not right now," he said. "It will take me at least six weeks to train one of the other legal secretaries to do your job . . ."

"My doctor says I have to quit, as soon as possible," she said, directing him to the attached note from Marco. "I'll get to that file of threatening letters after lunch."

She was firm, unequivocal, and Bo decided, all things considered, he would be glad to see her go, now that she'd suddenly grown a spine and an attitude. While she was at lunch, he scouted the other legal secretaries for her replacement, looking for just the right combination of low self-esteem, obedience, accuracy, and discretion.

In the coffee room, the underlings speculated about what was going on with these murders, and if there were a plot against Syn-EG. The number-one suspect was a rival corporation, Consolidated Companies, Con-COMP, until someone saw a news report that police were tracking a suspect, a crazy loner named Bruno Barotti.

The only people in the building who weren't talking about the Mad Dog Killer, it seemed, were Liz and Henry.

All Henry wanted to talk about was "Dear Tweets."

". . . yours truly got her crown jewels polished by a scrumptious lad in the back of a limousine at the end of the evening, making her one very happy princess," Henry read over the speakerphone to Annie and Liz in the green room. "Guess who the scrumptious lad is?"

"Who?" Annie asked. Liz shoved the *Downtown Eye* towards her so she could see the whole column.

"I'll give you a hint. The enchantingly evil queen he mentions is Rosemary Frost."

"Oh my God, you did the guy who writes Tweets?" Liz said.

"The Czarina couldn't get one of her regular walkers to take her to the party, so she took me. I gave him a little dish about Mrs. Frost and turned on my charm. And here I am, in the column."

"Yeah, but Henry, nobody knows it's you, so what good is it?"

"Liz, he may call me and invite me to some parties."

"He hasn't called you?"

"Not yet. But he will."

"Henry, you have to get him to come to my party tonight," Liz said.

"I asked. He can't. He has the Tomorrowland opening party *and* the Bowling for Breast Cancer fundraiser. Maybe next time."

"*If* – he calls you again," she said.

"Don't you think he will?"

"Henry, he probably has dozens just like you. Male models, aspiring actors. The competition is fierce."

"Yes, but I'm the only one who can give him the skinny on the Czarina and her friends."

"You were the only one I didn't guess from Tweets," Liz said. "Isn't that a riot? I guessed everyone else in the column."

Annie sat quietly, picking at some green-room fruit and crudités, while reading the back of the *Eye*. There was a new ad there for Miss Wolf.

"The doctor is not who you think he is. Be very careful," it said. "I think I love you."

"Annie? *Annie?*" Liz said.

"Sorry. What?"

"Henry just asked what the good cases were today."

"Oh. Well, a man is suing Syn-PHARM because its new impotence drug works too well. Now he can't get it down."

"Androx-Y?" Henry asked.

"Yes."

"That's great stuff."

"How do you know?" Liz asked.

"People are doing it recreationally in the clubs now," Henry said. "Anything else fun in the world of lawsuits?"

"Fun, no."

Finally, Liz brought up the unavoidable topic. "Beth is in a psycho state today. She's been interviewing bodyguards. You should see the guys parading through her office. It's like she's casting a Hercules movie."

"Why is she interviewing bodyguards?" Henry asked.

"Because two people who worked for Syn-EG have been killed by that Mad Dog Killer," Liz said. "She's afraid that, with her celebrity, she's a prime target."

"I hear that other victim, the foreign one . . ."

"Sunga," Annie said.

"Yeah, he was in the Bramble looking for anonymous sex. Some rough trade," Henry said.

Annie felt awful.

"I'm going back to my desk," she said. "I have a lot of work backed up from being out sick."

Even though she felt terribly guilty about the murders, she felt strangely good about the ad on the back of the *Eye*. When she read it, an involuntary pang of desire vibrated from her pelvis to the top of her head. It was as if someone had hit a tuning fork and then placed it on the top knob of her spine, and this despite knowing what she knew about Jim Valiente.

She had held out a small hope that Marco was wrong, that the other werewolf wasn't Valiente, just a case of mistaken identity that would be resolved when this guy was brought into the program. But the ad validated Marco. This werewolf knew who Marco was and knew she was with Marco. So how could her heart and libido respond to those words, "I think I love you," with such instinctive joy?

Later, in her session with Marco, she talked about how hard it was to have discovered these twisted things inside her, not just her desire to kill, but her desire for this other killer.

"It's not you, Annie, it's the wolf. As long as we control the wolf, you'll be okay," he said. "The wolf's sexual instinct is harder to control than the killing instinct. You're feeling increased sexual desire since your LMD became full-blown, and you're having trouble finding outlets. Have you tried masturbation?"

"Um, well, if I was in my own place I could but . . ."

"Have you been fantasizing more?"

She wanted to be frank with him, as he was her doctor after all, but she didn't want to tell him she'd been fantasizing about Jim – well, not Jim, she didn't even know who he was in real life or what he looked like human. But Jim in werewolf form. In her mind, she replayed that frantic werewolf sex at least three times a day.

It was as if Marco read her thoughts. "Have you been fantasizing about having sex again with a werewolf?"

"Yes," she said, the word escaping like a blast of vented steam. She was so relieved Marco had guessed and she didn't have to broach the subject herself. "Because it was . . . incredible. No hesitation, no words. Just sounds, moans, growls, howls, and smells, his smell – and sensations –"

"Yes, werewolf sex is supposed to be incredible," he said. "Free of all shame, going purely on instinct. There's no reason we can't work on your shame issues and provide a fulfilling sex life for you within a more civilized framework. I think we should get to that a little later and explore the root issues first. I want to know more about you and your family. How was sex treated in your childhood environment?"

"My grandmother remarried twice after I moved in with her and she must have had sex, but I never heard them talk about having sex. Her husbands drank a lot."

"She told you about sex."

"Oh yeah. She and Mrs. Mackie. They thought it was over-rated and my grandmother was always worried I was going to 'get into trouble' or get a bad reputation. I remember Mrs. Mackie said that sex was like eating cake in a dream. It looks so good, you have to have it, but you wake up and it's over before you get to the good part."

"How old were you when you lost your virginity?"

"Fifteen."

"And the circumstances?"

"Oh, there was this nice-looking boy who said he loved me. If I loved him too then, you know, I'd do it, he said, or else he'd have to go out with someone else, because he had blue balls, which is a very dangerous condition." She smiled. "We did it in the back seat of a car under the elevated train tracks in the old neighbourhood."

"And what did you think of it at the time?"

"This will sound so naïve," she said, "but I'd never seen human sex before, not even simulated in a movie. I somehow had the idea that the guy put his — you know — in and left it there, then something magical happened. When this boy pushed in, pulled out, pushed in again, in and out, in and out, I thought, 'What the heck is he doing?' I had seen dogs do it, so I shouldn't have been surprised, but I was. It was over very fast, and nothing magical happened for me. Afterwards, I just felt ashamed, and afraid I'd get a reputation."

"Did you?"

"No. If he told anyone else, they probably didn't believe him because I became a born-again virgin after that sorry experience."

"When did you next have sex?"

"When I was twenty-one."

"Five years later?"

"After the first time, I thought Mrs. Mackie was right. Sex was overrated and why risk a reputation or a disease or being an unwed mother for that?"

"Was the sex better when you were twenty-one?"

"Well, yeah, I was in love, and I knew more. That was Hayden."

"So you've only had sex with two men?"

"Four, counting the one in the park."

Marco's jaw clenched when she said that.

"I had a one-night stand after a party my friends Liz and Henry took me to, just after Hayden left me, a benefit for the Police Benevolent Association. The guy told me he was a cop. I was impressed, I guess, and drunk, really drunk. I never even got his name."

She was as red as a beet.

"I didn't even tell my friends about it, Dr. Marco."

"You don't have to," he said.

"So him, and then the werewolf in the park. Four."

Someone knocked on the door.

"Come in," Marco said. "Ah, Mike. Annie, this is my protegé, Mike Burke. Mike, this is the new werewolf, Annie Engel."

"Nice to meet you," Mike said, allowing himself only a glance at her. Marco had warned him to stay away from the female except on Marco's direct orders or when unavoidable, such as at dinner, as Carol often invited Mike to eat with them. Mike was a nice-looking young man, around Annie's age, and very quiet. Before he entered the program, he'd been in the army, Marco explained. Mike listened while Marco talked, adding a word here and there. He'd been at the Centre since just before Jim Valiente left, and had been kill-free for six years.

"Mike knows about Jim," Marco said. "He's going to help us bring Jim in."

"What do I have to do?"

"Nothing right now, Annie. Leave it to us. You have to go now, don't you? You have a movie date with Carol and Fritz."

After Annie left, Marco again said, "No fraternizing with Annie, Mike."

"No, no, I won't."

"Okay. She's very fragile and it's important we not do anything to disrupt the program."

"I understand. But won't Jim Valiente disrupt the program? How can we bring him back in after what he did to Sarah?"

"We have to do something. We can't leave him on the street. At the very least, we can drive him out of the city, send him to my father's program in Washington."

"I'll do whatever I can to help," Mike said.

Mike had been doing well. From Marco, he had learned to

master his lupine instincts, so he was able to suppress his full-moon transformation into wolf form. He'd learned about the drugs they used and how to judge dosage based on health, age, weight, and blood lipidity, although he wasn't allowed to mix or administer drugs except in emergencies. Marco did that, and Mike helped by hooking the patients up to their IVs. In his free time, Mike was working towards his degree in psychiatric nursing so he could one day take over the Centre when Luigi died and Marco took over the Washington practice.

Marco thought that Mike seemed loyal, but then, so had Jim Valiente. Jim had been so grateful when Marco first brought him in. He'd become Marco's star pupil, his right-hand man, his archangel, his confidant. Marco had taught him almost everything he knew. Many nights, Jim had dinner with Marco and Carol. After Carol went to bed, the two of them would stay up a little longer, discussing treatment ideas or arguing about philosophy, art, film, baseball. It had been difficult for Marco to make friends, due to his condition – or perhaps, as he sometimes believed, it had something to do with his inherent intellectual superiority, which intimidated other people and brought out their insecurities. What-ever the cause, he had not had many intimates, and Jim's betrayal had hit him harder than had it come from someone not admitted to the inner sanctum of Marco's soul.

With Mike, Marco had been more cautious and circumspect, less indulgent, less willing to show any vulnerability, and as a result Mike took fewer liberties and was obedient. Jim had come to think of himself as Marco's equal, Marco realized, and that's where the problems began when Sarah arrived. He was not going to make the same mistakes with Mike, or with Annie.

The next day he put an ad in the *Eye*. "Mr. Wolf, all is forgiven. Please come home. We love you." He let it run the week and got no response, but he hadn't expected one. Marco knew it wasn't going to be easy. The only way to get Jim was to wait for the full moon and go out with Mike and Annie, using her as bait. Jim, he was sure, would resist anyway, and would have to be killed. But at least that way, he'd be off the street, and the program would be safe.

⑥

On Sunday, Carol went with Annie to the nursing home to see Mrs. Mackie, and while there she helped serve fat-free frozen yogurt and watermelon cubes at treat time. On the train, Carol had mused that it might be a blessing to be sent back to one's girlhood, before one's dreams and illusions had been disappointed.

"Not with Mrs. Mackie," Annie said. "It turns out she was a terrible little girl, mean-spirited, selfish and bigoted. But she wasn't always like that. She had a wicked sense of humour and she had occasional moments of bigotry, but I don't remember her being so mean-hearted."

As soon as they arrived, Mrs. Mackie made fun of Carol's ears, which were slightly pointed at the tops. She asked to try on Carol's necklace, an anniversary gift from Marco. Against Annie's advice, Carol let her try it on. When she asked for it back, Mrs. Mackie shrieked, "No! Mine," and had to be restrained by a nurse while Annie forcibly removed the necklace from her throat. Before they left, Mrs. Mackie warned them darkly that the place was "crawling with Jews," and asked them to help her escape back to her family, who would surely be worried about her.

That afternoon, Fritz took Annie to a meeting of the LMD AA group, which Marco led in the living room of the penthouse. Here, she met more of the hetero werewolves, quickly and casually. They looked at Annie with understandable curiosity, but kept a polite distance as Marco had instructed. It made her feel a little strange, as if she were there but not there, a part of the group but apart from the group.

Not bad for a werewolf chick, one of the patients remarked quietly to another. At first look, she seemed not unattractive, but not the kind of girl who turned heads on the street. The longer

you looked at her though, the better she looked. That kind of girl.
She had medium length brown hair and a kind face, round with a
heart shaped mouth, a slightly pug nose, and nice brown eyes.

Substance abuse problems and LMD went hand in hand, it
seemed. One after another, the patients got up and told their
stories, "Hi, my name is Fritz, and I'm an alcoholic. I started drinking when I was fifteen and first realized I was gay but I didn't
become a full-blown alcoholic until I discovered I had LMD . . ."

Fritz told a story about getting drunk years before, the night of
a full moon, then transforming and going out into the night not
just as a werewolf, but as a completely hammered werewolf whose
prey that night was attending a performance of *Cats*. Normally, a
werewolf waits till the victim is alone and vulnerable before attack-
ing, but liquor and pills impaired Fritz's instincts and he ended up
sneaking into the theatre through an open door on the roof and
lurking in the vestibule by an emergency exit. The music, the
vodka, and the pills lulled him to sleep. The last thing he remembered was Betty Buckley singing "Memory." When he awoke, it
was morning, he was human and he was naked. Not sure what to
do, he snuck around backstage to a wardrobe room where the cos-
tumes were disembodied and hanging on hooks like the pelts of
mythical creatures – "such as werewolves," Fritz said, and the room
chortled. He grabbed the body suit for Rumpleteazer, complete
with tail, and put it on, sneaking out of the theatre to grab a cab
home, where the driver waited while this half-man, half-cat ran
upstairs to get the cab fare.

Some of the stories were grimmer, like that of a patient who
had been kicked out of the methadone program for missing three
days of treatment during a particularly aggressive full-moon cycle.
The following month, he went through transformation and with-
drawal simultaneously, and killed two heroin kingpins.

Though Fritz, and later Carol, when she dropped in, did their
best to keep the tone light, something about it reminded Annie of
the people at the Jesus Saves Tabernacle. The people here had the

same drawn, ashen faces, the gritted teeth. That look, Fritz told her, came as much from the physical rigours of LMD drug therapy as it did from their days of drinking.

That evening, Fritz went with her to Liz's party for the sixteen-year-old daughter of a garment manufacturer who'd had some business setbacks. He wanted to stick to the smallest budget possible, while his teenage daughter wanted the best of everything and was oblivious to his financial difficulties. Liz was almost schizo from running between them, and she took it out on her friends, as usual, even on Fritz, who bit his tongue and behaved himself, as he had promised Marco. The next night he accompanied Annie to a "Divahead" party Liz got them into. Fritz didn't even know what a Divahead – a Tweets term – was, as he didn't read "Dear Tweets" or the newspaper it was in, finding it too politically liberal. He wasn't a fan of gossip, in any event. A Divahead, Henry explained, was a small woman with a big head made even larger by an enormous hairdo. Cindy Adams, Eartha Kitt, and Imelda Marcos were the world's reigning Divaheads since Barbara Walters had gone for a flatter, more conservative 'do. Lara Flynn Boyle and Calista Flockhart were budding Divaheads. This party was crawling with Divaheads and other celebrities, including the guy who wrote the "Dear Tweets" column, which they could all quote like Scripture.

Fritz kept mum while Liz barked orders and Henry gossiped, but he was taking careful notes: Liz was selfish and snappish, Henry was needy and shallow and couldn't be trusted to keep a secret. In the short time Fritz spent with Henry, he learned that Rosemary Frost was addicted to painkillers and was husband-hunting with an elephant gun.

Liz thought Fritz was dating Annie, and at one point said to him, "I love her dearly, but she's not the sharpest knife in the drawer."

Afterwards, he reported all this to Marco, who asked Annie about her friends during their next one-on-one session.

"I've known them since we went to secretarial college together," she said.

"They don't seem to care about you," he said.

"They do. They just can't show it," she said, knowing she was lying. Ever since her LMD had manifested, she had sensed their souls as shallow pools of stagnant water. Liz's was slightly more dank, but they were otherwise identical.

"They sound terribly shallow, and I don't think they see the real you, Annie." Marco's voice caught in his throat when he said that. He took his glasses off and polished them to cover up for the moment of emotion. "You're very special. Maybe you shouldn't spend so much time with them."

So she made excuses with Liz and Henry and stopped returning their calls. Then one day, not long before the full moon, Marco said, "I think you should stay here a little longer. I'll let you know when you can go home."

All this was fine with her. Dr. Marco knew best. It was nice in the Centre, and safe. She liked the other werewolves she had met. After her last day at Syn-EG, which was marked with a standard-issue cake, a fifteen-minute party in the legal department conference room, and a search of her belongings by security to make sure she wasn't stealing Syn-EG property, Annie began working for the Centre, helping Carol in the kitchen and Marco in the office.

One evening a few days before the full moon, she was filing some financial information from a patient named Tom Voss when she decided to snoop for – and found – a file on Jim Valiente. Inside was a picture. He wasn't overly good looking; in fact, at first glance he looked sort of average. But he looked kind. His face was open, he was smiling, his eyes were blue, but an unusually deep blue. They projected intelligence and warmth. He had great charisma, even in a still photo.

Looks can be deceiving, Annie thought, closing the file and putting it away, then taking it out again to read about Jim, a writer. Before Marco had brought him in, he had killed twice, first a child pornographer and then a foreign student found to have the instructions and makings for a car bomb at the house he was renting.

There were copies of articles Jim had written for *Esquire*, *City Magazine*, the *Sunday Times*, and *The Washington Post*. There were some reports about his treatment. The file looked like it had once been fatter. Five years were missing between his initial admittance to the Centre and the last report, which said, simply, "Deceased."

26

Marco prepared Annie carefully for the full moon. As it approached and her lupine instincts strengthened, he upped the dosage of her drugs and began his hypnosis program. He knew it was risky to use her as bait to bring Jim in, but it was the only way without calling his father and asking him to send cousin Rudolfo, the tracker, up to help.

When Marco told her of the plan, she asked, "Is that safe?"

"We think so. We think you can get to him in a way we can't. Mike and I will be flanking you, close enough to keep your scent and trail, but out of sight. This is important, Annie. You must try to follow my orders. Listen for my thoughts in your head."

"Okay."

"Before transformation, I'm going to hypnotize you, just like I've done in therapy. Once you start to transform, I'll give you stronger drugs to suppress your sexual desire and calm you. This will make you more receptive to my thoughts. You understand?"

"Yes."

"We're going to do everything we can to keep you safe. It will be easier to do this if you relinquish control to me. Think you can do this?"

"I'm great at taking orders," Annie said.

"You're a good girl."

"Oh no, I'm not," she said. "But thank you for saying that."

"Oh yes, you are. You really light up the place. You're like . . . You . . . Well, I shouldn't say . . ."

He looked away. When he looked back again, he smiled and said, "Let's go over it again . . ."

Every day for two hours, one in the morning and one at night, he hypnotized and tested her. She responded well, but she responded best with a Zonex supplement, he found. He was confident they would be able to corner Jim and take care of him, whatever that entailed. Then the problem would be solved, and he wouldn't have to dodge his father's phone calls any more.

27

Jim knew that Marco would be coming after him the next night, using Annie as bait. That was certain. Marco wouldn't be alone. If his protégé was up to snuff, he'd bring him. If not, he'd bring in Rudolfo, who was not LMD but had a powerful sense of smell and been trained in all things werewolf. Rudolfo was cold-blooded, efficient and deceptive. When Jim had first met him he'd almost laughed. He'd been expecting some hulking muscleman with nostrils that flared and flapped like those of a bloodhound. Instead he met a short, slender man with wire-rimmed glasses and all the charisma and deadly skill of an IRS auditor.

He hoped it would be the protégé, whoever he was, because then he'd have a chance of getting away and getting Annie. With Rudolfo it would be tricky. Rudolfo did his tracking on a Vespa, armed with two guns, one a tranquilizer gun, the other a powerful shotgun, and there was no doubt in Jim's mind which one Rudolfo would use on Jim. Despite what the ads in the *Eye* said, or what Marco had probably told Annie, Jim knew they had no intention of bringing him back into the program. Marco couldn't risk it. He'd either kill Jim with an overdose as soon as he had him, or he'd have Rudolfo shoot him.

It didn't matter though. He was scared tonight, but he knew he had to go out looking for her the next night. He could feel it in

his bones. Whatever happened to Jim, Marco would not let the
female be killed – not tomorrow night, at least.

28

The Mayor was dining alone, except for his security guards posted
near the door and cops outside the restaurant, a mom-and-pop
Chinese place called the Lido Chop Suey House, not far from the
original Marva Foods store in his old neighbourhood. It was five-
thirty P.M., and the restaurant was closed to the public until seven
to allow the Mayor his privacy. Until now, these dinners had been
a closely-held secret, but tonight there were news media outside
the front and back entrances, waiting to ask him about the Mad
Dog Murders. The staff had to pull the shades on the windows to
keep the cameras from peering in.

The owner, Grant Ho, son of the original owner, Bing Ho,
apologized. "I don't know how they heard about it, your Honour."

"People talk. Don't worry," said the Mayor, though he was
worried, being caught out here without Seth to help him brave
the blinding cameras. He was waiting for a call from the Police
Commissioner. To keep anyone from surveilling his cell phone, he'd
asked the Police Commissioner to call the restaurant phone with
any updates on the hunt for Bruno Barotti, who was believed to
be somewhere by the airport.

In the old days, this place would be packed with people from
the neighbourhood, talking, laughing, clattering dishes, the exotic
sounds of Chinese punctuating it all. Bing was his own maître d'
and sometimes waiter, and his wife, Mai-Wen, presided in the
kitchen. When Grant and his sisters, Amy and Patsy, were old
enough, they helped out too.

How different things would be if the Mayor's son or daughter
had taken over Marva Foods. Then he wouldn't have sold the

business, he wouldn't be Mayor, and Marva might be sitting across the table from him sharing some House Special Chop Suey. Like in the old days.

Every Saturday night after they closed the store, they'd come here. Their first apartment had been across the street, before they had children and long before they left the neighbourhood for a large house near the river. At night, they could see the neon sign that said "Lido" in big turquoise letters with a red neon outline. Marva had made curtains that filtered out the brightness of the sign while letting in the glow. They'd thought it was romantic.

He felt tears pooling in his eyes, and closed his eyes to blink them back. He never used to cry like this, and it wasn't a good time to now, with cameras outside. That's all he needed, to be caught crying on camera. What would the media make of that, not to mention the interest groups and political hacks, or the men he defeated for this job? How would he explain without revealing that his wife wanted a divorce?

Most women would have loved to be the First Lady of a big city. As the *Downtown Eye* had asked, "How else could people like Rudy Giuliani and Marion Barry have snagged such hot chicks?" But not Marva. Marva couldn't take all the attention and she was trying to carve out her own identity as an artist. She didn't want anything to come to her because she was Mrs. Mayor. She didn't even like his politics that much, as it turned out, and had supported his run for mayor only, she admitted honestly, "because I didn't think you'd win."

Now he'd gained the world, or the city at least, and lost his wife. He thought he'd done almost everything right. He'd worked hard to look after the family, built a thriving business, consulted with Marva on all the big decisions. Not once did he forget a birthday or an anniversary. Most of all, he loved her.

He had finished his meal and was opening his fortune cookie when the Police Commissioner called and interrupted his blue-tinted reverie of youthful romance and marriage.

"Barotti and his dogs were sighted last night out near the airport. We're moving in on his suspected location now."

"I'll meet you there," the Mayor said.

29

Bruno Barotti watched the coverage on the cable television in his motel room and he was terrified. How soon before the police caught him? How would he prove he and his dogs had not killed those people?

He couldn't. Now he regretted all those times he'd threatened people with his dogs. The only damage they'd ever done was biting off that terrier's ear, and the terrier was provoking them. Clearly, this was part of the greater conspiracy against him, the one that had tormented him all his life and inspired him to buy the two dogs to protect himself from the secret police. But who would believe him? Madonna, maybe. Madonna understood.

Luckily for him, the motel was run by an old couple who didn't watch the news because it depressed them. He'd had groceries delivered and paid cash for them while wearing a germ mask over his face. But the dogs were a problem. They barked sometimes, and they had to be walked.

They were whining to go outside now. He wouldn't take them far, just around the back of the motel.

"Come here Lourdes, come here Rocco," he said, holding up their leashes. The dogs bounded for him. Once attached, they strained for the door.

As soon as he opened it, he heard a quick round of clicks and was blinded by the white of media lights and the strobing red police lights.

"Bruno Barotti, don't move," said a voice.

III

The Sturgeon Moon

August

30

The moon was visible all day, what Annie's late grandmother used to call a "sunshine moon."

"When the moon shows itself during the day, it means good things are coming to light," Grandma Kay had said, and she stuck to that belief even though shortly after she told Annie this, Grandma Kay broke her hip and her third husband, Mr. Fitz, had a stroke that left him unable to do much more than hum and blink meaningfully. While the other girls at Our Lady of Peace High School were going to shop at the mall or meet Puerto Rican boys at the park, Annie went home on the bus to tend to Grandma and Mr. Fitz after the private nurse left. Grandma Kay, a constant talker, commented on the television or complained from her bed, while Mr. Fitz hummed from his like an insane wasp, no longer able to argue with her or escape by wandering off to Ruth Flannery's bar when Grandma Kay's back was turned. Grandma Kay always thought he willed the second stroke that sent him to the hospital, where he died.

The sunshine moon didn't seem lucky or unlucky today, but it did seem powerful, as strong as the sun, casting a silver light more visible to Annie than the gold of the sun, and giving all the people on the street a strange luminescence.

After dinner, and after the patients in confinement had been dosed and tended, Marco took Annie aside to hypnotize her. When she seemed to be in a suggestive state, Marco tested it.

"Who are you going to obey tonight?" he asked.

"You."

"Who are you going to obey?"

"You."

"And only me."

"And only you."

"Snort like a pig."

She did. She was very suggestible.

"Mike, hand me the needle," Marco said. He gave Annie a shot of Depo-Provera to suppress her sexual desire, Valium to calm her, and Zonex to numb her emotionally.

"Help me take her up to the roof."

The sun was just setting. The full moon was due to rise at 10:03. It was now 8:50. Mike was to stay with her while Marco checked the patients downstairs in the confinement room, where Carol was supervising. Mike had scraped up some ketamine, but not nearly enough, and Marco had given them a lot of Thorazine mixed with some injectable Zonex to calm them down. It was going to be a rough night, and Carol was nervous. She'd handled confinement without Marco before, and without ketamine, but never without Mike, never all by herself.

When Marco got back to the roof, it was 9:25 and Annie was already in the initial stages of transformation. The hypnosis and the drugs had calmed her somewhat and made her suggestible, but they hadn't slowed down the physical metamorphosis. She was writhing on the roof, wearing just a bathrobe. The sounds of the evening became louder and the smells thicker. She felt a growing buzz inside her, which became a vibration which became a steady hum, like that of an engine, pushing something deep inside her to the surface. She was breathing very quickly.

"I'd better give you your shot," Marco said to Mike. Mike was getting an adrenaline and testosterone mixture. Like Marco, Mike had learned to suppress transformation, and now that they had to do the opposite, he needed a boost.

Annie watched Marco and Mike. She heard sounds coming from their mouths, but she could not longer understand the words. And then, the wrenching cramps began. Her body contorted. She thrashed on the ground, twisting and moaning in an inhuman way. She was changing much faster than she should, given the drugs in her system. Mike was only in the early stages, Marco hadn't started at all. He did so now, giving himself a shot like Mike's.

Annie's sweet, musky scent filled the air around them. Marco breathed it in. It helped him summon up his wolf. Annie's moan became a howl. Her limbs unclenched, and she jumped to her paws much more easily than in previous transformations. In the twilight, her eyes glowed a pale, luminous amber. She looked at Marco and growled softly, then turned and began to gallop across the roof, leaping across a wind shaft to the next building.

Mike was almost fully transformed. Marco pushed himself through the cramps until his limbs unknotted and he was able to jump up on all fours. Mike followed a moment later. Annie was gone, out of sight, but Marco had her scent. He took off running and Mike followed.

3 1

Across from Jim's apartment, Meredith was sitting in her apartment, writing at her desk while facing the window so she could watch Jim's window across the street. She did this every evening, hoping to catch a glimpse of him. Some nights he came out on the fire escape with a notebook and scribbled things down. When it was hot, he went shirtless.

It was clear this man was tortured by something. It had to be love because she never saw him with any women, or anyone, and besides, a man didn't have that look in his eyes unless his heart had been fatally broken. Okay, she was only twenty, but she had seen that look before in the eyes of her lovers. In one case, that of her father's best friend, she was responsible for it.

This was a wounded bird who needed her care. Ever since she had first looked into Jim's eyes, she'd known he was her destiny. The past heartbreak was blocking him from seeing it. He hadn't been married – or so he said after she asked him three times. It wasn't divorce. She'd pretty much decided that it was darker than something like catching a lover in bed with a friend. It was a dead girlfriend. He didn't seem to be in shock, so she probably hadn't died suddenly, but slowly and painfully.

Behind her, a voice said, "Meredith, are you spying on that guy across the street again?"

It was her roommate, Chrissie.

"I'm writing. I'm working on my Edie Sedgwick show."

Chrissie came closer and read over Meredith's shoulder. "'He had nursed her through a long and painful illness, enduring the progressive grief of watching her suffer and slowly slip away from him, and her suffering, to oblivion.' Oh my god. Stop obsessing. The guy's just an antisocial asshole with a crippling fear of intimacy. He's not fucking Heathcliff."

"You don't know him."

"Neither do you."

"I talk to him almost every day."

"Whatever. I'm going down to meet Ahmed and Ariel. Why don't you come?"

"Not tonight, thanks."

"He's probably a junkie."

"'Bye. Have fun."

"Yeah. You too, or whatever."

Obsessing. Please. There was no appreciation for the great emotions any more. This wasn't obsession, it was passion, fate, true love. All great love affairs were passionate, even a little obsessive. What great love affair would pass muster these days? The great French lovers Heloise and Abelard, whose graves she had seen during a semester in Paris? A clear case of an older man, a teacher, taking advantage of his power and years to lure a young, impressionable woman into a doomed affair. Taylor and Burton? Codependent pugilists. These days, everyone was supposed to follow rules, marry their "best friends," and either die of boredom or cheat after a few years.

Jim's window was open, but he hadn't come out. It was getting dark, and the light was off in his apartment. She didn't think he'd go out without closing his window. Maybe he was sleeping.

She saw something move, and reached for the opera glasses by the side of her computer. It was hard to see. His window was dark, but she thought she saw glowing eyes. After she focussed, she saw what looked like the face of a large dog. In a flash, it ran out the window and up the fire escape, then vanished.

When did he get a dog? she wondered. He seemed more of a cat guy. She watched for two more hours to see if he woke up, until her eyes grew tired and she fell asleep, still dressed, in the chair where she was sitting.

32

After saying a prayer, Gunther Hamernich went up to the roof with his gun. If the werewolf came back, he would shoot it. For this task, he had ordered special silver bullets from a company in Oregon. If the lore was true and a werewolf could be killed only by silver bullets, he was prepared. If it wasn't true, well, a silver bullet could kill as well as a lead one.

The police wouldn't listen to him. The FBI wouldn't listen to him. When he called the religious radio station they hung up on him. Even his pastor was skeptical.

"The devil himself is afoot, in the form of a werewolf," Gunther had told the leader of the Jesus Saves Tabernacle.

"The devil lives in all of us, until we accept Jesus Christ as our personal saviour and commit our lives to following the strict rules of God."

"No, I mean a real werewolf, a servant of the devil."

"Gunther, have you been drinking?"

"No, Pastor."

"You're sure?"

"I have not been drinking."

"Have you called the police, then?" the pastor asked, thinking he could pass the buck to the cops.

"Yes, and they told me to call the Special Werewolf Squad at 777-3456. You know what that is?"

"What?"

"Moviephone."

The pastor forced himself not to smile.

"I'm sure the police have it in hand. Didn't they arrest a suspect, Bruno something?"

"Unless he's a werewolf, he's not the killer."

"What you must do is go home, Gunther, and pray, pray hard for those people who still live with the devil."

Gunther himself wouldn't have believed his story, if he hadn't seen it with his own eyes. To see the beast twice in one lifetime seemed to him a message. For some time, he'd been struggling to determine his purpose in God's plan, other than to try to convert the ungodly and keep the knobs oiled and the foyer swept in the building he cared for.

When he saw the werewolf a second time, he knew his purpose. He had been chosen to hunt down the animal and reveal, definitively, the existence of the devil in a world that would not believe in the torments of hell that waited for those who broke God's laws. Everything in his life had led him to this, even those terrible days in the abandoned metro tunnel.

The tunnel had been hell, hot, crawling with vermin, the darkness lit only by the burning of badly ventilated cooking fires. Yet for a time he had preferred it down there to being above ground, where people might see his shame and judge him, a dirty alcoholic, "human waste," as one woman had called him.

Ironically, he had drunk to escape the very life he'd been living, more or less contentedly, since he'd become sober, a quiet life of menial work, rules, and humility before authorities and God. The pastor made him realize the common life he'd run from was his salvation. Compared to the life he'd lived as a drunk, it was paradise.

God had rewarded him by choosing him for a special mission, but even as he thought that, he cautioned himself not to get too grandiose about it. To be chosen was a test of faith and, as with all such missions, the servant should be more humble at completion than he was before undertaking it.

Let the brother of low degree rejoice that he is exalted, James 1:9.

33

Klaus Bendinger wanted to celebrate. He had just sealed a deal on behalf of his company to sell two million cans of special baby formula for lactose-intolerant children to an impoverished Asian country. He had thought they were going to have to write off that inventory after seizures and premature death in some South American babies who were fed the formula. If the mothers who prepared it added an incorrect amount of water, then yes, it could cause problems. But there was no proof yet that it was the fault of the product or the company, and it was unlikely there would ever be proof, since a sample from the supposedly contaminated lot had been secretly switched at the FDA lab with a sample from an improved version of the product that was known to be safe.

As far as Klaus Bendinger was concerned, it wasn't his fault there were so many illiterate people in the world who couldn't read directions. It was unfortunate, but any deaths that resulted were simply a form of Darwinian natural selection.

He was on a roll. The day before, he'd unloaded twenty million Numlex pills in Africa, where they were unlikely to be recalled as they had in the United States. So far, there was only circumstantial evidence linking the pills in that particular lot to the severe psychosis suffered by the 3,706 people who joined together in the class-action lawsuit currently before the courts, 3,706 out of more than a half-million who had taken Numlex with no effects other than a numbing of emotions, which was the point after all. Besides, Syn-EG legal had found a few severe loonies and litigious opportunists among those 3,706, and thought they could use those nuts to discredit the lot of them. They had a chance of wiggling out of it with nothing more than a moderate out-of-court settlement, perhaps even a win.

Officially, all these recalled products were said to have been destroyed. But Klaus had had a better idea. Why not re-label them with different lot numbers and send them to some poor country where people didn't have much and would appreciate them more? Damn, they were lucky to have Numlex and lactose-free baby formula. Most of them lived in huts, for God's sake. If the lactose-free baby formula didn't get them, something else would, dysentery or measles or one of those frightening tropical diseases. They didn't give a damn about a few deaths from side effects. They were too busy trying to get their next bowl of rice.

This would improve his bottom line by a few million instead of costing it, and every million in black ink counted these days if Klaus "Dinger" Bendinger was to get the upper hand and stay in Lord Harry's good books. This was a crucial time. Syn-PHARM and Synergy Biotech (Syn-BIO) were merging the following year into

Syn-HEALTH. Klaus wanted to head Syn-HEALTH. It would kill him to have to work below the head of Syn-BIO, Jed Sutton. Sutton was a young upstart, who at thirty-eight had gained a lot of media attention with Syn-BIO's experimental projects, but his company had been bleeding money like a late-1990s dot-com until recently, when a new antibiotic for resistant infections had come out and brought some profit to the place. Somehow, "Jedhead," as Lord Harry had dubbed him, was still golden in the Old Man's books. Most of his projects were long-term investments, which bought him a lot of leeway.

When the merger was first discussed, very quietly, Lord Harry made it clear he would not go outside Syn-EG, that Dinger and Jedhead were the top candidates to lead the amalgamated subsidiary and he would be looking at all factors before making a decision. As soon as Klaus heard that, he got together with a discreet private investigator he often used and hired him to not only check out Jed Sutton, but to find out if Sutton was checking him out. Sutton was dirt-free, and didn't appear to be investigating Bendinger. He was, however, pulling out all the stops in the media, leaking information about provocative new projects or rumoured projects at Syn-BIO. He got his pretty little face in *People*, *Newsweek*, *Time*, the *Times* business section, and even *City Magazine*, where he was listed as one of the city's One Hundred Most Eligible Bachelors ("a rich, brainy babe who can discuss genetics or particle physics with you before he goes out shirtless to chop you a cord of firewood," according to the writer).

Bendinger, fifty-nine and about as telegenic as Nixon, didn't give a flying fuck about particle physics unless they could make a pill out of it and sell a lot of them, and he hired people to chop firewood.

What he was counting on was his bottom-line achievements, and the need for Syn-HEALTH to have an older, more sober hand at the helm, a fellow South African who had been loyal to Lord Harry all these years, since he started out in the tobacco division in 1968. Klaus had one other thing going for him, something Lord Harry respected almost as much as he respected the ability to spin dimes into dollars – Bendinger would do anything for the company. He knew it was a jungle out there; he played accordingly, and very secretly. Confidence counted more than talent, money more than media, and might still made right, no matter how it was dressed up and spun through the PR machine.

Bendinger would never have admitted it aloud to anyone, but Sutton had shaken his confidence, to the point where he'd begun taking his company's own anti-impotence medication for a boost. One of the side effects of Androx-Y was that it made him feel more confident, almost immortal. Some men might find it distracting to negotiate a deal or chair a meeting with a battering ram in their trousers, but it always made Dinger feel like Superman, especially now that the police had grabbed a suspect in the murders of two of his brother Syn-EG executives.

When he was like this, he could screw all night.

He called his wife.

"I'm still tied up with business. Better have the doorman walk the dog tonight."

"Okaaaay. I'llllll calllll nowwwww," she said. She'd taken her Zonex-PM and would be asleep soon. He called the doorman himself and instructed him to go up to their penthouse apartment and get the dog.

After hanging up, he called one of his mistresses, a publicist he'd met while she was working for his wife's favourite designer. She was at a party downtown but offered to meet him in an hour at their favourite trysting spot, an unmarked, little-known bar that was popular with savvy city folk who were having affairs. The lighting there was somewhere between dim and dark. You could see your way to the bathroom easily enough, but it was hard to make out people's features unless you were up close. There was soft music, soft enough to blend with the whispered conversation to produce a kind of hum, but not so loud as to drown out the whispers. They'd have a couple of drinks, then head to her place. If he was lucky, her roommate would be there too.

Bendinger didn't want to be seen going into the bar, so he had the cab drop him off on a parallel street, a street of warehouses and garages, now closed. He was just rounding the corner towards the bar when something leapt out at him, pushing him to the pavement. The last thing he saw before he departed this Vale of Tears was a pair of wet, golden eyes staring into his.

Annie broke his neck with one snap and then tore at his throat before dragging the body behind a dumpster. Vaguely, in the back of her mind, she heard a wordless voice telling her not to kill, to come back, to obey, but once she'd got a whiff of Bendinger's soul, Marco's voice in her head was drowned out by the stench of rot, of curdled milk and open wounds and dying children – and by another voice that said, definitively, "Kill."

After she'd dispatched Klaus Bendinger, she stuck her snout in the air. She could smell Marco and Mike approaching and she could hear Marco more clearly signalling her to slow down and to obey. More responsive now that the need to kill was out of her system, she hesitated, then stopped to wait for Marco until she heard a low-pitched howl. Jim.

She struggled against it, trying to hew to Marco's commands but feeling the engine inside her driving her towards Jim. She sprang from her spot and ran north, past the piers. He was there waiting by the river.

"Come with me," he thought at her.

She did.

⑥

When Marco and Mike got to the piers, Annie was gone. Her scent lingered there, but when they tried to pick up its direction, they couldn't. It had disappeared, and so had she. Marco sent Mike east and south. He thought clear commands to Mike. "Kill him, bring her home."

Marco headed north, listening for her howl and trying to grab her scent out of the night air. The wind was blowing in from the south, making it hard to get hold of her smell, but every now and then he heard a howl and headed towards it, until the howling stopped.

(5)

Jim took Annie down into an abandoned sewer tunnel, where the air was dank and ripe. She followed him east, until they came up and headed to a small park, where Jim killed a representative of a theocratic Asian country run by a maniacal priest who harboured terrorists, flogged women for everything from unwed sex to wearing white socks, and passed laws make it illegal for children to play, lest it keep them from their religious studies. Annie killed his burly bodyguard.

They returned to the sewer and followed it until they got to an old freight train tunnel, no longer used. Not thinking at all, she followed him as he ran along the weedy, overgrown tracks. It was completely dark, and she had to rely solely on the smell of his body.

Somewhere along the line he turned north, and they surfaced a little farther on in River Park. There, Annie killed Gary "Gipper" Krebs, the head of Syn-FOODS, which made the popular Butternut cookie line as well as Malabar cigarettes. He had that day made a deal to grow and sell high-nicotine tobacco with the representative of a theocratic Asian country where women were flogged and terrorists harboured. This meant eluding certain UN sanctions, which meant the deal was done through a crafty middleman from Cyprus, who was with Krebs. Jim took him out.

They ran south to the river, and that's when Marco picked up their scent again. As he raced towards the river, the smell became stronger and stronger. He'd try to head them off.

Marco wasn't sure if Mike could receive him, but he sent a message anyway, hoping Mike would hear his thoughts, pick up the scent and join him. He couldn't waste time with Annie. He had to get rid of Jim, that was the priority. Once Jim was gone, unable to exert any more influence over Annie, she'd be easy to bring in. He had underestimated the power of the attraction between them, as he had with Jim and Sarah.

At the south end of River Park, Marco saw them approaching, running side by side in the shadows. The wind was now blowing from the west. That was good. It carried their scent to him and blew his scent away from them. That would give him an edge.

He moved swiftly, cutting towards them on a diagonal. Jim was closest to him. He stopped and coiled to spring. When Jim was just feet away, Marco sprang out of the bushes, going straight for Jim's throat.

But he'd misjudged the distance slightly and caught, instead, the bottom of Jim's jaw. He reacted quickly and attacked again. Jim fought back, pushing his forelegs into Marco's chest to keep him from getting a good grip on his neck.

Annie stood to the side, struggling against the competing voices in her head. Marco was exhorting her to come to his assistance against Jim. Jim was urging her to run.

She did neither.

She came to Jim's assistance, jumping on Marco's back and biting his neck. Marco howled in pain. He loosened his grip on Jim. Jim fell away, then got back to his feet. When he attacked again, he got Marco's foreleg, biting it to the bone. Marco collapsed to the ground.

"Run," Jim thought. He turned and headed east. Annie followed as he raced back underground.

The pain was crippling, but Marco knew he had to get up and get back to the Centre. With every bit of strength he had left, he raised his body from the ground and began to limp homeward, keeping to the shadows and moving in fits and starts to avoid being seen. It took him the rest of the night to get home. When he made it back to the roof of the Chelsea, he collapsed. Carol was waiting for him, but when she tried to approach to look at his wounds, he snarled at her, then passed out. Mike Burke was nowhere to be seen.

34

When Annie woke up she felt the sun on her face. She opened her eyes and was blinded for a moment by the brilliant light coming through the window. It took her a moment to realize she was in an unfamiliar room. This wasn't her apartment and it wasn't her room at Carol and Marco's. This was a small bedroom and obviously a man's. Even if the blue and grey colour scheme wasn't a tip-off, or the total lack of frippery, there was a weightlifting bench at one end of the room and men's underwear balled up in a corner. The wood-grain-finish clock radio said 2:35 P.M.

She was completely disoriented, but it only took a few moments to bring everything into focus. She had gone out the night before with Marco and Mike Burke to bring in Jim Valiente, and ended up on a killing spree that had finished here, with a bout of bestial sex before she and Jim collapsed in a heap – on the floor, as she recalled, though she was now in a bed. The bed of a ruthless murderer. Not that she could throw stones. How many had they killed the night before? She could recall killing two, maybe three. And loving it.

In the other room, music was playing quietly: sweet, surreal piano music. It sounded light and lovely and melancholy all at the same time. He must be out there, she thought, and wondered if she could sneak out the bedroom window and get away before he noticed she was gone. First, she'd have to find some clothes to wear, since she was buck naked. And she had to fight the post-kill nausea welling up inside her. She took some deep breaths to steady herself, inhaling and exhaling through the blanket so Jim wouldn't hear her. The blanket smelled like him. The scent smelled good, and, more importantly, it calmed her and settled her stomach for some reason.

As quietly as possible, she slid her sore body out of bed, stepping lightly to the closet. The soft click of the doorknob made her heart jump. She stood, frozen for a moment. Apparently, he hadn't heard her. But when she opened the closet door, it creaked. She stopped again, waited to see if he'd heard, opened the door another crack with another creak, stopped, waited, and managed to open it wide enough to slip a pair of jeans and a shirt off hangers.

The pants were too big so she took a belt off the dresser and cinched them up. Shoes would be a problem. There were fresh socks, still in their store packaging on the dresser, along with a crumpled ten-dollar bill and some change. The socks would have to do for shoes, she decided, and the ten dollars would get her back to the Centre.

When she went to the window, she saw a note, left on the night-stand next to a glass of water and a daisy.

> I had to go out to get some things. Please don't leave. Please trust that gut instinct that brought us together, and hear my story. Marco killed Sarah.
>   Love, Jim.

⑥

Across the street, Meredith watched Jim's window open and reached for her opera glasses. Someone was climbing onto the fire escape, but it wasn't Jim. At first, she thought it was a young man, but closer examination showed it to be a young woman wearing an oversized man's shirt over baggy trousers.

This is the type he goes for? she thought. No wonder then he hadn't yet responded to her, with her youthquaker retrogirl thing. And she'd been so proud of this look too, the Carnaby Street heavy eyeliner and frosted lipstick, the pink and green minidress with bright pink hose, and the silver and white checkerboard go-go boots she seemed destined for because the colours exactly matched the silver and white polka-dot hot pants she already had. It was girly and fun yet distinct from the ubiquitous *Sex and the City* style, which made its devotees look more like aging hookers than whimsical-yet-disturbed libertines.

Maybe it was time for a change of look anyway, now that others were copying hers, and not just downtown girls, but girls from, like, the suburbs.

She watched the woman climb down to the street and hail a cab. Only then did her thoughts turn from the importance of having a winning personal style to more serious questions. Who was she? Why did she leave via the fire escape? Maybe she wasn't a lover, maybe she was a burglar. If Meredith weren't convinced the police were fascist tools of the military-industrial complex, she would have called them. But, unwilling to do that, she had only one option: to use this information to get closer to Jim.

She saw him down on the street, carrying some shopping bags. She watched while he went into his building, then she looked up at his window. A few minutes later the curtains moved, but it was just a stray breeze. It was another five minutes before his head appeared in the window, looking out to survey the length of the street. Then he disappeared again.

Meredith put on her shoes, grabbed her keys off the plastic model of a human hand by the door, and went downstairs to catch him. He was fast but she was faster. When the steel door to his building opened, she was standing there.

"Jim, hey, were you burgled or something?"

"What?" He only gave her a quick glance before looking anxiously up and down the street.

"Were you burgled? I just happened to be looking out my window and I saw a woman leaving down the fire escape – and, well, if you *have* to call the police, I'll be an eyewitness for you."

"No. That wasn't a burglar. It was a friend. I guess my front door, it jammed or something, and she couldn't get out."

Meredith deflated. She'd hoped it was a burglar.

"Oh. And your dog?"

"My dog?"

"Your dog got out through the window last night. Did it come back?"

"It's not my dog. It belongs to a friend," he said. "The girl, when did she leave?"

"About ten minutes ago, maybe longer."

"Which way did she go?"

"She got in a cab and headed uptown."

He held out his arm and hailed a taxi, snapping a quick "Thanks" at Meredith before he took off.

"I need to get to the Chelsea the fastest way possible," he said to the driver.

He should never have gone out. He thought she'd be exhausted from the night before and that whatever drugs Marco gave her would make her sleep longer. He wanted to get a few things which would make her feel more comfortable, little things, like a fresh toothbrush. She could have used his. I mean, they'd licked the blood of their kills off each other the night before, what would be the big deal about using someone else's toothbrush? But women were weird about these things.

There wasn't much chance he'd catch her now, but he had to try. She'd written something on the bottom of his note. "I won't give you away. But please leave me alone and get help."

He looked at those two sentences from every possible angle. She didn't believe him. Or did she? Why would she promise not to give him away, unless she had some faith in him, and at least a seed of doubt about Marco?

⑥

She had seeds of both faith and doubt, and she felt the conflict between them, along with the nausea, as the cab neared the Chelsea. She asked the driver to pull over so she could throw up in the gutter. The driver wanted to make good and sure she was finished before she pulled herself back in the cab, and so insisted on waiting there a few minutes, to be certain there wouldn't be any aftershocks.

When she said she was fine, he said, "No, take some more deep breaths. Be sure."

"I'm sure I'm fine now."

If she had listened to the driver and waited, Jim might have caught up to her and stopped her from going into the hotel. But by the time he got there, she was gone, already in the elevator on her way up to the Centre.

35

The TV news was full of stories about the killing spree the night before – six victims: two executives of Syn-EG, a bodyguard, a foreign dignitary from an Asian theocracy, and two unidentified males. Which ones Mike had killed, or Annie, or Joe, Marco didn't know, but the city was going nuts. The police had arrested the wrong man, Bruno Barotti. The real killer and his mad dogs were still on the loose, according to the news media, and the Mayor was looking more and more embattled.

Marco watched CCN, while ignoring his father's frantic phone calls, every hour on the hour.

Not only had Marco lost Annie, Mike Burke hadn't come back either. Marco had thought he could count on Mike. Ah, but then, he had thought the same thing about Jim, years earlier. In fact, he'd thought much better of Jim than Mike, as Jim was brighter. Still, Mike was more obedient, easier to get along with. He seemed unlikely to challenge the status quo. With Mike it was clearly a case of mentor and pupil, and Marco expected he would return soon.

That had been his mistake with Jim, he thought, elevating him to his own level, which gave him the confidence to take liberties and, ultimately, to leave. Marco had taught Jim chess, and taken him with Carol to the opera; Jim had taken Marco to baseball games and weird downtown theatres, one night to Billy's Topless à Go-Go. Sometimes they'd broken the beer rule and gone up to the roof to shoot the shit, talk about their fathers and first loves, or just generally whine about how hard life was for a wolfman.

Then Sarah had arrived in Camelot.

Thinking about all this again got him into such a stew that when Carol knocked on the door and said, "Annie's back," he snapped, "Where the hell was she? Get her in here. Then bring me some tea. With caffeine in it!"

Instead of being relieved, he was furious.

"You took off, you killed, ignoring my instructions," he barked as soon as Annie stepped into his office. "You fought me."

"I'm sorry," Annie said. "It was the wolf in me."

"That shouldn't have happened. I hypnotized you and gave you shots so —"

"I couldn't help it!"

"I don't expect you to be able to control yourself on your own," he said. "But if I can't control you we've got a problem. Where's Mike?"

"I don't know. Isn't he here?"

The phone rang and the answering machine picked up.

"Marco, this is your father! For God's sake call me about this mess you've —" Annie heard before Marco got to the volume button and turned it down.

Marco was so embarrassed to have been chewed out by his father in front of Annie, he lost his temper completely.

"I don't know what Jim told you, but he's to blame for Sarah's death, not me. He mixed the drugs that killed her. That's why he faked his own death. I had nothing to do with it. Sarah may have imagined I was in love with her, but she imagined a lot of things, and so did Jim!"

Annie hadn't mentioned a word about Jim's note. Marco just assumed Jim had spoken with her. "I don't know what you —" she began to say.

"He killed her, not me. Sarah broke up with him and Jim cracked."

"Yeah, that's what Carol said before —"

"Where is Jim? He's got to be dealt with."

"I don't know where he is." That was a big fat lie. Before she'd
gotten into the cab, she'd turned and noted the address. Why this
instinct to protect Jim?

"You don't know?" Marco said.

"I was disoriented. I don't know where I was. I found some
clothes and put them on."

"How did you get home?"

"There was money in the pocket so I used it to get a cab back
here."

"I didn't kill Sarah," he said again. "I didn't."

"Okay."

"I'm going to hypnotize you to see what you can remember
about Jim."

"Dr. Marco, I'm exhausted. I'm about to drop. Jim Valiente isn't
going anywhere."

"How do you know?"

"He was unconscious when I snuck out and he didn't look like
he was going anywhere for a day or two," she lied, again.

"Can't risk it. I'll give you a little something to perk you up
a bit."

"May I take a quick shower?" she asked. "The smell of killing
and everything, it's making me ill."

"I'll hypnotize you first —"

"Can I at least . . . pee?"

"Okay," he said.

In "her" room, she sat for a moment on the bed. Why was
Marco so defensive? He had made her feel really uncomfortable,
and now she didn't know what to believe. Unable to sense either
man's true soul, she was lost. She wanted to believe Jim. But why
would Marco kill Sarah?

What she needed was to get out of there, she decided, go somewhere to clear her head and look at things more objectively.

She left a note: "I had to go home. I'll be back." Then she
changed into her own clothes and grabbed her purse. While Marco

was in his office and Carol was in the kitchen, she slipped out, running down the stairs to the lobby and out to the street, planning to go home, sleep in her own bed, and get her bearings.

At the corner Jim saw her. His cab crept up beside her.

He rolled down his cab window. "Hi. Remember me? From last night?"

He looked different from his picture. His hair was short now, almost a brush cut, and dyed sandy blond. He was heavier and wearing dark glasses.

"Get in," he said.

"I'm not going anywhere with you. I'm don't want to be around any of you right now." She started to walk away, stopped and turned around.

"Marco wants to hypnotize me to find out where you live so you'd better go away," she said. "I don't know why I should care —"

"Come on, get in. We'll go somewhere safe where we can talk. I know a nice soup place, a public place."

"A public place?"

"Yes," he said.

"Why?"

"We need to talk," he said.

36

"Green pea and ham," Jim said to the waiter.

"Vegetarian vegetable," Annie said.

As soon as the waiter left, Jim said, "I wasn't responsible for Sarah, not directly. But I did break the fraternization rule, and I fell in love with her."

He felt funny saying that. What woman wants to hear a man talk about the last great love of his life on their first date? And this was a first date in a sense, even though they had killed together and had sex already – naked, grunting, public sex. It could be the last date too. He had one shot to convince her she should give up her old life and the Centre, and live as a free werewolf, with him. He didn't want to blow it.

"It happened by accident. I was helping her adjust to being a werewolf and spending a lot of time with her and Marco and Carol. Then I started seeing her on the sly, by myself. Marco was trying to keep her away from the other werewolves as much as possible. They're a bunch of lonely guys. Even if they weren't werewolves, most of them would have a hard time maintaining a relationship."

"Who doesn't?"

"Yeah, well, it's harder if you're a werewolf, and female were-wolves are scarce. Drop a female in the middle of that bunch of horny misfits and you're going to have trouble. Every straight guy in the program fell for Sarah. Even Marco fell for her. I bet he didn't tell you that."

"No."

"It was obvious. He started dressing better, wearing cologne. He took most of the grey out of his hair. Everything Sarah said was charming and everything Carol said made Marco cringe. He was completely charmed by Sarah. But I didn't think it was serious at first."

"Did Carol know Marco was in love with Sarah?"

"I don't know, she never showed it. But you know Marco keeps her on Valium and who knows what else," he said. "We figured Marco would come around because we were in love. Rules have to bend for love. When we told him, he seemed annoyed, but he didn't seem psycho."

"Marco said you gave her the IV that killed her."

"Yes, but Marco prepared the IV, I just hooked it up. He gave her the initial dose of ketamine, then left me to hook up the IV while he went down to do the other patients. I always hooked up her IV, but I wasn't allowed to mix the drugs. Program policy." Jim swallowed hard. When he spoke again, he said, "She was on the bed, manacled. She was sedated but conscious. We joked around a bit. We said, 'I love you.' I hooked up the IV and she said, 'See you on the other side of the moon, babe.' That was the last thing she said to me."

The waiter brought their soups and a basket of hot bread.

"I checked her the next morning. She was dead."

"It could have been an accident."

"It could have been. But in this case, it wasn't an accident. It was murder."

"How do you know?"

"Because he accused me of it. He accused me of loading the IV with an intentional overdose. The best defence is a good offense, right? We were alone in his office and we both knew he'd mixed the IV, but he could stand there with a straight face and accuse me. I knew he'd done it, and I knew then that he had been more in love with Sarah than she or I realized. If he had the balls to lie barefaced to the one guy who knew the truth, what chance did I have to make the others believe me?"

"Wouldn't the other werewolves —"

"The other werewolves were completely dependent on Marco and they all loved Sarah and needed to blame someone. I got the hell out of there."

For two weeks, he stayed in a cheap hotel in the Meatpacking District, he told her, the kind of place that always smelled of boiled cabbage, and where he shared the bathroom with two disgruntled bachelor postal workers and an elderly lady who had recently been released from a mental institution.

"I couldn't go back to the Centre, but even if I could have, even if I'd wanted to, Marco would do me in. I knew it. I thought I could control the wolf on my own with tranquilizers and self-hypnosis, but the grief of losing Sarah, and my anger — it was overwhelming. I no longer had that control. The next full moon I transformed and killed two men. I knew Marco was hunting me and that he'd probably brought in Rudolfo, his father's tracker. I had to get out of the city."

"So you faked your own death."

"And I fled to India to look for this werewolf I'd heard about, who lived as a man and a natural werewolf in a wildlife preserve. About six months ago I came back."

"Why?"

"It was time. I can't explain it any other way," he said.

She was silent.

"Do you have any other questions?"

"I have a hundred," she said. "I don't know what to do now. Even after what you've told me, a part of me wants to go back to the Centre. If I go back there, I can live a more or less normal life."

"Less, not more, and for how long? There's a fifty per cent chance a patient will die of an overdose during the first four years of his treatment program. Or the ketamine and other drugs may just fry your brain, make you permanently insane. It's rarely a long life at the Centre."

"What's the alternative?" Annie asked. "One can't go around killing people during the full moon."

"Why not?"

"It's wrong!"

"Is it wrong when a frog kills a fly? Annie, everything in nature has some purpose. In us, it's nature, not nurture. It's not a bad childhood because your mom didn't love you or your daddy beat you. It's not selfishness or cruelty or any of that human misery. It's nature's plan. Our purpose is to prey on predators, thin the herd of villains, and help maintain the balance of good and evil in the world."

"Villains? I've mainly killed men who worked for my company, Syn-EG. Businessmen in grey suits married to, like, Miss Flaming Gorge Utah —"

"That oil man, Bingham?"

"Yes."

"He ran Syn-PET operations in a small sub-Saharan country where they were crucifying the people of the south for not con-

verting to the north's religion. These people were literally being
crucified, on crosses in the hot desert sun. When they were dead,
their orphaned children were sold into slavery," he said.

"That's terrible! But that's not Syn-PET's fault. And it's not their
job to solve all the problems of the world. They are there to
develop the economy, which is good for a country –"

"Company girl," he said. He smiled a little when he said it. Very
disarming. "Some companies do that. But Syn-PET and its parent,
Syn-EG, do not. They suck out everything they can and send it
home to Lord Harry. Loot and leave. They impoverish countries
they work in, they don't enrich them."

"Well, it isn't their right or responsibility to get involved in the
internal politics of a country," she said, not smiling back.

"But they did get involved. They do all the time, Annie."

He was very passionate as he spoke. It turned her on – against
her better counsel.

"In this case, the southern rebels fought back and were making
gains. The rebels were getting close to the oil company's operations, which are in the southern part of the country even though
the proceeds go to the dictatorship in the north. Bingham appealed
to the government to crush the rebels and hired its own merce-
naries, supposedly to protect their property but, in fact, to help the
government brutally put down the rebellion."

"I never heard about that."

"It was being investigated, but witnesses died, people were paid
off, the oil company got a big PR firm and implicitly threatened to
pull its advertising from any media organ which covered the story.
It was covered, despite that, by CNN and some newspapers, but not
widely. It happened in Africa. That whole continent would have
to explode before it registered here."

"Why didn't Bingham go to the government and say, stop the
crucifixions and child slavery or we'll yank our business out of
here?" Annie asked. "Don't answer that. I know the answer. The
government would just give their oil leases to some other company."

"Right."

"How do you know this about Syn-PET?"

"I did some research on your victims."

"What about Peter Gorgon?"

"Heads Synergy Defense Industries. What is their motto? 'Protecting Democracy'?"

"Protecting the Free World," she said.

"An awful lot of their weapons end up in the hands of dictatorships the government is friendly with, and from there into the hands of unfriendly dictatorships and private armies. People who torture and execute . . . and crucify dissidents. You want to talk about killers, Annie?"

"Armin Sunga, the importer-exporter?"

"I don't know, but I'm sure he was up to no good. Import-export can be used as a cover for everything from guns to under-age Albanian girls," he said.

"But it's not right to go around being judge, jury, executioner —"

"You didn't judge Robert Bingham. You didn't think, there goes a man whose greed empowers other evil people and kills the innocent, I think I'll rip his throat out. You smelled evil, and your natural instinct told you it was your job to take him out."

"Why me? I was an altar girl. I'm nice," she said, her voice trembling. "I don't think I'm cut out to be an assassin. I feel guilty if I hurt people's feelings."

"You were born to do it. And you're good at it," he said. "Look. Stay with me. We'll get to know each other. If, before the next full moon, you want to leave, you can go."

"I can?"

"I didn't tie you up, did I?"

"No."

"I left you alone in my apartment. You were free to leave then, and you did. You're free to leave now if you don't believe me," he said.

Annie was silent, not knowing what to believe. It all boiled down to whether she wanted to return to the Centre, be reintegrated into the normal world, perhaps at some risk to her health, and rat out Jim to Marco – or shack up with a known serial killer.

She took a big whiff of his body smell, which was wafting over the table at her, and hers at him, and to everyone in the restaurant, as neither of them had had time to shower. She remembered what Marco had said to her during one of their sessions, how this was just a physical attraction, and she could resist it if she mustered up the will.

But she didn't.

"I can leave any time?" she asked.

37

Jim's living room was a sunny shade of pale blue and lightly cluttered with books. It doubled as his office area. By the window was a desk with a computer, a coffee cup and stacks of clippings. Above it, taped to the wall, was a large calendar, with the phases of the moon marked.

"Make yourself at home," he said.

"Can I take a shower? I feel gross."

"Let me put fresh towels in the bathroom for you. Oh, and I bought you a toothbrush this morning, before you took a flyer."

"You bought me a toothbrush?"

"I thought you might not want to use mine, that it'd just be nice for you –"

She looked at him, hard. "Thanks. That was . . . thoughtful."

While she showered, he changed the sheets on the bed and placed a vase of flowers beside it. She came out of the bathroom wearing a pair of his pyjamas and a bathrobe, her hair wet and slicked down.

"You can sleep here. I'll take the sofabed," he said.

"Great," she said and crawled into bed. It was just dusk, but Annie was feeling very tired. Jim turned off the overhead light. The waning moon made their faces glow a dim silver.

"You look" – he sought the word – "ethereal in this light."

"Oh. Uh. Thank you," she said, looking away for a moment. She'd never been good with compliments on those rare occasions she'd received them.

"You need anything?" he asked.

"No. But can we . . . talk?"

"Yeah." He sat down on the edge of the bed. "Annie, Annie what? I don't even know your last name."

"Annie Engel. You're Jim Valiente."

"I go by Jim Black now. What do you do?"

"I was a legal secretary at Syn-EG. I recently quit, on Marco's advice."

"Stopped seeing your old friends? Your family? That's Marco's M.O., his 'control strategy.'"

"I have no family left."

"I'm sorry to hear that."

"It's okay. I'm used to it."

"So, uh, you were a legal secretary. But that isn't what you wanted to be when you were a little girl."

"I wanted to be a painter."

"Do you paint?"

"I dabble. I'm not very good. What do you do?"

"I'm a ghostwriter," he said. "I write books for other people. I get no credit, but the money's very good and the hours are flexible."

"Have you written anything I've read?"

"Did you read Pam Jacoby's book about her time working with Mother Teresa in India?"

"You wrote that?"

"Yeah. Did you read it?"

"No, but I heard about it. She was on *The Beth Tindall Show* talking about it. A friend of mine works on that show. What else have you written?"

"I just turned in a book about quarterback Bud Beckman's emotionally troubled childhood as a circus kid."

"Why don't you write your own book?"

"With my luck it'd be an *Oprah* pick and I'd get famous. We werewolves can't afford to bring any attention to ourselves so we can't ever become too successful. I work hard at making my writing good, but not too good, and publish under the client's name only, to avoid any kind of fame."

"What an odd problem to have. I have friends who are working as hard as they can to become famous."

"We're odd creatures," he said. "Anyway, that's why I ghost-write."

"A werewolf and a ghost!" she said. "But you could write under a pseudonym."

"I wrote a lot of stuff from India under the name Jim Black, magazine pieces mainly. But things are different in America. It's risky to expose yourself or your work here, especially if you're a werewolf," he said.

"Where did you grow up?" she asked.

In quiet voices, they gave the first-date summaries of their childhoods. She was an orphan raised among the elderly in the old neighbourhood; he was raised by his father, now dead, after his mother vanished one night.

"Mom did that a lot," he said. "She'd take off for a night or two at a time, no word to anyone, and she'd come back dishevelled and naked. One night she took off and never returned. The whole neighbourhood thought she was a drunk and a tramp. So did I. She was the great family shame."

"She was —"

"Yeah, I realized later she was a werewolf, and had probably been killed. That's why she didn't return."

"I'm sorry."

"Me too."

"My Grandma Kay used to talk about her grandfather in Belfast. He used to disappear for days at a time and come home naked and filthy," Annie said. "She said it was because he was English. She was kind of a bigot when it came to the English. I never thought about it before, but he must have been the werewolf in the . . ."

"The werewolf in the woodpile?"

"On one side. I don't know much about the other side of the family."

She yawned, then apologized for yawning.

"Don't apologize. You're tired. You should get some sleep," he said.

"No, I'm fine," she said. She yawned again. "What was India like? I've always been curious about it."

"India. India is an amazing country," he said. "It's like a trip through the collective id. The beautiful things in your dreams and the horrible things in your nightmares, they're real in India —"

She was asleep. He watched her sleep for a while. Her mouth fell open. She snored lightly.

@

He'd been up before her that day, and stayed up later, but the next morning he was up before her again.

"How do you have so much energy?" she said. "I'm exhausted."

"You get used to transformation, and it gets easier. It's a lot easier than confinement and ketamine. You want some coffee?"

"Yes. Please."

"I'll run down and get some."

"I could make you coffee," she said.

"I don't have a coffee maker."

"I could go get you coffee."

"Nah. It's better if I go down. I'll just throw on some clothes. Cappuccino?"

"Thanks, yes. That would be nice." She was craving caffeine.

Before he went to the Pink Pony, he stopped to get newspapers and a bottle of vitamins specially formulated for women. There'd be other things to buy soon. She'd need clothes and they'd have to dye her hair and do a few other things to make her less recognizable.

At the Pink Pony he went straight to the counter to order from the barista. Meredith sidled up to him and said, "Hello! Getting your coffee to go? Why don't you sit a while?"

He almost didn't recognize her. Gone was the thick black sixties eyeliner, artificial mole, and frosted-pink lipstick. She was almost bare-faced and instead of one of her go-go-girl minidresses she was wearing a too-large men's shirt over pants that bagged at her ankles. When she reached into her pocket, he saw that the pants were way too big for her too, and were cinched at the waist with a plain brown belt.

"Can't. Work," he said.

"When will you be finished work? Because I'm doing a script reading of my Edie show at Over Here next week –"

"Next week's terrible, but break a leg, okay?"

The barista put two double caps in takeout cups on the counter.

"Those both for you?" Meredith asked.

He almost said "No," but caught himself in time, and just smiled.

When he gave Annie the flowers, the vitamins, and the coffee, she said, "You thought to get me vitamins?"

She looked up at him in such a grateful, sweet way, he wondered if anyone had ever been thoughtful with her. He couldn't help it – he leaned over and kissed her. She kissed him back. Human, she was shy, but there was still enough of the wolf coursing through her to overcome that. The foam dissolved and the coffee grew cold while they got to know each other in bed.

3 8

"**W**e're going to have police boats all around the city and choppers above. The bridges and tunnels will be manned by teams on each end," the Mayor said, pointing to a large map under a sign that said, "Operation Harvest Moon." The Police Commissioner was flanking him on one side, his media guy, Seth Kirk, on the other. They were speaking to the leading cops on the force, liaisons from the FBI and the army, along with Lord Harry Teufel and other members of the Mayor's task force.

"Every beat cop, bike cop and patrol car in the city will be on the job. The FBI and the Green Berets are sending men and K-9s. The military are lending us night-vision equipment. As you see, we've divided the city into different-coloured sectors. The killer always strikes in a deserted area after getting his victim alone. We want to concentrate on the most vulnerable areas.

"Each team will have a name corresponding to the sector it is in charge of. You will radio to each other and to the command post set up in each sector. The command posts will report to us here at Command Central.

"Memorize the codebook because you will have to use the code for all radio contact. We don't want anyone to know what we're up to. Anyone. Do not tell your colleagues who are not directly involved in the operation. Do not tell your wives or girlfriends, your priests, your shrinks, or your bartenders. Don't leave any information about this anywhere. Either lock it up safely, shred it, or carry it on your person. We will tolerate *no* leaks of any kind. We have a gag order in place. If one word of this gets out, we will find out who leaked and you'll be prosecuted."

They went over the schedule for test runs, how meetings would be conducted, who was in charge of the various parts of the operation and what the chain of command would be. There was a Q and A, and then the Mayor said, "We have less than a month. That's not much time."

The meeting broke up. At this point, Lord Harry, used to being the biggest potentate in any room, stood up and barked, "Let's get it together fast, and do it right. I've lost four of my best men. I can't afford to lose any more."

Meaning what? The Mayor wondered. He could afford to lose four men? Those four lives were disposable?

On the way out, Lord Harry added, almost as an afterthought, "And their wives and children can't afford to lose any more husbands and fathers."

What an ass, the Mayor thought. It wasn't Teufel's solecism that irritated him. The Mayor had been Mr. Misspeak since his election. In one fell swoop he'd alienated several interest groups at once when he'd said, "Gays and lesbians, blacks . . . er, African-Americans, Muslims, and Orthodox Jews should be free to live the same way as normal people." Normal? Are you saying we're not normal? they shouted back at him. He didn't mean they were abnormal, but there were more white people, heterosexual people, non-Muslims, and non-Orthodox Jews in the city, and so that was the statistical norm.

The Mayor had been misunderstood, and maybe insensitive – but his heart was in the right place. He was just an old-school guy who hadn't caught up to all the new rules about these things yet. But the more he tried to explain, the more trouble he got into, until the party that had run him for mayor asked him to put a lid on it and sent over the best media guy they could find, Seth Kirk.

Lord Harry was different. The man didn't seem to have a human bone in his body. He'd changed his citizenship according to his business interests. He'd once said that smoking was good for the economy, because its addicts died young, thereby saving on the costs of caring for an elderly person. When people jumped on that statement, he ignored them. He could afford to. He was rich and he had a great deal of power and control, none of it contingent on pleasing voters or being re-elected.

In spite of all that, putting Lord Harry on the task force had been the right thing to do. The gag order meant Lord Harry and the entire media arm of his operation were straitjacketed on this story. The Mayor didn't have to worry too much about them. It was that guy at CCN he was worried about, Sam Deverell, who by all accounts wasn't smart enough to find his ass with both hands. Yet, somehow, he kept finding out things nobody else in the media knew.

In the afternoon briefing the previous day, Deverell had stood up and asked about rumours that Armin Sunga had been involved in the illegal arms trade. The Mayor looked at him and said, "Sam, you of all people know not to pay any attention whatsoever to rumours."

Everyone in the room laughed. Sam looked around, looking puzzled and annoyed.

"Well, that's why we ask about them and check them out," Sam said earnestly.

Apparently, he didn't know about his wife, Candace, and her co-anchor, Wallace Waring. The Mayor had half a mind to tell him, just to shut him down for a while, but he couldn't. He felt for the guy. Sam seemed so damned nice, and he was covering the biggest story in town without his wife at home to love and support him. Whereas the Mayor had the wife at home in the mayoral mansion, but she might as well have been on the moon most of the time, since she was living completely separately from him under the same roof. Marva did call once or twice every day to be support-ive, and twice a week they still had lunch in his office. Her voice was kind, she said all the right things and made the right noises to pump him up, and though it made him feel better in the moment, when he hung up the phone or she went back to her side of the mansion he felt worse than before. She was there for him up to a point, but no further.

So when he looked at Sam, he saw another guy who had lost his woman and whose heart was breaking bit by bit. A man who, like him, had to buck up, look strong, go out there in the jungle and be a man.

The Commish said, "Man, I just want to call that Deverell up and tell him about his wife. Take some air out of his sails —"

"No," the Mayor said. "That's his personal life. Stay out of it. But take care of the leak problem. No leaks. No kidding. What are we going to do about the guy suing us?"

"Barotti? I'm waiting to hear from the lawyers," Seth Kirk said. "He's a nut; we may be able to use that against him."

"In this city?" the Mayor asked.

39

Jennifer Ray was being run ragged – not by the story, though that was hectic enough. What was wearing her down was running interference so people didn't tell Sam about Candace. She and Cooper screened his calls, his mail, and his e-mail to weed out the messages that said, "Your wife is cheating on you with Wallace Waring, you dumb fuck." She even screened his voice mail at home, since Sam cleverly used the same PIN, his birthday, for everything. All she had to do was call Sam's home number, punch in the code, and she could delete any messages about Candace.

Even trickier was heading off people on the street. Sam's hearing wasn't what it should be, thank God, so he missed the construction workers yelling at him from above, "Hey Sam! Your wife's a whore." Surprisingly, most people said nothing, and Sam was so consumed with the Mad Dog story, he didn't understand when people did. But sooner or later some badass was going to clue Sam in and he was going to find out not only that Wallace was boning his wife but that the whole city knew. The longer it went on, the harder it was going to be for Sam, as she pointed out to Cooper.

"I've got to tell him," she said.

"Do you?"

"I do."

"You're a brave girl. Aren't you afraid of how he'll react?"

"Yeah, of course. I'm worried he'll be distraught and get depressed," Jennifer said. "And he won't be able to do his job."

"I hope he's not one of those guys who snaps and blows his wife away."

"Sam?"

"It's almost always those mild-mannered ones. You know, they go along, being the nice guy, being taken advantage of by one ambitious, sweet-faced woman after another," Cooper said. He had a bitter edge to his voice. "Until one too many of those sweet-faced women ditches him for an asshole –"

"Hypothetically speaking."

"He's gotta have a dark side somewhere, J.R. So be gentle."

"Of course."

"But not so gentle he doesn't understand what you're saying."

"I'll take him for dinner," she said. "Aww, poor Sam."

"He'll be okay, I think. Maybe. He reminds me of Swee'pea," Cooper said. "You know, the baby from those old-timey *Popeye* cartoons?"

"Why?"

"That baby was always crawling on high-rise ledges and through burning buildings with frantic adults in pursuit, completely oblivious to what was going on. He always came out of it okay."

"Or Mr. Magoo. Blind as a bat, just getting missed by falling anvils and speeding buses," Jennifer said. "He's lucky in some ways. Love doesn't seem to be one of them. It's sad, Coop, he calls her from the job, leaves these sweet messages for her."

"What does he say?"

"He loves her but he understands she needs her space, and he's sorry."

"*He's* sorry? That's pathetic. Do you think he's pretending he doesn't know, just to save face?"

"No, I don't think so."

"Why doesn't she just divorce Sam? What is she waiting for? Is she trying to get even with him for something?"

"Jesus, Cooper, I don't know. Maybe she really does just need some space. Or maybe she's giving him the old pocket veto."

"Pocket veto?"

"A passive-aggressive tactic. She wants to move on with Wallace, but Sam's such a nice guy, she can't bear to tell him to his face. So she stays away a while, goes out with another guy, hoping Sam will get the hint and get out of the way."

"Women do this?"

"Men do it too. You've probably done it," she said. "But her plan backfired because Dear Tweets got the story, and now it's out of control."

"Yeah, that's why I don't think we should get involved. We don't know what's going on and when you get between couples without full knowledge, you can get burned," he said. "Maybe you should wait. Now that it's out, maybe she'll tell Sam she wants a divorce. Unless she's trying to punish him."

"I'll wait a little longer," she said. "As long as I can. It's all I can do sometimes not to take him by the shoulders, shake him and yell, 'Wake up!'"

On her way out, she stopped at Sam's desk to check his voice mail. There was a message from a loony guy who thought he'd seen the werewolf, which, he was sure, had eaten a young woman who had lived in his building and since vanished. There was a message from an agent who wanted to represent Sam, followed by one from some anonymous man who said, "Buddy, wise up. Your wife is screwing Wallace Waring."

Jennifer deleted that message and listened for the next.

It stopped her in her tracks.

"Sam, this is Micki. I just wanted you to know that your wife knows about our fling and she wants me to go public with it because people are talking and she looks like the bad guy. In return, she'll get me a job in TV."

Jennifer hung up the phone after jotting down the number.

That fuck. *He* had cheated on Candace, that's why Candace left him – the same thing had happened to Jennifer's mother, and to her, because she'd had to suffer through the subsequent divorce and her father's marriage to a shallow homewrecker, whose chronic over-spending delayed J.R.'s orthodontia, ate up her college fund, and ulti-mately sent her father to bankruptcy court. Fucking men. Let Sam find out about Candace the hard way. She wasn't going to tell him.

But for the sake of CCN, they had to do something about Micki. After Jennifer told Cooper, Cooper called Micki.

"Why don't you come in and talk to us," he said.

⑥

Sam was at Griffin's, in the back room with Ivan.

"You weren't followed here, were you?" Ivan asked.

"I came in the back way, like you said," Sam said. He handed Ivan a packet of money.

"It's very dangerous for me to give you any more information. I have to declare a news blackout for a while," Ivan said, as he counted the bills.

From beyond the imitation Oriental rug hanging in the doorway came the sounds of people in the bar having fun, music, laughing, the clinking of glasses. Things had worked out well for Ivan and his partners, Vincent and Marguerite. Business had started picking up at the bar just as Ivan's information business was closed down by the police department's new secrecy rules.

"How long?" Sam asked.

"I don't know."

"What will I do without you?"

"What do the other reporters do?" Ivan asked.

"I don't know. When will it be okay to talk again?"

"I don't know. Don't call me. I'll call you," Ivan said. "Good luck with . . . you know." He meant Sam's wife.

"Thanks." Sam thought he meant the story.

It was late and Sam had to get home to water Candace's plants and feed the goldfish, also named Sam and Candace, that he'd given her for their last anniversary. No matter how exhausted he was when he got home from the story, he looked after these things

before he went to bed. Tonight he hoped to stay up long enough
to watch *All the President's Men* again, maybe even crack some of
the books on reporting that Cooper had given him.

He had the cab drop him off at the Chinese restaurant near his
apartment to pick up dinner to go. The driver said, "God bless you.
Women are the devil."

"Sure. 'Night."

At the restaurant, one of the other customers, an older woman,
smiled at him and said, "You're a nice-looking man. You could
have your pick of the ladies."

"Thanks," Sam said. He wondered why people complained about
being famous. All it had brought him was a lot of compliments.

He was feeling pretty good when he got back to his building.
There were cops there, talking to the doorman.

"Someone robbed?" Sam asked.

"Sam Deverell?" A cop said.

"Yeah."

"We need you to come with us."

⑤

Cooper was still at work when Sam called.

"I need a lawyer," Sam said.

"Oh my God, what happened?"

"I've been picked up as a . . . material witness or something.
Cooper, they want me to reveal my sources. They say my reporting affects public safety."

"No, don't reveal your sources. You don't know anything that
would assist in apprehending the killer. This is clearly an attempt
to intimidate the press and keep information from the public. It's
withholding information that might affect public safety, not
reporting it." Cooper's relief that Sam hadn't blown up his wife
gave way to enthusiasm about this delicious new twist.

"I haven't said anything. I know it's a violation of my rights
under . . . some amendment. The fifth? No, the first, right?"

"Right."

"But if I don't give them names, they could put me in jail."

"Don't reveal your sources, Sam. Do not. You're a reporter now. You're representing the entire fourth and fifth estates."

"I won't, boss," Sam said. "Will you get me a lawyer?"

"Right away. Listen, if you have to go to jail for a day or two, can you handle it? They won't put you in with any hardened criminals. You'll probably have your own cell. We'll bring you things . . ."

"Will I have to shower with the other inmates?"

"No. We'll make sure you're looked after and protected, Sam."

"Just a day or two?"

"I'm sure of it. You'll be a hero, Sam."

"Okay."

"Good luck. Say nothing until the lawyer gets there. Cops are tricky, they might try to scam you into giving information."

"Lips zipped," Sam said.

Sam went to jail, and CCN had a live crew there when he did.

40

Dear Tweets,

You know how our conscience bothers us when we get something wrong. How we gnash our teeth and wail and send ourselves to bed without dinner, and sometimes alone. This *may* be one of those extremely rare occasions.

We can't name names, but a certain oblivious husband may not be as heroic as we thought. Very reliable sources say his confection of a wife left him because *he* had an affair – with a younger woman. So if Wifey's now getting her frisson from elsewhere, who would begrudge her or her new paramour?

We can't confirm, and you know how hard we work to get the facts straight. Don't touch that dial.

Oh when will those besotted idealists who choose to marry

ever learn? Don't do it, kids. Abandon yourselves to meaningless sex! Comme moi, or comme . . .

. . . a certain actor known for working-class roots and intelligent acting who has been nicknamed "The Gopher" for his sexual ubiquity on set. (Gopher: in one hole and out another. Get it?) While our Gopher is plumbing tunnels in France, his titled fiancée manages to order champagne (Krug) and candied almonds (gold- and silver-coated, imported from Switzerland) for their upcoming wedding reception, and all this while her head is buried in the sand! That's quite a trick, dear. Do come up for air and take a look around before you make a terrible mistake. We've tried to warn you before: there's a reason gophers and ostriches don't mate in nature. When you return to our reality, perhaps you can tell us what it is you have on that handsome burrowing creature that got him to agree to marry you in the first place.

Lest you think it's only men giving into their animal natures, let me assure you, the girls are striking a blow for equality. Leader of the pack is a certain Oscar-nom lovely who has her honey's name tattooed in a place she claims can only be seen by her beau or a board-certified physician. Well, it seems a few others have been peeking down there: a married movie mogul who makes delightful family fare, her current co-star, and a cameraman on her last film who left his wife, got his heart broken and is now in rehab. And no, the it's not the Usual Suspect, Tweets. Think blonde. Think perky. Think wholesome.

41

"I'd like to help you out. I have a soft spot for Sam," Micki said, lighting a cigarette in defiance of the No Smoking sign on Cooper's wall. He knew it was in defiance, and not that she didn't see it, because when she walked in and sat down, she'd looked at the sign, smiled, and pulled out a smoke.

"But I have to look out for myself too," she said. "Candace Quall says she can get me a job as a production assistant at Syn-TV and will help me become a reporter."

"How long was your affair?" Cooper asked.

"As far as the sex goes, it was just a day. But what a day. That guy hadn't fucked in ages," she said. "He was a wild man. Then it turned into a lot of talking."

"Talking about what?" Jennifer asked.

"His wife, how he felt bad cheating on her. Two words: mood killer." She looked around for an ashtray. Cooper, fearing she might just drop the ashes on his rug, emptied a candy dish and pushed it towards her. She flicked the cigarette into it.

She was a big girl, not what they were expecting. Tall, plump, and curvy, what some might call zaftig, with big breasts, big eyes, and a round doll face framed by dark curls. Sexy, for sure, but they'd been expecting some grasping anorexic bimbo with cold eyes and fake tits.

"What kind of job are you looking for?" Cooper asked.

"I want my own talk show. *Pro Sex*, straight talk on sex with a pro."

"Are you a pro?" Jennifer Ray asked.

"I work in the sex industry, yes."

"And you want your own show right off the bat?" Cooper asked.

"I took communications in college, before I dropped out. I do a public access TV show twice a month. I know what I'm doing." She handed Cooper her tape.

"I can't offer you an on-air job just like that," Cooper said. "But I could possibly bring you in as a production assistance to our entertainment news department, to start."

"Well, let me think about it," she said, butting out her cigarette. She stood and shook hands with Cooper and Jennifer Ray. "Oh, I have a videotape of me and Sam too. Having sex. Our little secret. For now."

After she left, Cooper said "She seems . . . what's the word?"

"Jolly," Jennifer provided.

"Yeah, real jolly for a blackmailer." He stared at the lipstick-stained carcass of her cigarette in his candy dish. "Is this ethical?"

"Giving her a job to save Sam? I don't think so," Jennifer Ray said. "Maybe we should just let Sam go down. The shit."

"Let him go down? While he's in jail for not revealing his sources?"

"Yeah. He made his bed," she said.

"It was one weekend. He hadn't had sex in ages . . ."

"How long is an age in the average man's sex life?"

"It depends. A couple of months?" Cooper said.

"Two months?"

"Men are —"

"Yeah yeah, men are men are men. That doesn't mean I have to violate any more of my ethics to protect this one," Jennifer said.

"This Micki can't seriously believe we'll give her a show of her own straight off." Cooper said. "What are we going to do about the story while he's in jail? The police aren't talking, City Hall isn't talking."

"More sidebars."

"What haven't we covered already?" Cooper asked. "We've looked at killer dogs, how to defend against killer dogs, previous unsolved murders by the same method, pepper-spray sales —"

"I dunno. I'll think about it. Shit. I'd better get down to the jail, bring that cheater some things, keep him quiet."

"I'd go but I have to be here," Cooper said.

"Yeah, whatever. I'll call you after I talk to Sam."

On her way out, she stopped by the assignment desk to see if they had anything new on the Mad Dog story.

"Nothing worthwhile," the assignment editor said. "Just a couple of film students who claim they saw a bizarre animal, half-bear and half-dog, on the night of one of the murders."

"A werewolf!" One of his assistants said, and then howled like a hound.

"Yeah, thanks for nothing," Jennifer said.

⑥

Sam was waiting for her in his cell, unshaven, looking kind of gloomy.

"I'm really glad to see you. It's so lonely in here," he said.

"Sam, I have to tell you something," J.R. said. "Micki contacted us."

"Micki?"

Jennifer Ray counted to ten.

"The Micki you had an affair with."

"Yeah," he said. "I don't know how that happened. I was stupid."

"You're a grown man, Sam. Didn't you think of the consequences?"

"J.R., I don't know if you can understand this. Promise me you won't repeat this."

"I promise."

"It's very personal."

"I promise!"

"When we moved up here, Candace disappeared into her work. She was never around."

"That happens."

"We hadn't had . . . marital relations in a long time and I was lonely. It was my birthday, just before this whole Mad Dog thing broke. Candace was away. I felt old and ignored, this girl approached me, we had a few drinks –"

"Where was Candace during this wild weekend?"

"At the big TV and radio convention in New Orleans."

"RTNDA."

"Right."

"Sam, why are men such asses?"

"Aw, Jennifer, don't get mad. I know it was stupid. It was just one weekend. At her place, not mine. After that all we did was talk, until Micki told me she couldn't see me again."

"And how long is a long time to go without sex, Sam?"

"Let me see. It started when we were still in Atlanta. Candace and I hadn't done it for nine months."

"Nine months?"

"A whole year if you don't count hand . . . you know."

"Hand jobs?"

"Yeah."

"A year without anything but a hand job? Did you go for counselling?"

"I suggested a . . . sex therapist but Candace said she was just tired from working so much."

"Before that year everything was fine?" Jennifer asked.

"Well, yeah. I mean, Candace was never really into . . ."

"Candace didn't like sex?"

He didn't answer that question. "Candace is a great woman. I must have been doing something wrong. It's entirely my fault, all of it."

"Candace is a great woman?"

"In her way."

Jennifer looked at him. Was he being a gentleman?

"How did you meet?"

"Her first day at the station, in Albuquerque. She'd just been hired as a junior reporter. She was a frightened, insecure young woman," he said. "And I was the city's top-rated anchorman . . . and I'd just been dumped by my first wife."

Just dumped, and here came Candace, so young and beautiful and classy, looking for advice and a helping hand. He was feeling rejected by his wife and was only too happy to help the pretty girl. Back then Candace had been so needy, he had to tell her he loved her five times a day and reassure her that she was indeed the most beautiful reporter in Albuquerque. She was the one who wanted to get married, and he'd gone along with it. They got married in a small ceremony in the desert, with his family and a few friends from the TV news community. She never knew her father, and her mother, she said, was dead. He didn't tell Jennifer this.

Even Sam didn't know the truth for the first two years they were married, until her mother tracked her down, showing up on their Albuquerque doorstep when Candace was in Taos reporting on an arts festival. Sam invited "Ma" in, where she told Sam everything she knew about Flora, er, Candace. She "asked" for a large "loan," while promising Candace's secret past was safe with her, then drank all Sam's beer and passed out on the table, which knocked her upper plate out of her mouth and sent it skidding across the floor.

Knowing this about Candace made him love her more. Looking into her mother's beaten-down face, hard and mean, for five minutes, he learned more about Candace than he had in all the time they'd been together. Until then, Sam thought Candace was a nice, if snobbish, middle-class girl who didn't believe in pre-marital sex – or much post-marital sex for that matter – daughter of a dead mother and an unknown father. Her background was to blame for her problems with intimacy, he thought, and her obses-sion with class and appearances. After he met his mother-in-law, he understood Candace had pushed down that vulnerable little poor girl and grown a lead-lined shell around her that could keep radioactive waste intact.

Sam paid the old woman, put her on a bus back to Arkansas the next day before Candace got back, and never told his wife about the visit. Every month he sent his mother-in-law some money, until one month the money came back. Written on the envelope were the words, "She's dead. Retern [sic] to sender." He never told Candace about that either, and he didn't tell J.R. now.

Maybe he should have told Candace, he thought, flushed her out of her bomb shelter, opened her up.

"Sam, Sam, Sam," Jennifer Ray said. "What is it about arousal that makes so many men's brains shut off? I mean, a hooker?"

"I'm sorry. I was thinking about Candace and I missed something. What hooker?"

"Micki."

"Micki's not a hooker."

"Call it what you will, if you pay them, they're pros."

"I didn't pay Micki," he said.

"You didn't?"

"No."

"Did you promise to get her a job in television?"

"She wants a job in television?"

"She didn't tell you that either? Sam, did you make a videotape with Micki?"

"No. Why would I do that?"

"A sex videotape."

"God no, I'm not that stupid, J.R. Jeez."

"Okay, but she did make a video of the two of you."

Sam buried his face in his hands. "Oh, good grief. I have to talk to her. When am I going to get out of here?"

"Soon, Sam," she said.

Nine months without anything, not even a blow job, J.R. thought. Even she couldn't completely fault a guy for giving into temptation after nine months of celibacy. It didn't surprise her that Candace Quall wasn't a sex fiend. The few times Jennifer had seen her at industry events, she'd come across as a real cold one, and an acquaintance who'd worked with her briefly when Candace first arrived at Syn-TV confirmed it.

"Where that woman walks, a cold wind blows and the ground cracks with frost," she'd said.

This Micki thing was very fishy. Sam was a nice guy, and not bad looking for a man his age, but he had no clout back when he and Micki were mixed up. If Micki had been sleeping with him to get ahead, it was worse than that old joke about sleeping with a screenwriter in Hollywood. Her sense of Micki was that she didn't do anyone unless she was getting paid somehow. Making a secret tape to blackmail Sam wasn't a good career move, at least not before the Mad Dog story broke. What could she get, a few hundred bucks cash?

Further investigation was needed.

42

"'Free Sam!'" the Mayor read from the *Daily Post*. "We've turned this guy into a hero."

Seth turned to the Police Commissioner and said, "You should have called me. I could have spun this differently. Instead, CCN got the jump, making it look like Sam Deverell was protecting the public safety with his reports."

"Can we still spin it our way?" the Mayor asked.

"Not without giving away information about the investigation and Operation Harvest Moon," Seth said.

"Well, what the hell do we do now? We can't keep him in jail. We look like shits. We have to let him go."

"Then we look like losers who have backed down. No. I have a better idea. We find this girl he allegedly had an affair with – according to 'Dear Tweets.' We get her to go public, and when we spring him from jail, he's not a hero, he's a schmuck."

"That didn't work with Clinton."

"Clinton's wife wasn't cheating – allegedly – on him. Sam has public sympathy because of his cheating wife. But if it turns out his wife sought comfort with another man because Sam cheated on her, the tide turns," Seth said. "People will feel like suckers for sympathizing with him when he was the guilty party and they'll be pissed."

"I don't know. I hate to kick the guy when he's down," the Mayor said. "You better have proof he is the guilty party."

"We don't need proof –"

"I need proof," the Mayor said. "Everyone is entitled to one mistake."

The Mayor had to believe that, since he'd made that mistake. Lately, he'd been thinking a lot about his mistake in the 1970s, and whether that was what caused him and Marva to grow apart the way they had.

It wasn't like he was wearing gold chains and tight pants and getting down at the discos, like so many forty-something men did back then. Some of the guys he knew went nuts out there. The husband of Marva's best friend had left her to become a swinger, only to end up a bloated fixture at a singles bar, lamenting the wife, kids, and community property he'd left behind, before going home to a grim studio apartment, the only place he could afford after he paid the alimony and the child support.

For the Mayor it happened differently, while he was advising a previous mayor on the garbage strike. Between the grocery business and the strike, he wasn't getting home much, and when he did, Marva was busy with her own things. There was this sharp young attorney working with him, Catherine Thompson. One night he told her she reminded him of the Charlie Girl, from the perfume commercials popular at the time. That was his only image of the new breed of modern career women, the confident, independent Charlie Girl who wore pants and strode down the street leaving men goony-eyed in her wake.

When Catherine had laughed at this, he'd been as embarrassed as a six-year-old – he'd even blushed – because he'd meant it as a compliment, not a joke. Before he could apologize, she'd kissed him, square on the lips, slipping her soft tongue into his mouth.

No tongue but Marva's had touched his since he'd met Marva, aside from beef tongue in a sandwich once in a while. Catherine's felt sweet, and maybe it was her particular kiss, or just the sensation of a strange, forbidden kiss, but it was so erotically charged it almost made him dizzy. He ended up that night, and almost every night of the garbage strike, in her uptown apartment.

How Marva found out, he never knew, but he came home early one night after the strike was resolved, and found his dinner in a dog dish with his name written on it in black marker. Marva was gone. She'd taken the kids and gone to visit her best friend, M'Lou Greene, the one whose ex-husband was trying to be a swinger. He called and M'Lou told him, "She can't come to the phone. She's busy smoking cigarettes, drinking whiskey and reading *Ms.* magazine." In the background, he heard Marva cough. She really was smoking cigarettes, which she knew he hated.

The next day, he went over there and spied on them through the slats of the fence. They were lounging by M'Lou's pool, both of them in T-shirts and shorts, sunglasses, their hair in foam curlers. He couldn't hear what they were saying, but he heard Marva laugh. She didn't seem to miss him.

Many phone calls, several bouquets, and a copy of Johnny Ray singing "Walkin' My Baby Back Home," and Marva came home. After he asked and got her forgiveness, he returned one of Catherine's many calls to tell her he couldn't see her any more. He had to be faithful to his wife.

Marva said she forgave him, even acted like she forgave him. They worked it out, but on some level, things were never the same between them. He wondered sometimes if Marva had had an affair after that, when she was taking classes at the college and the Art Students League, but he never asked her and she dropped no clues, other than a kind of distance and absence he recognized in himself when he was having his affair. And now there were those visits from Serge, her sculpture teacher.

43

The girl was missing and Gunther was sure her disappearance had to do with the werewolf. The hair on her broken window, the boyfriend who tied her up, the werewolf, and then Annie just vanishes? The beast got her for sure. And nobody would listen to him.

He wasn't the only one who missed her. A very friendly woman named Carol had stopped by, looking for her.

"She has vanished," Gunther said. "I believe a werewolf got her. I'm not crazy. I saw the animal one night, and I found blood and coarse hair on a broken window in her apartment. One night I –"

"Did you call the police?" Carol asked.

"Yes, and they told me to call 777-3456. You know what that is?"

"No."

"Moviephone."

"I'm sure it's just a coincidence," Carol said.

A day or two later, a blind man stopped by to ask about Annie. He was a friend of hers and hadn't heard from her for a while.

Gunther was taking no chances. He had his gun, and he had the silver bullets he'd ordered from Oregon. And he was going to keep calling people until the authorities did something. And whether or not they acted, he was going to do something. A girl just doesn't disappear like that.

44

One of the hardest things Marco ever had to do was call his father to ask for Rudolfo's assistance in bringing in the two rogue werewolves. Three now, as Mike Burke had not returned, but Marco decided not to tell his father that when he finally spoke to him on the phone. Naturally, in their last phone call, Marco's father had reminded him yet again that Rudolfo, who had only one of the needed werewolf genes, on his father's side, was a better tracker than Marco, a true werewolf, was.

Rudolfo was due to arrive at the Centre around noon, and Marco didn't want to be there when his non-werewolf cousin arrived. It was a power thing. He didn't want to wait for Rudolfo. He wanted Rudolfo to wait for him.

Carol didn't mind being the welcoming committee. Rudolfo, to his credit, was one of the few Potenzas who appreciated Carol, but that was probably because she, like him, was not a werewolf. He was an expressionless man, so for years she didn't realize Rudolfo liked her, until he sent her a present after a particularly horrible Thanksgiving in Washington with Luigi and the clan. The present was a bracelet with an amethyst, her birthstone, inscribed, *You are a Jewel in the Potenza Crown. Rudolfo.* Rudolfo made Marco uneasy, but Carol liked him and had baked his favourite cake and stocked his favourite tea, the smoky and very caffeinated Lapsang Souchong.

Not only did she like Rudolfo, but it made her feel better, with all the problems and chaos recently, to have him coming to stay until the full moon at least. Something about Rudolfo . . . when he walked into a room, crooked pictures seemed to right themselves. That was the aura he carried, one of safety and order. When a werewolf appeared in a place outside the main LMD centres, Rudolfo was sent to get it. He usually did, one way or another, more often alive than dead, as he secretly hated to kill. He never said so, but one Thanksgiving when the other Potenzas were bragging about bringing down particularly resistant werewolves, she'd noted that Rudolfo hung his head over his dish and ate quietly.

While he had a freakishly powerful sense of smell – he could correctly identify the ingredients in a cookie – he also did a lot of groundwork, asking questions like a private detective. Under other circumstances, he could have been a private detective. He brought in many werewolves while in human form just by doing his research and legwork.

When Rudolfo arrived, Carol was delighted, until he stepped out of the way and she saw Luigi there behind him.

"Carol," Luigi said.

"Hi, Dad," she said. He hated being called Dad. He preferred the august sound of the word "Father."

"Tell Marco we're here," Luigi said, manoeuvring his Orson

Welles–like bulk into the foyer with the help of his cane, his blessed bloody cane made of wood from some forest in Germany where they'd cleared out a bunch of werewolves in 1933. At the top of the steps into the sunken living room, he held his free arm out and Rudolfo took it. Luigi was getting old and had to be helped down stairs. This made Carol soften a little towards him.

"Marco had to step out but he'll be back shortly. Where are your bags?"

"Rudolfo's luggage and equipment are coming separately. I am not staying the night," Luigi said.

Thank God, Carol thought.

"Well, come in, have a seat," she said. "May I get you some tea? A piece of fructose-sweetened cake perhaps?"

"Mint tea, on ice, with Equal, not Sweet'N Low," Luigi said, picking up a newspaper from a pile on the table.

"I don't have Equal, Dad. Sorry. Just Sweet'N Low."

"If that's all you have, that's all you have." He didn't look happy about it.

"Lapsang Souchong?" she suggested to Rudolfo.

"Oh yes, thanks," he said. "May I . . . help you?"

"Oh no, Rudy, you sit. You've been on the road."

Carol put the kettle on and sat down on a pink and yellow chair at the matching Formica table. In the living room, Luigi was talking loudly about the news coverage. This was all Marco needed, Carol thought. He was already in such a shitty mood. He hadn't been this snappish and critical in ages, since . . . just before Sarah died, come to think of it. It was normal for him to be mildly critical, but lately she and everyone else had to walk on eggshells around him or risk a blast of sarcastic anger.

But she understood he was just reacting to his father's dissatisfaction. Even if they didn't speak for weeks, Luigi had some ability to transmit his disapproval by remote. Marco so hated dealing with his father, he'd intentionally played telephone tag with him for two weeks, only calling when he knew his father would be out, and reporting to him about events by faxed letters. When he'd finally had to talk to him and ask for Rudolfo, it had been very humiliating. Carol wasn't sure how far back this trouble went between Marco and his father – probably to the very beginning. Most of what she knew, she had picked up just by watching the Potenzas together. For a family of shrinks that talked so much, they were remarkably close-mouthed about their own emotional issues. The competition between the men just seemed to get in the way.

To be fair, the women were pretty competitive too. When she was alive, Marco's mother, Mary, had set the tone by pitting the other women against each other. When the women were properly miserable, Mary turned her attention to the men.

Mary had disapproved totally of Carol but still could be counted on to compliment Carol in a way that diminished Enzio's wife, Audrey, if Audrey was getting too big a head. As she was eating a piece of cake Audrey had baked, she'd say, "Carol, you should give Audrey the recipe for that delicious lemon-walnut cake you make," for example, while saying nothing about Audrey's cake, perhaps even making a bit of a face as she swallowed. Carol's kitchen skills and her ability to stretch a buck were the two things the Potenzas appreciated, if they absolutely had to and could score points against a relative that way.

The tea kettle whistled.

When she got back to the living room, Luigi and Rudolfo were reading through the local newspapers. Luigi was reading the *Daily Post*.

"This publicity is terrible," Luigi said. "This is completely out of control. How did this get bungled so badly, Carol?"

"You'll have to discuss it with Marco. He has been working very hard on this. Tea, Dad?" She poured from one pot for Luigi, another for Rudolfo, who was quiet, as always, but smiled at her and mouthed his thanks.

"How is everyone in Washington?" she asked.

"Well, not good, obviously," Luigi said. "This situation is causing trouble for all of us."

"Of course it is. Aside from that, is everyone healthy? How are Enzio and Audrey? I've been meaning to call them."

"Audrey is pregnant. A boy."

"Isn't that nice? Gee, I wish she'd called to tell me. How far along is —"

From the foyer, Marco called out, "Carol, I'm home. Is Rudolfo here yet?"

She jumped up, hoping to head him off so she could prepare him. Before she could, Luigi shouted, "Yes, he's here, with your father."

Carol got to the door just in time to see the pained expression on Marco's face, as if a large shard of glass were passing through his lower intestine.

"Father, how good of you to come," he said.

"Not a moment too soon. I should have come up at the very beginning, instead of trusting you to take care of this. But I can't babysit you through these crises. I have problems of my own in Washington."

"It's not my fault," Marco said. "If it hadn't been for Jim Valiente, I'd have brought the female in. There was nothing I could do about Valiente."

"You could have —" Luigi stopped. "Carol, will you excuse us please."

"Carol, go out to the garden," Marco said, looking down and to the side but not at her.

"You call me if you need anything," Carol said.

Just as she was closing the door, she heard Luigi say, "You could have euthanized him."

Being banished by Luigi made little difference to Carol. The little window by the door to the roof garden was open. Beneath that window was a table, where she sat and paged through the *Downtown Eye*. The front was headlined, WHO IS KILLING THE EVIL

PEOPLE OF THE CITY?, with half the sentence at the top and the other half below photographs of the victims laid out in a mosaic. Carol ignored the story and opened the paper to the "Dear Tweets" column. That and the horoscope were all she dared to read these days. It always distressed her to learn about the patients' victims, and it made it easier for her to help the patients if she didn't know the details, how many children the dead left behind, and so on.

But this headline nagged at her and she found herself going back to read the story on the killings. The *Eye* had uncovered proof that a man named Armin Sunga, an importer-exporter, was really an arms dealer known by the alias Mr. Singer, though the CIA had nicknamed him No-See-Him. He was one of the world's top brokers of land mines, was believed to have entered the nuclear trade in the early 1990s after the break-up of the Soviet Union, and had supplied weapons to governments, terrorist organizations, and rebel armies all over the world.

Among other things, Klaus Bendinger, president of Syn-PHARM, had authorized drug experiments on unwitting children in a remote African village, experiments linked to a sudden increase in cancer cases. Syn-PHARM denied there was any link between the experiments and the cancer and had wiggled out of any legal ramifications, because the kids' parents had all signed consent forms. As the *Eye* discovered, the parents were largely illiterate. Those who could read couldn't read well, and certainly not small-print legalese.

Mohammed Abdullah was a high-ranking official of a theocratic Asian country run by a maniacal priest with one eye. Abdullah was rumoured to be a highly talented torturer, which had eventually earned him a plush assignment in America. Peter Gorgon was an arms maker, Robert Bingham was involved in the suppression of a poor minority in support of a sub-Saharan dictatorship, and so on.

In the living room, Luigi and Marco were still arguing about Jim.

"You should have done it as soon as you discovered he'd killed the female. What was her name?"

"Sarah," Marco said.

"Why were you letting him fill the drug IVs anyway? You know that's against policy. Only trained physicians should be handling the drugs. That was your decision, Marco. You have to accept responsibility for that and for the mess it has spawned."

He berated Marco's performance before he wound down a bit, let out an exasperated sigh, and said, "Let's look at his file and decide how we're going to approach this. I have to be on the shuttle back to D.C. at 10:22 tonight."

For the next hour they went over their options, trying to come up with a foolproof plan for the next full moon. Luigi declared he was hungry and told Marco to call Carol in to fix them something to eat. Without a word, she went into the kitchen and began preparing their lunch. She thought of calling Audrey to congratulate her on her happy news but figured she'd better wait until Marco knew. With luck, she'd get a chance to tell him before Luigi did.

It wasn't Marco's fault they couldn't have children. She'd been infertile when she was younger, and was now menopausal. But Luigi blamed Marco for choosing not only a normal wife but one incapable of popping out heirs. Audrey had already plunked two ill-tempered daughters into the world and was now gestating with a male Potenza, a future count, if he outlived Marco. A little werewolf boy.

Oh, that "werewolf thing." On one hand, the Potenzas were proud of it. They weren't just men, they were "powerful beasts," and any skill in their family was attributed to "the werewolf in him." Enzio was a champion-class tennis player because of the "werewolf thing." Luigi had been a world-class runner in his youth because of the werewolf thing. But in the patients, it was seen as a disease which had to be controlled at all costs because they were not strong enough to handle it. The Potenzas saw themselves as being above the rest, special werewolves sent here to manage the others.

After one emotionally brutal family gathering, Carol had told Marco her observations.

"Carol, remember the last time I cooked dinner? The pasta was gluey, the vegetables were mushy, the sauce had too many onions? I'll leave the cooking to you if you leave the psychoanalysis to me."

Because she didn't have anyone to talk to about it, she sometimes blurted out things about the family or cracked a rude joke about Luigi to the patients, until Marco reminded her to keep family matters private. It was at times like these she missed Sarah and even Jim, in spite of everything, because she had been able to talk freely with them about the werewolf thing, about the Great Potenzas.

The Great Potenzas. That wasn't Carol's nickname for them. That's what they called themselves. Even though she snickered a little when she heard it, she understood their need to exalt themselves.

In the truly great families, there is a shared profession and passion. The Barrymores have acting, the Kennedys have politics, the Wallendas have the trapeze and the circus, the Gruccis have spectacular fireworks, the Redenbachers have popcorn, and the Potenza family had werewolves. But, unlike those other noted families, the Potenzas had the unique frustration of being a great family whose greatness had gone completely unrecognized for the last two hundred years. Nobody outside the community acknowledged them at all, so they had to pat themselves on the back a lot and talk endlessly about their illustrious history.

The Potenzas had been in medicine, specializing in mental afflictions, long before Sigmund Freud was an Oedipal gleam in his father's eye. They were physicians, men of science who travelled Europe countering superstition with proven medicine. In one famous case, history records the visit in 1456 of "a fysician Potenza of Savoy" who was summoned to a small Swiss village to treat its teenage girls, believed to be possessed by demons. The previous spring, the girls had started cursing their parents, talking brazenly to men, and playing cards. Exorcism had been unsuccessful, and a clear-thinking rationalist on the town's council decided science was needed. Potenza came, and diagnosed the problem as one of body, not spirit. He treated the girl's bodies by removing their uteruses, followed by postoperative treatment of their sexual organs with "cauterization, camphor compresses and cold rainwater enemas" to rid them of their "ill humeurs." Several of the young women died of septic infections, but those who survived, it was written, "became meek and goodly wives" who never misbehaved again.

During the 1500s, Niccolò of Savoy gained renown by curing a young Italian prince of his fear of women with a combination of anatomy lessons, bloodletting with leeches, and the careful ministrations of some of Europe's finest courtesans. This early form of sex therapy enabled the young prince to marry and produce two heirs. His father, the king, was so grateful he granted Dr. Niccolò Potenza the title of count, a title the family still carried.

There was no shortage of nervous or completely mad aristocrats in the inbred noble houses of Europe. Phobias and manias were commonplace. Frigidity and its opposite, nymphomania, were epidemic among princesses, homosexuality and stuttering among princes, particularly the first-born heirs of powerful autocratic kings. One Polish-Lithuanian prince, whose twin had died in the womb, suffered from a severe case of sciophobia, the fear of shadows. A French dauphin had a pathological fear of eyes, ommetaphobia, and could not look at any eyes, even his own in a looking glass.

Often their own court doctors were guilty of shocking malpractice, preferring herbal teas and leeches (which the Potenzas had since abandoned), to the more modern therapies of bloodletting by opening veins, sugar of lead cataplasms, opium enemas, and shock treatment, which the Potenzas had pioneered. It used not electricity, but delivered physical pain with toe and wrist vises whenever an abnormal behaviour was exhibited. This combination was highly successful. When it was not successful, the Potenzas usually got lucky. For example, when the idiot and multiphobic son of a Scandinavian king died during treatments, his father did not hold it against the Potenzas, taking solace in the fact that his second son, hale and intelligent, was now heir instead of his first-born, who was afraid of chickens, fresh air, and looking up – not the kind of things that inspire confidence in a nation or in a father who wishes to see his dynasty carried on into infinity.

At the height of the Potenzas' success, when they were the toast of the crowned heads of Europe, endowed with titles and lands in Italy, Germany, Russia, and Spain, disaster struck.

It was in Germany in the late eighteenth century that the family became cursed. Two Potenza brothers were summoned to rid the Black Forest of werewolves. The Potenza brothers, Count Giuseppe and his brother Vittorio, had gone believing that ignorance, superstition and poor food-storage practices were causing the locals to hallucinate werewolves where there were just wolves. One night, Giuseppe was walking around the village, making rounds of the afflicted patients, when he saw an abnormally large wolf, almost as big as a bear. He followed it into the forest, tracking it all night and cornering it just before dawn in a small cave. When he went in, pistol drawn, he discovered a scared, and naked, woman. Something about her large, frightened eyes, her aromatic musk, and her glistening naked skin moved him. For the first time in his life, he experienced a love greater than the mere affection or lust he sometimes felt for women, and he understood the kind of love the poets wrote about, which he'd always derided as sentimental madness that weakened a man and made him look foolish to all but himself.

Taking her tiny, shivering hand in his, where it felt like a small bird, he convinced her to tell him her story, and promised to keep her secret and take care of her always. She then took him to meet her family, an entire family of werewolves who would become the first of their kind to be treated for their malady by the Potenzas. Giuseppe married the young woman, whose name was Inge.

Inge was said to be quite lovely, and Giuseppe was himself quite a looker by the standards of the day, though by the standards of Marco's time, this great beauty was hard to see in the portraits of the count and countess on his wall. Carol, looking at them in her husband's study, thought they looked plain and grim. Inge had a bony face, no visible eyelashes, and no light in her eyes. Giuseppe was a big man with a doughy face and haunted eyes. His face had been pulled downward into morose jowls. His wrinkles all pointed downward. It was clear that marriage to a werewolf wasn't all bestial sex and roses.

Treatment back then consisted of confining the werewolves in a stone dungeon and placing them in iron restraints. There was no good sedation beyond a simple opium solution that wore off very quickly. Though mesmerism produced some results, most of the werewolves were conscious through their transformations, thrashing against their leg irons and the stone walls until they exhausted themselves. Over time, this had crippling effects that none of the modern medicine in the eighteenth-century world could alleviate. Within a few years, Inge and all the members of her family were dead, with the exception of a brother, Heinrich, who escaped into the forest before a full moon and was never seen again. Inge was the last to die, but not before giving birth to Giuseppe's only children, a son and future count, Giovanni, and his sister, Constanza.

Giovanni and Constanza seemed very normal and the Potenza family shrugged off the difficult episode of Giuseppe's marriage. But just as Queen Victoria harboured the hemophiliac gene that would bring down crowned heads all over Europe, so the Potenzas harboured Inge's werewolf gene. For several generations, it was unseen, as the gene was recessive. For all the Potenza family knew, it had died out with Inge. It didn't show its feral face again until Augustus Potenza married another carrier, the Scottish Lady Mary McDee, while he was treating Albert, the prince consort of Queen Victoria, for migraines. The twin sons of "Auggie" and Mary were both full werewolves, which manifested itself when the boys turned thirteen and killed two members of the House of Lords on a foggy night in the poorest part of London's East End. When the twin wolves killed them, the two peers were on their way to have sexual intercourse with child virgins in the belief it would cure their syphilis.

The boys returned home half-human and dripping with their victims' blood. Fearing discovery, Auggie sent Lady Mary and the boys to a family estate in the Austro-Hungarian Empire. One of the twins had contracted syphilis from the attack and would die an agonizing death. The other, Augustus II, became his father's guinea pig for experimental treatments of the disorder, which Auggie dubbed Lycanthropic Metamorphic Disorder. Fear of their secret getting out, coupled with the powerful attraction Potenza men felt for werewolf women, led them to breed from then on with other werewolves whenever possible.

Wars, famine, colonialism, and revolutions would drive most of the werewolves out of Europe and Asia to the New World, though they retained a hold in Germany until the 1930s. The Potenzas followed after the Second World War.

⑨

The sound of the Cuisinart grating raw potatoes and apples for her red-potato and apple torte topped with smoked Gruyère drowned out both Carol's thoughts and the voices in the living room. When the blades stopped spinning, she heard Luigi say, "We procured some ketamine for you. It's arriving tomorrow with Rudolfo's equipment. I had to call in some favours so don't waste any of it."

"We'll need some for the hunt."

"No. No tranquilizers for the renegades. The troublemakers have to be removed."

Carol opened the refrigerator slowly so it didn't make a sound and took out the milk and the smoked Gruyère. She listened to Luigi dictate the "goals of the operation" as she made a thin sauce of cheese, red wine, and cinnamon and poured in the potato mixture.

They were going to kill them, Jim, Mike, and even Annie. Even though she knew these things were sometimes necessary, it made her feel sick. Enzio and Luigi had no qualms hunting down and killing werewolves who resisted treatment and tried to get away. They didn't have the heads of their trophies mounted above the fireplace, but they might as well have. A few years earlier, Carol had overheard Luigi and Enzio bragging about how they went after and "bagged" some guy named D. B. Cooper who appeared to have outsmarted everyone . . . everyone except the Mighty Potenzas.

Marco had been very successful in luring stray werewolves into the pack and keeping them there. Once he got them into the Centre and Carol had fed them a meal and given them some TLC, they wanted to stay. Sometimes a patient went incurably insane from the drugs and had to be euthanized. Anybody who had seen the agonizing effects of a werewolf trapped in a K-hole knew this was an act of pure mercy. Sometimes there were overdoses in patients whose systems had been weakened by time or other ailments.

But Marco had always been privately opposed to intentional killing.

Carol stirred in two eggs and topped the torte with grated Gruyère and crumbled walnuts that had been coated in oil and a little chili powder, and heard Marco say, "Yes, they'll all be taken out."

"Are you sure it'll be done?" Luigi asked. "Those Valientes were always difficult. His mother was very difficult to bring down."

Jim's mother? Carol had known his mother was probably a werewolf because Jim himself had told her the story of her full-moon absences, when she'd come back naked and dishevelled. Until now, Carol hadn't realized that the Potenzas had tracked and killed her. She started crying, but she couldn't be caught crying in front of Luigi. She took an extra Valium before she put the torte in the oven and began her cold cucumber cups, and popped another before she served the men in the garden.

45

There were a few bad moments for Annie and Jim in the beginning. They were both taking it slow, opening up to each other. Even without the "werewolf thing," there were the usual problems of relationships, often so insurmountable in this city that the average relationship was shorter than the average mortgage approval.

One day Jim was in the living room working on a novelization due before the new moon and Annie was in the bedroom putting white base paint on a canvas while watching *The Beth Tindall Show*. The subject of the show was "Is Love Blind, Deaf and Drunk?" It was a rerun about the girlfriends of serial killers on Death Row.

Annie remembered Liz's tale of having to referee the girls in the green room, since two of them were dating the same serial killer. At the time, she thought these girls were absolute idiots.

Now she thought about how complicated life was. Jim was thoughtful, smart, and he seemed sincere. She found him very attractive. After sex, he held her and they talked. A guy who could stay awake after sex? Exceedingly rare, from what she'd been told. And he was the kind of guy who thought to get a girl a fresh tooth-brush after she'd spent the night. Most guys wouldn't think of that after a night of routine sex, let alone a night spent running all over town killing people. Then he brought her vitamins, and the next day art supplies and canvases. He lovingly washed her hair, cut it, and applied the dye to make her a blonde. There seemed to be nothing he would not do for her.

More than that, he was patient. If she was nervous, or shy, he held her until the feeling passed and she relaxed. Right after the full moon, the sex was wild and intense. The further they got from the full moon, the slower, more skilled and tender it was.

But . . . he was a killer.

Marco had welcomed her in, given her a place to feel at home and made her feel safe and normal. On the other hand, Jim made her feel loved. Then again, those girls who went on *Beth Tindall* and other such shows and declared their love for serial killers on Death Row thought they were loved. How was she any different from them, aside from the fact that she was also a serial killer?

Jim was obviously different. He didn't kill sixteen aging prosti-
tutes or three previous wives just for kicks, as two of the heart-
throbs on the show had. But he was still a serial killer, and, despite
the success of the incarcerated men on the show, it couldn't be easy
for serial killers to get girls. They pretty much had to take what
they could get. Maybe that was the case with Jim, she thought.
Maybe he wanted her only because she was a werewolf and he
didn't have a lot of girlfriend options.

He was working and she didn't want to disturb him, but the
question was eating at her. Her future was at stake, she had to
know, and finally she went out to the living room and said, "Jim,
would you like me if I wasn't a werewolf? Or if you weren't?"

He hesitated. Not because he didn't like her. He was sure he
loved her. But if she weren't a werewolf, they probably wouldn't
have met. If he weren't a werewolf he'd probably still be a high-
flying magazine writer, pounding out a true-crime book every year
or two, divorced from the woman he'd been dating then and
playing the field like so many of the guys he used to know. If he'd
continued on that track, he probably wouldn't have even noticed
Annie. Guys like that didn't date shy secretaries, they dated models,
actresses, and attractive woman journos.

Of course he couldn't tell her that. He was trying to avoid all
the past relationship mistakes he had made because he didn't want
to fuck this one up. He didn't want her to feel she was in competition with his work, and he didn't want to hold back gifts or
affection. He wanted to be strong enough so she could be honest
with him and he could take it, not be oversensitive and defensive. He wanted to be honest with her while being sensitive to
her insecurities. He had to say just the right thing without bull-
shitting her.

"Maybe not. We might never have met," he said. "And that
would have been a tragedy."

Good answer, she thought.

Later that night, after they'd made love and were lying in bed talking, he had a bad moment when she told him about Hayden and Clark Barrow Lipp.

"Do you miss him?" he asked.

"No."

"You sound like you miss him," he said.

"It's not that," she said. "I did love him, or think I did, but I'm over it."

"Why do you still sound so hurt?"

"It's dumb, I guess, but it still makes me angry that she's living my dream, and she didn't play fair to get it. I supported him through law school –"

"Your dream?"

"Yes. I had this dream, he and I together in our own house, he'd be writing in one room and I'd be –"

"What?"

"I'd be painting in another room."

"Go on."

"We'd make love in a series of blue rooms . . ."

She looked at Jim, who had just made love to her in a blue room after finishing a chapter of a novelization.

"Almost like this," she said.

"Like this."

"It's not exactly as I dreamed it. It's not our own house, and I don't remember Hayden and I killing people in my daydream. But it's eerily close."

He kissed her.

"Tell me about India," she said.

"It's a big story. Can you be more specific?"

"Why did you go there after you faked your own death?"

"Have you heard of the ironically named Wolfgang?"

"No."

"No, you wouldn't have yet. You weren't in the program long enough," Jim said. "He's from another branch of the Potenza family.

His mother named him. Evidently she was one of the few Potenzas with a sense of humour. The rumour was that he was living naturally as a werewolf on a wildlife preserve in northeast India. I went there to find him."

"And you did?"

"It took me six months but I found him, working as a wildlife officer and running a kind of commune for werewolves in the Sunderbans, a swampy mangrove forest. God, it was beautiful, but strange. Weird things happen there. The animals there can drink saltwater. Fish climb trees, tree roots grow up, not down, and tigers behave like no other tigers in the world."

"How so? They have good table manners?"

Smile. "No. They attack from the front instead of from behind and they go for the throat. The werewolves taught them that, going for the throat to rip it out."

"Were you happy there?"

"More or less. It was a good group of people and an amazing place. But almost everyone there was paired up. Some of the werewolves had families. I was alone. After five years, I felt it was time to go back, gut instinct, and Wolfgang agreed," he said.

"Who did you kill there?"

"Poachers mainly, though every once in a while we'd hop trains to other places to take out a warlord or a ring of men who were stealing little girls and selling them into prostitution."

"Were there Indian werewolves?"

"Oh yes, but their numbers have been in great decline, a process that has gone on for centuries, thanks to factional wars and colonization," he said.

"Do you miss India?"

"Sometimes."

"Do you want to go back?"

"To visit, not to live," he said. "Tell me about the Centre. Is Fritz still there?"

"Yes."

"Is he Marco's protegé?"

"No, that would Mike Burke."

"Fritz had been my pick to succeed me."

"Fritz likes being a dentist," Annie said.

"Fritz was the smartest of the bunch and had the best self-control," Jim said. "Is Lucien still there?"

"Lucien. I don't remember a Lucien."

"Dark-haired guy, glasses. He looked like a rounder Groucho Marx."

"I'm sure I would have remembered him."

"He must have died then. I'm not surprised," he said, sadly. "He had trouble with the ketamine. Did anyone die while you were there?"

"Any of the werewolves? No. Not that I know of, but I was never in confinement. Do a lot die?"

"They lose a few every year. I lost one of my friends there to an overdose, Bernie, a composer. Another one went into a K-hole one night and never came out. Marco euthanized him."

"What's a K-hole?"

"An inescapable nightmare state caused by ketamine overdose," he said. "Carol put together really beautiful memorials for those guys."

"She really loved you."

"Carol? I loved her too," he said, his voice very soft. "Does Marco still treat her like a half-wit?"

"I wouldn't say half-wit. He can be pretty patronizing at times," she said.

"He was more than patronizing when I knew him."

"He loved you, too."

"I don't think he was capable. He's an emotional cripple."

Annie said nothing. On this point, Jim was firm.

She felt strong enough to ask Jim about Sarah.

"What do you want to know?"

"What she was like?"

"Oh, God. Sarah. Well, she was funny. Didn't take a lot of shit. Liked to shock people. And tell lies." He laughed. "Big whoppers to strangers, just for the hell of it. It would crack us up, because the truth was more unbelievable than the lies she told. But she had a heart of gold."

He looked at Annie to see if she was displaying any signs of jealousy and insecurity. She seemed fine.

"But her heart wasn't as big as yours," he said to her.

46

During his time in jail, Sam had a lot of time to think. He couldn't say he liked being in jail, but he had his own cell, and he was finally getting a chance to read some of those reporting books Cooper had given him. The guards were downright pleasant. They let him have visitors whenever he wanted, and even let Jennifer Ray bring him takeout food and printouts from the news wires about the Mad Dog case. All in all, the timing had been very lucky, being thrown into jail just as his source, Ivan, was clamming up. It saved him from trying to come up with new angles on the story.

"The rumour at City Hall is that the Mayor would like to let you out but he's keeping you in to save face," Jennifer said, handing him a sandwich and a root beer. She still hadn't told him about Candace and Wallace.

"Despite the huge public outcry?" Sam asked.

"Uh, yeah," she said, unable to tell him that the outcry had diminished since rumours spread that he'd had a fling with another woman and that's why his wife was now canoodling all over creation with Wallace Waring. Sam wouldn't notice here, where he was surrounded by men, and she kept the *Downtown Eye* and "Dear Tweets" from him. Men still by and large supported Sam, according to the private poll CCN had taken. Support from women had dropped off significantly.

"Sam, Micki wants CCN to hire her in exchange for keeping quiet about you and the secret video."

"Hire her? To do what?"

"She wants to do her own show and be a reporter, and she's playing hardball." Since Cooper's offer, Micki had gone to Candace and Syn-TV to get a counteroffer. They were willing to bring her on part time as a junior showbiz reporter. The ball was now in CCN's court.

"Sam, can I ask you some more personal questions?"

"Yeah."

"How did Candace find out about you and Micki?"

"Micki called her up and they went for dinner. I don't know what was said except that Micki went into some detail about . . . what we did . . . in bed. Candace came home, told me this, and said she was leaving."

"What else did she say?"

"Candace? You know, that she was deeply hurt and disappointed and . . . God."

"Better tell me, Sam."

"It made her sick to hear of the things Micki and I did . . . in bed. She was going to stay with a friend for a while, a sorority sister. She said we needed some space to get perspective."

"How come you didn't go to RTNDA with her?"

"I was working the weekend shift at CCN. And the year before, I didn't go with her to the convention in Vegas because I was hosting a celebrity frog-jumping contest in Atlanta, to raise money for kids with leukemia. I wish I'd gone to that Vegas convention, because that's where Syn-TV first started talking to her about a job here in the city. If I'd been there maybe they'd have offered me a job too. Not that I'm unhappy at CCN –"

"I know, Sam."

The microchips in Jennifer Ray's head began to multitask. When she got back to work, she called the news library and asked them to pull all photos of Candace Quall for the last two years and she sent an e-mail to her friend who used to work at Syn-TV.

"If you want all the gossip on Syn-TV, you should call this girl who works on *The Beth Tindall Show*. Her name's Liz," she e-mailed back, and gave Liz's number.

"Yeah, I've been following that Ace story for some time," Liz told her. "Yesterday I heard from a friend of mine who knows the guy who writes the 'Dear Tweets' column that the other woman, the one Candace's husband had an affair with, she has a videotape."

"Thanks for your help," Jennifer said. Please God, don't let the *Downtown Eye* print the stuff about the videotape and please don't let them find out that Micki's a hooker.

An intern came by and dropped off a stack of photos, organized chronologically. J.R. didn't even know what she was looking for, until she found it: a photo of Candace and Wallace from RTNDA, but not the RTNDA earlier that year. It was from the previous year in Vegas, the convention Sam couldn't attend because of the celebrity frog-jumping contest.

There could be a logical explanation for Candace being photographed there with Wallace. They were both at the convention, Syn-TV was courting her, and Wallace was part of Syn-TV's efforts. It could have been completely professional.

But there was no logical explanation for the third photo in the stack, Wallace and Candace again, a bald man hiding his face, and just behind them, a girl smiling broadly for the camera.

Jennifer took the photo in to Cooper.

"Take a look at this. It's Candace and Wallace at RTNDA in Vegas last year."

Cooper looked at it. It took a moment before he saw what she saw.

"That's Micki in the background."

"Bingo."

"What's going on?"

"I'm not sure, but Candace Quall is up to no good. You know Sam and Candace hadn't had sex in nine months? Over a year if you don't count hand jobs. Don't tell him I told you that. I promised I wouldn't repeat it."

"Poor guy. Even you have to cut him some slack —"

"I do. I mean, after that long I'd chip in to buy a guy a hooker," she said. "I think Candace set him up. I'd like to spend the rest of the day on this. I'm afraid 'Dear Tweets' may already know there's a video."

"Shit."

"How's Micki's video, by the way, the other one, the one of her public access show?"

"It's a talk show, called *Pro Sex*, sex talk from a pro, a prostitute," Cooper said. "The thing is, she isn't bad."

"Not on TV maybe," Jennifer Ray said.

"I'll ask her to come in."

⑥

Micki looked at the photo and said, "So, we were all at RTNDA in Vegas. Big deal."

"It's a big coincidence," Cooper said. "What were you doing there?"

"See that bald guy covering his face? He's a client. He took me and I tried to pitch my TV show while there," Micki said. "He'll never admit it, though. He's married."

"That's where you met Candace," Jennifer said.

"We may have met. I don't remember."

"This looks bad, this picture," Cooper said.

"And we're journalists, we can find out a lot more," Jennifer added. "And we can make it look even worse than it is. We have that power. We're the news media."

"Micki, any ex-bosses or -boyfriends out there who might talk to us?" Cooper asked. "Who might have something less than flattering to say about you? J.R., go call around some escort agencies, see which of them have employed her –"

"Oh shit," Micki said.

Yes, she admitted, she had met Candace at the last RTNDA, and Wallace and Candace probably first got involved there, though she didn't know that for a fact. She didn't see Candace again until she crashed a Syn-TV party in January, just after Candace started there. Candace asked her if she was going to the next RTNDA and Micki said no. Candace asked if she was still working as a call girl to support her public-access TV show.

"I said yeah, but I was hoping to get my show on legit TV and give up prostitution. I asked if she could help and she said she didn't think so. But a week later, she called my escort agency and booked me for an evening."

"To have sex with Sam?" J.R. asked.

"No, to have dinner with her. She was paying, I went. Anyway, she told me her husband's birthday was coming up, and she wanted to get him something special. She wanted me to spend a weekend having sex with him, being nice to him, but not tell him I was a hooker or that I knew her, so, I dunno, he'd feel attractive."

"You said yes."

"Yeah, I thought it was really cool of her to do that. I've done that kind of job before. Lots of wives don't mind if their husbands have a roll on the side every once in a while as long as they don't get emotionally involved, or, like, pick up a disease or have unwanted children. You'd be surprised how many long-time wives have a 'less work for Mama' attitude towards prostitution. And sometimes, the wives join in."

"And the videotape?"

"She asked me to make it secretly and give it to her so she could surprise him with it for their anniversary."

"But you didn't give her the videotape," Cooper said.

"No, because I got suspicious about why she wanted a tape. Once I read about her and Wallace in the 'Dear Tweets' column, I knew it was more valuable to me than to her, so I made a copy and put it and the original in two safety deposit boxes."

"Smart girl," Cooper said. "So Candace wanted the videotape for the divorce?"

"I guess. It's grounds for a quick divorce in this state, adultery."

"And Candace would want Sam to be the bad guy in the divorce," Jennifer said. "For PR reasons."

"Yeah, plus, it turns out the apartment and this big house they own in Atlanta are in Sam's name, and she wanted the apartment and half the proceeds from the sale of the house," Micki said. "I felt bad for him though. He's a nice guy."

"How did she pay you for having sex with Sam?" Jennifer asked.

"Cash. I didn't want to give my agency a cut for the Sam thing, so we negotiated a private deal."

"Damn. No receipt."

"Not for my weekend for Sam," Micki said. "But when she booked me for dinner she went through my agency, so she had to have paid by credit card."

Jennifer and Cooper looked at each other and smiled.

"Can you get the receipt?"

"I can try, but not until later. After I leave here I have to go to City Hall to meet with the Mayor's media guy."

"The Mayor's media guy?" J.R. asked. "Seth Kirk?"

"He wants the tape too!" Cooper guessed. "So they can leak it to the media, make Sam look bad, and justify keeping Sam in jail. Goddamn. This town."

"Micki, we're pussycats compared to City Hall. They'll put you in jail to get those tapes," Jennifer said. "But we can help you. Can you keep your mouth shut about Sam?"

"What's in it for me?"

"We won't report that you and Candace hatched a scheme to seduce Sam and that you've been using the tape to try to blackmail yourself into a job. How's that?" Cooper said. He pushed his phone over to her. "Call the Mayor's media guy. Tell him there is no video-tape and you didn't have an affair with Sam, that it's just gossip."

Micki did as she was told. After she hung up, Cooper said, "J.R., wait about five minutes then call the Mayor's media guy and see if you can convince him the Mayor has saved enough face and Sam should be sprung."

Micki got up as if to leave.

"Hang on, Micki, we have to get those videotapes," Cooper said. "I'll go with you."

47

If you took an empty sixteen-ounce Evian bottle with cap, a tiny bit of superglue and a toothpick, you could fill it with tap water, reseal it, and sell it for a two bucks to hot commuters or joggers, three if you wore dark glasses and carried a cane.

The beauty of the water scam was that nobody would ever suspect anything so low-profit of being a scam. The profit on twelve bottles of refrigerated tap water was only about thirty bucks. But it was a great cover for other scams, and it was a motherlode of free entertainment for Razz. It was fun to watch people strug-gle to get the caps off. It usually took four or five good twists to break the grip of the superglue. When the cap finally broke open it was with enough violence to spill water all over some stock-broker's expensive suit or some pretty young woman's outfit.

It was also fun, as well as profitable, to give people the wrong change back. Razz punched tiny holes in the money, ten tiny pin-holes in a ten dollar bill, for example. He'd punch ten holes in a bunch of ones as well, and mix them liberally in with the tens. When, after going through the motions of feeling the pinholes to make sure it was a ten, he handed someone a one instead of a ten, the customer felt like a jerk asking for correct change. Razz would feel the bill again, pull another one dollar bill from the ten dollar pile and give it to the customer with his most sincere apologies. If the customer mentioned it again, Razz acted suspicious. He didn't say anything, but his demeanour and tone said, "How could you rip off a poor old blind man?" Nine times out of ten customers just wrote off the nine dollars as a donation to the visually impaired, rather than cause a scene in which they might come off badly.

To make it more believable, he always slipped a few mispunched tens into the pile of ones, clustered near the bottom, so if someone came back with a cop, Razz could show that he sometimes erred in favour of the customer. He made about fifty, sixty bucks on top of the water profit this way, and then, if the forces of the universe were with him, he might have the opportunity to snag a fat wallet before he sold his last bottle and beat it to a new spot.

Singing in the subway was good too. The worse he sang, the more money he got, but it was never enough to justify the time he put in, unless he grabbed a wallet. It was always easier to make money if his cousin Lewis was in town. Lewis would play his elderly sighted brother, helping Razz around. Lewis wasn't that old, he was in his fifties like Razz, but with the right sad expression, the right stoop to his shoulders, and a certain arthritic way of walking and moving his arms, he could make himself look seventy. Few people could resist these two Damon Runyan characters, or their bullshit. One of them would distract a victim while the other picked his pocket, plucked her purse, or swiped a mink jacket off a garment rack.

Lewis never stuck around long, though. He was a track hound and followed the big races, always just two steps ahead of an outstanding warrant or a vengeful woman he'd bilked out of her life savings.

Razz got lonely, and he was tired too. He was working almost as hard as some slob with a job, as Lewis would say. When Razz was younger and good looking it was easy to find some naïve young do-gooder woman to take him in and look after him for a while. Lewis, even at his age, still never had any trouble, but Lewis never looked for women in this city.

"They're too hard, too suspicious, too selfish, and too greedy," Lewis complained, before he moved on to Pimlico and a widow who owned a bar.

There was one nice girl left in the city, a girl named Annie, who looked like a good prospect. Razz actually felt something for her, a combination of lust and need that he thought might be love. Even better, he was sure she felt the same way. If only he hadn't been so aggressive with her, she might be with him now. He had waited and waited for her to make the first move, but after realizing she was a nice Catholic girl, he'd decided it was up to him. All he'd done was scare her off. When he'd tried to talk to her, to apologize and explain, she'd run from him.

He shouldn't have run after her, he thought. She probably suspected that he wasn't blind after that incident. When he finally caught up to her again, he was going to have to do a real song-and-dance about his heightened sense of smell and his love guiding him in his chase. She might buy it. She'd bought his story about how his late seeing-eye dog, Fred, went blind without Razz knowing until Fred was hit by a bus that just missed Razz by inches.

Why wouldn't she accept that he was not just following his nose but his heart when he chased her down the street that day? All he had to do was find her again and talk to her, one on one, without the cops being involved, and he was sure she'd come back, or his name wasn't Razz, a.k.a. Bill Smith, a.k.a. Moe Bloom, a.k.a. Donald Black . . .

Since then, he'd seen her once near a health food store, and lost her. So when he saw her again, he was determined not to let her get away.

It was a sunny Saturday and Razz had just sat down in front of a discount clothing place in a busy shopping area, with his water bottles and his cigar box of change, when he saw her getting out of a taxi and going into the shop with a man. At first he didn't recognize her because she'd changed her hair colour and was wearing dark glasses. Razz was sure she hadn't seen him.

When she and the man came out and hailed another taxi, he had manoeuvred himself close enough on the sidewalk to hear the address the man barked out to the driver.

Twice in two months he had run into her by accident. But as Lewis always said when he was on his way to the track or an off-track betting shop to wager some lovelorn divorcee's money on a horse with a serendipitous name, there are no accidents. This was cosmic. Razz had to find her, the last nice girl in the city, and win her heart.

48

Meredith was talking to the barista at the Pink Pony when Jim walked by with a girl. It was a different girl from the one she'd seen crawling out of his window. This girl had short blond hair and was wearing regular jeans and a sleeveless tee. She was cute, but lacked the breezy, oversized style of the girl on the fire escape.

What does he see in this one? she thought. Meredith's momentary jealousy was eased by the thought that Jim was at least dating again after whatever horrible romantic tragedy had been tormenting him, and he was playing the field, which meant she now had a chance.

When she saw the girl with Jim again the next day, getting out of a taxi with a bunch of bags from Mother Earth's Bounty, she got a little worried. She couldn't tell how cute the girl was, as she was wearing dark glasses, but she looked pretty cute. Worse, Jim really seemed to like her.

That night, thanks to her new telescope, she got an even better look when the girl leaned out the bedroom window. The girl was drinking wine and staring up at the sky. Jim joined her, and

Meredith watched them, framed in a warm golden window against the dark night. Something the girl said made Jim laugh. He said something that made the girl laugh. They kissed, a long kiss, both of them propped on their elbows in his windowsill, and then they disappeared inside and shut the curtains.

Meredith tilted the telescope down and refocused on Jim's door, to see if they were going out. A black man with a pale pink buzz cut came out, a blind man walked by, tapping his cane, and a group of kids went in. She looked back at Jim's window. The light was out but there was still a faint glow from behind the curtains like a lamp or a candle.

That should be me, Meredith thought. I'm the one who has spent almost every day trying to coax him out of his shell and cheer him up. I should be drinking wine under the stars and kissing that man. I should be the one being undressed by him now, his masculine hands cupping my breasts . . .

"Will you please stop?" her roommate Chrissie said from behind her. "A telescope? You are now officially a Stalker with a big S."

"I'm looking at the stars," Meredith said, subtly tipping the telescope upward.

"Sure you are. I'm going over to Kafka's. Come out with us, meet some real guys."

"I can't. I have to find . . . Orion and do some work on my Edie Sedgwick stuff."

"Meredith, this was a cute crush at first but it just gets worse and worse. You never go out socially any more. You don't read, you don't even watch TV. It has become an unhealthy obsession. Get out and get help."

"Thanks for the tip. 'Bye." She put her eye to the telescope and looked at the night sky until she heard Chrissie close the door to the apartment, then she tilted it down to Jim's window.

49

Dear Tweets,

When, oh when is a superior race of beings going to invade our planet and save us from stupid people? I've been waiting and waiting. I've blasted high-frequency radio signals into the ether. I've put out cookies and milk. I've placed ads in the back of the Eye. "Help! I'm being held captive on Planet Imbecile."

We are surrounded by the . . .

Self-Deluded

You'd think the Queen of an Empire who pulled herself up by her bra straps would know when she's licked, and not continue chasing a certain major mogul who has told her he's not interested. Sir, you will need hints as big as battering rams to break through this Czarina's ego, not to mention that bomb-grade corsetry and that force field of makeup and perfume. She thinks you're just playing hard to get.

We are surrounded by the . . .

Self-Destructive

You'd think a former pretty boy on the comeback trail would keep a low profile so soon out of rehab. Nobody's going to want to hire you for those romantic Latino Lover roles if they find out you were snorting with a half-naked leather boy in the john at the Black Bull. By the way, how did you repay him for his opiate generosity?

We are surrounded by the . . .

Just Plain Stupid

You'd think a man in television would know better than to make a sex video with his girlfriend, especially when that man is a married man. Stupid. That's why Aces beat jokers.

50

"**Y**ou'd better be careful," Liz said to Henry. "The Czarina is going to figure out it's you feeding Dear Tweets this stuff."

They were sitting on two wooden chairs in the waiting area of the police precinct, waiting to report Annie as a missing person as soon as a cop had a free moment. The Mad Dog murders had sucked so many people into their investigation that the rest of the force had its hands full with the day-to-day crime fighting. Missing girls didn't rank very high on their list of priorities at the moment.

"Do I care?" Henry said. "I've had it with her, and her mink oil, and her Caspian caviar and her patronizing references to gays."

"What did she say about gays?"

"'I love you homo people,' and she said it the way you might say 'munchkins' or 'retarded kids.'"

"What do you expect from a woman who thinks famine is a Darwinian thing?"

"Not that we care about famine victims. Fashion victims, yes."

"At least we don't say mean things about famine victims," Liz said. "Where will you go if you leave Rosemary?"

"My new beau thinks he can get me on with this actress he knows something about. I can't tell you who, but think blonde. Think perky . . ."

"Not her! We are in, Henry! If you get her to come to just one of my parties . . ."

"Excuse me," a policeman said. "Can you come this way?"

The cop, clearly pressed for time, sat them down by his desk and said, "So this woman has been missing for how long?"

"A week? Two weeks?" Liz looked at Henry.

"I'm not sure." Henry looked at the cop. "We've been really busy, we lost track of her. Her super says she just vanished."

"He also says she was eaten by a werewolf. But we haven't seen her and she hasn't returned our calls. She quit her job. So we think the part about her vanishing is true." Liz said.

"Uh huh. You have a picture of her?"

"Just a couple of Polaroids from a party," Henry said. "This is her here, behind me and Liz. And this is the three of us behind Rosemary Frost. That's her there."

"Uh huh. Did she have a boyfriend?"

"She broke up with her last one. He's married now. But her super said she had a new one," Liz said.

"And she brought a guy named Fritz to one of your parties, Liz. But I thought he was gay," Henry said.

"I didn't get that vibe off him at all," Liz said.

"My gaydar went off –"

"Your gaydar went off like a pachinko machine for Wallace Waring too. I think you're confusing your gaydar with your wish-dar."

"Excuse me. I'm very busy. Can we get back to Annie Engel?" the cop said.

"Oh, sure," Liz said.

"Where does she live? We'll send someone over when we can," said the cop.

51

When Sam went into jail, everyone was being very nice to him. When he got out of jail, something had changed. Men were still being nice to him, saying things like, "Hey, everyone's entitled to one mistake" and "Better luck in the future."

Women, though, were very cold, and saying puzzling things like, "It serves you right" and "Not one of you can be trusted." One woman shouted at him, "Pig!"

"Why are they doing that?" he asked Jennifer. "Do they know about Micki?"

"I dunno," she said.

"They couldn't know, could they? Unless Candace said something somewhere . . ."

"Let's get you home, Sam. A nice hot shower, some clean jammies and then you can crawl into your own bed. Cooper's given you the day off to recuperate from doing hard time."

Nothing was leaking out and nobody had new information on the Mad Dog story. About all they had was some sidebar stuff. There'd been some sightings of strange doglike creatures, and Jennifer Ray thought it would make a good weird story about werewolves and mass hysteria. The story had a bit of a news angle, because one of the guys she wanted to interview was the super at a building of a young woman whose friends had just filed a missing persons report on her. Jennifer was surprised to see one of the missing girl's friends was Liz at Syn-TV. It was true what people said about the city. It's just a big small town, and everyone's path crosses everyone else's eventually.

It's also true that one stone can kill two birds. When Jennifer called Liz to ask her about the missing girl, she mentioned that she'd heard that Candace had made up the story about the girl and the videotape, and that Candace's affair with Wallace Waring had started long before Candace moved to the city.

Jennifer waited to give Liz time to call her friend who knew Dear Tweets, and for that friend to call Dear Tweets. Ten minutes later, Jennifer called the *Downtown Eye* and reported the same thing to the Dear Tweets assistant. Dear Tweets was unable to take the call, as he was out having a green-tea facial.

"You're the second person to tell me this in the last five minutes," the assistant said.

Technically, gossip was against every journalistic ethic J.R. still had after six years in TV news, but these were exceptional circumstances, and fire had to be fought with fire.

⑥

Sam was raring to go the next morning when she picked him up, cleaned up real nice, in his work clothes, his Burberry, his hat, and his Clark Kent glasses. Dear Tweets had not yet retracted the story about the videotape, claiming he hadn't received the messages about it until after the column "went to bed." He promised Jennifer Ray he'd make a little mention in the next column, but only after she threatened him with an unflattering profile on CCN. God, she'd always hated people who abused their power the way she was doing now, but man, it was a jungle out there. She consoled herself now that what she was doing was in the interests of a kind of justice beyond simple rules.

"Who are we going to interview?" Sam asked.

"Gunther Hamernich," Jennifer read from her sheet. "He's a super, a nut. He thinks a werewolf ate a girl in his building. After that, we talk to two film students who think they saw a cross between a bear and a dog on the roof. I'm betting they were totally fucked up at the time – they were when I called. But they should be amusing. We also have an old woman who thinks she saw a coyote last full moon, and then one last interview, with a psychiatrist who will speak about mass hysteria."

"No real news about the murders?"

"Nope. What about your sources?"

"Still clammed up."

"Work on 'em, Sam. The full moon is coming."

ⓖ

Gunther was waiting for them, all scrubbed up and his hair combed and slicked back with an aromatic pomade that smelled like auto grease and apples. He was wearing a shirt and tie.

"I saw it one night during a full moon, two months ago, and it wasn't the first time I saw a werewolf. When I was a drunk and a bum, I lived with the Mole People in the tunnels under the city. I saw one down there. It looked right at me. So when I saw it again recently, I knew what is was. And when the girl disappeared, I knew what had happened to her."

"Werewolf ate her?" Sam said, with a straight face.

"Yes. I think he was her boyfriend. He would tie her up. One night, her window was broken. There was dog hair stuck to the glass . . ."

"Her boyfriend had a dog?"

"Her boyfriend is the werewolf!" Hamernich said.

"And you say you were a drunk when you saw the werewolf."

"The first time. I was sober the last time. Five years ago, a man from the Jesus Saves Tabernacle found me and sobered me up. I have not touched a drop since I accepted Jesus Christ as my personal saviour. This is what happens when people turn away from God: women work, children run wild in the streets, whores and homosexuals freely practice their sins," he intoned in a flat voice. "Werewolves and demons appear and you know the devil is afoot. Judgement is coming."

"Okay. Thank you so much," Jennifer Ray said brightly.

"I have a picture of her, Annie," Hamernich said. "She was a nice girl before the werewolf got her. A good Christian girl."

"Where'd you get this?"

"From her room."

"Can we see her room?" J.R. asked. "Has it been sealed off by the police?"

"No. They're too busy. They took my statement about the missing girl, they looked around her apartment, and they left. You know what they did when I told them a werewolf was responsible for this and for all those murders?"

"What?" Sam asked.

"They told me to call 777-3456."

Sam looked blank.

"Moviephone," explained Jennifer. "A friend of mine used to give that number to pick-up artists in bars."

"Come up," Hamernich said.

The apartment was very clean. The hallway opened into a small kitchen, and beyond was a door to a bedroom/living room, where a clock radio on low volume played Dionne Warwick asking, "Do You Know the Way to San Jose?" There were several bottles of Bergerac organic wine on the kitchen counter. In the fridge, some soy milk and some now wilted, rotten, or liquefied fruits and vegetables. In the freezer compartment, J.R. found tofu breakfast sausages, a box of frozen Gardenburgers, and a half pint of Vanilla Fudge Rice Cream frozen dessert.

"She's a vegetarian," Jennifer said.

They couldn't use any of this for the mass hysteria story. Annie Engel didn't remotely fit the profile of the other murder victims, who were rich, greedy and evil. Her only connection to the Mad Dog case was through this lunatic super who thought he saw a werewolf.

But Jennifer Ray was curious to know how a young woman, about her own age, could vanish like that, leaving food in her pantry and her moisturizing cream open by the side of the bathroom sink. It happened far too often. Where did these young women go?

Slowly, she put together a sketch of the girl from the things Hamernich said and what she observed around Annie's apartment. Annie Engel was the girl people called when they wanted their cats fed, their plants watered, or fifty dollars to pay the electric bill until the pension cheque came. She had three pairs of sensible but pretty Naturalizer shoes in her closet, one pair still in its box and its Shoe Savers bag. The businesslike suits in her closet were off-brands. There were some cute party dresses, also off-brands.

In her pictures, she looked plain-pretty, plain on first glance, but prettier the longer you looked at her.

"She looks sweet," Sam said.

"Yeah."

"I wonder what happened to her?" Sam said.

Jennifer put the picture frame down on the dresser and moved to the desk. There was a cabinet beside it with paints and brushes organized in orderly cubicles. On the desk was a computer, turned off, and a yellow legal pad. At the top, Annie had written: Suicide.

Underneath were two columns, Pros and Cons. Under Pros she had written,

Nobody else will get hurt
No more guilt
Nobody will find out

Under Cons there was nothing but a pencil drawing she'd doodled. It was well done. It looked like a snowy field, fringed by a few trees, under a full moon.

"Well, I don't think a werewolf got her," Jennifer said, quietly, showing the legal pad to Sam.

"Aw, you think she —"

"This would explain the lack of interest on the part of the police."

"That's sad. Aw. I wonder what it was she felt so guilty about she had to kill herself."

"I bet it was some dumb commonplace thing, something connected to a broken heart." She turned to Hamernich. "Did she have any family here?"

"She had no family left," he said.

"What a shame," Jennifer said.

"She had two friends who stopped by, Henry and Liz. Liz works at Syn-TV. I have her card somewhere . . ."

"I have her number," Jennifer said.

Sam left Annie Engel's name out of the finished report, except for a mention of a missing girl and a quick shot of the photo. The tone of the piece was too light for the story of a young woman's suicide. But Jennifer couldn't stop thinking about her. She called Liz at Syn-TV, and got Henry's number. After she talked to him and to the manager of the nursing home where Annie used to visit a Mrs. Mackie, she talked to Annie's former fiancee, Hayden Lipp.

"I'd like to do a report, Coop," she said later, over Buffalo burgers and beers at the station hangout, Bobo's. "About this girl Annie Engel, who presumably killed herself. She sounds like she was a nice girl and, you know, she was just a year older than I am. She had her whole life ahead of her."

"What's your angle?"

"Human interest. She had a bad break-up with a guy earlier this year, but there was no sign of serious depression. Why does she take her own life?"

"Presumably. No body has been found."

"No, and where is the body? I dunno. It's raggin' on me, Cooper. A nice girl, eaten up, not by a werewolf, but by the big city."

"Keep talking."

"Everyone I've spoken to said pretty much the same thing. She was too nice, too kind, too good. Even her ex-fiancee said that. How can you be that and survive? I have to break my own rules at least once a day to keep the upper hand with the assholes in this city. Jesus, just to protect Sam, I've lied, gossiped, threatened, broken promises, and otherwise abused my power as a television journalist. And I'm one of the good guys."

"You are."

"Not like her. She lived here all this time, and she stayed good, truly good. I mean, a really good person."

"She probably wasn't much fun."

"Coop."

"Sorry."

"The question isn't just, How does one do that, stay truly good in this crappy world, but, Does one want to? Is this what happens? One way or another, do those good people just get –"

"Eaten up by this crappy world?"

"Exactly. I was thinking it would be a good piece for the *Great City Show*. It'll take some time to do properly and I'll have to do it

on the side but nothing's coming out on the Mad Dog story now
anyway –"

"I had Justin Berg work his sources and they're dry too."

"Sam's working on his sources. Maybe he'll get lucky."

"He's a lucky guy," Cooper said. "He's not the shiniest quarter
in the cash box, but luck's as good as brains."

"Better, maybe."

"Okay, go ahead and do it," Cooper said. "I have something else
I want to talk about."

"Yeah," Jennifer said.

"I think we're going to hire Micki."

"To do what?"

"We're going to make her the sex reporter, and twice a month
do a half-hour digest of those reports with a call-in segment where
she gives sex advice."

"A version of her public access show, *Pro Sex*."

"You saw the tape."

"Yeah, I watched it last night."

"And?"

"You're right, she is good, really good, actually," Jennifer said.
"She's sharp, witty, tells it like it is, is neither pro-male nor pro-
female –"

"Just pro-sex, with a pro."

"It's a great hook. But she's also a liar, a blackmailer, a gossip –
oh damn. So am I. I just admitted it five minutes ago," she said.
"Fuck it. Hire her. She'll fit in great."

"Really?"

"Sure. She did the right thing – eventually, and under duress,
but she did the right thing," Jennifer said.

"She didn't come forward with this until someone, Candace
maybe, leaked the information to Dear Tweets. Think about it. She
was just protecting herself."

"You'll have to clean up her language for our air."

"I was going to ask you to teach her the approved names of body parts, functions, and sexual acts, so we don't have to bleep her."

Jennifer laughed. "One or two bleeps per episode might be kind of fun."

"Genius, J.R. That's why I love you . . . uh, I mean, I love you as a journalist, of course. So will you do it?"

"I'll think about it. Ask me again after the full moon. What time is it? Oh shit. I gotta go to a party this woman Liz is having. Dear Tweets is supposed to be there." She took out a small hand mirror and a tube of lipstick. "How do I look?"

"Great."

"Nah, but cute enough for this crappy world. Talk to ya."

⑥

"I'm worried about Sam Deverell," the Mayor said, picking at his cold Hungarian goulash. Another late night at City Hall, staring into a plate of cold food with orange, waxy fat congealing around its edges, while people hammered at him from all sides. Life was good at the top.

"Well, we couldn't keep him in any longer. It was too controversial. The *Downtown Eye* called you a fascist, even the *Post* got on you about jailing a journalist," Seth said. "I tried to get some dirt on him, but none of it panned out, so —"

"We're not going to smear him. No proof, no smear," the Mayor said.

"If he gets wind of the dragnet —" the Commissioner said.

"Sssh," the Mayor said. He closed his eyes. "I feel an idea coming."

That day at one of their "amicable" lunches, Marva had suggested the Mayor "kill Sam with kindness."

"Invite him to City Hall, talk to him like a person and explain you don't want this information getting out," she said.

He had smiled. Marva had always been the one he'd gone to with "people questions," whether they concerned a cashier going through a bad divorce who kept breaking down in tears in the middle of checkout, meetings with franchisees or stockholders, or negotiations with Teamsters. How he missed her.

But sitting here now, her advice twisted itself into another idea. He wouldn't kill Sam with kindness, but the way to secure Sam Deverell might be to give him what he wanted.

6

For over an hour, Sam had been waiting at the bar at Griffin's, counting the varieties of vodka and hoping Ivan would come in. Marguerite told him he shouldn't wait, Ivan wouldn't talk to him, but he insisted on waiting. He needed to get something, anything on this story.

"So you made a videotape, did you?" Marguerite said.

"I make them every day," Sam said.

"Pah," she said, and walked away.

He was reaching for the free pretzels when his cell phone rang.

"Sam Deverell."

"Sam, this is Seth Kirk."

"Who?"

"I'm the Mayor's media liaison. The Mayor would like to speak to you. Where are you? We'll send a car. No cameras. Come alone."

6

The Mayor had welcomed him in, shaken his hand and introduced him to his Police Commissioner and media guy.

"You've just shone on this story, Sam," the Mayor said. "It hasn't made our job easy, but we respect the work you did."

"Well, thanks! But I can't reveal my sources."

"We're not going to ask you to reveal your sources. We have an offer for you. We want to give you an exclusive."

"You'll be the only reporter inside the investigation," Seth the media guy said.

"Great!"

"But . . . the story is embargoed."

"Embargoed?"

"You can't report it, or say anything about anything you see, hear, or learn until we say so, on the night the operation is launched. You'll have access to the cops, to us, the task force. You won't be in the Mayor's or the Police Commissioner's private meetings, but you can attend all the other meetings," the media guy said.

"Gee, that sounds pretty good. I'll have to clear it with my managing editor, but I'm sure he'll be happy."

"I'm sure he will, Sam," the Mayor said.

"You and CCN will be legally bound to honour this embargo. If you break the embargo, you go back to jail," the media guy said.

"I understand," Sam said. "And I want to thank you for this opportunity."

"No, thank you, Sam," the Mayor said. "And I'm sorry about your wife."

"My wife? You know about my wife?"

"Word gets around," the Mayor said.

52

Mike Burke awakened after the full moon naked in an abandoned building with no idea of where he was and how he was going to get home. Looking out a smeared window, he saw only black and Hispanic-looking people on the street below. He wasn't a bigot or anything – he just didn't think a naked white man with blood on his face and chest would fare real well in this neighbourhood. But Mike was a former soldier, trained to obey, be resourceful, and find his way out of unfamiliar territory.

All he could find to wear was a black trash bag, which had to be emptied of plaster and nails before he could poke a head hole in it and wear it like a dress. He waited until well into the night, about three in the morning, before he crept out of the building.

He was uptown and had no money. After he washed the blood off with the muddy water from a puddle, he went looking for something better to wear, poking in dumpsters and sidewalk trash barrels until he found a pair of ripped brown trousers and a stained T-shirt that said Nike on it. He had no shoes. New full-body turnstiles in the metro stations made turnstile jumping impossible. He started walking, slowly, because he was still a little stiff from transformation.

A few blocks farther on, he saw a bunch of guys, dressed as badly as he was, going into a soup kitchen. He went in too, figuring he could get a hot meal and maybe make a phone call to Marco – better yet, Carol – to come get him. Marco was going to be furious. It wasn't the first time Mike had gone out with Marco to bring a stray in, but he'd never disobeyed Marco's commands before. His latest kill was the first since he shipped back home from Somalia, where he'd devoured a warlord and a magician who had convinced an army of young boys that they were invincible to bullets and could attack a rival warlord's forces with complete confidence.

The pastor at the soup kitchen gave him a hot breakfast and promised him change for a phone call after he attended a prayer service. While he ate, he thought about what Marco might do to him. Demote him maybe, back to the patient pool, just long enough to punish him. He'd hate to go back to the patient pool. That meant mandatory confinement and heavy drugs. He hated the drugs. That was one reason he'd worked so hard on transcending.

He had to go back, he knew that. But he didn't feel like going back just yet. Maybe if he made up a story about where he was, said he'd had amnesia. Marco might buy that. Yeah, he woke up naked in an abandoned building, and then he wandered into a soup kitchen. And if he was going to have amnesia, he needn't go back right away. Give Marco a couple of weeks, and instead of being angry, he'd be relieved when Mike came back.

It would serve Marco right to have to worry a while, and Mike was in no hurry to face his temper. Mike knew how to take orders and not show emotion, but that didn't mean Marco didn't get under his skin. If he wasn't being critical, he was being condescending. Marco had to be smarter than everyone else in the room. Most of all, Mike didn't like the way Marco treated Carol. Sometimes at dinner, Carol would tell a funny story and Marco would shoot her a look and say, "You're digressing." Carol would stop and Mike would have to find her during a free moment later to discover what happened to her former roommate who ran off with the roadie from Moby Grape (had a bad trip, ended up in an emergency room, joined a cult for a couple of years, now an insurance adjuster with two college-age kids in St. Louis). Or what she thought of Abbie Hoffman or Jimi Hendrix when she met them both at a party in the Canyon when she was living in California. ("They were both very smart and very thoughtful," she said. "Jimi asked me if I was having a good time, and Abbie asked me my opinion of the war. Then a man named Carlos came by and asked if I wanted to eat some peyote and I don't think I remember much of the party after that unless God was there with seven smooth-faced blue angels and the Rolling Stones. It was the sixties, so anything's possible.")

Something else was bothering him too. Marco had said after Sarah died that Jim Valiente had mixed up her drug IV that night. At the time, Mike knew nothing of procedures, and just accepted what Marco said. But Mike had been Marco's protegé for five years now, and Marco never let him mix the drugs, except to train him to give an emergency shot if Marco wasn't there for some reason.

Mike hadn't known Jim or Sarah that well, but Marco's version bothered him. If Sarah had broken up with Jim, and Jim was heartbroken, and if Marco knew it and was a trained psychiatrist, supposed to be sensitive to these things, why would he have let Jim mix the drug IVs and give Sarah hers? Even if Marco didn't think Jim would kill her, why would he make a guy treat the girl who just broken his heart? That would just be cruel.

After his hot, and not bad, breakfast, Mike spoke to the pastor and asked if he needed a hand, and maybe knew of a place he could stay for a few weeks, until he got back on his feet. As Mike was a veteran and seemed like a nice young man who had just taken some wrong turns in life, the pastor decided to help him. Mike went to work in the kitchen, sleeping at night at the church's shelter. He was very quiet and hard-working. Two weeks became three.

Mike could have stayed there. He liked it. But the full moon was coming and he had to go home.

"Wish you'd stay, but I hope you'll find a good life at home," the pastor said, pressing some money into Mike's hand. Mike protested but the pastor insisted. Mike kept enough for cab fare, and dropped the rest of the bills into a donation box at the door on his way out.

⑥

Carol was relieved to see him, wrapping him in her warm maternal embrace.

"Oh, thank God you're okay, Mike. Thank God. Marco! Marco! *Marco!* Mike's back."

Marco came out of his office with his reading glasses on. "What the hell happened to you?" he asked.

Mike gave him a stony look. "I had amnesia," he said. "I was staying in a men's shelter uptown until I got my memory back."

"I thought you'd joined Valiente," Marco said. "I've been worried sick. This, on top of everything else . . ."

"He had amnesia, Marco. Don't be angry. Go back to your office," Carol said. "Mike, can I get you something to eat? Come into the kitchen. A lot has happened but I expect Marco will get you caught up on most of it later. Rudolfo's here. Enzio and Audrey are expecting a baby, and Max has a fashion show coming up in the fall . . ."

In the kitchen, Mike said, "You sit, I'll cook us something."

"You can cook?"

"Nothing fancy. I make good soup. What else is going on?"

"You know Annie didn't come back."

"I didn't know, but I kind of sensed it."

"She went with Jim Valiente. So Lwee-Gee came up with Rudolfo and read the riot act. Marco will fill you in more, but I warn you, Marco is in a terrible mood. He's under so much pressure."

Mike didn't tell her his suspicions about Marco and Sarah and Jim. The honourable thing, he felt, would be to talk to Marco first. After he and Carol ate, he found Marco in his office with Rudolfo, going over a large map.

"I'd like to speak to you, Marco," he said.

"We need to speak to you –"

"Alone, please," Mike said, in a tone Marco had never heard before.

"Excuse us, Rudolfo."

As if reporting to a superior officer, Mike reported his suspicions. Marco listened and then said, firmly and with barely controlled anger, "I did not kill Sarah, and I deeply resent your accusation. Jim was further along in his transcendence than you, so I decided to let him mix some of the drug IVs. We had more patients in the program then, if you recall. I let him give her the IV because he asked to and because I didn't realize he was heartbroken, I thought he and Sarah were 'cool' " – he made quotation marks in the air when he said this – "about the break-up. I never in a million years thought he'd kill her. Now go talk to Rudolfo and ask him to bring you up to date on our plans. I need to take care of some other things."

After all these years, Sarah was still making trouble for him, Marco thought.

From the beginning, Sarah had caused trouble. Female werewolves had become rare and she was an even rarer creature, a lovely young woman, smart and spirited. All the men at the Centre fell in love with her and, yes, Marco did too. For the first time in his marriage, he wanted another woman, not just a fling, but a relationship with another woman. Sarah gave every impression she wanted the same with him, at least as he interpreted it. She didn't say so, not overtly, but he could see it in her smile, the way she laughed and the way she looked at him.

Sarah was perfect for him, he realized. She was a werewolf, like him. All those things he couldn't quite explain to Carol, he could explain to Sarah. Not only was she younger and probably able to bear the children Carol couldn't, she would satisfy his family's desire for a werewolf wife for him. This at a time when he'd grown more than bored with Carol.

But even if all this weren't true, he would have wanted Sarah. He was madly in love with her, emphasis on the *madly*. A strange, surreal mood overtook Marco. He could not see reason, as far as Sarah was concerned. He wanted her, he had to have her, and he deserved her.

After that, everything Carol did annoyed him and seemed like part of some passive-aggressive strategy to weaken him or manipulate him. Her every mistake tested his temper. When she went into one of her endlessly expanding stories it was like chewing tinfoil. Even when she did something that seemed purely kind, he saw it as an attempt to make him feel guilty because she sensed they were growing apart and he'd soon take a mistress.

One day, while he and Sarah were discussing her sexual history in great detail, she said she hoped to have sex again soon.

"Oh?" Marco said. "Do you have someone picked out?"

Sarah turned, looked right in his eyes and said, "Well, yeah."

There was no mistaking that look, he thought. She wanted him and this was her way of telling him so. He was sure of it. A lock of her brown hair fell over her eyes and he reached down and brushed it away gently. He stopped taking notes and rested his chin on his hand, gazing at her like a schoolboy.

"What you need, Sarah, is a man like me," he said, to encourage her.

"I already have you," she'd said.

"Not as a doctor, as a companion, an intimate."

"Jesus, Doc, yesterday I told you about screwing a guy in the back of a Trailways bus on my way home from college. You know every detail of my sexual history. You know my menstrual cycle! How much more intimate can we get?" she said, and from the look on his face, she realized what he was really saying. He had a goofy look she'd seen before on infatuated men – pink-faced, glossy-eyed, nervously wiggling his lips.

"How much more intimate can we get?" she repeated, adding, "Seeing that you're married to the fabulous Carol, and I have that strict rule about married men because of all my father's affairs."

She hoped this would mollify him. After all, he was a mature man, a professional, married to a woman who waited on him hand and foot and treated him like he was God's gift to mankind. All that and a bag of chips too. Even if he hadn't been married, she wouldn't have gone for Marco – too pretentious and snobbish, a know-it-all, constantly correcting everyone, most especially Carol. Okay, he was a decent shrink, and, in any event, the only game in town for werewolves. He was really smart, devoted to his patients, and she did respect him. But as a boyfriend? And even though she knew it was his job as a dispassionate headshrinker to ask about her sexual history, he seemed to be overly interested in that lately. Whatever she brought up, he'd find some thread in it that led to her sex life. In the past, she had shrugged off all of this, but once she saw that look on his face, she reconsidered. It was kind of creepy.

Wisely, when he asked her who she was planning to have this big affair with, she didn't tell him, even though she had brought up the subject in hopes of getting his blessing for her relationship with Jim.

"I just have a feeling something wonderful is going to happen, soon," she said.

Then she flashed that meaningful look and smile at him again. She had done it to say, "No hard feelings, right, Doc?" but he read it as, "Your wife is in the way of our great love affair of the ages."

It never occurred to him that he might be projecting his feelings, his body's desire or his ego's desire on her.

The night after that conversation with Sarah, he lay in bed and thought about what to do with Carol. Would she divorce him without spilling the secret of the Potenzas, or the Centre? Too risky. Maybe he could pawn Carol off on Rudolfo. Rudolfo was always sweet on her. Marco had done all right by her, she had no cause to complain, and he had no reason to feel guilty, in his mind. If he hadn't rescued her from her life of drugs and casual sex, she'd probably have been dead long ago anyway. The patients might have trouble with it, but they'd have to learn to live with it.

Over the next few days, while he was transferring some of his assets into a Swiss bank account and fantasizing about the blissful life ahead, he kept a close eye on Sarah, which is why he saw her as she left the building after a session.

That day, she wasn't alone when she left. A dark-haired man was walking beside her. He must have said something funny, because Sarah laughed, threw her arms around him and gave him a deep, soulful kiss. When they finally pulled apart, Marco got a good look at the rogue's face.

It was Jim.

The two of them turned, walking very easily with each other. At one point Jim playfully pushed her away and she grabbed him and kissed him again. It was a long kiss.

It made Marco sick. There was a strict No Fraternization with the Female rule, and Jim, his trusted right hand, was breaking it behind his back to take advantage of a vulnerable young woman. His heart was broken. For the rest of the day, Marco wept like a French depressive, alone in his locked office with a Serge Gainsbourg CD playing over and over.

After the tenth or eleventh play, he stopped weeping and got angry, at Sarah more than at Jim, because he loved Sarah so much more than Jim. All the hetero werewolves were in love with Sarah, though he had expected Jim to show self-control and put the program ahead of himself. That Jim didn't put the program first made Marco think Sarah was the problem.

Sarah had played Marco, she had led him on, he realized. He was thinking of divorcing his wife for her, his long-suffering wife. It was obvious to Marco that Sarah was playing Jim too. Sure. Jim was a big magazine writer and she was an aspiring author. Jim could help her career. What could Marco do for her, other than enable her to lead a near-to-normal life? She turned those selfish, ungrateful siren eyes of hers on Jim and he was a goner.

He had a thought – perhaps she intended to play Jim and Marco off each other, as Marco's mother had played him off his father and brother. Boy, here he was, a middle-aged man, and he was still being taken in by the tricky games of women.

Cautiously, he kept his knowledge of their affair from them, but in the days leading up to the next confinement, Marco was very critical of both of them, particularly Sarah. He thought he was masking it well, being very civil to her, but Sarah heard sarcasm and insults. Sarah complained about one of the other werewolves, Kyle, who had been acting hostile and jealous, as if there had been something going on between them, and Marco said, "Well, you must have done something to lead him on." And when she talked about her frustrations with her job, he said, "Let's face it, you haven't been getting by just on your brains so far, have you?" She asked what he meant, and he was very cold, enumerating her faults – promiscuous, selfish, manipulative, opportunistic – then said, "I know you're strong enough to hear this, Sarah, and I only tell you all this because I care about you. I know you want to be better than this. I have to be honest."

Then she had the honesty to ask, "Is this because you have feelings for me, Dr. Marco?"

"Of course I care about you, Sarah. You're my patient. I'm just doing my job."

The next day, Jim came to him, looking nervous – unusual for Jim – and said, "Marco, I've been seeing Sarah."

"Have you?" Marco sounded genuinely surprised.

"I wanted to let you know. It just happened. I know we aren't supposed to 'fraternize' but . . . well, we're in love. I want to marry her," Jim said.

"Jim, we have the No Fraternization with the Female rule for a reason. The others –"

"I think it would be less disruptive to the others if Sarah and I were married than if we snuck around and got found out. She thinks so too."

"You discussed this with Sarah?"

"Yes."

"Jim, there's a lot you don't know about Sarah." Marco put his hand on the younger man's shoulder in a way that was sympathetic on the surface, but with a too-hard squeeze, to send the message of one man's domination over another. "I can't go into detail or explain. Just be very careful who you trust. You know she's ambitious and – well, I can't say any more. It's not a good idea. We have this rule for a reason."

Marco thought Jim had heard him and understood. Marco reminded Sarah of the rule too, and she said nothing, but smiled a little and looked down and away. Marco felt very satisfied later when he watched Sarah leave the Centre alone – until she got to the corner and he saw that Jim was waiting there for her. She threw her arms around him and hopped up on him, wrapping her legs around him. When Jim put her down, she took his hand and they walked out of sight.

Sarah had not only led Marco on, made him consider divorce, broken his heart, she had now taken his protegé and his best friend from him. They were defiantly ignoring his wishes. If this continued, Marco would either have to submit to their wishes – a thought he couldn't stomach – or risk them leaving the program, which was

not an option Marco even wanted to consider. That would mean
two werewolves in the city living outside Potenza control.

The next full moon seemed routine. The patients had been in
confinement for one day already, Sarah in her own room, now
Annie's room. After Marco checked vital signs, he loaded each
patient's IV with drugs, mixed specifically to their needs and capacity. Jim usually hooked Sarah up to her IV, and he did that night
too. But Marco had mixed it.

In the morning, Sarah was dead of a massive overdose.

Marco hadn't done it consciously. But he was very angry with
her and he had wondered since then, in the rare moments when
he would allow himself to sit alone with the truth, if he had
unconsciously mixed a fatal dose because a part of him wanted her
dead. He allowed himself these moments very seldom, because he
had a program to run and he couldn't give in to sentiment or guilt
for too long. He had to think like a general at war, for the sake of
the program and the sake of the family.

53

The full moon was just a week away, and Annie still hadn't committed to staying. But she was still there in Jim's apartment. Jim
felt that with every day she stayed, the less she was likely to go back
to Marco, but he couldn't call it with confidence. They had a good
time together, they loved each other, and Annie was even getting
into the "life on the lam" part of their existence.

But he worried she might be one of those good girls who takes
a walk on the wild side and then returns to normal life. Downtown
was full of nice girls who rebelled by dating self-involved artists or
heroin-addicted musicians who they hid from view when their
families came to visit. After a few years and maybe one too many
trips to the emergency room at three in the morning for a stomach-
pumping, a good number of these girls ended up back in a place

like their hometown, working in stable jobs, and married to hard-working, stable guys. The wildest girl he'd known in college had been a girl named Cindy who arrived looking like a missionary but left with black spiked hair, a black eye, and a restraining order in hand. When last heard from, she was happily married with a kid in Virginia, where she had joined the Junior League.

Everything he knew about Annie weighed in that direction. On top of that, she refused to believe that Marco had killed Sarah, except by accident. When he asked her if she missed her old life, she said, "I'm not sure yet." She was still a bit shell-shocked from having her whole life yanked from her by an aberrant gene.

Time was running out, and she seemed to be making a passive-aggressive de facto decision by not making any decision.

Then she said, "Okay, I'll stay." She had walked into the living room holding a picture he'd cut out of a magazine and put in a stack to be filed later. It was a photo of a field of snow in Alaska, fringed by trees, under a full moon, and for some reason, it made her cry so hard she couldn't say any more than just, "Okay, I'll stay."

There was a week to the Harvest Moon and he had a lot to show her. He told her how to use the old metro, freight-train and water tunnels to get around if they got separated.

"Travelling above ground should be minimized to avoid being seen," he said. "Follow me if you can, I know the lay of the underground. Fresh graffiti is a good sign the rails are dead, because someone has obviously crossed to paint the wall, but it's best to run between the tracks to be on the safe side. If we get split up, I've stashed clean clothes and money in paper bags at two locations, one in a little room off a tunnel about a block from here, and another on the roof behind the water tower. Beyond that, trust your instincts."

To ensure that the information would imprint, he took her out on some trial runs through the tunnels. Other girls probably wouldn't have found it romantic to be slogging through dark, weed-choked tunnels or in a half-foot of stagnant water puckered with water bugs or other sewer creatures. She did, though she probably wouldn't have before all this happened, or if she were with anyone else.

On the way back from the last test run, they saw a missing-person poster on a light pole, taped at the top and the bottom so the sides fluttered in the wind.

HAVE YOU SEEN ANNIE ENGEL? it asked.

"Someone's looking for you," he said.

"Nobody I want to find me."

"We're going to have to lay real low until the full moon," Jim said. "And we're going to have to have a plan . . ."

54

That same blonde girl had been with Jim every day. Meredith saw her from the big picture windows of the Pink Pony during the day and from her window at night. This looked serious. When Jim came in to buy coffee she asked him who the girl was and he smiled and said she was "his mate." The two words went off in her chest like a bomb of fire and icicles, and for the first time since Jim met her, she was dumbstruck. In her mind, it just wasn't possible. She just knew, in a cosmic kind of way, she and Jim were destined for each other, despite her daily protests at her mirror, "Fuck men, fuck 'em all." This girl, this spoiler, had come in and skewed Meredith's destiny.

At work, she was completely distracted. While watching out the window for either one of them, she mixed up orders, presented bills without bringing coffee, and couldn't hear the calls of customers, "Miss, miss, *miss*! I wanted an iced espresso, miss!"

The only person able to break through this distraction was a blind guy who came in every day. He sat where the shadows were and moved when the sun moved in order to stay in the shadows, always facing the window. One day he showed Meredith a flyer, one corner ripped and another with a piece of tape stuck to it, like it had been torn off a light pole.

HAVE YOU SEEN ANNIE ENGEL?

Underneath was a picture of a young woman who looked vaguely familiar to Meredith. She had to look at it a while before she realized who it was.

"Have you seen her?" the blind man asked.

"Not sure," Meredith said. "Who are you?"

"I'm a friend of the girl's. Her boyfriend."

This didn't seem right to her.

"How do you know it's her? I mean, if you can't see . . ."

"A friend told me it was her," Razz said.

"What does she do?"

"She's a legal secretary."

"Oh yeah?" A hip guy like Jim with a legal secretary? Clearly this blind guy had this Annie Engel confused with some other Annie Engel, or was working some scam, or his friend was playing a joke on him.

"How old is she?"

"Twenty-nine." She looked about twenty-nine. "She may be with a man, about thirty-five, blond."

"How do you know what he looks like?"

"A friend told me."

Meredith would have loved to see a little trouble befall the girl, though she wouldn't have admitted it. But she didn't want anything bad to happen to Jim. And while she didn't know what was going on, she knew this "blind" guy meant to cause trouble.

"Can I make a copy of this?" she asked, and took off to make one without waiting for his answer. When she came back, the blind man was talking to the other waitress.

After work, she put the flyer up on her bulletin board next to her computer and studied the face. Annie Engel, not a very exciting name, she thought. What is it he sees in her that he doesn't see in me?

55

Enzio had arrived to assist Marco and Rudolfo, and he was driving Carol nuts with his frequent calls to Audrey in front of the others, asking how this test or that test had gone. Carol was trying very hard to be generous about all this and "understand." It was sibling rivalry and Enzio was jealous that Marco was next in line to be count, but she wished Enzio would try being a little bigger and not rub Marco's nose in talk about the Potenza fetus. It was bad enough Enzio had to take digs at the way Marco ran his Centre, and harp on the problems that had ensued as a result.

Try as she did to turn the other cheek and be kind, she couldn't help being snippy with Enzio. Enzio had been a playboy who married relatively late, waiting for Audrey, a second cousin and full werewolf, to grow up to marrying age. She was twenty when they married. After seven years of marriage they had two daughters and a son on the way. Enzio boasted often about his young, fertile wife. Carol knew this wasn't aimed directly at her. It was Enzio's way of criticizing Marco through his choice of Carol, once again. She didn't know what came over her, but after listening to this kind of thing quietly, night after night, she finally said, "I hope it isn't true what they say about the higher risk of problems with children of, you know, cousins who marry."

With the Potenzas, it was as with royalty. There weren't that many suitable mates of one's own fine blood, so they often had to resort to dipping into the family gene pool. But to Carol, it wasn't much different than the Eaton family in Coosa County, Alabama, who liked each other so much they bred a sprawling clan of descendants with flat foreheads and pink eyes, a story she then told at the dinner table.

"Carol, please," Marco said, giving her a dark look.

"Please yourself," she said, getting up from the table to go into the kitchen to get the next course. It wasn't like he hadn't said the same thing way back when he married her, a red-blooded commoner who he'd hoped would thicken up that thin soup. If she had been able to have children, things might be different. But things work out the way they work out.

Luckily, she didn't have to spend much time with the "boys," who were busy either in Marco's office arguing strategy and poring over maps, or out on exploratory missions. Enzio, Marco, and Mike went out to survey the topography; Rudolfo went out to gumshoe and ask questions to try to find Annie. The men kept Carol busy bringing them snacks or topping their tea, but outside of sit-down meals, Marco and Enzio had little need for her and apparently no desire to talk to her. Most of her attention went to the patients, who were feeling a little ignored by Marco.

Rudolfo and Mike, on the other hand, went out of their way to pay attention to her and include her in things. Rudolfo invited her along on some of his gumshoe trips. They spoke to Mr. Hamernich, hiding their amusement when he told Rudolfo he was sure Annie had been eaten by a werewolf. As they rode the subway to Annie's former place of employment, Syn-EG, Rudolfo surprised her by discussing the family. She was taken aback just to hear him talk at length – period. Usually, he just asked her questions, and then listened. To hear him say a bad word about Luigi and his clan was unprecedented.

"It's hard to be a non-werewolf in our family," he said.

"It sure is. Sometimes I feel like Marilyn on *The Munsters*."

"Even I get tired of hearing the tales of their great triumphs," he said. "It must be much harder for you."

"I try to tune it out and think about menus."

"I'm so tempted sometimes to bring up some of those triumphs they don't ever mention."

"Oh, like what?"

"Berchtesgaden, 1933. The Potenzas were hired to clear the woods of werewolves, where they'd been massing. And they did. No treatment. They slaughtered them."

"Well, it was a different time. There was more prejudice and less advanced treatment —"

"Do you know Berchtesgaden?"

"It sounds familiar. Wait — was that Hitler's country place?"

"Yes."

"Nineteen thirty-three. Is that significant?"

"Hitler met with a group of his top lieutenants there a month later."

"Oh."

"The family doesn't like to talk about that one," he said.

"Yeah, I can see why."

"I'm not sure about things these days," Rudolfo said.

"I understand," Carol said, taking his hand and squeezing it.

"But I have a job to do. I can't let werewolves kill people," he said. "Can I?"

"I'm confused too," Carol said.

"May I ask you a personal question?"

"Yes, of course, Rudy."

"Why do you stay with Marco?"

She took a deep breath, held it, smiled, exhaled and said, "I love him. And I think his work is important. I think it's important to give people with LMD a shot at a normal life. Rudolfo, please try not to kill them. For me."

Rudolfo was quiet.

At the end of the night, in a kitchen lit only by the light under the stove hood, she and Mike had "their time," an hour of quiet chat about everything except the "werewolf thing." Ever since he came back, Mike had been even more quiet than usual. He was quiet in a different way than before. He seemed lost in thought more often. A few nights before the moon, after Marco had fallen asleep on the sofa, Rudolfo on the floor on top of a large map of the city, and Enzio in a recliner with his arms akimbo and his mouth hanging open, Mike came into the kitchen and made her some tea.

"Carol, how come Marco doesn't let me mix up the drug

combos?" he asked her. "He made such a big deal about teaching me how to do it."

"It's against policy. You have to be a trained doctor or nurse," she said. "Except in an emergency. You know that."

"He let Jim Valiente do it, the night Sarah died."

"Well . . ." She stopped. "Well, maybe that's why he doesn't do it any more."

"It was risky of him to let Jim do it, after Sarah broke his heart and all. Didn't Sarah object?"

"I wasn't here. I was away visiting my sister, so I don't know."

"When I break up with someone or someone breaks up with me, I don't want to see them," Mike said. "I avoid them. Wouldn't Sarah object to having Jim hook her up that night?"

"You should discuss it with Marco," she said.

Later, asleep next to Marco, who had to be carried into bed by Mike, she thought about it again. She knew what Marco would say. He'd say he had been extra busy that full moon because she was away, so he bent some rules and let Jim help. There was no way of her knowing the truth and she subscribed to the "Serenity Prayer": change what you can, accept what you can't, and be wise enough to know the difference. She couldn't change Sarah's death or Jim's disappearance, so she had driven all questions out of her head, and accepted what had happened and Marco's explanation of it. He was her husband, after all, and Jim's "death" had seemed to confirm his version of events.

Normally, she would take a sleeping pill now, and put the questions and herself to sleep. But tonight it was dogging her mercilessly.

Marco was out like a light. She got out of bed and went down to his office to find all the things she'd pulled from the files on Jim, including his suicide note, a typed note.

I loved her and I didn't mean to kill her. I just lost control. I don't think I can get it back. I know I can't have her back. Please forgive me. I love you all.

"Though I am old with wandering
Through hollow lands and hilly lands,
I will find out where she has gone,
And kiss her lips, and take her hands;
And walk among long dappled grass,
And pluck till time and times are done
The silver apples of the moon,
The golden apples of the sun"
　– W. B. Yeats

She looked at it more closely under Marco's pink and orange Venetian-glass desk lamp, and then she took out a sheet of clean paper, found Marco's old typewriter stashed under his computer desk, and slipped the paper in.

"What really happened to Sarah and Jim while I was away?" she typed, one letter at a time so she wouldn't wake anyone in the house.

Putting the pieces of paper side by side, she compared them. She had seen this on *Murder, She Wrote* or *Perry Mason*, one of those shows. The *w* jumped a bit on Marco's typewriter and the *s* was cropped slightly, the same as in the note. While it was possible Jim had typed his note on Marco's typewriter, when could he have done that, if he'd disappeared right after Sarah's death and his argument with Marco, as Marco had said?

56

Jennifer had wanted to tell Sam about Candace, but by the time she realized he wasn't the bad guy, he was sequestered. It wasn't something she wanted to tell him on the phone, especially while he was having so much fun at City Hall. You could hear it in his voice.

When the Mad Dog story was over, Candace was going to serve him papers and this tawdry episode would be over too. And yes, it was in large part due to her, Jennifer Ray. She had manoeuvred

Sam out of his marital media mess with little damage to anyone, after chasing Dear Tweets all over town and finally finding him at the same party as Candace Quall. With Micki at her side, a credit card receipt from TR Billing, and the backup paperwork to trace it back to the escort agency, she'd gone up to Candace at a cocktail reception for the Committee for a Free Media and said, simply, "Candace, the jig is up. We have evidence you hired Micki to —"

At that point, Candace shushed her and pulled her aside. "Okay," she said. "What do you want?"

"You tell Dear Tweets that Sam did not have an affair with anyone. He was a great husband but you grew apart or whatever. Go ahead and save face but make sure you save Sam's face first," Jennifer said. "You tell Dear Tweets tonight. He's here somewhere."

"And then?"

"And then it's case closed, unless you pull something like this again."

Candace looked at her with ice-hard blue eyes. "Okay," she said finally.

"Sam's a really good guy. He deserves better," Jennifer said. "A lot better."

"Well, so did I," Candace said. "You weren't married to him."

"You shouldn't be either. File for divorce, cut the poor guy loose, and let him keep everything."

"I worked hard on our house in Atlanta —"

"Everything."

Candace drew her face tight, turned, and walked away.

"I bet she drinks hot tea and pees ice water," Micki said as they watched her walk away.

"I don't know the whole story, but my bet is that it's the old story. Candace latched onto Sam when he was a big local TV star and she hitched her wagon to his star," Jennifer said. "After he pulled her as far as he could, she began looking for another star to haul her a little farther up the mountain. I guess she figured Sam couldn't do that for her here."

"Sam felt for her," Micki said. "He told me she never knew her father. He could have been one of several men who frequented the rib-and-chicken shack where her mother worked on the interstate. She may have been looking for a father figure —"

"— that she could punish over a long period of time," Jennifer finished. "Maybe. Sam's a really good guy. It's always the good ones who fall for women like Candace."

"And he's great in bed, or at least he was with me. I'm telling you, the first round was fanfuckingtastic. I was ready to pay him," Micki said.

"I don't know if I want to hear this," Jennifer said. "Yeah, I do."

"He was a wild man. We screwed for a whole day. If he'd kept screwing me instead of doing all that talking about Candace I could have fallen for him," Micki said. "You know he and his wife hadn't had sex for about a year?"

"Nine months, twelve if you don't count hand jobs. Yeah, he told me that too."

"Sam didn't tell me. Candace did. She said she just wasn't into having sex, especially with him. That happens. Big deal. It was nice of her to buy him a prostitute, I thought, since she didn't want to do it."

Jennifer was warming to Micki. She couldn't hold the video-tape thing against her. Cooper was right. Micki had kept quiet about it, until someone — Candace — had leaked word of the affair to Dear Tweets. At that point, Micki had to protect herself and, as the girl had a head on her shoulders, she found a way to work it to her advantage.

"I'm glad you're going to be working for us," Jennifer said.

She was more dubious about Sam's exclusive.

⑨

"It sounds like a scam to me," Jennifer said to Cooper the next morning. "Neither Sam nor anyone at CCN can report anything

Sam learns until the full moon? He and his tapes will be sequestered at CCN expense until then?"

"It's all legal. If they try to take his tapes, we'll sue their asses, and they don't want any more bad publicity," Cooper said. "They're letting him take his Gizmo everywhere and shoot what he wants. We just can't see any of it until the embargo is lifted."

"He's there alone, Coop. He's doing it all by himself. I don't know if he's up to that yet."

"We don't have a choice," Cooper said.

Even if it was a scam, Jennifer figured Sam would get something out of it somehow. He was lucky that way, and he was having a great time. Nothing was coming out about the investigation anyway, and with Sam away and Justin Berg reporting the Mad Dog sidebars, she'd had more time to work on her in-depth look at the missing, and presumed dead, Annie Engel.

After Jennifer Ray's piece on suicide ran on CCN, her phone lit up. Young women, young men, mothers, fathers, and doctors called to thank her for it, ask for referral numbers, give referral numbers, or just tell their own stories of losing someone good too young.

It was odd, she'd never wanted to be a reporter, but she had really enjoyed doing that piece herself, under her own name. She wanted to do more.

She had put it together using Annie Engel as the centrepiece of a larger look at suicide among young women in the city, careful to note that Annie was missing and presumed dead, but that no body had been found.

She was glad she had when she got a call from a man who gave his name as "Moe Bloom."

"That girl is living somewhere near Logan," Razz said. "I've seen her."

"Do you know the exact address?" Jennifer Ray asked.

"No."

"Will you go on camera?" she asked.

"No," he said, and hung up.

She would have discounted this guy as a crank if she hadn't taken another call about fifteen minutes later from a woman identifying herself as "Chrissie."

"My roommate has that girl's missing poster on the wall," she said. "She lives in this neighbourhood, on Logan."

"Do you know the exact address?" Jennifer asked.

"No, but it's someplace that can be seen from our apartment with a telescope," Chrissie said, and yes, she would go on camera.

6

Chrissie's roommate, Meredith, wasn't home when Jennifer arrived with her Gizmo.

"She's out at a reading somewhere. She's an actress," Chrissie said. "She'll be back tonight."

Chrissie had seen the young woman walking down the street with a man about thirty-five, with short blond hair. The girl had short blond hair too now. Though Chrissie couldn't pinpoint the building, she walked with J.R. down the block while J.R. showed the picture to other neighbours. A drugstore clerk remembered her buying hair dye.

When she had enough for a quick update, Jennifer Ray gave Chrissie her card.

"Have your roommate call me as soon as she gets home," she said, and then headed back to CCN to edit the story for the afternoon newscast.

Meredith was furious.

"What if this girl is wanted by the police?" she asked. "Jim would be an accessory. He'd go to jail. How will that help me?"

"People think she's dead, Meredith," Chrissie said. "People are worried about her."

"Why did she disappear if she didn't do something wrong? Or maybe she knows something about someone, someone powerful who will track her down and kill her and Jim . . ."

"Your imagination —"

"I don't want Jim dead, or in jail," she said. She did want the girl gone, but she didn't want to go on camera and rat her out, thereby alienating Jim forever. If Jim got wind of this, he'd leave, and she might not find him again, and how would she be able to be there for him when his current relationship inevitably went belly-up?

☾

Gunther saw the report on CCN while he was heating up some fish sticks and rice for lunch. For the first time, he questioned his theory about Annie being eaten. It was worse than that. She had been lured away by the werewolf. If the legends and Hollywood movies he'd seen on the subject were true, she had probably been bitten, and she might be a werewolf too. Or was that vampires? And did this means she was beyond redemption? Didn't Jesus say all those who accepted him and followed him to God would be saved?

IV

The Harvest Moon

September

57

When the Potenzas saw the report on Annie, Enzio took control.

"Rudolfo, you go down there and see what you can find out. Marco and I will scout the area for rooftops. Mike, stay here with Carol and the patients."

"I'm going with Rudolfo," Carol said.

"Carol, you'd help out more if –"

"I'm going with Rudolfo," Carol said.

Since her discovery, she'd been uncharacteristically quiet. She continued to make dinner and clean and bring the men fresh pots of tea and snacks, fulfilling all of her housewifely duties except for sex. When Marco turned to her on one of the rare nights when he wasn't collapsing from exhaustion, she said no, she wasn't in the mood, and turned away from him. She knew there were women who would have walked out, knowing what she knew about Marco, but she felt an obligation to the patients, and now, to Jim and Annie. She stuck around and paid attention. The men might think she was stoked up on Valium or Zonex when she smilingly waited on them, if they noticed her at all. But she was hyper-sober and listening to everything.

Down on Logan, she and Rudolfo split up to cover more territory. Carol had suggested they poke around together, but that
seemed daffily inefficient to Rudolfo. He took the west side of the
street, she took the east.

6

As if Meredith wasn't annoyed enough with the world, the other
waitress came in to work wearing a big men's shirt over baggy men's
pants cinched in with a belt. What an imitator, Meredith thought.

"Nice outfit," Meredith said.

"Oh, thanks. You know the blind guy who was in the other day?"

"Yeah."

"Look over there across the street," the other waitress said.

"Where?"

"In the shadow of that stoop down the block. See? That's him."

"Oh yeah."

"Do you think he's really blind?"

"I don't know."

"I don't think he is. I think he's standing there watching that
guy Jim's building."

"He asked me about that. About Jim's girlfriend actually,"
Meredith said.

"He asked you? Then why did he ask me?"

"He asked you about the girl? What did you tell him?"

"I told him where she lives," she said. "But now I don't think
he's blind. I think he's a stalker."

"Excuse me," Meredith said. She looked out the door.

"I'll be right back," she said to the other waitress.

She knew what apartment Jim lived in geographically from her
window, but she didn't know the apartment number. She ran a
fingernail down the buzzer board. Only about half the tenants
were listed on the board.

Carol was walking north on the last block of Logan when she
saw a girl frantically pressing intercom buttons, shouting "Jim!"

"I'm looking for Jim too," Carol said to her. "I wonder if it's the same Jim. He's about thirty-eight, a writer."

"Why are you looking for him?" Meredith asked, sharply.

"He's in danger," Carol said, simply.

"Maybe from you?"

"Not from me," Carol said.

Carol's eyes made Meredith want to trust her, but then a man who looked like either an FBI agent or a Mormon crossed the street and walked up to Carol's side.

"My Jim is black, about six foot two, writes sports stories," Meredith said. "Is that the same guy?"

"No," Carol said. "Thanks anyway."

"Sure."

When the woman left, Meredith heard her say, "Any luck?"

"They're somewhere in this neighbourhood," he said. "But I don't know where. You?"

"Not a sign of them," the woman said.

After they left, Meredith pushed the last remaining button on the intercom.

"Jim? This is Meredith. I need to talk to you."

There was no reply, though she was sure she heard breathing.

"Fuck you, then," she said, and let the button go. Fuck him, and the girl. Here she was, trying to take the high road and warn him that people were after him and his girlfriend. Chrissie was probably right. He was an antisocial asshole and probably a heroin addict or something. Fuck him. Fuck all men. She had to think about her career.

58

Jim and Annie were upstairs eating when a strange woman buzzed and said, "Jim? Jim? It's Meredith. I have to talk to you. It's important."

"Who's Meredith?" Annie asked.

Jim shrugged.

"Are you scared?" he asked Annie.

"No."

She knew she should be, but the closer she got to the full moon, the less she felt human fear and the more she just felt wolf energy. She could feel it now, building inside her. Now that she was used to it, it didn't make her queasy or strange. All she felt was excitement, energy, and some mild discomfort. And hunger. She'd eaten a whole box of tofu sausages and four Gardenburgers, and had washed it all down with two soy milkshakes and a quart of orange juice.

"We just finish what we have to do tonight, and then we'll get out of town," he said.

"Okay."

"If I lose you, or you lose me, you know where to wait for me."

"Yes."

"I love you."

"I love you too."

59

Marco and Enzio were planning to take up positions on three roofs around Logan. Rudolfo had implanted a tracking device inside each man's ear, so he could follow them. When they had the other two werewolves cornered, Rudolfo would move in and shoot them. He'd be carrying a gun, and with the help of the werewolves, would then dispose of the bodies.

At seven, Marco did his second-last check of the patients in confinement. He'd do one check at eight, and then he'd head downtown with his brother, protegé, and tracker. There wasn't much time. The full moon would rise at 9:17. Carol had to act fast. After pouring most of a jug of glycerine down the sink, she took the near-empty jug out and said to Marco, "We're almost out of glycerine. I'm just going to run down to the pharmacy and get some more."

"We need you to cook dinner and help Mike with the patients."

"Order out," Carol said.

"Carol?"

"What?"

"Is something wrong?" Marco asked.

Enzio was looking at her funny too.

"Nothing."

"We need you here. You can't leave right now, Carol, for God's sake," Marco said. He picked up the phone and called down to the pharmacy to order up some glycerine.

Mike followed her into the kitchen.

"Don't worry," he said.

60

Dear Tweets,

Oh how we wish we had a proper substance abuse problem, or 127 personalities, like a certain zaftig TV star, or a terrible childhood trauma, like [insert name of favourite shamed celebrity here] we could blame things on. But we don't (though we were a chubby child and our other personality Firmamentia did poorly in math, but that's not an excuse, just an explanation for what you're about to read).

After consulting with the Council of Queens (my mother's bridge group), we realized that we have to take responsibility and admit:

We erred. Again.

Remember those two Aces we told you about, the ones who spent so much time making the beast with two backs while the lady's unwitting husband was busy rooting out evil and informing the public? Remember how we then told you she had left her spouse because HE had cheated first, and there was a videotape? Wrong. No affair, no videotape. Hubby was a "great husband" but the couple simply "grew apart." This from the Lady Ace herself, who also says the Bachelor Ace she's been seen with all over town is "a great friend who has been a comfort during these difficult times, and that is all." Yawn. Evidently, she's not just blowing smoke up our rosy pink derrière. It's for real, Tweets. In the words of Paulette Goddard in the 1939 movie The Women: "Aw, why can't those mouldy old rags leave a successful divorce alone?"

Point taken, Paulette, wherever you are. We are contrite.

On a brighter note, we were absolutely right about that Ripe Queen and her autumnal pursuit of a certain titled megamogul. Having failed to attract him with her heaving bosoms and painful repartee, she has hit him where he lives by offering up her company and massive land holdings. The Great Omninational Trader is said to be very interested in this highly lucrative enterprise of hers. We can't say what her company is, but on a completely unrelated note, do you remember a story last year about a cosmetics company that was testing its products on the tender skin of young Indian girls in the orphanages it "sponsors"? Neither here nor there.

61

Sam was having the time of his life inside Operation Harvest Moon. Hell, this was like D-Day or something. And he was the reporter of record, just like that guy Ernie who covered the Second World War. Ernie Kovacs? No, that couldn't be right. Ernie Kovacs was funny.

He was dying to tell someone all about it, about the day he went on a training run with the K-9 cops, or the time he went out on a ride-along in a police chopper. He got to see the communications centre, he lunched with the Mayor in his office, he pretty much had the run of the place, as long as he didn't "touch any of the buttons." Except for a few of the Mayor's closed-door meetings, Sam was in on everything.

He was allowed to call Cooper and Jennifer every day, but only under Seth's supervision, which meant he couldn't say much. At the end of every day, a police escort took him to a hotel room and stood guard outside his door. The phone had been removed and he was frisked to make sure he wasn't packing a cell phone. Sometimes, Sam was able to convince the cop guarding him to break the rules and join him for some room service and some pay-TV.

This was the life.

Seth had been against it.

"It's a huge risk. If we blow the dragnet, this guy's got a fucking documentary, *Anatomy of a Disaster.*"

"If we blow it, we blow it. At least people will see everything we did to catch the killer," the Mayor said. "If they want to impeach me after that, let them. Go ahead, make my day."

Although he didn't say it aloud, it was no secret to Seth that the Mayor would have given anything to go back to the day when the party came and asked him to be their candidate for Mayor.

The Mayor would have gone back a little further, to the day he decided to sell his grocery business to a big conglomerate and retire. He and Marva had started with one store and built it to a chain in twelve states. Along the way, Marva quit work to raise kids and he converted Marva Foods to a franchise operation, so that every store but the original one was quasi-independent, offering the benefits of a chain and the special service and local knowledge of a Mom-and-Pop.

Bigger fish had tried to swallow them up before and they'd turned them away. Then an enormous shark swam up with an enormous cheque, a cheque so big that he and Marva sat for a day just looking at it, passing it back and forth – "Let me look at that cheque again" – before they put it in the bank. The buyer had offered to wire the money into their account, but they said no. He was the son of a greengrocer, Marva the daughter of a fishmonger, people who had done a dollar's work for every two-bits' pay. They wanted to hold that cheque in their hands and look at it for a while.

All those years while he was working like a dog he had dreamed of the day he could quit and enjoy the fruits of his labours, get out before he fell dead of a massive coronary, as his dad had done when he was just forty-five, collapsing into a pyramid of jewel-like citrus fruits he had only just finished stacking.

For the first couple of months, retirement was easy. He and Marva took a cruise and travelled all over Europe, sleeping late, eating, and visiting museums. But when they got home, alone together for whole days sometimes, tensions started to appear.

While he was working all those long hours and the kids were growing independent, she had needed something to fill the time, she told him. Since the children had grown and left home, Marva had made a nice life for herself, taking courses at the Art Students League, volunteering at the Museum of Postmodern Art, making sculpture.

After they sold the business, she was busy with her life and he was at a loss. Even when she was there, he was home alone in a way, since she went into her studio for hours at a time and didn't like to be disturbed. One day he had followed her in, and sat talking to her while she was trying to work, until she asked him not to bother her while she was creating. She suggested he find a hobby.

A hobby? He hadn't had a hobby since he collected stamps in grade school. For a time, he toyed with starting his own business, but the only thing he'd ever known was grocery, and when he sold the business he'd signed a non-competition clause barring him from the grocery business for five years.

Bored, he called his kids and talked to them about the old days until they started finding excuses to get off the phone. Gradually, they became harder to reach. He suspected they were screening his calls.

Finally, his daughter said, "Dad, I'm really busy here. You remember what it's like. Remember all those times I came to visit you at the store and you put me to work pricing cans and stacking carrots?" Then she laughed and said, "I got my work ethic from you, Dad, thanks. I gotta go."

He hung up the phone, put on his coat and took the metro out to his first store in the old neighbourhood. The new manager didn't know who he was and he had to be vouched for by an old butcher who was the only person remaining from the old days. Everyone was very polite, in a chain-store way, as if the identical demeanour of the employees had been ordered from the home office along with the signs, display cases, and store-brand coffee and detergent.

Politely, the manager told him they were very busy, but he was welcome to walk around the store. They didn't have time for stories about his run-ins with Teamsters and unreliable fruit wholesalers way back when.

Alone, he wandered the aisles, remembering all the times he had walked around the store with his son and daughter when they were young, teaching them the finer points of stocking and display, expecting they would follow him into the business one day, though neither did. He thought about the time a woman had gone into labour in the canned goods aisle, and the time a robber had held a gun to Marva's head while he'd emptied the safe and handed over the day's receipts.

Just then, the silliest of things got to him, a little shrivelled-up carrot on the floor in the produce department. For some reason, that moved him, that little shrivelled-up carrot, like a thousand he had swept up in his childhood. Tears welled in his eyes. Fleeing the store without saying goodbye to anyone, he grabbed a cab to take him home, so nobody would see him cry on the metro. In his whole adult life, he'd only cried a dozen times, if that; only once in public, and that was at his mother's funeral.

After that, he stayed home and watched television. Mainly, he watched the news channels, talking back to the pundits and politicians on CCN and Syn-TV. One winter morning, while he was yelling at Senator Trent Lott, the phone rang. It was Eddie Schimmel, a guy he'd worked with on a mayoral task force during the garbage strike of 1975. Eddie was now on the executive committee of his political party.

"I got your cheque," Eddie said.

"Just now? I sent it last month."

"Yeah. I meant to call you sooner to say thanks. Very generous of you, but I wonder if you'd be interested in doing more. Can you come down here for a meeting?"

As soon as he'd walked in the door, Eddie had asked him, already knowing the answer, "How did you get here?"

"I took the metro," he said.

The men and one woman in the room smiled and nodded. They asked him some more questions about his business, his family, his old neighbourhood, and what he thought of the city now. They already knew a lot about him, statistically. They'd already had him checked out by a fine private investigative firm before Eddie ever picked up the phone and called him. But they wanted to get a feel for him as a man.

About halfway through the meeting, they knew. Here was a family man – a successful businessman – who had dealt with unions, government, customers, the marketplace, the executive suite, and people of every race and creed. His wife was on the board of a museum, which gave him some cultural credibility, and both his children had gone to public schools. Long before social pressures and laws made it necessary, he'd hired blacks, Hispanics and women, and promoted them according to merit.

A true hometown guy, an insider, but a political outsider. He was neither liberal nor conservative. He was pragmatic, a self-made multimillionaire who still rode the subway, for God's sake. They had their man.

"How would you like to run for mayor?" they asked.

Six months into his term, the paint was barely dry on his mayoral portrait and the honeymoon was over. The "refreshing no-nonsense candour" that endeared him during the campaign had just pissed everyone off after the election. And now there were mad killer dogs on the loose he'd not been able to have captured. At least, not yet.

⑥

The Mayor had given strict instructions that nobody was to mention Sam's marriage, so Sam was able to live fairly happily in his bubble. The only problem was, he couldn't call Candace, as he had every day – despite the fact that she didn't return his calls except when she knew he wouldn't be home. It had been over three months since Candace had walked out, he realized. Time had really flown while he was working on this story. That seemed a long time for Candace to think about things. He didn't want to rush her because, after all, he was the bad guy who had cheated on her, but three months . . .

She gave him so little, he thought now, but he couldn't help loving her.

Yet, he didn't miss her that much, he realized. In the three months since she'd left he'd been fine. What if she did come back? What would he get out of the deal? Emotional support? Nope. A hand job once every month or two, or, if he was really lucky, a blow job during which he'd have say, over and over, "Watch your teeth. The teeth! Careful with that. *The teeth!*"

It was over between them, he realized, and although he felt a sadness when he thought that, it was a distant sadness. Like the memory of a sadness.

As soon as the operation was finished, he would file for divorce, he decided.

His police guard drove him from his hotel down to city hall. Today was the day, Operation Harvest Moon. Tonight, Jennifer

Ray would be allowed to join him to coordinate the coverage from city hall. Then, hopefully, it would all be over.

And then what?

Sam was going to miss this story.

62

Lord Harry was not happy with the way this operation was shaking out. He'd accepted the position on the Mayor's task force, and agreed to the gag order, because he wanted to have some influence over the way things were being handled, only to find he had no influence and couldn't even feed information to his newspapers or TV network.

"This Mayor has got to go," he said to one of his aides-de-camp that day. "He is mud in my newspapers as soon as that gag order lifts. Send the word to all the editorial boards."

Being snookered never sat well with Lord Harry, and he'd been snookered. Nothing could cheer him up, not the news that a record six million schoolchildren were now taking Z-Junior, used to treat Attention Deficit Disorder, not the news that overall profits were up twenty-five per cent, and not the news that his lobbyists had won two more senators over to their side on an upcoming bill that would allow him to circumvent antitrust legislation to buy the world's number-one global telecommunications company.

Nobody got the better of Lord Harry, ever, he told his young Russian mistress Ludmilla, not since his days as a lad in Cape Town, selling day-old newspapers to bleary-eyed commuters.

"You are king of the world," she said. His back was to her, otherwise he might have seen her rolling her eyes at his bodyguard while she fingered one nipple suggestively.

"A king snookered by a mayor," Lord Harry said. If it hadn't been for the high cost to his executive ranks, he would have wished failure on the Mayor's operation and done everything he could to ensure that failure.

"What time are you going to City Hall?" she asked.

"I'm having dinner with Rosemary Frost in her apartments and then going to City Hall."

He caught Ludmilla making a face and mistook it for a comment on Rosemary Frost.

"You're not jealous of Rosemary?" he said.

"Should I be?"

"No," he said, and laughed. He didn't find Mrs. Frost at all attractive. Now, her holdings were another matter. Not only did she run the number-one perfume and cosmetics company in the industrialized world, but she had a garment company and extensive real-estate holdings he wanted, not to mention the hearts and minds of millions of young women and the editorial and ad pages of the top beauty magazines. The trick was going to be getting all that from her while giving her as little as possible in return. He'd dealt with some tricky business people in the past, but she was the trickiest. It was clear she wanted to be the next Lady Harry.

"Don't worry about that old mayor," Ludmilla said. "He is nothing compared to you."

Yes, the Mayor was nothing, a grocer. Lord Harry was . . . a lord. And so what if he'd got his original holdings in Cape Town by marrying the widow of his boss? It was what he did with it, parlaying that one newspaper into two dozen major dailies around the world, then into a multimedia empire, and then a conglomerate with holdings in almost every industry, touching almost every country on the planet. That was him, all him.

About the only enterprise he didn't have a piece of was cosmetics, a booming business and one of the biggest scams ever.

⑥

"Fifteen cents' worth of ingredients, and we sell it for fifty dollars an ounce," Mrs. Frost said, holding up a small jar of Formula Jeunesse

Creme. She was taking him through a mini-museum for Frost Cosmetics in her penthouse apartment, while her valet, Henry, prepared her boudoir for a private dinner there. The museum ended at the boudoir, so there would be no escape for the canny Lord Harry.

"The lovely opalescent blue jar costs a dollar, more than the cream inside," she said.

"A dollar fifteen, pretty good. What's the labour cost?"

"Negligible. It's packaged in Bangladesh. The factory there can put out five thousand jars a day at full capacity. Total cost of the product with shipping and labelling is a dollar ninety-seven."

"Very good," Lord Harry said.

"Now, these are marvellous," she said, showing him a container of Dew Drops, teardrop-shaped gelatin capsules with a pearl finish that contained "emulsifying enzymes to tone and balance your skin, giving it the glow of a girl the morning after."

"Five cents per capsule for the ingredients. We sell them for two dollars per."

"Remarkable."

"Ah, and this is my private room. We'll be dining here," she said, ushering him into her boudoir, where Henry, in white tie and tails, was waiting to serve arugula salad with caviar cream dressing. It was his last day on the job.

63

After Marco, Enzio, and Rudolfo left, Mike turned to Carol in the confinement room and said, "I'm going out."

"You have to?"

"It feels like my duty, you know?" Mike said. "Will you'll be okay here?"

"I'll do my best," Carol said. "Be careful."

"I will, but if I don't come back . . ."

"Oh, Mikey."

"I want you to know how much we all love you. I love you."

"I love you too, Mikey."

"Leave him."

"I'll think about it."

He kissed her cheek and went up to the roof to begin his transformation.

Even though she couldn't see the moon, Carol knew it had risen when the patients began to transform in the confinement room. They were more heavily sedated than in previous months because the clinic finally had some ketamine to give them, scraped together by Luigi and Enzio, though the dose was only half as much as usual. Still, it was painful to watch as their bodies seized up and contorted, as their limbs pulled inward and then stretched out, and they began to thrash against the restraints. It always made her cry to see them struggling against the manacles.

6

Marco and Enzio were positioned at a diagonal. Marco had taken position on the roof of a grocery store on one end of the block, Enzio at the other. Between the two of them, they could scan every roof on this stretch. Enzio transformed first, quickly and easily, show-off that he was. Marco took a little longer.

The moon was full, and very close to earth. It appeared larger than usual and was golden.

Enzio saw something, a shadow, darting over a building fronting a cross street. He stood up on all fours and stuck his snout into the air, moving his head back forth. Then he spotted it. It had stopped, and was looking right at him. He ran after it.

Marco, watching this, expected to see the other wolf come up, but instead saw two emerge from a building just down from the Pink Pony. Who was the first werewolf, then, the one Enzio was chasing?

The two wolves began to leap across rooftops. Marco followed them.

Down on Logan, the blind guy saw it all.

⑨

Gunther was up on his roof with his gun and his silver bullets, waiting. He had put out two big raw steaks as bait and then taken position behind a skylight. He'd been watching the roofscape for the better part of an hour, his mind wandering to thoughts of God and heaven, the living hell he'd endured with the Mole People, his long-dead wife, Gerda, who he'd put through her own living hell, a son somewhere he'd lost track of. He prayed to God to send the werewolf to him, and he prayed some more, then drank some iced tea and prayed some more.

God answered.

A werewolf bounded past him, not twenty feet away on a neighbouring roof. But by the time Gunther flicked the safety off his gun, he couldn't get a good bead on the beast. As he was cursing the swiftness of the devil, a second werewolf jumped onto his rooftop. This time, Gunther was able to get a shot off, wounding Enzio in the foreleg. He took another shot and blasted one of his back legs. The wolf hobbled and fell to the tarpaper. Gunther approached, holding his gun with both hands. The wolf snarled. Gunther kicked it in the head with his heavy boot, then kicked again until it was unconscious. He was going to put a bullet in the wolf's head when it occurred to him it might be Annie. In that case he wanted to keep her alive and bring her back to God, after proving to the world he had caught a werewolf, of course. He would need some rope. And a camera.

⑨

Rudolfo couldn't figure out why Enzio was not moving on his scanner. He had to make a decision, either follow Marco's signal, or circle back and find out why Enzio was still. He decided to follow Marco.

64

Jennifer had been allowed to come down to City Hall in the morning to begin looking through Sam's tapes for material to feed back to CCN when the embargo was lifted. She had written intros to the behind-the-scenes footage of meetings, to the demos of the equipment and Sam's field trips with the K-9 cops and his jaunts on police boats and choppers. When that was done, she and Sam had dinner in Sam's temporary office at City Hall, during which both Seth and the Police Commissioner poked their heads in to pay their respects.

"Nice guys," Sam said.

"Not as nice as you, Sam," Jennifer said, and decided to test that theory. "I don't know if this is the right time to tell you this but . . . CCN is hiring Micki."

"Micki? My Micki? . . . I mean, the Micki that I –"

"Is this going to be a problem for you?"

"For me? No. I like Micki. I was dumb to have that affair but –"

"Sam, you're only human," Jennifer said. "And you're a good human."

"Is it a problem for Micki? Working at the same place as me?"

"No, she likes you," J.R. said.

"She does?"

"How's your wife? I guess you haven't spoken to her –"

"No, but . . . that's over," Sam said. "I called her every day and she only called me four times, and always when she knew I wouldn't be home. You know what I'm sayin', J.R.? It's been over three months since she walked out! She didn't have sex with me for a year before that. I can take a hint."

Jennifer coughed. "You're better off without her," she said. "Seriously."

"Yeah," he said. "Can we change the subject?"

"Of course."

"Did they ever find that girl? Annie?"

"No. We heard she'd been sighted downtown, but we couldn't locate her. It was probably a different girl."

"Aw, too bad," Sam said. "Damn."

The door opened. A uniformed officer said, "Mr. Deverell, Operation Harvest Moon is about to begin."

"Wait until you see this, J.R.," Sam said.

Jennifer followed him. He was popular here. Almost everyone they passed said hi or high-fived him.

"This is the command centre," Sam said. "Don't touch any of the buttons."

"I won't," Jennifer Ray said.

They entered a large conference room that had been converted to Command Central. A map was covered with lights. A bunch of police officers wearing headsets manned consoles that looked, Sam said, "like they're right out of *Star Trek*."

"Cool," J.R. said

"They've got patrols ringing the city, working their way from the outside into the centre," Sam said. "Every one of those lights is a cop. Then they've got extra patrols in the parks, police boats patrolling the waterways, and choppers flying everywhere."

This was the deal: Sam was going out with a police chopper and as soon as the Mayor gave his okay, he could begin broadcasting. J.R. would stay at Command Central to coordinate. Cooper was back at CCN, where he'd supervise incoming feeds.

"Look at these," Sam said, pulling out his night-vision goggles. "These things are neat. The Mayor and I turned out the lights in some of the offices last night and tried them out —"

The Mayor came in with the Police Commissioner and some members of his task force.

"Operation Harvest Moon is underway," he said.

☾

After Mike lost Enzio, he headed towards Marco. He was able to catch up quickly, because he was so much younger than Marco.

At 26th and Remfry, he cut his former mentor off on top of a tenement.

Marco faced him. He wasn't sure why Mike was there, but he was glad he was. Enzio had vanished and Marco would need help tracking the two wolves. But when he tried to rush ahead, Mike jumped him and fought him.

Jim and Annie went underground and travelled up to Parker Avenue, unencumbered.

⑥

Mrs. Frost was reclining provocatively on a seventeenth-century chaise longue, her bosoms nearly spilling out of her blue dress. They had just had their coffee and Mrs. Frost had dismissed Henry from the boudoir. Lord Harry knew it was time for him to get out of there.

"Oh, stay a while longer," she said.

"I can't. I have to go to City Hall."

"The Mayor can wait. Go some other time."

"I can't."

"Why?"

"Top secret."

"May I go with you?"

"No, it's a private meeting."

"At this hour?"

He said nothing.

"You're going to walk out on one of your biggest — and most charming" — she smiled again — "stockholders?"

"It's business, Rosemary," he said.

"Finish your cognac, at least," she said, filling his glass to the rim.

He could not refuse without being rude, and he didn't want to be rude, because he wanted her property. Somehow, he had to get her to agree to a business merger without having to agree to a personal merger, but that was proving sticky. There was a reason this daughter of an immigrant picklemaker had married three progressively richer men and become one of the wealthiest women in the world. He suspected she was trying to get him drunk so she could get him into bed and use that against him somehow. She was beyond breeding age so he didn't have to worry about her getting pregnant. But no doubt she had other ways to manoeuvre him.

He thought he had her game figured out. She put him into the position of having to either insult her outright or go along with her. As she was a tremendously powerful woman, with influence over the hearts and minds of millions of young women, and the editorial and ad pages of their popular beauty magazines, many people went along with her. To insult her was to declare war on her, and she was a vicious warrior who, it was rumoured, had killed her first husband and reduced the other two to twitchy drunks, their wallets lighter by hundreds of millions of dollars.

Lord Harry was much richer and more powerful than she was, and he had a newspaper and a TV network at his disposal. Still, she worried him (he'd never admit she scared him a little), because, after all, he hadn't even figured out how to get safely out of her apartment, let alone how to counter her ballsy mating strategy.

When she stepped out for a moment to talk to her valet, he dumped all but the last dregs of the obscenely expensive brandy into a Ming vase.

Rosemary was frustrated. She had tried everything to get him to relax, but whatever she did, Lord Harry responded by bringing up business. She was a businesswoman, and she understood – but only up to a point, because she was also a woman, and he was a man. Just as her business holdings would fill a big gap in his empire, so he could fill the gap in her.

Well, she knew he wasn't the sentimental type and was going to be a hard nut to crack. After all, he had sued his own mother over a property dispute. He had two children who rarely spoke to him, one a dissolute heiress who yo-yo'd between detox and retox, and a son who had become a Buddhist and denounced his own father in rival newspapers pretty regularly. He was so disappointed in his daughter and son that when they were twelve and thirteen respectively, he had gone to court to get a paternity test to make sure they were really his, and then had the results double-checked when it was proven that the two were, indeed, the spawn of Teufel.

Rosemary had no children, which had always made her a good prospect for marriage because she brought so little emotional baggage and so much money to her unions. It had been easier when she was younger, before supermodels became the trophy wives of choice for moguls. Back in the days of Slim Hawks Hayward Keith and Pamela Churchill Hayward Harriman, moguls went for spirited women with broad shoulders and substance – women who knew how to shoot big game and were almost as ruthless as the men they married. Alpha women. What had happened to men, she wondered, that they now went for reedy, blank-eyed girls whose brain cells had been progressively destroyed by protein deficiencies caused by eating disorders, and who seemed to come mostly from Estonia and Ukraine?

"Thank you for a lovely dinner, Rosemary," Lord Harry said as soon as she stepped back into the boudoir. "But I must go now."

"Oh no!"

"Yes."

"I'll go with you to the helipad," she said. "Your bodyguards are waiting up there."

This was a big fat lie. She had instructed Henry to keep the bodyguards and chopper pilot in the kitchen for at least fifteen minutes, so she'd have some time alone with Lord Harry in her private elevator and again up on the windswept roof, with the great city at their feet. Then she would tell her story, how she rose from the little girl the kids knew as Picklehead (because of her father's trade and the smell of brine that always clung to her clothes) to become the world's beauty empress and owner of the number-one selling perfume, Frost. Perhaps then he would see what they had in common, and what they could have in common if they united their houses.

⊚

Following gut instinct and the smell of moral rot, Jim and Annie came up in the parking garage of a ritzy Parker Avenue building via an abandoned sewer line. From there, they climbed the stairs upward, all the way to the helipad on the roof. There they took cover behind the water tower, and waited. The smell of evil was wafting up to them, the sickly smell of an embalmed corpse, burned skin, and rose incense, followed by a smell so huge and horrible it would defy translation into human terms. If you took every foul-smelling thing you could imagine, a dead rat, a lump of cheese that had been mouldering in a cave, a maggoty dead man, and mixed it up with raw sewage, it would smell like rainwater in spring next to the smell of this soul.

A door opened and two people emerged, first Rosemary Frost, then Lord Harry.

Annie was in spring posture a second before Jim. When the two victims got within range of the water tower, the werewolves leapt, teeth bared, at the same moment. Jim went for the woman. Annie went for the man.

In moments, Rosemary Frost and Lord Harry Teufel were dead.

⊚

When Marco finally broke away from Mike, he knew it was too late for the victims. The smell of death-by-werewolf coming from uptown was strong enough for his sensitive nose to pick up blocks away, even if he hadn't heard the post-kill howls. Enzio was nowhere to be seen, and Mike had turned on him. He could only hope Rudolfo was still picking up his signals.

⊚

"We're not sure what they are," said the cop in the police chopper, in a crackling radio voice. "We zoomed in as much as we could. Looks like . . . wolves."

"Big wolves," Sam said. He was in the chopper.

A shaky picture appeared on the video feed at Command Central. Two large, brown animals were galloping away from two bloody people.

"Wolves?" the Mayor said, his unblinking eyes glued to the feed. "Wolves don't kill people. That's a myth."

"They've probably been crossed with something else, some fighting dog like a mastiff," said a Schutzhund expert who was on the task force.

"Where's their trainer?" the Mayor asked.

"Out of sight," said the Police Commissioner.

"We just had another wolf sighting on Lincoln," said one of the cops at the command console.

The Mayor turned to the Schutzhund expert. "Parker Avenue and another on Lincoln. How does the trainer control them from such distances?"

"And they seem trained to kill specific victims," the Commissioner added.

"I don't know," the Schutzhund man said. "They may have been trained to respond to radio signals. They may have receivers implanted in their ears."

"Another sighting on Hearst," shouted a cop.

"We've got a pack of wolves trained to kill loose in the city!" the Mayor shouted. "This is unheard of!"

"We've had coyotes here before, wild pigs in the old neighbourhoods, and a crocodile was pulled from the lake in the park a couple of years ago," a park services man said. "But never wolves."

People and resources were diverted to the east side. The K-9s were headed over there, along with choppers and foot and car patrols.

"We have to go to air with this," Jennifer Ray said.

"The embargo —" Seth Kirk said.

"Seth, you have to tell people there are wolf-dog killers roaming the streets," J.R. said. "You owe it to them."

"She's right, and the public could help," the Mayor said.

"Your Honour, I don't think it's a good idea," Seth said.

"Lift the embargo," the Mayor said.

"Turn around that tape and feed it to CCN. Sam, stand by," J.R. said into Sam's earpiece as she speed-dialled Cooper's cell phone. "Cooper, we're ready to go live from the police chopper. Tape is being fed now, two more victims. We'll do a quick three minutes live from the sky, then feed you the pieces we've already done. You'll want to get a crew to the scenes of the murders as soon as we get an address."

"You're a genius, J.R.," Cooper said.

⑥

Henry had never liked the sight of blood, and the sight of it all over Mrs. Frost's blue Narciso Rodriguez dress was almost too much for him. He might have fainted to the ground if an incredibly gorgeous bodyguard hadn't caught him in his beefy arms. He was only just able to recover his senses and check his hair by the time the police arrived, followed closely by Justin Berg and a crew from CCN.

65

Annie and Jim travelled in a water tunnel that was used for overflow and coated with a strangely opalescent slime, running side by side on the west side, heading downtown. Their work was done in this city and they knew it, even if they didn't think it in those words. Annie felt powerful and she felt satisfied. But the feeling lasted just a moment. A sudden roar filled the tunnel, followed by the sound of rushing water. An adjacent water main was emptying into the tunnel ahead of them, and water was flooding in.

"Run back," they both thought at the same time. Annie turned and ran. Jim was behind her.

And then, as she emerged to the surface through a manhole, using every bit of force she had to push the cover open, she realized Jim wasn't behind her. She was panicked for a moment, and wanted to go back down, but the water was now rushing below.

People were shouting. She looked up, almost blinded by the neon on all sides. It was the Theatre District. A group of tourists who had just left a performance were screaming and snapping pictures. Annie took off, running past tourists and street preachers, knocking over a sidewalk artist's display of caricatures and another merchant's stand of postcards. She was looking for the entrance to a tunnel that would take her below the train station. From there, she could travel south to the place where she was to meet Jim if they got separated.

When she found it, she had lost the screaming tourists but picked up Marco and, behind him, Mike.

Marco followed her down into the tunnel. Mike followed him. She didn't want to lead them to Jim, so she headed north instead of south, ducking off into an abandoned metro tunnel and circling back, but failing to lose them. And then she heard human voices in the tunnel.

"Police," she thought, and at that point, her thoughts connected with Mike's.

"Run east," Mike thought.

She did; Marco followed, and Mike followed him. More human voices echoed from the east. They were now coming from the east and west.

"Marco, stop," Mike thought. "We have to save her. We have to."

Marco ran a few more yards, and then he stopped.

It was an instinct, and a surprising one.

"Run south," Marco thought to Annie, as he turned to stand with Mike.

Marco and Mike waited until the police trackers and K-9s had them in view, and then they took off running north, taking the trackers with them. Human sounds came from the north, a block

or so away, and just as that patrol came into view, they cut east,
jumping down a level to a lower tunnel, a sewer, then pushing
open a valve to emerge in a culvert, and into the river.

@

"Three wolves were seen going underground in the Theatre
District," Sam shouted above the roar of the chopper blades to the
viewing audience. "The police have dispatched foot patrols to
the tunnels in the area."

He pushed his earpiece in farther. "Just a second. What? We
now have preliminary IDs on the Parker Avenue victims. We're
going live to Justin Berg with that."

@

"We lost the trail at the river," the radio dispatcher said to the
Mayor. "The boats can't find them."

"They've got to be somewhere!" the Mayor shouted.

@

Gunther had taken two rolls of pictures of the wolf. Because he
was a good Christian, he removed the bullets from the unconscious wolf and bandaged its legs to staunch the bleeding before
he took the photos. Then he sat down in a chair and watched the
beast while he waited for the police to come. They were taking a
long time.

The emergency operators had taken dozens of calls about wolf
sightings before they got the one from the strange man who said
he'd caught a werewolf. Once the video footage made the TV news,
all the lines lit up. The operator he spoke to was ready to move him
up the list when he said he had one in his custody, until she asked
his name and he said, "I am a servant of God here to reveal the existence of the devil to the world. My name is not important."

"Another nut," she mouthed to the dispatcher beside her, and
then she hung up on Gunther.

While Gunther was waiting, he prayed and recited the books of the Bible, Genesis, Exodus, Leviticus. . . . The repetitive rhythm lulled him to sleep.

Enzio awakened on the floor, trussed up like a rodeo calf. But as he transformed to human, his arms slipped the bonds. He groaned. He was in a lot of pain.

Enzio had been shot twice and it took a great deal of effort to hoist himself up. He covered himself with a blanket and picked up the gun from the floor. He was trying to creep out silently, dragging his wounded leg, when the man in the chair woke up.

"Wha –" Gunther said, and turned around. He reached for his gun and the phone. The gun was gone.

"Don't move," Gunther said. "I'm calling the police."

Enzio pointed the gun at him. Gunther continued dialling. He wasn't afraid of death.

"I'll tell them you forced me to come back here at gunpoint to perform sick sexual acts, then you shot me," Enzio said.

"I have pictures of you –"

"Thanks. I'll take that camera." Enzio said.

6

Seth was frantically strategizing behind closed doors. The wolves had all escaped, and the Mayor was furious. They'd mounted a big, expensive dragnet to stop this killing once and for all, and all it had yielded were some garden-variety criminals they'd stumbled across and some strange guy in a suit on a Vespa, carrying a high-powered shotgun, picked up near the river.

"We'll continue to track them until we find them," Seth dictated to the Mayor. "And we'll mention all the other criminals we accidentally arrested during the dragnet, to try to put a positive spin on things. We'll announce that an investigation will be launched to see who's responsible –"

"We?" the Mayor said.

"You –"

"You can go."

"But —"

"Please leave."

The Mayor buzzed his administrative assistant. "Is Sam Deverell back? Good. Send him in here," he said. "Tell him to bring his producer and his camera. And get Marva on the phone, see if she's free for lunch."

When Sam and J.R. came in, the Mayor said, "How long will it take you to go live?"

"Minutes," Jennifer said. She miked him, and set up the shot.

"Tell me when we're live," the Mayor said, and sat quietly until he got the signal.

"We didn't catch the person or people responsible for the Mad Dog Murders last night," he said. "Nor the animals used to commit the murders. I take full responsibility for this, and I apologize to the families of the victims and to the entire city. I will continue to do everything I can to ensure a successful conclusion to this investigation, until such time as the people of this great city find a better man for this job, at which point, I will humbly turn over power to him. Or her."

That was it.

⑤

Marco and Mike rode a trash barge down the river while they transformed, then piggybacked on a dumptruck back to the city. Mike had shown Marco how to use a trash bag to cover himself, and that's what they were wearing when they walked into the Chelsea lobby later that morning.

"What happened to you?" the guard at the desk asked.

"Don't ask," Marco said.

Carol was downstairs in the confinement room. After hosing down the now-human patients and changing their sheets, all by herself, she had to hook them all up to their breakfast IVs so they could sleep off the transformation. She was almost done when

Mike came in. After he told her what had happened, he took over for her.

"I'm glad you came back," she said.

"I did it for them," Mike said. "The patients."

She nodded. "You're a good guy. You're going to stay?"

"For now. I don't know about the future," he said. "I want to keep my options open."

"Me too," she said.

66

Annie huddled in the little maintenance alcove off a freight tunnel that Jim had shown her on their earlier trip underneath the city. Nobody came after her. Her trail had gone cold. Jim had not come.

Here she transformed back to human, waking up naked and damp on the stone floor. They'd stashed clothes, money, and some miscellaneous items here. By the light of a flashlight, she dressed and brushed the mud and twigs out of her hair. She wiped her face and hands with some Wet-Naps, sprayed herself with cologne, and put on dark glasses.

They'd agreed that they would wait just past sun-up, and then if still separated would each proceed with their plan alone, hoping to meet up with each other later.

It was well past sun-up now, by her watch.

She went to the surface and hailed a cab. While she rode to the airport, she turned around and watched the city skyline shrink and fade behind her.

At the airport, she picked up her ticket to Alaska. Jim hadn't picked his up yet. After washing up more thoroughly in the ladies' room, she went to the gate, where she watched for him nervously, distracted only for a moment by the news on the monitors suspended around the waiting area. Henry was on TV, talking excitedly about how Mrs. Frost and Lord Harry Teufel had been killed by wolves the night before.

"Rosemary was a queen," he said. "She came from nowhere, daughter of an immigrant picklemaker, and she became a queen, with a heart of gold and a devotion to bringing more beauty into the world. We were very close, you know, best friends. I can't believe she's dead!"

The attendants were boarding people with small children, and others who needed assistance, and still Jim wasn't there. Maybe he had been captured or was dead, two possibilities she wouldn't let herself consciously consider before now. She closed her eyes to hold back the tears, a futile effort. They slipped from between her eyelids and tumbled down her face, dripping off her chin.

When she opened her eyes again he was there.

"Traffic was a bitch," he said.

Epilogue

On the way up to the penthouse, Carol thought about what she was going to do. She walked up the stairs, all the way to the top, to give herself time to consider everything. She had always been a big believer in love and forgiveness, to the extent that she'd been willing to welcome Jim back into the program, even when she believed he had intentionally killed Sarah. But she was human, and she was angry at Marco. Things that had jarred her when Sarah was with them, things she had mentally set aside because she didn't have enough information to understand why they jarred her, now fell into place.

Things like, how mean Marco had been to her when Sarah was there, how solicitous Marco had been of Sarah, how he had started wearing more cologne and fussing more about his appearance, and how Sarah had seemed uncomfortable with his attention and in turn had become more solicitous of Carol.

Marco had been in love with Sarah.

Love was probably not the right word. He was infatuated with her. He lusted after her. He wanted to impress and possess her. He

295

had mixed the drugs that killed her that night, though Carol knew it was an unconscious impulse, the wolf in him. For all his talk about control, there were things in him that he couldn't control. Keeping a lid on them so long had brought out the very worst in him.

But last night he had helped Jim and Annie escape. Because she had known and loved Marco for so long, she knew what he had felt in the moment he made that decision. It had been his instinct to help. He had, in that moment, become a man, his own man, and that, she thought, should be rewarded in some fashion.

When she walked into the penthouse, he was sitting in a chair in the living room, looking ahead with haunted eyes. The phone had been ripped out of the wall beside him, taking the jack with it, trailing its broken wires like veins. Luigi would be having a coronary trying to call.

"I'm sorry," he said to Carol. "I am so sorry."

"I know," she said. "But that isn't enough. Things have to change. You have to change."

"I will. I have. I'm just . . . so confused."

"Well, yeah. You're human, Marco. Mostly. That means confusion sometimes. Not always knowing what the right instinct is," she said, and this time he didn't say anything about her armchair psychoanalysis.

"Will you stay?"

He looked so helpless, and his eyes were full of fear she'd say no.

"I'll stay for the patients, until further notice. But I am not cooking for you or sleeping with you, at least not for a while. This is going to take time to work out," she said. "I'm not sure I can forgive you."

"Okay. I . . . I understand."

"And I think the wolves should be given the option of staying in the program or living free, despite the risks."

"My family will never go for it . . ."

"Too damned bad. If they object I go to Beth Tindall, and I take Mike with me. If the Great Potenzas get in my way, or hurt me in any way, Rudolfo will come forward. Or one of the patients will, or two, or three. . . . The patients love me, Marco."

"*I* love you, too."

"Then you'll agree to my terms."

"Whatever you say, Carol. You're all I have. You're the only thing that has kept me —"

"I know. We'll talk later. I need some sleep now," she said. "I'll take the master bedroom. You sleep wherever else you want."

When she woke up, it was almost night. She heard a noise in Annie's room and went to check. Enzio was there, snoring. His arm and leg were bandaged. He looked bad.

She sat down across from Enzio, crossed her arms, and stared at him until he snorted awake.

"Wha —?" he asked.

"Things are going to change," she said to him.

"What? How?"

"I'm not sure. But things are going to change. The program is going to have to become more humane. That's all I wanted to say. Get some sleep."

@

The only person Razz could tell about what he'd seen was his cousin Lewis. But Lewis was incommunicado at the moment. When Razz called the woman who owned the bar near Pimlico, she cursed Lewis's name and hung up.

@

Nobody believed Gunther. But he didn't care. God knew. The werewolves would return, he was convinced. And when they did, he'd be waiting for them.

@

Rudolfo was bailed out by Carol.

"I don't want to do this any more," Rudolfo said.

"I understand," Carol said. "You don't have to do anything you don't want to do from now on."

"The family –"

"The family can kiss my half-Polish ass," she said. "After this fiasco, I'm calling the shots. If they don't like it, I'll blow the whistle on them."

Rudolfo looked at her with an even greater admiration. He found this take-charge attitude incredibly erotic.

"So what is it you want to do, Rudy?"

"Don't laugh," Rudolfo said.

"I'd never laugh at you."

"I've always wanted to be a forensic accountant," he said.

"Really? Why?"

"I love numbers. I want to make numbers add up."

"And if they don't add up?"

"I want to find the paper trail and hunt down the culprits."

He spoke with such fervour, it moved her deeply.

"You'd be great at that!"

He blushed.

"Are you going to stay with Marco?" he asked, without looking at her.

"For now," she said. "For the patients. Then I'm going to visit Bonnie Mae, my sister, walk by the ocean, figure things out."

"Oh."

"Maybe we can have dinner when I get back," she said. "Just the two of us."

⑤

Jennifer Ray was sitting at Sam's desk, doing his expense reports for him as a favour, when the phone rang.

"Hi," the man said. "May I speak with Sam Deverell?"

"He's not here," J.R. said. "He's in Aruba for a few days. Can I help you?"

"I'm not sure." He told her his name and said, "I wasn't going to call, but Sam seems like a nice guy and I thought he should know the truth."

After Jennifer hung up the phone she went into Cooper's office.

"Guess who I just spoke to," she said. "Just between us."

"Who?"

"Wallace Waring's ex-boyfriend."

"Boyfriend?"

"Ex."

"You sure?"

"I believe him, Coop. He knew too much, not just about Waring, but about Candace."

She sat down, put her black-booted feet up on Cooper's desk, and told him about the conversation. The ex-boyfriend's name was Boyd, and he and Wallace had been together for four years. He wanted Wallace to come out, be an example to young gays and lesbians everywhere. These days, being gay wouldn't cost a guy his job, so why not be honest, Boyd thought, and be a role model. But being able to keep his job and being a gay icon wasn't enough for Wallace. He wanted to be a superstar, and felt he could never be a superstar if people knew he was gay. Fifty per cent of the population was female, Wallace pointed out, only ten to twenty per cent gay or bisexual men.

"Boyd said he was the closet lover and Candace was the display model. But Boyd got tired of the dishonesty and he broke up with Wallace. He wanted Sam to know so Sam's feelings wouldn't be too hurt," Jennifer said. "He said Wallace and Candace are two of a kind, ambitious, superficial, completely self-serving. The only thing they don't have in common is sex."

"He's gay, and she hates sex. It kind of works out for them," Cooper said.

"They're perfect for each other in a way."

"Life is strange."

"Love is stranger," she said.

Their eyes met for a moment.

"What time is it?" Cooper said, looking down at his watch quickly. "It's time to go. Want to stop at Bobo's?"

"Sure," she said.

"On second thought, let's go somewhere quieter. There's this little Lebanese place in my neighbourhood, a Mom and Pop place," Cooper said. "We can talk there, you know, without shouting over the jukebox."

                                          ⑤

At Syn-EG, the board elected Jed Sutton, head of Syn-BIO, to be the interim CEO. Everyone liked him. Even the *Downtown Eye* approved, in a gushing editorial:

> Jed Sutton may well represent the new breed of activist executive. He has a short history with the company, but in that brief time he instituted many reforms at Syn-BIO and spearheaded micromedical technologies and innovative strategies to get the jump on emerging viruses and bacterial infections.
>
> But his most dazzling success to date is Lysinex corn, a hardy, high-protein plant, unveiled last week at a corn cook-off and news conference. Lysinex was Sutton's passion, a projected he started as a grad student in western Canada. He developed it on his own, living, he said, "Like an independent filmmaker, juggling six credit cards and borrowing from Peter to pay Paul." When he sold it to the late Lord Harry Teufel, it was on the condition he be made president of Syn-BIO with complete responsibility for the project, stock options, and a 51 per cent profit stake in the corn.
>
> It was a good move. According to seven years of rigorous independent tests completed last month, Lysinex is safe for humans, animals, and other vegetation, while remaining resistant to insects and fungus. And guess what? It's delicious. Lysinex has a sweet, slightly nutty taste. At the cook-off, some of the city's best chefs made a variety of dishes using the corn – ground, on the cob, off the cob, and popped. (See page C-7 for Syn-TV chef Jon Jordan's

recipes for butter-browned polenta with black truffles, and a roasted-pear, Roquefort and cornflour soufflé that will make you believe in God again. There are no atheists in Jon Jordan's kitchen.)

While Lysinex is sure to be a favourite on the American dinner table, Sutton says its real value will be as a food crop in the developing world, where it could greatly reduce famine and hunger. Yesterday, he announced plans to donate 50 per cent of the seeds from the first harvest to the United Nations World Food Program.

The Downtown Eye heartily congratulates Mr. Sutton on his corn and his program. One suggestion: Please change the name. Lysinex sounds like something you'd use to strip paint.

⑨

Jim and his girlfriend had vanished, completely. Meredith watched every day, waiting for them to return or, better yet, for Jim to return alone from wherever they had gone. But every day she spent less time watching Jim's window until, one day, she forgot to care, and went a whole day without thinking about him at all.

⑨

"I miss you," the Mayor said. "I know I fucked some things up. The affair —"

"You're having an affair?" Marva said, incredulous. "Really?"

"I'm not having an affair now. I haven't . . . you remember, *that* affair."

"Oh, in the seventies," she said. "I knew you weren't having one now."

"Is it so far-fetched to think another woman would find me attractive?"

"No, no, don't misunderstand me. Women love you. But you felt so guilty about that affair you had during the garbage strike I couldn't imagine you ever being with another woman. You're not the type."

Grant Ho brought their House Special Chop Suey.

"I know that affair planted the . . . seed, or whatever, that led to our . . . lack of communication," the Mayor said.

"Hon, it started long before that. It wasn't the other woman. It was the business."

"The business? But you loved the business."

"You were always at work, and once the kids came along and I wasn't at work with you, we started to drift apart," Marva said. "I was distant from you too. I know that's one of the reasons you had that affair. I was starting to find my own life, apart from you, the kids, and the stores."

"You're not to blame!"

"It's not about blame, hon, it's about understanding why things happen the way they do. I was very angry when I learned of it, but I had time to think about it. Neither of us was really present in the marriage at that time. You were under a lot of pressure. I wasn't there for you, and she was, making you feel desired."

He didn't ask if she'd had an affair. He didn't want to know.

"I still love you," he said.

"I know," she said. "I still love you too. I watched your statement on CCN at the end of that dragnet, and I thought, what a good man he is. What a rare man."

"Will you come back, be my wife again?"

As much as she loved him, she wasn't sure what she wanted just now. She couldn't quite bring herself to say yes, but how could she say no to a man who took her for their reconciliation dinner to the place they'd gone so often when they were young and madly in love, who remembered that she had made curtains that screened out the light of the Lido's neon sign, but let in its warm glow. He never used to remember things like that. His head was full of prices and Teamsters and pounds of carrots.

"We can try," she said.

⑥

The Hunter's Moon, came and went, and no one was killed. The Snow Moon came and went and nobody was killed.

⑨

Dear Tweets,

What a year it has been, a year that flung us from bed to bed, from frolic to fear, from glee to grief. It was a great blow to us to learn of the tragic deaths of the great cosmetics queen Rosemary Frost and mighty mogul Lord Harry Teufel. Our conscience was sorely pricked by the fun this Royal We had with them before their unfortunate murders. Mrs. Frost was romantically inclined towards Lord Harry, and we have taken some comfort in knowing that these two corporate titans went together, side by side. If there is a mogul heaven, we imagine them there, trying to turn the angels into cheap labour and corner the market on harps.

We've been trying to find out what straw finally broke the back of a certain sang-bleu fiancée of a certain peasant-prince actor. This just in: ten days before the wedding, she decided to fly to Europe to the set of her beloved's latest movie and surprise the world-class beardsplitter. He was surprised! So was she! So was his naked co-star! So was his naked co-star's hunky husband when our titled jiltee called him up and told him what she'd walked in on. We weren't surprised though, were we? The wedding is off, the naked co-star (think perky, think wholesome) is headed for divorce court, and that reclusive director's long-awaited next movie is in peril because the peasant-prince and the hunky star he cuckolded were supposed to co-star in the big-budget chiller. Shooting was scheduled to begin next month in the South Pacific. All we don't know is: who got custody of the ten-thousand Balinese tangerine blossoms?

Unhappy endings, Tweets. But we take heart. There are some happy beginnings as well.

Someone must have slipped some Androx-Y into the microbrews at a widely watched city news network. Fresh off a new six-figure contract to be head anchorman, our favourite nice-guy reporter has been looking doe-eyed at the voluptuous host of a new show about . . . well, the art of love, to put it delicately. And she is looking back. Lucky man. The zaftig lady and her anchor look almost serious. We asked their managing editor about this May–October pairing and got the perfunctory "no comment." Well, Mr. Managing Editor wouldn't be one to share any secrets, would he? Not when he and a certain producer have been looking so tight.

The way love has been breaking out all over the city lately, you'd think it was spring, that the world was warm and green, instead of this frozen winter monochrome. Really, have you seen the Mayor and his missus lately? I don't mean to be impertinent, kids, but GET A ROOM!

But nothing can top the surprise last weekend sprung by two TV news aces. "We're just friends," they told us, over and over. Then right under our noses, they ran off and eloped, and are now honeymooning in Key West. We hear that hot new promoter, Party with Liz, is organizing a big reception for the newlyweds when they return to the city.

As for me and my house . . . Eros has touched our Royal We as well. Want to know who the lucky lover is? Check out the next edition of City Magazine and its story called Dead End Kids about the sloppy-guy chic so fashionable now among slumming boys and girls. He's one of the models, formerly a man-in-waiting for an illustrious Grande Dame. That's all I'm going to say.

All's well that begins well – temporarily. Season's Greetings, and a Happy NEW Year.

Acknowledgements

My deepest thanks to the following:

Victor, Victor, Victor (Hernandez)! Sorry I missed ya.

Dinah Forbes, for giving me the opportunity and holding on tight while the deadline came and went and I was pleading, "I just need to rewrite this middle section. Just a few more days . . . weeks . . . a month." Ditto: Russ Galen and Danny Baror.

Diana Greene, Jennifer Gould, Yvonne Durant, Susan Seelandt, Siv Svendsen, Casebeer, Joe Myers, Jan Reddy, Victor Navasky.

Martin Levin.

The Chelsea, especially Stanley and Jerry. When I'm broke and madly rewriting, they tell me not to worry, just keep working, and they smile so I know they're not worried either.

Sammy, David, Uncle Mike, Robbie, and the guys at the Aristocrat Deli, who kept me fed and watered during the crazy rewrite phase, with special thanks to the night shift, Yusef, Rafael, and Abdul.

Scott, Louise, Laura, and Chris Hannant, and Sgt. Reinaldo, NYPD, for taking good care of them.

Rob Schultheis, Steve Masty of the faceted gallstone tiara, David Bernknopf, Jake Gold and Leesa Butler, Salmaan, Andrew Miller Griffin, and the Gordfather.

Caroline White.

Cec.

The Light ex-23, IWALY.

Ion and Jerry at No Exit.

Tania, Fabienne, Xavier, and everyone at Serpent Noir and Serpent à Plumes.

Yann, Bruno, and Tim.

Jed Sutton.

Charlie Cale, Wendy Jewell and Nina Young for that beautiful day, and the American Library of Paris for that wonderful evening.

Brian and Violenne at the Abbey Bookshop in Paris.

Shakespeare & Company and the Village Voice in Paris.

Damon Jones and Pete Padilla.

Charles Northcote, secret agent man.

Norm Gosney.

All the real-life villains in the world who committed such over-the-top crimes in the name of profit that I hardly had to make up anything.

And last but not least, the late Pam Smith, the Scottish spitfire and God's gift to writers. I can still hear that laugh.